PRAISE FOR NEWTON THORNBURG

"Thornburg has a way of setting up a story on familiar ground and then, with a deft twist or two, jerking that ground out from under the reader. . . . [He] is a spare, muscular writer whose stories walk the reader into the darker corners of the human psyche. . . . The one thing Thornburg doesn't do is disappoint."
—*Los Angeles Times* on *A Man's Game*

"Tense, funny and despairing. . . . Charged with a passion that makes even grotesques seem likable and, more important, credible right up to the last, startling sentence!"
—*Time* on *Cutter and Bone*

"A searing knockout. . . . A thriller. . . . It will make you wince, but it will hold you until the very last shattering line!"
—*Business Week* on *Cutter and Bone*

"Thornburg is a born storyteller, riveting his readers with a book so galvanically charged that it truly is nearly impossible to put down. Characterization here rings true in every case, the details . . . are frighteningly accurate, and the plot line surges ahead with the brutal force of madness."
—*St. Louis Post-Dispatch* on *Cutter and Bone*

"The plotting is tight, action episodes are fast-paced and graphic, and the suspense is built skillfully to a climax."
—*Washington Times* on *Black Angus*

"A superlative novel. . . . A weird and fascinating trip with two fictional characters so strongly set in a plot so complex and satisfying that one marvels at their creation."
—*Los Angeles Times* on *Black Angus*

Books by Newton Thornburg

A
MAN'S
GAME

NEWTON
THORNBURG

A TOM DOHERTY ASSOCIATES BOOK
NEW YORK

This is a work of fiction. All the characters and events portrayed in this book are either products of the author's imagination or are used fictitiously.

A MAN'S GAME

Cover art by Alan Ayers

A Forge Book
Published by Tom Doherty Associates, Inc.
175 Fifth Avenue
New York, N.Y. 10010

Forge® is a registered trademark of Tom Doherty Associates, Inc.

ISBN 0-812-55374-8
Library of Congress Card Catalog Number: 95-42567

First Edition: April 1996
First mass market edition: May 1997

Printed in the United States of America

0 9 8 7 6 5 4 3 2 1

To Janet

A MAN'S GAME

ONE

He stood at the front end of the bar, looking out over the cavernous room with boredom and contempt. His straight, brownish hair was pulled back into a ponytail held by a silver clasp that matched the ring in his left ear, and he had silver-and-turquoise Indian jewelry around his neck and wrists and fingers. He wore old jeans and cheap snakeskin boots and a matching vinyl snakeskin vest with nothing underneath except his lean, muscular torso. Even then he did not stand out in the college-age crowd, any more than did the deafening young grunge band performing on a low stage at the rear of the room. Ragged and emaciated, they looked almost tame compared to those they were playing to, who had bright green hair and purple hair and dreadlocks and shaved heads and wore junk rags and see-through pajamas and black dominatrix lingerie over white longjohns. Some of the crowd were dancing, but most stood around in the dimness drinking beer or wine and studying each other in the eerie lambency of a lightshow.

The man, who appeared to be in his mid twenties, lifted a bottle of Mexican beer to his thin lips and chugged it. When he lowered the bottle, his attention focused on a very pretty young woman standing with friends on the other side of the room, beyond the dancers. College kids, he thought with contempt. Yet he could not take his eyes off the girl, who was small-boned and curvaceous, just the way he liked them. He watched her for a while longer, then started toward her, picking his way through the crowd. As he drew closer, his upper lip lifted in a kind of smile, a smile oddly like a sneer.

"Hey, purty lady," he said, "you wanna dance?"

Startled, she looked at him for a moment, then mumbled "No thanks" and turned to the girl closest to her, reaching for her. And they practically collapsed in each other's arms, sputtering for a few seconds, then letting go and laughing out loud, laughing *at him*. Moving on, he heard the girl's voice again, addressing not him so much as the world in general.

"Give me a break, okay? Just a break—that's all I ask."

The man made his way to the front door then, still smiling his odd smile, pretending nothing much had happened. But his body had become slick with sweat and he could feel himself trembling with the effort to control his rage. Outside, he pushed through a couple of teenage boys, who started squalling until they caught his look, and then they skulked away.

He walked down the block and got in his car, a seventies' Chevy Impala, not in the best of shape. But it started right off for a change and he drove closer to the rock tavern, parking finally in a loading zone so he could watch the entrance more carefully. He got a pint of rum from under the seat and took a deep pull on it, washing down half a meth in the process. He wished he could have taken them all on one at a time, the boys the same as the girls. College kids—he should have known better. Christ, how he hated them. Someday, when he got control of the whole local market—acid, grass, all of it—then they'd change their tune, the bastards. He'd have a penthouse looking out over the whole fucking Sound, and they'd be pounding on his door then, begging to be let in. He could just see himself sitting out on the deck in one of those lounge chairs, looking off into space, indifferent, while some college bitch worked on his joint.

Right now, though, all he wanted was to see the girl come out alone and leave by herself. Or even both girls, if it came to that, because he didn't doubt for a second that he could handle the two of them at the same time. Shit, all it would mean is that he would have twice the fun, giving them each a lesson in manners, like who it just didn't pay to laugh at.

But they came out in a group finally, three girls and two boys, one of the boys a football type, bigger than the man. Disappointed, he smashed his fist into the dashboard and the thing cracked open, the hard old plastic splitting like the shell of a turtle in a vise: a childhood memory. In a rage now, he started the car and took off, burning rubber and scattering the stinking college kids.

The rock joint was located practically in the shadow of the Space Needle, an area much too crowded for what he had in mind. So he drove east past the freeway and went up onto Capitol Hill, for once not to pick up some pitiful fag but just to cruise the neighborhood surrounding the park: dark, leafy streets with old mansions set back amid the great trees, dimly lit and solid, fortresses people like him could breach only with a jimmy and a flashlight. But that was not his interest this night as he rumbled slowly up and down the quiet streets, nursing his rage. There were a few couples out late and some solitary males, fags looking to score, he figured. But it wasn't until he drove alongside the park and turned at the yellow-brick mansion that he saw what he was looking for: a midnight jogger, a young woman running with a dog on a leash.

The man grinned ruefully, figuring the bitch had to be a yuppie, a college girl, to be so stupid, so reckless, running these streets at night, thinking some fucking mutt would save her. Already his heart had begun to hammer at him and the sweat came again, prickling his skin in the cool night air. He drove on for two blocks and turned at an unlit corner, parking a few hundred feet down the side street. He put on a pair of gloves, workman's leather gloves with the smooth side in. Then he got a tire iron from under the seat and slipped out of the car, moving quickly back to the corner. The house there was a ramshackle gingerbread type set back in a lot overgrown with bushes, some as tall as trees. So he had no trouble concealing himself as the girl came toward him, her tennis shoes slapping steadily louder on the sidewalk.

He hit her first, lunging out of the bushes and throwing a forearm into her face. As she fell, the dog—a boxer—jumped straight up into the air and yelped even before the man caught it with the iron, right on its snotty head, hard enough to make the stupid thing flail along the sidewalk for a dozen feet, as if it were trying to run on ice. Then it found its legs and scampered off, yipping in terror.

The man hurriedly dragged the young woman back into the bushes, then lifted her and carried her closer to the unlit house, where the brush was even thicker, making for better cover. But by then he didn't care if he was seen or not as the rage came founting out of him like arterial blood. With his half-gloved fists, he punched the girl twice in the face as hard as he could. He pulled her sweats and panties down and pushed her sweater and bra up around her neck. Yet even as he lowered his own pants, he knew he was not going to make it, knew that he was losing it, that he would not be able to penetrate her. In a fury, he began to hit her again, in the face as well as the body. Then he rolled her onto her stomach and tried once more, grinding desperately against her buttocks. But it was no use.

Desolate now, crying, he lay across her limp form and masturbated on her. And afterward he stayed there for a time, holding onto her, even kissing her, as if she were a lover.

Finally he pulled off her sweatshirt and wiped her carefully, trying not to leave any cum on her. He belted his pants and picked up the tire iron and for a few moments stood there in the shadows looking down at the girl, wondering whether to waste her. College kids. Christ, how he hated them.

Despite the troubles in his marriage, Jack Baird was feeling reasonably happy. For one thing, he'd just had a very good day, calling on only nine of his accounts, yet billing over seven thousand dollars, which meant a commission of at least four hundred for him. His new Buick was purring along just fine, and then there was the day itself, clear and warm after a spring of seemingly endless rain. The city looked burnished in the bright sunshine.

To his left was the long green sweep of Volunteer Park and the cemetery; on the other side, a row of handsome old Victorian houses giving way to a couple of new condo buildings, after which came Baird's own street, angling off Fifteenth Avenue and heading straight for his house before cutting back to the avenue.

Even when Ellen was on her high horse, Baird still enjoyed coming home and seeing the big old house dead ahead. It was a blocky red-brick affair with a dazzling view to the east of Lake Washington and the Cascades. As far as he was concerned, though, its best feature was that he had stolen it fifteen years earlier for sixty thousand dollars, about a tenth of its present market value. As such, the house represented almost his entire net worth.

But it was as he pulled in and drove around to the garage that he came upon the real treasure in his life: his daughter Kathy, who was eighteen. At his arrival, she had come out onto the back porch, and now she came down the stairs as gravely as a funeral director, though she certainly didn't look the part in her denim shorts and a sleeveless blouse knotted under her breasts.

Groaning as if he'd spent the day in a coal mine, Baird got out of the car. "And what have I done to deserve all this?" he asked. "You gonna hit me up for a loan?"

"That's not fair."

He kissed her on the forehead. "Just kidding, baby. Whatever reason for the welcoming committee, I'll take it."

She made a face, a kind of pout. "The creep followed me home again."

"You're kidding."

"I wish I were. He got on the bus downtown and got off with me at the park. Then he walks me home. I try to run, he runs. I can't shake him. And all the while he keeps talking his special brand of filth."

Baird felt a surge of anger. "Goddamn—that settles it. Tomorrow I'm gonna find out who he is, and then we'll go to the police, let them handle it."

"Really? You think they'd bother with something like this?"

"Of course. Why not?" He patted her bottom with his briefcase. "Come on, let's go inside."

Going ahead of him through the back door, she turned and smiled, and Baird had no trouble understanding the creep's taste in women, for his daughter was hauntingly beautiful, though in a style not altogether modern, in that she looked sweet and shy rather than tough and assertive.

Ellen, working at the kitchen sink, glanced over at the two of them as they came in.

"Daddy's going to find out who he is," Kathy said. "Then we'll go to the police with it."

Ellen went on rinsing a bowl of lettuce as if she'd found it in a neighbor's garbage. "The *police?*" she said. "Aren't we over-reacting just a bit?"

"How can you say that?" Baird went over and kissed her on the cheek, then turned back to Kathy. "What is this, honey—the fourth or fifth time he's done it, right?"

Kathy nodded. "Five times. In two weeks."

"Right. I'd say that's enough harassment for now."

Ellen placed the salad bowl on the butcher-block table and began snipping and slicing vegetables into it. "I don't know," she said. "I admit he looks creepy. But for heaven's sake, he hasn't even tried anything yet. He hasn't even touched her. All he does is talk. He's probably just some poor jerk with a crush."

Kathy gave Baird a baffled look. He made a face and shook his head, indicating for her not to let it bother her. She knew her mother. They both knew her mother.

"What do you suggest we do then?" Baird asked.

Ellen shrugged. "Drive her to and from work for a while. Make her inaccessible."

"If I have to hide from somebody, I'd just as soon know who the devil he is," Kathy said.

Her mother looked at her, giving special attention to her skimpy attire. "You know, if you didn't get yourself up the way you do, maybe this sort of thing wouldn't happen."

"Oh, Mother—for God's sake!" The girl dismissed her with a wave of the hand and left the kitchen, crossing the dining room and heading upstairs.

Baird shook his head. "That was just great, Ellen. Nothing like backing up your kids."

"She is not a kid. She's a grown woman."

"The hell she is. She's our little girl, and there's this maniac out there making her life miserable."

"Why maniac? How do we know that? Because he's got a ponytail?"

"Don't be ridiculous. You've heard the things he says to her."

"Have I?"

Baird was shocked. "Jesus Christ, you don't believe your own daughter?"

"It just sounds so weird, that's all."

"That, Ellen, is the fucking point."

She picked up a large zucchini and began to pare it into the salad. "All right. Okay. You find out who he is and we'll go to the police. I'm just saying that there are all kinds of jerks out there hitting on women all the time. And I wish she'd be more of a woman and not such a wimp. Sometimes you just have to tell men to fuck off, that's all."

Baird wearily dropped his briefcase onto the table and went over to her again. He took the knife out of her hand and put it beside the salad bowl. He placed his hands on her shoulders and gently backed her against the counter.

"This is our daughter we're talking about," he said. "And with her, we don't play it casual. We don't take chances."

She did not blink. "Why not just call the police?"

"Because I don't want some cop jerking me around on the phone. First, I find out who this guy is, then we go to the station and lay it out for them face to face—*make* them do something about it."

She lifted his hands off her shoulders and moved away, still intent on getting dinner without interruption. "Whatever," she said.

Upstairs, Baird knocked on Kathy's door even though it was slightly ajar. As usual, an opera was playing softly on her stereo, one of the romantic arias she loved so much more than her father did. For that matter, her bedroom was not much to Baird's taste either, since it was without question the most relentlessly feminine room he'd ever seen, all pink and white, with gossamer curtains and mounds of silky pillows and teddy bears and huge stuffed bunnies and kitties, as well as a white four-poster bed trimmed in rose sateen and needlepoint. Also painted white was her drafting table, where she endlessly drew beautiful young models wearing clothing of her own design.

Kathy and her mother had fought over the bedroom for years, Ellen insisting that they toss out "all this baby-girl shit" and make it into a proper room for a college student, one that other students could visit without Kathy becoming a laughing stock. But the girl had checkmated her—by dropping out of school, by never having guests.

Now Baird found her lying facedown across the bed. He sat next to her.

"Why is she so hateful to me?" she asked.

"That was a bit much, I agree. This creep is scaring you to death and she can't seem to get over the fact that you're not going to be a lawyer someday."

Kathy smiled wryly. "You know what? There's a bunch of new law-school brochures downstairs. But they're not for me— they're for *her*."

Baird had seen them. "Yeah, I know."

"She'd be fifty by the time she got out of law school."

"Don't remind me." Baird was the same age as his wife.

Kathy punched him lightly on the arm. "Oh, come on, you're not old. You could pass for sixty-five easy."

"Thanks a lot."

She laughed. "No, really. When you pick me up at work, the other girls all start primping. '*That's* your father?' they say."

"Yeah, I'll bet."

"Well, they do."

"Anyway, we've got more pressing things to talk about. If we do end up going to the police, I want you to tell them everything he's said. Everything he's done. You'll probably have to sign a complaint. What we want is to get a restraining order against him."

Kathy rolled over and sat up. She looked frightened. "Do I have to do that?" she asked. "I mean, tell them what he's said. All that filth."

"I'm afraid so, baby."

"God, he's so weird. So sickening."

"What'd he say today?"

She sighed. "Oh, just more junk. He was running on about my body, you know? My looks. Judging every part, like I was a show dog or something. You know the thing he likes best?"

Baird was embarrassed. "You don't have to tell me."

"My eyes," she went on. "He likes the look of fear in them. Like a horse in a fire, he said. That's the look he wants. Like a horse in a fire."

For Lee Jeffers, it had not been a good day. In fact, it had been a perfectly miserable *two* days, considering that she had spent most of that time helping Joe Daniels on the Munson case, which meant reinterrogating a lot of people who hadn't wanted to be interrogated in the first place: welfare mothers mostly, down and dirty sisters who as usual seemed to despise Lee on sight, even more than if she'd been some snooty blond chick from the suburbs. Then, midway, she had arrived home yesterday at seven, desperately looking forward to chilling out with her one true love—her very own, recently purchased old Wallingford bungalow—only to discover that there was no water pressure upstairs and four inches of the stuff downstairs, covering the basement floor. Three hours and almost five hundred dollars later, the bandit plumber cheerfully informed her that the water pressure was back and that most of her plumbing was lead pipe and would have to be replaced with copper. He himself could do the job for as little as three thousand dollars.

As a result, Lee got to bed late and slept poorly, counting thirty-five hundred disappearing dollars instead of sheep. She never seemed able to save any money. The house was already mortgaged to the rafters, and now it had lousy pipes, just like one of her ex-lovers, who toward the end of their relationship had begun wheezing during the act, a turnoff if ever there was one. So this morning, sleepy and cranky, she had set out on another day with Daniels, whose great size and shaved black head and weary scowl seemed to command instant respect, even from the sisters. Which definitely was not the case for Lee, and for reasons not entirely clear to her, though she imagined it had something to do with her café-au-lait color, her green eyes and wavy black hair. And some of the sisters, the serious carboloaders, probably didn't like the way she dressed either, accentuating her trim figure with tight jeans and no blouse under a sharp, tailored jacket.

"I'd like to ask you a few questions," she would say.

"Well, you can ask all you want—don't mean you gonna hear nothin back, though."

This, while looking at Lee as if she were a gaudy Sea-Tac hooker instead of a detective appointed to Seattle's elite Metro Squad. Unfortunately it was a scene that played right into Lee's growing alienation from her own people, or at least those people everybody considered to be hers. In reality, Lee's mother was white and her father was probably an octoroon, that horrible word she had learned as a child in Louisiana. And in anybody's math, that meant she was fifteen-sixteenths white, maybe not enough to be *judged* white, but certainly more than enough not to feel any overwhelming affinity with the ladies in the projects.

For that matter, she really didn't care one way or the other. Like most police officers, she had come to feel that there were only two races in America now anyway: us and *them*, cops and the rest of the population. So it was not an identity crisis she was having so much as a crisis of competence. She simply wasn't getting the job done. Not yesterday. Not today. And it galled her.

The Metro Squad had been formed originally to handle cases that spilled over into suburban and other jurisdictions. But as time passed and the squad's reputation grew, it increasingly was brought in on the department's hardest cases, important ones that had gone unsolved too long as far as the brass was concerned. Though Lieutenant John Pearson was nominally in charge of the squad, Sergeant Bleeding Hart Lucca—Lee's partner—pretty much ran the show. Each of the squad's eight detectives had his or her own cases, assigned according to workload and specialty, but they also had to assist each other a good part of the time, the assignments usually coming from Lucca, as in this case.

The Munsons were brothers, ages five and three, wide-eyed little black boys who had disappeared from the Alder Vista apartment complex four months before. A week later their mutilated bodies were found in a downtown dumpster, each enclosed in a green plastic trash bag, which predictably resulted in the media labeling the unknown culprit "the trash-bag killer." Since the boys had disappeared from the project playground, left there by their mother while she went shopping, the police figured that somebody somewhere in the area had to have seen something.

The project after all was not some high-rise monstrosity like Chicago's Cabrini Green, but a handsomely laid out apartment complex not much different from private ones nearby. Its two-story, eight-unit buildings were set among trees and green space, with covered parking, a playground, even a swimming pool.

In one apartment after another, Lee continued to get the same response. Young or old, the tenants complained that they already had given their story to "them other poh-leece"—the homicide detectives—and didn't have anything new to add. And over and over Lee heard that the two little boys had run wild and that their mother was no damn good, a crackhead, a ho.

When Lee groused to Joe Daniels about her lack of success, he gave her a pep talk.

"Hey, babe, it ain't you—they dish out the same shit to everybody. You just gotta roll with the punches and keep comin back at 'em, like you can't hear nothin negative."

"I don't know," she said. "Maybe if I shaved my head and put on three hundred pounds, maybe then they'd open up a bit."

He laughed loudly, shaking his big bowling ball of a head. "Man, I don't know about you. You as mean and low-down as any of 'em."

"That's for sure," she said.

Despite the pep talk, Lee was not irritated in the least when Sergeant Lucca had her beeped and she was told to meet him at Harborview Hospital. And not until she had arrived and roused the sergeant from one of his semi-slumbers did she learn that she was there in regard to one of her own cases, the Heifitz rape-murder, which happened during Christmas week and was followed three months later by a rape-and-attempted-murder with similar characteristics.

She found Lucca in the old main lobby off Ninth Avenue, sprawled across a delicate little loveseat like a bear dozing in a bed of posies. As usual, he was wearing one of his lumpy tan sportcoats, shiny polyester brown pants, Hush Puppies, and a shirt and tie that looked like a unit, something he put on and took off together, saving to wear later, unlaundered. His colorless hair was almost gone on top, his face drooped, and his red, weary eyes looked as if they hadn't gazed upon anything of interest in decades, which definitely was not the case, since he had one of the best conviction records on the force. He was widely unloved.

Seeing Lee, he sat up a little straighter to give her room. But there was no greeting.

"What's up?" she asked.

"A rape. Went down last night, over near Volunteer Park, in some hermit's front yard. Rape Unit didn't think it was anything special, so they sat on it all day. But one of the uniforms who rolled on it—Mister Ambition, I guess—he also rolled on your Miss What's-her-name, the Seafirst Bank gal. And he saw certain similarities. Rape didn't give him the time of day, so he eventually calls us. I guess he remembered you were working the other one. Probably wants to get in your pants."

"That's sexual harassment, Sergeant."

"So sue me."

"What similarities?" Lee asked.

"The severity of the beating. Man used either some kind of rough gloves or a meat tenderizer—it's hard to tell. Also there was no penetration. And her sweatshirt is missing, like he might have used it to wipe her off with, keep us from having a semen sample."

"That's kind of a stretch, isn't it?"

"It's something at least."

"I guess so. Anyway, good for the uniform. Hope he's chief someday."

"Be an improvement."

"What do you think?"

Lucca shrugged. "I don't think it's our boy. Crandall, in Rape, she says the girl hadn't reported any harassment—no one walking her home from the bus and rhapsodizing about his joint. And there weren't any cuts. No little red symbols carved into her body."

"Just the possibility he masturbated on her. And the beating."

"Yeah—the beating." Lucca shook his head. "Kid's face looks like a black-and-blue pumpkin."

"We can talk to her now?"

"Why else would I call you?"

Lee smiled coldly, a habit she figured all Lucca's partners

had to develop sooner or later. Either that or transfer. "This Crandall, she still around?"

Lucca grinned. "Jeffers, will you stop being such a goddamn wimp. That's what being in Metro means—you just move in and snatch their cases right outa their grubby little mitts. They say anything, you spit in their eye."

"I wanted to ask her a few questions, that's all."

"Sure you did."

Lee suddenly became aware of an elderly woman sitting bolt upright in the chair next to them. The woman looked more appalled than frightened, much as if she had overheard a couple of teenagers planning a cruel prank. Using a laquered bamboo cane, she got to her feet and set out across the carpeted floor toward the espresso shop. She was an impressive-looking woman, expensively dressed, with an air of casual refinement and elegance that fit beautifully into the tasteful old art-deco lobby, with its golden banisters and marble wainscoting. Watching her, and knowing that they must have shocked her, Lee wondered if she and Lucca had not become some sort of modern barbarians, persons so steeped in violence and brutality that they had lost all sense of proportion, all sense of decorum. The thought frightened her, enough so that she pushed it away.

"Well, let's go talk to the girl," she said. "We can't make any money here."

TWO

Sitting in his car, watching the distant bus stop, Baird came to the conclusion that he would have made a lousy private investigator. Even as keyed up as he was, as anxious for the thing to be over and done, he still found it hard to just sit there and do nothing. For the first time in ages, he wished he still smoked. It would have been so easy to reach into his shirt pocket and flip one up, light it, drag. It was a warm day again. The car's windows were down. He could almost see the blue smoke drifting out the passenger side, fouling the air and turning up the noses of the joggers and power-walkers as they chugged along the cinder path that came within twenty feet of his car. He had pulled onto the grass alongside the park's curving blacktop drive at a point about two hundred feet from the park entrance on Fifteenth Avenue, across which was the bus stop where Kathy would be arriving soon.

His original plan, once he saw the man get off the bus behind her, was to jump out of his car and follow the two of them on foot, do a little power-walking of his own. From the bus stop it was about a quarter mile to Baird's house, so he would have had plenty of time to catch up with them, be right behind Kathy in case the guy stepped up his campaign and did something more

than just walk along and utter his sweet nothings about violent
sex or violent death, the one apparently as attractive to him as
the other.

But then Baird decided that it would be better to stay in his
car, since he wasn't as likely to be discovered that way and yet
would still be close enough if Kathy needed him. The important
thing, once she was safely home, was to follow the guy and find
out who he was and where he lived. According to Kathy, he liked
to refer to himself in the third person, as "old Jimbo," as if he
were some sort of folksy country character, someone people just
couldn't help loving. But Baird, like Kathy, preferred to think of
him as simply "the creep."

Meanwhile the minutes passed as slowly as the joggers on the
path. Baird absently reflected that at least he had a pleasant spot
to sit and wait, for the Park Service did what it could to maintain
the place, despite all the picnics and parades and flag-burnings
and drunks in four-wheelers, who would tear up the sod at night
doing figure eights as large as football fields. To Baird's right,
out the passenger window, the scarred lawn stretched for a quarter mile, shaded by scores of trees, everything from towering firs
to modest dogwoods, some set in flower gardens and others edging the avenue, above a thick undergrowth where two weeks earlier the body of a murdered drug dealer had been found. It
shocked and worried him, a killing so close to home. But even as
he was thinking about it, he saw the bus coming up Fifteenth,
virtually soundless, drawing its power from the hot wire overhead. He started his car and waited.

The bus stop was situated just off the avenue, on the narrow
street that ran downhill from the park. As a result, the huge vehicle practically had to stop as it negotiated the tight corner. Pulling alongside the curb, it then hissed to a full stop and its doors
flew open. Baird felt his body tense as the passengers began to
emerge, stepping down from the back door. Kathy was the third
one off, an eyecatcher even at that distance, with her wavy dark
hair and trim figure, a short electric-blue dress showing off her
long legs. As she came back to the corner and started across the
side street, Jimbo was already after her, a muscular young man
wearing jeans, boots, and an open leopard-skin vest over his bare
torso. His hair was pulled back into a ponytail, and even as far

away as he was, Baird could see the man's earring sparkle.

By the time Kathy reached the other side of the street, heading home along the avenue, the creep caught up and began to walk backwards in front of her, like a teenager with a crush. Baird put the Buick in gear and pulled onto the blacktop drive, moving slowly. At the park entrance, he saw that the traffic was going to be too heavy for him to crawl along following Kathy, so he accelerated onto Fifteenth and drove ahead two blocks. At the street there, he turned right and proceeded downhill for a short distance before pulling into a driveway and backing around. Then he came up toward the avenue again, parking finally just short of the corner. To his right was Lookout Park, which ran along the escarpment that eventually would angle behind Baird's house. From this second park a person could see much of Lake Washington and the Cascades; and from where he was, Baird could see anyone crossing the small, narrow park and heading down Alton Place, Baird's own street.

When the two of them appeared again, they were less than fifty feet from where Baird was parked. So he got his first good look at Jimbo's face, which was unremarkable except for its pale gray eyes and the way he held his mouth, the upper lip arched in a frozen sneer. Heading through the park, the creep started walking very close to Kathy, ostentatiously sticking his face in front of hers, as if he were mugging with an infant. But she went on as if he were not even there, striding along with her eyes downcast, her face set.

Next to him, she looked so small and vulnerable that Baird came close to jumping out of the car and running to her rescue. And if he had, he wouldn't have gone empty-handed either, would have carried the sawed-off pool cue he kept under the car seat. He didn't even consider the gun he had in his briefcase, probably because the only reason he'd bought it was for protection when he dropped off his orders at the warehouse at night. But even intervening with a pool cue would have been stupid, he knew, ending probably with the police charging *him* with a crime, not the creep. And that was not the kind of help Kathy needed.

So he continued to sit there in the car, tense and sweating, watching his daughter as she came to the end of the park and went on down the street, heading for home. Twice the man put his hand on her, first on her shoulder, then on her hip, and each time she angrily slapped it away. Finally she broke into a run, but he went right along with her, laughing and flapping his arms like a chicken, ridiculing her pathetic attempt to get away from him.

Because Baird's house was situated at the corner, where the street angled back toward the avenue, he was able to watch the two of them all the way to the front door. If Jimbo suddenly had gotten rough with her or had tried to force his way into the house, Baird would have been there in a few seconds. Then too, he saw his wife's car already in the garage. A part-time librarian at the university, Ellen worked such a varied schedule that Baird seldom knew when to expect her home. As it turned out, though, Kathy didn't give the man the opportunity to do much of anything. The moment she reached the front walk, she made a sudden dash for the door, leaving Jimbo standing there in front of the house. He yelled something at her, then turned and headed back. Halfway across the small park, he stepped off the sidewalk long enough to kick at a flower bed, sending an explosion of bright color into the air. An elderly woman sitting on a nearby bench said something to him, and he gave her the finger as he walked on, not even bothering to look back at her.

Baird kept watching him until he crossed the street and went out of sight, blocked by the houses and apartment buildings along Fifteenth. Even then Baird didn't follow until he judged that Jimbo was close to the bus stop. But when he finally started his car and turned onto the avenue, he was surprised to see Jimbo crossing to Volunteer Park and walking up the same drive where Baird had parked earlier. For a time, Baird figured that the creep was heading for his car, evidently having left it somewhere in the park earlier. And this would have been good news, since it meant that Baird would have been able to get his license-plate number right off—the one bit of information the police probably needed most. But when Jimbo reached the museum drive, he crossed it and kept on walking, heading out over a broad open space toward an outdoor-theater stage, behind which was the park's men's room, widely known as the city's most notorious pickup spot for homosexuals.

Rather than get out and follow the man across the lawn,

Baird stayed in his car and took the winding road that circled below the restrooms, a road he and Ellen sometimes followed in the course of an evening walk, even though it was often bumper-to-bumper with the parked cars of men and boys who carried on as if they had never heard of AIDS. Feeling decidedly uneasy, Baird parked and waited, and in time he saw Jimbo emerge from the restroom and head down the hill in the company of an older man in a business suit. The two of them got into the man's BMW and drove away.

Baird followed them to a new apartment building that overlooked the interstate and Lake Union. The BMW disappeared into the building's underground garage for almost an hour, during which Baird again sat and stewed, though now with the added burden of knowing that the creep could kill his daughter without even intending it, could get the job done just by raping her, just by having sex with her.

When the BMW reappeared, Baird again followed it, this time to a downtown street only a few blocks from Bond's department store, where Kathy worked as a salesclerk. Jimbo barely had time to get out of the car before the driver roared away. Jimbo yelled something at him, then went over to another car, which had a parking ticket stuck under the windshield wiper. He removed the ticket, wadded it, and shot it basketball-style into the bed of a nearby pickup truck. Then he got into the car, which ironically was a 1972 Chevy Impala hardtop, the very same model Baird had owned more than twenty years before. Only this one was a rattletrap, with cardboard windows, doors that didn't match, and a muffler that hung almost to the pavement. But it was the car's license plate that interested Baird most. He had the number written down even before Jimbo pulled away from the curb.

The old car left in its wake a virtual contrail of exhaust gases, so Baird had no trouble following it through the city. Jimbo drove south past the Kingdome and then took the bridge to West Seattle, pulling in finally at a rundown motel that according to the sign out front, now rented its rooms as "Furnished Efficiency Apts.—$95/wk."

Getting out of his car, Jimbo went over to a row of country-style mailboxes and looked inside one of them, then generously inspected the contents of two others before going on to his room, which was located at the far end of the single-story, L-shaped structure. Baird waited a short time before driving into the parking lot. He went slowly past Jimbo's room, which had the number "12" above the door, then he stopped and checked the mailboxes. In the name slot for the Number 12 box, a piece of heavy white paper had been inserted. On it, crudely printed, was the name "Slade."

Baird did not bother to write it down. It was not something he was likely to forget.

For Baird, the one great advantage in working on commission was that he never had to worry about being late for work or even missing a day entirely. Most of his customers required only two calls a month, since paper supplies didn't turn over very fast. Because of this, he was always able to juggle his various daily routes in such a way that no one slipped through the cracks. In fact, the only reason he showed up at the warehouse at all in the morning was because a few of his customers inevitably would call in for an emergency delivery of one item or another, which he would take to them himself during the course of the day, eventually billing the item on their next invoice. As for his daily orders, he almost always dropped them off in the evening, so the warehousemen would have more time to put them up, especially those that had to be delivered the next day.

The Norsten warehouse and office were located just north of the downtown, in the largely commercial area called the Denny Regrade. Named after one of the city's pioneers, it was once a hill as large as the others that still ringed the downtown, including Baird's own Capitol Hill. So steep that horse-drawn wagons could not negotiate its streets, the hill had been simply washed out to sea at the turn of the century, sluiced away with power hoses in the same manner that gold was then mined in Alaska. In the company office there was an antique framed photograph of a house during the regrade, sitting all by itself atop what appeared to be a butte of mud, its owners obviously having refused to go along with the regrade. Reputedly the house of a Norsten forebear, it perfectly symbolized the family tradition of resistance to change. At the Norsten Paper Company there were no computers, no forklift trucks, no power equipment of any kind except for the massive, rickety elevator that carried incoming freight to the upper floors and outgoing orders down to the loading docks.

It was a place Baird went to five mornings a week without a trace of dread. He liked kidding with the girls in the office—and that is what they were still called at Norsten, "girls," no matter what their age—and he enjoyed the heavier raillery with the other salesmen and the warehousemen and truckdrivers. He also liked the coolness and the smell of the old warehouse, its fragrance of freshly minted paper—boxes and rolls and sheets of it—stacked in the huge old rooms, which were twenty feet high, with thick brick walls and the original oak floors and great ax-hewn rafters a yard in diameter and sixty feet long. But probably the thing he liked most about the place was simply its antiquity, the privilege—rare for a contemporary American—to work in a building erected in another century.

On this day, though, he had gotten in and out of Norsten as fast as he could, kidding with no one, just picking up the call-ins and heading out on his route. He had known that he had to be in the park by five o'clock, waiting for Kathy's bus. At the same time, he knew that he couldn't let it show that he was in a hurry, not if he wanted to keep his customers. Baird's ten years in the business had persuaded him that shopkeepers in general disliked salesmen instinctively, convinced that the bastards didn't really work for a living, certainly not the way the shopkeepers themselves did, putting in the long hours of the self-employed. Given this mind-set, they quite naturally were always on the lookout for an excuse to dump their current supplier in favor of someone newer and cheaper. Baird of course tried not to give them that excuse. He was not a glad-hander or joke-teller, but he was affable and steady, and he knew the paper business inside out.

Ironically, it was these same small accounts—the bakeries and restaurants and corner groceries—that he could have lost without seriously denting his income. Most of his commissions came from sales to factories and hotels and restaurant chains, large orders of specialty packaging and food-service items, most of it printed. And as luck would have it, most of his customers that day had been these larger, more important ones. Though the purchasing agents for such companies didn't share the shopkeepers' hostility to salesmen, they were acutely aware of the largesse at their disposal, how easily they could make or break a salesman's day.

So by seven o'clock that evening, when he reached Leo's Bar & Grill, Baird was very much in the mood for a few cool ones. He not only had to unwind from the long, hard day, but now he also had cause to celebrate, having learned Jimbo's identity. On the drive back from West Seattle, he had phoned home with the good news, adding that this meant they would be going to the police in the morning.

"Oh, God," Kathy said. "I won't sleep a wink tonight."

"Sure you will."

"Come home soon, okay?"

Baird had promised he would.

Leo's was located only a few blocks from the Norsten warehouse. Though its clientele was mostly working-class, a number of newsmen from the two local dailies could often be found there. Like all hard-liquor bars in the state, by law the place had to be part restaurant, in fact had to gross half its income from the sale of food. It was said that the owners, Leo and Sally Donato, reached this magical number by classifying as food any drink with an olive, cherry, or twist of lemon. The place wasn't open for breakfast and had only a small crowd at lunchtime and virtually no one in the evening, so the regulars like Baird naturally assumed that the books were cooked. Still, it was difficult to imagine a state examiner—or anyone else for that matter— arguing the point with Leo, who weighed three hundred pounds, only the last fifty of which were fat.

The food-liquor schism divided the place physically as well. On the left, as one entered, was the bar, a long antique thing as massive as the man who tended it. The mirrors behind it were old and beveled, and the wood floor was worn in ruts where the bibulous had trod through the decades. To the right were naugahyde booths backed by a waist-high wall, on the other side of which was the empty restaurant. On top of the wall were plastic ferns and flowers that looked as old as Baird. In the rear, past the bar, there were a pair of pool tables and a juke box that played nothing later than the Beatles.

As Baird slipped onto a bar stool, Leo gave him his usual

greeting, cupping his hand and calling back to Sally, who was working at the reception counter, making change for one of the pool players.

"Hey, Sal, you better go fix yourself up. Your lover-boy is here."

As was his custom, Baird signaled for her not to bother. "No, just as you are, Sal. Anytime, anywhere."

"I'm coming, baby! I'm coming!" she cried, to weary laughter from the regulars, even as she came over behind the bar now. "Where the hell you been?" she complained. "Don't you love us no more?"

"I love you fine. I'm here, ain't I?"

"That you are," Leo said. He had already delivered Baird's usual vodka-tonic, made with Russian vodka and Schweppes. Since he was not a very heavy drinker, Baird figured he could at least imbibe the best.

"You just don't look your usual supercool self," Leo went on. "What is it, Jack—living up there on Fag Hill got you down? You been strolling in that damn park again? You let them naughty boys pull down your panties and do all that nasty stuff they do?"

Baird took a long, cool drink, looking at the two of them, beauty and the beast. Actually, Sally wasn't a true beauty, just trim and very cute for a forty-year-old. She was also a good deal tougher than any man in the place. Not that Leo was a gentle giant, just a little slower to rile. He was bald and neckless, with sleepy eyes, a squashed nose, thick lips, and arms that looked like logs. Legend had it that in his first and only year of college, he had been slated for the Husky varsity, but on an off day had picked up the line coach and shaken him so hard that the poor man lost a dental plate—and a top prospect.

"As a matter of fact, I was in Volunteer Park this afternoon," Baird said.

Leo wagged his head in sorrow. "Oh Jesus, they've gotten to him. Next thing you know, he'll be coming in here tacking up Gay Pride posters."

Sally lit a cigarette from what was probably her third pack of the day. Though she rarely coughed, her voice had begun to sound like Lauren Bacall's. "Aw, come on, let's get off his case. When Jackie's blue, then I am too."

"And very poetic."

"Naturally. So you wanta tell Sally all about it?"

Baird had long thought that the worst thing about bars, other than that drunks congregated in them, was that everybody was always playing to the crowd, only rarely managing to be himself. A perfect example of this were the Donatos, who one-on-one were each caring, intelligent, straightforward individuals, which was the reason they were two of his closest friends. Yet at the moment, these two "friends" were patronizing him as if he were a cretin who had just wandered in out of the rain. But then everyone was fair game, including the Donatos.

"I'd tell you, Sally, but you'd only blab it to Leo. Like that afternoon we spent together at the beach."

She sighed wistfully. "Don't I wish."

Leo winked at the other men at the bar, all but one of whom Baird knew. "Me too," Leo said. "A relief pitcher now and then, that's all I ask."

"*Pitcher!*" Sally barked. "Is that what you call what you do? Catcher is more like it." She smiled at Baird and the others. "The only way Leo knows he's had sex is if I tell him so."

She had to hurry back to the counter then, to collect from an actual restaurant customer. Leo took her place in front of Baird.

"No bullshit, man," he said. "Everything okay?"

Baird shrugged. "Sure. Nothing serious."

"Which means everything ain't okay."

"I guess you could say that. Some ponytailed creep's been harassing my daughter. He hounds her all the way home after work, telling her how much she's gonna enjoy being stabbed and raped and—well, you get the picture."

"No shit, Jack."

"No shit."

"Maybe we oughta pay the fella a visit." Leo made a fist and tapped it into his palm. His hands looked like a pair of baseball gloves.

"I've been thinking along the same lines," Baird said. "Only it's my problem, Leo. I appreciate the offer, though."

Sally had come back by now. "What problem?" she asked. Leo told her and she shook her head in disgust. "God, that really pisses me. There are just too damn many sickos out there these days."

"California's getting too crowded for 'em," Leo observed. "So they come up here."

"And your Kathy's such a lovely girl," Sally said, turning to Leo. "You remember Kathy, don't you? Jack brought her in here for lunch around Christmas, wasn't it? God, what a knock-out! Brunette hair and violet eyes—I love that combination."

"Only she's got brown hair and blue-green eyes," Baird said.

"Whatever. All I'm saying is, if I looked like that, I'd make a beeline for Hollywood. I'd be bigger than Madonna."

Leo laughed. "Oh, sure. What do you think, there's a short-age of beautiful girls down there? You gotta have talent, Sal."

"I'd take acting lessons. If the Boz can do it, I can do it."

"I ain't talkin about actin."

"What then?"

Leo had moved down the bar to refill a couple of mugs of beer. "*Talent*, Sal."

One of the other men, a retiree named Ralston, chimed in. "Yeah, the kinda thing a girl does with her lips and tongue—"

"And teeth," said another, old Wyatt. "The kinda talent, Sal, that can make ugly old bald guys like me feel like Frank Sinatra."

"Who's an ugly old bald guy," Leo said.

"That's the joke," Wyatt explained.

Sally stood there looking at Leo and the others. Making a face, she turned back to Baird. "Not exactly a convention of rocket scientists, you know?"

Baird was not surprised to see old Wyatt at the other end of the bar. A dentist with an almost nonexistent practice in the Re-grade, Wyatt was a dead ringer for the Uncle Ben of rice fame and the only black among the regulars. His real name was Dr. Earl Hadley, but he'd made the mistake one day of bragging that a dentist had to have the eyes of a hawk and the steady hand of a Wyatt Earp. Ever since, his name was Wyatt.

Baird smiled. "If it wasn't for the two of us, Sal, this'd be a pretty tacky place."

Sally picked up his glass and topped it off with a good deal more vodka than tonic. "You can say that again," she said.

It was close to ten in the evening and Jimbo Slade was feeling no pain. He had scrubbed himself good in the shower, making sure he got rid of even the ghost of an odor from his job: the stinking dishwasher detergent and the food itself, especially the goddamn leftover fish, which he liked to say smelled like midnight pussy by the time it got to him.

Afterward, he put on the long blue-velvet robe Murray had given him and turned some rock music on the radio. He filled a glass with ice and Red Label Scotch, then lit a reefer and lay back on the bed to enjoy himself. He liked the word "reefer." Old Murray had taught him that too, along with a lot of other bullshit, like what to wear and which fork to use and how to pronounce "chic" and other asshole words, the old fart trying to turn him into a proper little Hollywood fag. And Slade had gone along for a time, what with the old creep gone all day designing sets or something like that, and the streets absolutely running with primo pussy. Murray had even let him use his car occasionally, a prissy little BMW that Slade nevertheless had managed to score with more than a few times, usually in his special way, the cunts down there being just as gutless as the ones up here, scared to death of a real man.

Finally, though, he hadn't been able to get up even a limp one for Murray, and when the pitiful old fag started bitching about it, Slade had simply unloaded on him—too much, as it turned out, since the bastard almost died. Slade had squeezed everything he could into the fucking BMW and was almost out of state when some gung-ho trooper checked the car's license and pulled him over. Originally charged with attempted murder and grand theft, he plea-bargained it down to assault and grand theft, and did eighteen months at Soledad.

But he was smarter now, more cautious, taking his time. The dishwasher job kept the parole officer happy, and when the police came sniffing around—especially that bitch, Jeffers—he was able to tell them that he was straight now and that he had a job and paid taxes just like everyone else. As for the measly minimum hourly wage, at least it kept him in smokes. And meanwhile, he was moving ahead slowly but surely, selling mostly to his johns and their friends, nickle-and-dime stuff maybe, but it was adding up. Then too, there was more product now, with acid becoming big again, like Murray said it was back in the sixties, when the old fag was a fucking hippie.

The only problem was the brothers, who wanted to hog it all. You had to move so goddamn carefully with them that he sometimes thought he was going to get an ulcer. But it was the only way. You crossed them and before you knew it you had a bunch of twelve-year-old jungle bunnies running up your ass with Mac-tens. They were wasting each other even faster, though, so Slade figured things eventually would go his way. All he had to do was kiss a little black ass on occasion, be patient and careful, and he was confident he would wind up where he belonged, up there on top of the mountain.

Of course that meant he had better not lose his cool anymore, like he had the other night. Sometimes it just got to him, though, the way some rich, stuck-up little cunt would give him the shoulder. It really pissed him, because it made no sense at all. It certainly wasn't because of the way he looked; the fags proved that every day, practically standing in line to have a shot at him. And it wasn't the way he talked or acted either, because some of the cunts would turn away the minute they saw him looking at them, smiling at them. All he could figure was that he must have scared the hell out of them, with his hard face and hard body, right out there for the whole world to see. He dressed the way he did, like a rebel, because that's what he was. What they saw, that's what they would get, and he figured they just didn't have the guts for it. That was the only logical explanation.

Nevertheless he knew he couldn't let it happen again. The lady dick, Jeffers, was still on his case about the Ravenna thing, he was sure of that. But he'd been smarter this time, wiping the girl off with her own fucking sweatshirt and deep-sixing all of it—the sweatshirt, gloves, and tire iron—in the Duwamish River, on his way home. Still, he promised himself that there would be no more of that, no more blowing his cool. He had too much to lose. And anyway, the girl who worked at Bond's was really beginning to get to him. He couldn't even think about her anymore without getting a mega hard-on. She was so goddamn beautiful, and she seemed so sweet and pure, he would have bet a gram that she was still a virgin. Maybe he would send her flowers and ask her for a regular date, start taking her out to dinner and shit like that. Maybe she wouldn't be so shy and skittish then.

Smoking and sipping at his Scotch, he lay there in his crummy bed, in his crummy room, thinking about the two of them up in his penthouse, out on the deck. He would be lying back in a real fancy lounge chair and she would be kneeling beside him, timidly running her hand back and forth over his flat gut, moving gradually, maddeningly, lower. Then he would look at her and smile, giving her permission, and she would lean forward, her beautiful hair falling across his body. And he would feel her mouth then, like warm honey running over him.

This was the picture in his mind when he heard the car pull in and park outside. At first he figured it was his neighbor, the spic cleaning lady in the next apartment. But the footsteps on the porch were a man's. Then there was a knock on the door. Slade placed the roach in an ashtray and flicked open his knife, holding it ready, next to his body, on the side away from the door, which he hadn't bothered to lock yet.

"It's the police," he heard. "Open up."

"Come on in," he said.

It was Jeffers' partner, Lucca, the big soft slob who had joined her in questioning Slade after the Ravenna thing, three months before. Slade let go of the knife and raised the glass of Scotch, preparing to take another drink.

"Well, Sergeant, what brings you here?" he asked. "Come on in. Sit down. You want something to drink? Coffee, beer, Scotch—you name it."

Lucca shut the door behind him, but made no move to sit down. "This ain't a social call," he said.

"I figured that."

The sergeant took out a cigarette and lit it, gumming it like some toothless old woman, all the while looking down at Slade through his Coke-bottle glasses as if he were studying a very large, very dead, snake. Slade had to admit it was a pretty good act.

"What can I do you for, Sergeant?" he asked.

"The night before last. Where were you?"

Frowning hard, Slade pretended to concentrate. "Jesus, lemme think. One day's purty much like another, you know?"

Lucca shook his head. "Don't fuck with me, Slade."

"Hey, I'd never try to fuck with you, Sergeant. I'm trying to remember—honest."

"Between midnight and two in the morning."

"Well, let's see—I was here last night."

"Not at this hour, you weren't. My partner and I came by then too. No one was here."

"Detective Jeffers came by last night? No shit? Jesus, I'm sorry I missed her. What a fox, huh? You know, I'm beginning to think she's got a thing for me—I mean, the way she keeps after me, even though I ain't done nothin wrong."

"Midnight and two A.M., asshole. Where were you?"

"Night before last, huh?"

"Right."

"Why? What happened then?"

"You tell me."

"Hey, I wish I could help. I really do. But all I draw is a blank."

"You want to do this downtown?"

Slade did not respond to that. "Midnight and two in the morning, huh? Lemme think. Oh, yeah. I was at that rock club near the Needle. Some new band was playing."

"What club? What band?"

"Well, lemme put the old thinkin cap on, okay? Let's see now. The band was this buncha creepy kids—Alien something, I think. Yeah—Alien Beings, something like that. And the club—well now, let's see—they keep changing owners so often, you know? Lemme think. Oh, yeah—the *Semi* Hard Rock Café. You know, a typical Seattle name. Real cute."

"Anybody see you there?"

"Well, I'd think so, wouldn't you?"

"We'll check it out."

"Naturally."

The sergeant just stood there for a while then, saying nothing, staring down at Slade with a sour look, as if he had a gut ache.

"Mind if I look around?" he said finally.

Slade shook his head. "Not at all, Sergeant. Not if you got a warrant."

"You think you're real cute, don't you?"

"Jesus, Sergeant—I'm just dumbfounded, you know? I mean, you ain't got a warrant? You came all this way just to ask me where I was a couple nights ago?"

"You're never out of my way, scum."

"Why? You live here too? You live in West Seattle, Sergeant?"

"Where I live is my business."

"Well, sure. Naturally. I was just making conversation."

Slade was enjoying himself immensely. He had drawn up one leg, letting his robe fall away to the point where he was almost exposing himself. And it made him want to howl, the way the ugly old bastard kept glancing at him there, as if he was afraid some giant snake was about to come slithering out, spitting fire at him. Slade hadn't forgotten what one of his johns had told him about Lucca. Supposedly, years before, when the sergeant worked Vice, he'd had the habit of picking up teenage male prostitutes—runaways—and giving them a hot meal and a sermonette, all for the price of a blow job. Slade didn't know whether it was true or not, but he was inclined to believe it. Lucca was just too weird for his own good, coming here like this alone at night, and the way he stood inside the door like some kind of giant stuffed owl, ogling everything but touching nothing.

Slade had known a lot of cops over the years, and Lucca was the only one he could think of who wouldn't have leaned on him by now. At the very least, they would have made him get up and put on some clothes. Most of them, taking in his filthy sink and crummy furniture and tacked-up porn, would have kicked over a few chairs and slammed him up against the wall. And they would have poked around too, with or without a warrant.

Not Lucca, though. He seemed content just to stand there and gawk, like some kid who had lost his way. Well, Slade was not above helping him try to find it again.

"I just had a long, hot shower," he said.

Lucca sneered. "Who gives a shit?"

"I'm so squeaky clean, I bet if I got a hard-on, my dick would squeak."

"What are you, losing your mind?"

Slade grinned. "I just thought you might be interested, Sergeant."

"Well, you thought wrong, buster."

"It's just that . . . well, I've kinda heard certain things, you know?"

"Heard *what?*" The sergeant's eyes looked as if they were about to pop right through the Coke bottles.

"Or maybe it's I've got this sixth sense, you know? After a while—doing what I do—a man begins to recognize certain kinds of people, you know?"

At that, Lucca finally moved, coming straight over to the bed and tipping the flimsy thing, spilling Slade onto the floor. "I guess your sixth sense didn't tell you to expect that, huh?" he bawled.

Slade got to his feet slowly, apologetically, holding out his empty hands, for it suddenly had occurred to him that the wacko cop might just up and shoot him.

"No, I sure didn't expect that," he said.

On his way out, the sergeant stopped and looked back at him. "We'll check out your story," he said. "Meanwhile, don't leave town, understand?"

"Why would I? This is my town."

"Lucky us," Lucca said.

Baird would have had to eat alone that night if Kathy had not joined him at the kitchen table. Even microwaved, it was a delicious dinner—a stuffed pork chop, baked apple, and scalloped potatoes—food that Ellen had painstakingly prepared. So he could understand her added coldness to him, not coming home till almost nine o'clock. Kathy of course wanted to know all about his trailing of Slade, and he told her what he could, omitting only the creep's homosexual transaction, if that was what it was. He told her that Slade had left his car in the park, near the art museum, and he had followed him home from there.

Later, in the family room, he finally got Ellen to agree to go with him and Kathy to the police station in the morning. She grudgingly conceded that the university library could probably go on functioning without her part-time labors at the magazine checkout desk. And she even went so far as to ask Kathy about "this Slade character," what he had done that day, what he had said.

Kathy spoke softly, as if she found it more embarrassing to tell her mother these things than she did Baird.

"Oh, just more of the same junk. Only today he had a name for it—oxygen 'depovation,' as he pronounced it. He seems to think that if a woman lets a guy choke her while he's making love to her . . . well, for her, it just doesn't get any better than that."

Baird came close to spitting out a mouthful of coffee. "Jesus Christ! I ever get my hands on that—"

"Oh, come on," Ellen cut in. "To me, he sounds like a poseur. The Great Pretender. Probably read it in *Playboy*."

"I don't think he reads much of anything," Kathy said.

Ellen made a face, an expression of mild distaste. "Well, we'll have to see what the police say."

For the rest of the evening the three of them said very little. Across the room, on television, the Candice Bergen sitcom had come to an end. Though Baird wasn't very interested in it or any of the shows that followed, they at least were conducive to dozing, which he did, lying on the couch while Ellen sat knitting in one of two easy chairs that faced the TV. As usual, Kathy had taken some pillows off the couch and rigged herself up on the floor, close to Baird. And finally she sat back against the couch in such a way that his hand rested on her shoulder. Sometimes she would squeeze in at the head of the couch, making him scoot down and rearrange his pillow halfway onto her lap. Then she would play with his hair, twisting it around her fingers, even as short as it was.

"Pepper," she would say. "And here's some salt."

Ellen occasionally would look over at the two of them and shake her head in disgust. But Kathy was oblivious to her mother's disapproval, and Baird wasn't about to shove his daughter away. Not unexpectedly, he and Ellen had had a number of quarrels about the problem, Ellen accusing him of encouraging the girl, even reveling in the "childish crush" she supposedly had on him.

"What do you suggest I do?" he'd say. "Get up and move? Push her away? Slap her hands?"

Ellen did not lack for answers. "A little fatherly coldness would do the trick. I know I certainly got plenty of it from my old man, and yet I managed to grow up! At eighteen, I sure as hell wasn't Daddy's sweet widdo baby girl."

For the life of him, Baird couldn't imagine what Ellen expected him to do about Kathy. Just because she didn't want to be the kind of young woman currently fashionable—some hard-assed, hard-nosed future doctor, lawyer, merchant chief—what was he supposed to do? Reject her? Throw her out? As far as he was concerned, she was precisely the kind of daughter parents should have been proud to have: not only beautiful, but thoughtful and loving, a girl who wasn't a slut or a drug addict, a girl whose only crime seemed to be that she was in no hurry to grow old and hard. She had dated in the past. She'd had friendships and opportunities. She'd had good grades in her one year of college. But she had not been happy there, and for now, her job and her home and her parents seemed enough for her. Which was all right with Baird.

Unfortunately, Kathy was not the only thing his wife was unhappy about. And that unhappiness had been going on for almost four years, starting even before their son Kevin had gone off to college in Bellingham, ninety miles north of Seattle. Ironically, for the previous eighteen years Baird and Ellen had been "the happy couple," the envy of most of their friends, the one couple who seemed to know how to make a marriage work. It hadn't seemed to bother her any more than it did Baird that he was not a professional man like most of their neighbors. He had made his choices and Ellen had gone along with them, beginning with the move to the Northwest after the two of them graduated from the University of Illinois, their home state.

Because the Vietnam War was then at its unpopular zenith, they had married while still in school, hoping to keep Baird from being drafted. Partly for the same reason, he had decided to take a job teaching English Lit in a Seattle high school. But after five years, as the war wound down and the job began to bore him, he joined a fledgling advertising agency formed by two of his friends. Because he was the best writer of the three, he became the ad creator, the inside man, while the others worked as account executives.

Though the business prospered, Baird eventually found himself having to deal with the same feelings of boredom and frustration he had experienced in the classroom. And finally he figured out that the problem was not the kind of work he did—not the frivolousness of advertising nor the annual sameness of teaching—but *where* he did it: inside a building, in a room, at a desk. So he eventually found his way into the sales job with Norsten. As a college graduate, he knew he was overqualified for the work, but it paid well enough, certainly more than he could have earned as a schoolteacher, and he was not confined to an office or tied down to a desk. He was content, and he had thought Ellen was too.

Then suddenly, four years before, she had informed him that his job was a laugh and their lives were a waste. Overnight she became a dedicated feminist and an ardent defender of minorities and gays and whales and spotted owls. It seemed there was not a single liberal cause that could have survived without her tireless support. She marched on Gay Pride Day and Martin Luther King's birthday and was even on the scene, cheering wildly, when Seattle's lunatic fringe set fire to the American flag at the local post office. She resented the money that could have been donated to "good causes" but which Baird instead "wasted on pleasure." In time she refused to go out fishing with him or even boating on Lake Washington, and finally she typed up a statement and magnetized it to the refrigerator, a rundown on just how much his favorite hobby was costing them—exactly four hundred and eleven dollars per fish per year. Since their kids were nearing college age at the time, Baird went along with her and sold his boat, a twenty-four-foot Reinell that he had kept moored in Lake Union, just a few blocks from home.

In time, though, Ellen began to lose her political fervor and eventually even expressed a total indifference to it all, as if some lingering fever had finally released its grip on her.

"It's just a lot of sound and fury," she said, "like everything else."

Unfortunately this newfound reasonableness did not extend to family matters, and especially not to her daughter. Ellen simply could not accept the girl's refusal to become the kind of woman her mother wanted her to be.

That night in bed Baird as usual had to deal with the paradox that while his marriage was increasingly loveless, he still desired his wife as much as ever, even though maturity had made her more handsome than pretty. Ellen was a tall woman, only two or three inches shorter than Baird, who was five-eleven. Her hair was colored a shade of strawberry blond and she had a nice strong smile and a steady, blue-eyed gaze that would have made a judge squirm. Though she had gained about ten pounds since college, it only made her seem more voluptuous to him.

Like him, she slept naked, just as they had done from the very first. And this puzzled him, because she otherwise tried to discourage his general horniness. Whatever her reasons, he was grateful for the lapse. Cuddling close, he put his arm around her, holding her breasts, and his cock rose between her buttocks. He edged a little lower, hoping to enter her, but she straightened out on the bed and pulled away.

"I'm almost asleep," she sighed.

He kissed her on the cheek and rolled onto his back, disappointed but not in the least surprised.

"Good night," he said.

THREE

The next morning was a little too perfect for an old Seattleite like Baird. There was a stiff breeze blowing out of the north, holding the temperature in the high sixties and scouring the air so vigorously that the city's streets and buildings seemed to sparkle in the brilliant sun. Flags spanked and trees shimmered, and down the hill the Sound was a lake of blue fire rimmed by the green of the peninsula, above which the Olympics soared snowcapped and jagged, as if they had been placed there by the Chamber of Commerce.

Baird knew the effect a morning like this could have on tourists, for he had been one himself the summer after his sophomore year in college. He had caught salmon and climbed Mount Si with a pair of fraternity buddies, and he had decided then that once he graduated, he too would become a citizen of the great Northwest. The only problem was that over the next quarter-century so many other tourists had followed his lead that the place was turning into Southern California. He wished that before making the big move all future immigrants would visit the city in December, sit gridlocked in their cars on Interstate 5 at six in the evening, listening to the drone of their windshield wipers and dreaming nostalgically of that halcyon time, months before, when they had seen the sun. But it was already too late. Even now, Baird had to drive around for fifteen minutes before he found a parking space near the Public Safety Building.

As usual, Ellen had set the mood for the three of them, saying absolutely nothing as they drove the few miles from their house on Capitol Hill. She was dressed for work, wearing a white blouse, one of her voluminous artsy skirts, and a cardigan. Back at the house, she had tried to make Kathy change out of a short-skirted, low-cut lavender dress suit, saying that she might come across as a more believable victim if she weren't "half-naked." But Kathy had stood her ground, reminding her mother that she would be going to work later and that the lavender suit was the kind of "garment" the store wanted its clerks to wear. She worked in the costume-jewelry department and often had to model items for customers. Though she never said it in so many words, Baird had little doubt that the most important part of her job was simply to look the way most of the store's clientele wished they could have looked.

Biting his tongue, Baird stayed out of the argument. He wanted there to be as much harmony between them as possible when they finally sat down with the police. He didn't want the three of them to come off as so solitary and uncommunicative that the police might sense they were not in total agreement about the threat to Kathy. So he walked a fine line between his wife and daughter, trying to keep Kathy's spirits up without giving Ellen reason to believe he was coddling the girl.

Like most structures in downtown Seattle, the Public Safety Building was situated on the side of a hill. Being fairly modern, it was a drab edifice, a high-rise box with a skirt of reddish marble at the base and no-nonsense steel and glass above. In the lobby, Baird stated his business to an officer sitting alone at a raised desk. The officer, who looked like a clone of Jimmy Carter, told Baird to go up to the third floor, where one of the uniformed desk officers would be able to help him.

"I know the man's name," Baird said. "Jimbo Slade."

The officer pursed his lips. "Slade, huh? The name rings a bell. Listen, go on up to five—the detective division." He picked up his phone. "I'll give them a call. You just wait in the hall there. Someone will come for you."

Baird thanked him, and the officer smiled almost as sweetly as the ex-president.

On the fifth floor, along the corridor wall, there was a pair of benches, both partially occupied. While Baird stood and waited, Ellen and Kathy squeezed in between two elderly Asians and a young black woman who had the look and attire of a hooker. In time, a man came and got them, not introducing himself, just saying the one word, "Baird," then indicating for them to follow him. He appeared to be in his late forties, a heavy, balding man with a dour, professorial look that he underscored by wearing thick, horn-rimmed glasses and walking like a duck, slapping along with his feet pointed out as he led the three of them around the perimeter of the bull pen.

Baird, who liked detective shows on television, was surprised at how quiet and orderly this bull pen was compared with the video variety, which usually depicted police stations in New York and Los Angeles. Here there was carpeting and partitions and the decorous chatter of computer keyboards, not law officers and felons screaming at each other. Still, the detectives *were* armed, and there was at least one handcuffed man sitting next to a desk. On one side of the room there was a row of windowed offices with closed doors. Inside the bull pen, however, there was no real privacy, just clusters of three and four desks separated by the chest-high partitions.

When the detective reached his desk, he pulled two nearby chairs over to the one already there and indicated for the Bairds to sit. As he sat down himself, he finally managed to tell them who he was, though still not offering his hand.

"I'm Sergeant Lucca. What can I do for you?"

Baird introduced himself and Ellen and Kathy, then briefly told the sergeant about Kathy's situation. "It's been going on for over two weeks now," he said finally, taking a paper out of his suitcoat. "Last night I followed the man home to West Seattle. The name on his mailbox is Slade. He calls himself Jimbo. And this is the license and make of his car. Also his address." He handed the paper to the sergeant, who glanced at it, then turned his attention to Kathy.

"You're how old, Miss Baird?"

"Eighteen."

"And you want to make a formal complaint against this individual?"

"Yes," Kathy said.

Looking vaguely troubled, the sergeant began to tap a pencil against the top of his desk. "You understand that this can't be just a matter of language the man has used, or the fact that you don't like him."

"I know that."

"Even under the new stalking statute, there has to be something the man does or says that constitutes a threat," Sergeant Lucca went on. "A threat against your life or a threat to harm you in some way, force you—something like that. And even then—in the beginning—about all we can do is get a restraining order against him."

Kathy told the detective that Slade carried a knife and that he had taken it out as he walked along with her, that she had felt threatened by it.

"What kind of a knife?"

"A switchblade. When he took it out, it was just a pearl handle. Then he pushed something and the blade jumped out."

"Well, it's against the law, of course, carrying a switchblade. But these days, with so many kids packing automatic weapons . . ." Sergeant Lucca shook his head in futility.

"How about threatening someone with it?" Baird said.

The detective barely glanced at him before turning back to Kathy. "Just what was the threat? What specifically did he say?"

Kathy sat silent for a few moments, as if she didn't know where to start. Then, breathing deeply, she began. Baird wondered whether Lucca could even hear her.

"He said that I was going to be his woman and that I had no choice in the matter. He said I'd soon be on my knees, begging him to . . . to make love to me, and—"

"*That*'s how he said it?" Lucca asked. "In those words?"

Kathy looked at Baird and he nodded slightly, frowning, urging her to plunge ahead. And that was exactly what she did, in a way Baird had never heard her speak before. She took another deep breath and let it come.

"No, he said 'fuck.' He said I'd be begging him to fuck me

and suck his cock every chance I got. He said I'd learn to love the feel of his blade as much as his cock. And that the 'coolest' experience a woman could have was to be stabbed or strangled while she's having an orgasm."

At this, even Ellen squirmed.

But Sergeant Lucca still looked bored. "That was the way he put it—the coolest experience *a woman* could have, not necessarily you?"

Kathy was leaning forward slightly in her chair, her hands clasped in her lap. She turned from Lucca to Baird, who wanted to reach across the desk and give the sergeant a good shaking. "For Christ sake, can't you hear her?" he wanted to shout. *"Can't you see her?"*

"Yes," she said now. "Only he didn't say 'woman.' "

"What did he say?"

" 'Cunt.' He calls women cunts."

At the nearest desk, a woman had just sat down. She appeared to be in her mid-thirties and was unusually striking, with heavily lashed green eyes, olive skin, and short, wavy black hair. Because her desk was at right angles to the sergeant's, and slightly behind it, Lucca couldn't see her without turning and therefore wasn't aware of her obvious interest in Kathy and what she was saying. The nameplate on her desk read: "Det. Lee Jeffers."

Lucca shrugged. "Well, there you go. As long as it was impersonal like that—I mean just a general comment about women, even a threat against women—it still wasn't a specific threat against you."

Kathy looked as if she had been slapped. Baird gestured at the paper he'd put on the sergeant's desk.

"What about his name and license here? Jimbo Slade— aren't you going to check to see if he's got a record, or if he's wanted?"

At the mention of the creep's name, the female detective looked up from her desk. "Slade?" she said to Lucca.

Swiveling in his chair, Lucca lowered his glasses and gave her the kind of look a teaching nun might have given a noisy pupil. "You weren't here," he said.

The woman shrugged. "I know. I'm sorry. Just go ahead."

Lucca's smile was venomous. "Well, thank you very much, Detective."

"Look," Baird said, "if you two know something about this Slade, we want to know it too. Does he have a record or not?" At the moment, he was looking across Lucca's desk at the woman, but she suddenly had become engrossed in some papers before her.

"Well, what about it?" he asked Lucca.

Just then the sergeant's phone rang and he answered it, saying nothing but an occasional "Yes, sir" or "No, sir" through most of the conversation. The moment he'd answered the phone, the female detective had got up and left her desk, almost as if she were afraid Baird would start directing his questions at her. She went over to a desk occupied by a black man with a shaved head, her every move followed closely by the other men in the room, for she had a good figure and didn't bother to hide it, wearing tight, faded jeans, cowboy boots, and a green-jersey turtleneck. As she spoke with the black man, she looked over at Baird. But seeing that he was watching her, she turned away.

When Lucca finally hung up, Baird repeated his question. "I was asking about Slade. Does he have a record or not?"

The sergeant obviously didn't like being put on the spot. Assuming the same pained expression as before, he took off his glasses and absently began to rub the lint off them. He glanced at the female detective as she returned to her desk. When he finally answered, he did so without even looking at Baird.

"Well, let's just say the man is known to us. He's got a juvenile record, but of course that's sealed. And he served time in California for assault. Since then—up here—a couple of arrests, but no convictions."

"No *convictions?*" Baird said. "What was he arrested for?"

"Suspicion of rape and assault. But we had no case. For all practical purposes, he's got a clean slate."

"And you know all this just off the top of your head?" Baird pressed. "You don't have to check his record? Punch it up on a computer or something?"

"That's right," Lucca said. "It was a recent case. The charges were dropped. Which means he's just like you or me. He enjoys

the same rights as any other citizen. We can't just haul him in
and arrest him because he's got a dirty mouth and a switchblade.
But—as I said—that doesn't mean we can't try to get a restraining order against him. Your daughter doesn't want him bothering her, and that's understandable."

"Well, let's do that then." It was the first time Ellen had spoken. "Let's do what's possible at least."

The sergeant was grateful. "Exactly. For now, that's all we
can do."

"And what if he doesn't obey the restraining order?" Kathy
asked.

"Then we can arrest him. If it's a flagrant violation, he'll find
himself in jail. But usually in cases like this—not involving ex-
wives and kids and such—usually the feelings don't run so high.
The offending party learns that his obsession is going to cost
him, and he backs off. That's what I think will happen here."

"And what if you're wrong?" Baird asked.

"We cross that bridge when we come to it—not before."
Lucca smiled coldly at Baird. "It's the law," he said.

Baird had planned to pretend on the way out that he had forgotten to mention something to the police. He was going to ask the
women to wait for him in the corridor while he went back. With
Kathy and Ellen safely out of earshot, he was going to tell the
police about Slade's apparent homosexual whoring, figuring that
this would impress upon them the gravity of the situation, the
need to move swiftly against the man. But this was a plan made
before Baird had dealt with Sergeant Lucca. Now he figured he
already knew what the detective would say: that there was no
proof Slade had engaged in prostitution, that homosexuality was
not a crime, and that Baird would do well to calm down and
leave police work to the professionals. Which was exactly what
Baird had decided to do. He couldn't see that he had any other
choice.

As they were driving Kathy to her job, Ellen couldn't resist a
casual dig. "Well, I'm certainly glad I came along. Can't imagine
what you'd have done without me."

"For one thing," Baird said, "I might have punched out Sergeant Lucca."

"That would have been a big help."

"It would've helped me. I'd be feeling a lot better right now."

"I didn't like him either," Kathy said. "He made me feel like the guilty one."

Ellen sighed. "The man isn't paid to worry about our feelings. He was just doing his job."

When he pulled up at Bonds, Baird told Kathy that he would pick her up at four-thirty.

"I know, Daddy," she said. "And I really appreciate it. Bye now. I love you guys."

She leaned forward from the back seat and kissed him on the cheek, then kissed her mother and got out. Baird did not drive away until she had reached the department store's door, where she turned and waved.

Ellen laughed and shook her head. "You'd think she was going to Europe."

"I wouldn't."

"You wouldn't what?"

Not answering, Baird turned onto Olive Way, heading east toward home, so Ellen could pick up her Volkswagen and drive on to her job at the university.

"You notice the kind of kiss she gives me these days?" she said. "You, she kisses on the cheek. Me, she gives one of those high-society busses, kissing the air about six inches away. You'd think she was Princess Grace."

"Princess Grace is dead."

"Princess Di, then."

Baird looked over at her. "Tell me, when was the last time *you* kissed her?"

She shrugged and looked out her window at the freeway passing underneath them. In both directions, it looked like a parking lot filled to capacity.

"When I felt her flinch," she said.

Normally Baird stopped in at Leo's only three or four times a week, usually having just a couple of drinks before going home to a late dinner with Ellen and Kathy. This night, though, he seemed to need the vodka and the time alone, time to think through the problem of Jimbo Slade and an indifferent police department. He had known from the beginning that a restraining order against Slade was probably the most they could hope for, and apparently it was already in the works. But he suspected that Slade in all his swaggering splendor—ponytailed, leopard-vested, half-naked—would barely glance at the thing before wadding it up and tossing it away, just as he had the parking ticket. And Baird couldn't help wondering what he himself would do then. What he *could* do then.

Tempting as Leo's offer of assistance was, he knew he wouldn't him up on it. The problem wasn't Leo's; it was *his*. And anyway, Baird knew that when it came to protecting Kathy, no one was going to do the job better than he himself would. He knew he wasn't as young as Slade, and probably not in as good shape, but then he wasn't planning to box the man or race him in the four-forty. All he figured he would have to do was communicate with him, somehow get across the message that Kathy was simply off limits to him and that if he persisted in bothering her or harmed her in any way, there would be consequences beyond just another police arrest and interrogation. In other words, Baird would probably have to threaten the man, exactly how or with what, he wasn't sure yet. But he had never lacked for imagination.

Nevertheless, for a paper salesman, as for any law-abiding citizen, the idea of meeting and threatening someone like Slade was a scary one. If the creep became violent—well, Baird still had his pool cue, not to mention the gun in his briefcase, the tiny .25-caliber Colt automatic he had bought for cash from the late Bill Chambers, an ex-Norsten salesman who had been assaulted and robbed one night in the company parking lot, all without once reaching for the gun, which he too had kept for protection.

Because Baird didn't want to worry Ellen or Kathy, he had never told them about the gun, any more than he had mentioned the uneasy feeling he often had at night dropping off his orders at the darkened warehouse, the day's collections in his coat pocket. At home he also kept a .38-caliber revolver in the table beside his bed. And finally, there were the rifles and shotguns bought back in the days when he had been an occasional hunter.

At that point he caught himself and smiled at his sudden

flight of paranoia. After all, it was thoroughly possible that Lucca might have been right about Slade, that the man would back off once he learned what his obsession was going to cost him. Or perhaps Ellen saw the creep clearest of all, judging that he was nothing more than a poseur, a fake, the kind of man who would not take a restraining order lightly. In any case, Baird felt decidedly foolish in letting his fears for Kathy run away with him, even to the point of counting his weapons, none of which had ever been fired in anger.

He pushed his empty glass toward Sally. "This is my last. Gotta be on my way."

"If you insist."

"I do. But it's been real."

"It was good for you too, then?" she said.

"But definitely."

When Sally served the refill, Baird took a third of it in a single draft. It felt like a sliver of ice going down.

"You know a cop named Lucca?" he asked. "A detective?"

She gave him a withering look, then turned herself into the Godfather's meanest, most Italianate daughter, gesturing with a cupped hand. "Whatta you tink, huh? You tink every paisan inna world knows every udder paisan? Tell me, you know every mick in town?"

"I've told you before, Sally—I'm not a mick. I'm a high-class Wasp-type fellow. I only come here to slum."

"Well, you sure picked the right place for it." She shook her head. "Naw, I never heard of him. Why?"

Leo came up behind her like a breaching whale. "What'd you say his name was?"

"Sergeant Lucca."

Leo crooked a bratwurst finger and tapped the side of his head. "Boy, when it goes, it really goes fast, huh, Jack? And to think, she's only forty."

Sally looked puzzled. "Why? You know the guy?"

"Hell yes, babe. Don't you remember, right after we bought the place from Kelso? We had a burglary—guy took mostly cigarettes and booze."

"And ruined the damn cash register too."

"Right. And who was the detective on the case? How the hell

could you forget our old pal, Sergeant Lucca? Christ, I practically had to toss the asshole out on his ear."

Sally was indignant. "I didn't forget, smartass! I just forgot
his name!"

"What happened?" Baird asked.

Leo shook his head, remembering. "Well, the sergeant had
finished his investigation and was about to leave, you know? So I
poured him a freebee, and what does he do? He turns it down.
I say, 'Hey, what kinda paisan are you anyway?' And he says, 'I
ain't no fuckin paisan. I'm three-quarters *Nordern European*.' By
then I'm already a little pissed, so I say, 'Nordern European,
huh? Is that like in Nazi?' Well, he stands there for a minute just
lookin at me, you know? And mind you, there ain't all that much
to him, just another pasty-faced, overweight little fucker with
glasses. And he says, 'Yeah, that's right—like in Nazi. Only next
time, we ain't gonna do the Jews—we're just gonna do *ghin-
nies*.'"

At that, old Ralston and Wyatt whooped with laughter, while
the others looked more aghast than anything else, undoubtedly
trying to picture someone crazy enough to call Leo a ghinny to
his face.

"And—?" Baird said.

"I was coming out from behind the bar, that's what. Cop or
no cop, I was gonna toss his ass out the door." Leo laughed now,
glancing at Sally. "You remember what the asshole did then?"

"Hell yes, I remember! I almost peed in my pants!"

"Get this," Leo said to Baird. "Mister Nordern European
reaches down and *unbuttons his sportcoat!* Yeah, like old Wyatt
down there. Like he was some fuckin gunfighter, for Christ sake,
and we was gonna have a fuckin shoot-out!"

"No shit," Baird said.

"No shit. He unbuttons his coat! And he slips his hand underneath, up near his chest, cuz he's wearing a shoulder holster.
Well, of course I stop dead. I can't believe my eyes. And I say,
'So what the fuck is this? You gonna shoot an unarmed man
right in front of his wife and friends?' And then he kinda catches
himself. He just stands there for a couple seconds, like he's froze
stiff. Then he drops his hands and gives me this shit-eater grin.
'Naa,' he says. 'It was just a little joke, that's all.'"

"Yeah, like hell it was," Sally put in. "He just lost it. He panicked."

"Can't figure that out," Ralston said. "Leo come after me, I'd just kick his ass."

Baird and the others laughed.

Leo picked up his bar rag and wiped at a spot. "I'll say this for the guy, though—he knew his business. By the next morning, he already had our burglar. Knew exactly who he was, just by the way he broke in and what he took."

Sally had lit another cigarette. "What about him?" she said to Baird. "He gonna help you with this creep bothering Kathy?"

"He's the one we talked with anyway."

"You didn't like him?"

Baird shrugged. "Well, the man did give us a few precious minutes of his time. But he made it clear he had a lot more important things on his mind than our little problem. He kept tapping his pencil." Baird looked up at the Donatos and smiled. "I sure wanted to break that pencil."

Later, as he was about to leave, Baird saw Detective Jeffers come in off the street, frowning slightly in the dimness. Since women seldom came into the place alone at night, especially any that looked like Jeffers, the men at the bar swiveled and gawked as if Cleopatra herself had come to entertain them. Though Baird suspected that the detective was there to see him, he didn't want to make a fool of himself by getting up to greet her, only to have her pass on by. The regulars would have enjoyed that too much. So all he did was glance at her as she came striding back. She came straight to his stool.

"Could we talk?"

"Of course." Taking his drink, he got up. "Why don't we go into the restaurant section? It's quieter over there."

She nodded and led the way, still wearing her tight jeans and boots, though with the addition of a suede jacket. As the two of them passed the reception counter, Sally gave Baird a look of comic disapproval, as if she were scandalized. And he could see that she already didn't much care for Detective Jeffers, who superficially at least was a younger, taller, sexier version of herself. Following them to a booth along the far wall, she got out a lighter and flicked it on, about to touch the flame to a candle in a red glass bowl.

Detective Jeffers waved her off. "That won't be necessary."

Sally didn't like that. "Whatever you say."

"Would you like a drink?" Baird asked the detective. "Or something to eat?"

"Just a beer," she said to Sally. "A Henry's, if you've got it."

Sally gave her a killer smile. "I think we just might have one or two."

Baird touched his glass and nodded. "I guess one more, Sally," he said.

She turned the smile on him. "Of course, sir."

Before Baird could introduce the two of them, Sally abruptly departed.

The detective smiled coolly. "Mister Baird, I'm Detective Jeffers. Sergeant Lucca doesn't always observe the amenities."

"I noticed that."

"Mind if I smoke?" She was already getting out a cigarette.

"No, go ahead."

As she lit it and dragged, Baird found himself wondering about her, the touch of exotica in her looks. Along with the dramatic green eyes and olive skin, she had full, shapely lips and teeth that were an almost indecent white. He noticed that she wore no wedding ring.

"I called your home and your wife said you might be here," she said now. "First of all, as I told her, the hearing for the restraining order is the day after tomorrow in district court. Judge Ruskin. You should be there by ten. Room E-Twelve."

"That soon, huh? Thank you. Or was it Lucca who pushed it?"

She shrugged. "I know Slade a little better, that's all. I served him this afternoon. I doubt that he'll show up, though."

"That won't matter?"

"No. It's not like a trial. I'm sure the judge will grant the order."

"Good."

Jeffers dragged again and blew the smoke away from the table. She looked solemn, almost grim. "I could have called you about the hearing," she said. "But there are some other things I felt you and your wife should know, and your daughter too."

Baird was already feeling uneasy. He knew he was going to hear things he didn't want to. "About Slade," he said.

She nodded. "The rape case Sergeant Lucca mentioned—it's my case actually. I was the arresting officer. If I'd been there when you came in, I'm the one you would've talked with, not Lucca."

"What about the case?" Baird asked.

"The woman came to the department with the same complaints your daughter has. She was in her late twenties—I mean, she *is* in her late twenties—and she's very pretty, like your daughter. But there was nothing we could do then either, except help her get a restraining order, which she says Slade totally ignored. No one was able to catch him in the act, though. There are so many cases like this, most of them domestic complaints. And of course we've got our hands full just trying to keep up with crimes that have already been committed."

"I understand that." Baird was feeling a growing impatience. "But what happened with the woman? What did Slade do?"

Sally brought their drinks then, so Baird had to wait a few more seconds. And even after Sally had left, Detective Jeffers didn't answer immediately, just sat there looking at Baird, her eyes cold with anger. She dragged again and stubbed out her cigarette.

"He beat her, and he raped her, and he cut her," she said finally. "The victim knows it, and I know it, and I imagine even Sergeant Lucca knows it. Unfortunately that isn't enough for a conviction. Or in this case, even an indictment."

Baird was holding his drink so tightly he wouldn't have been surprised if the glass had shattered. He felt shaky with fear and rage. A rill of sweat slid down his spine.

"I don't understand," he said. "Why wouldn't Lucca tell us this?"

"Because we don't know for sure that Slade did it. And we're still working on it, still trying to nail him. Also, Lucca doesn't like civilians getting in the way."

"And my daughter—what about her? Do we just leave her out there dangling, like live bait?"

Jeffers sighed. "I know," she said. "That's why I'm here."

Baird felt like an idiot. The woman had come on her own time, had gone out of her way to help Kathy, to help him.

"I'm sorry about that," he said. "I do appreciate you coming here. I know it's above and beyond—and I thank you for it."

"That's all right. I couldn't leave it the way it was."

"And Lucca doesn't know?"

She shook her head.

Baird sat there for a few moments, saying nothing, thinking. "About the woman," he said finally. "The victim. I have to know what Slade did. Like how, where, when?"

Jeffers nodded. "Yes, I know." Despite her look of anger, she went on in the flat, offhand way of police officers everywhere— or at least those on the TV news—calmly speaking about the unspeakable, the mundane horrors of their workaday lives. The victim's name was Barbara Evans. She was twenty-nine, a divorcée, a loan officer at Seafirst Bank. Like Kathy, she rode the bus, in her case to the Ravenna district north of the university, where she shared a small house with her mother. Slade was often her co-rider, boarding the bus where she boarded it, getting off where she got off and tagging along beside her, telling her about stabbings and orgasms and her inevitable desperate need for him. She was also visited by Slade at work. She would look up from her desk and see him watching her. He would smile, lick the air salaciously, then disappear, only to show up later at the bus stop.

Then, on a wet February night two weeks after the restraining order had gone into effect, the woman was walking hurriedly from the bus stop to her home, her hand thrust into her open purse, gripping a can of Mace, when she was suddenly struck from behind and dragged senseless into some bushes. A rag was stuffed into her mouth and her clothes were slashed from her body, the knife finding skin and blood with every swipe. Then she was sodomized "in the mouth *and* anus," Jeffers said, making sure Baird fully understood the woman's violation.

"After that, he beat her with his fists," she went on. "Barbara said the man wore rough leather gloves. She was in the hospital for almost a month. She lost three teeth and most of the vision in one eye. She needed three hundred random stitches and was operated on for internal bleeding. She limps now and will never have any children."

Baird took a deep drink of the vodka, hoping it would calm him. "And Slade did it? You know Slade did it?"

"She says it was him. She says she *smelled* him, a cheap cologne he uses. Her wounds were consistent with a large, sharp knife. And of course there was his record with her, all the harassment, the restraining order."

"Yet he walked?"

Jeffers nodded. "His word against hers. And the hospital somehow lost the hair and semen samples. Also, we didn't come up with anything. His room, his car—everything was clean. We didn't find a knife. There were no gloves, no marks on him, not even a scratch. And a buddy alibied him. The D.A. wouldn't prosecute, said we had no case. So that was that."

By now Baird was so overwhelmed by the problem, so frightened for Kathy, that he found himself just sitting there staring at Jeffers, unable to focus his thoughts.

But Jeffers had more for him, much more.

"I'm afraid it doesn't end there either. Last Christmas a teaching assistant at the university was found dead in Discovery Park. She was very pretty and had complained to friends that some guy was harassing her. Only she never named him or described him to anybody. She lived alone, near the park. We assume she was on her way home when she was abducted and taken to the park. As wild as it is there, her body wasn't found for days. She was just lying out there in the rain."

"Yes, I remember reading about her," Baird said.

"And then there was the jogger two nights ago, in your area."

Baird could barely find his voice. "You think Slade did that too?"

Jeffers shrugged. "We don't know yet. In all three cases, there are similarities, but not enough of them. The student's clothes had been cut off her, and she had knife wounds, and she was severely beaten. In fact, it was a blow to the head that killed her. But there was no semen in her, no sign of penetration anywhere. The jogger was badly beaten too and never saw her assailant, but there are no knife wounds, and once again, no semen. It seems that only Barbara Evans got the full treatment. So it's hard to know. Maybe we're talking about three different men—three different animals. That's what Sergeant Lucca thinks."

Baird said nothing for a time, just sat there looking at Jeffers, this lovely messenger with the terrible message. When he finally spoke, his voice almost cracked.

"This whole thing—it's a bit much for me. I don't know what to do."

"Just do the obvious," she said. "Protect your daughter. Go with her everywhere for a while. Maybe even send her away."

Earlier Baird had considered that very option: sending Kathy to stay with his brother and sister-in-law in Illinois. But then, as now, he kept seeing Slade's face, the look of insolence and fanaticism. "You think he'd lose interest in her then? Would he turn to someone else?"

The detective lit another cigarette. "I can't answer that."

"Incidentally, he's either bisexual or a prostitute. When I followed him last night, he stopped at that sewer in Volunteer Park and picked up a guy."

She nodded. "Yes, we know he does a little hooking. After Barbara Evans' rape, we surveilled him around the clock. He also pushes drugs and works in a restaurant. Washes dishes."

"I didn't want to bring it up in front of my daughter."

"She should know," Jeffers said.

"I suppose so." But Baird didn't want to think about that now. "Sergeant Lucca—" he said "—what is it with him? Why didn't he tell us all this? Instead, he acts as if it was damned impertinent of us to come in and waste his valuable time."

Jeffers smiled wryly. "It's hard to say. I'm his partner, and I'm usually in the dark too. I think he felt the desk made a mistake, that you should have been sent downstairs for the uniforms to handle. Protocol, you know."

Baird drained the last of his drink. "No, I'm not sure I do know. If he knew about these other cases, then he knew we weren't making some candy-ass complaint."

"What can I say? He's second in command of the Metro Squad. He's my boss."

Baird made no response to that, and Jeffers fell silent for a short time too. Finally she sighed.

"There's one more thing," she said. "You remember what Lucca said about Slade's juvenile record? That those records are sealed? Well, they're not—not to us. If we have a crime suspect and it would help to have his juvy record, we can get it."

"Which you did with Slade?"

Nodding, she took a final drag on her cigarette and put it out. "When he was twelve, he molested a seven-year-old girl. Two years later he beat his foster mother with a broom handle. Almost killed her. While she was helpless, he repeatedly raped her."

"Jesus Christ."

"He spent most of his childhood in one juvenile facility after another. Foster families in between. His mother was a heroin addict. Father's unknown."

"I don't care about reasons," Baird said. "I don't give a damn why he's like he is."

For a time, Jeffers just sat there looking at Baird, not even blinking. Finally she spoke.

"I don't either. We don't have that luxury anymore."

On the way out, Baird finally introduced her to Sally, knowing that if he hadn't done so, his hostess would have made him pay in the days ahead. But as for Leo and the regulars at the bar, he decided to let them enjoy their salacious suspicions, at least until Sally deflated them with the truth.

Outside, Baird asked Jeffers where her car was parked, and she gave him a look.

"You're going to walk *me* to my car?"

"Of course."

"Mr. Baird, I'm *armed.*"

"Good. Then you can protect me."

Shaking her head, but smiling, she led the way to her car, parked half a block down, on the other side of the street. Before she got in, she put out her hand and he took it in both of his.

"I want to thank you again," he said. "I'm indebted to you."

She shrugged. "It's my job."

"Not everyone does their job."

"No, I guess not." She started to get in her car, then stopped and turned to him. "Remember, I told you all this so you can protect your daughter—not try something against Slade. That would be—"

"Stupid?" he said.

"Yes. And dangerous."

"Don't worry. I'm not the vigilante type."

"Good."

FOUR

Two days later, at eleven in the morning, Kathy got her restraining order. Jimbo Slade was now forbidden by law to come within one hundred feet of her. The hearing itself lasted only a few minutes. The judge was a chubby, unkempt woman with a voice like a chain saw. After scanning the report that Jeffers gave her, she asked the detective a few questions, ascertaining that Slade was absent by choice, having been served his papers the previous day. She then asked Kathy a few questions, seemed satisfied with the girl's answers, and granted the order. Finished, she shoved the paperwork toward a clerk, tapped her gavel, and bawled "Next!"

Though Baird was pleased that everything had gone smoothly, he couldn't help feeling that Kathy and the other litigants were being served a McDonald's Hamburger version of justice. And out in the corridor, as he and Kathy were leaving, Detective Jeffers only added to this feeling.

"I'll see Slade gets a copy," she said. "But I want to remind you—if he violates the order, don't call us—I mean me or Sergeant Lucca. Just dial nine-one-one and get the uniformed police. They'll handle it."

"Understood," Baird said.

They were heading down the front steps, in the cool shadow of the massive building, which was located across the street from the police station, on the same steep hill. It was a bright morning, with a strong wind blowing. Like Kathy, Jeffers did not bother to hold her hair in place.

"We know you went out of your way on this," Baird said to her. "And we do appreciate it."

The detective smiled coolly. "Don't forget—nine-one-one." Turning away, she walked hurriedly toward the police station.

Kathy smiled at her father. "I think she likes you," she said.

"How can you tell? If she was any cooler, I'd have frostbite."

"I can tell, that's all."

"A gal sort of thing, huh?"

"Of course."

"It's so limiting, being a man."

Kathy patted him on the shoulder. "I know. Poor thing."

From the corner, the two of them walked downhill, toward the parking lot where Baird had left his car.

"Why not drop me at home instead of work?" Kathy suggested. "The day's half gone, and I'm feeling lazy."

"Your mother won't be there till four," Baird reminded her. Ellen had insisted that she could not take time off for the hearing.

"So?"

"So I don't want you home alone. Not yet."

Kathy put her hand in his. "You treat me like I'm still your little girl," she said.

"Sorry."

She looked up at him and smiled. "I'm not."

That evening, checking on Kathy, Baird went into the back hallway behind the kitchen, where she was repainting a small wicker rocker that her favorite teddy bear—the one she called Freddy Bear—sat in all day, every day, as if he were waiting patiently for a return of the good old days when he had been admitted to her bed, along with the rest of her menagerie.

"Slade probably has the restraining order by now," Baird said. "From now on, he stays a hundred feet away."

"Unless he chooses not to."

The comment surprised Baird, for Kathy at the moment looked anything but thoughtful and pessimistic, with spots of white paint on her nose and cheek and bare legs.

"That's true," he admitted. "And maybe that's reason enough you should visit Uncle Ralph and Aunt Dollie."

She went on painting. "I'm sorry, Daddy. I just can't do that. I don't want to go there or anyplace else. I feel safer here."

"Slade is here."

"And he'd be here when I got back. Do you want me to leave for good?"

"Of course not."

"So I'll stay then."

"As you wish." He touched her cheek. "You missed a spot here."

She laughed and pretended to go after him with the paint brush as he scooted out of the kitchen.

He still had not told Kathy the full truth about Detective Jeffers' visit to Leo's. He judged that would only terrify the girl needlessly, learning that Slade was a suspect in a murder as well as in the rape of the Ravenna woman, not to mention the rape of the jogger only days before, only blocks away. For that matter, Baird hadn't given Ellen the full story either, knowing from experience that she would disagree with his decision not to tell Kathy and would promptly give the girl the whole story.

All Baird told them was that Jeffers felt they had been short-changed by Sergeant Lucca and had a right to know about Slade's juvenile record. Minimizing that record, Baird said that the creep had been convicted of child molestation and had served time in various juvenile facilities. He made no mention of Slade's brutal rape of his foster mother.

Now he went on through the dining room and the living room and into the den, where Ellen was curled up in her favorite chair, reading a book titled *Introduction to Contract Law*. Feeling at loose ends, he simply repeated what he had just said to Kathy.

"I imagine Slade's been served the restraining order by now."

"Good," his wife said.

He waited for a few moments, wondering whether she would say anything else. "Must be fascinating reading," he said.

She looked up at him. "What would you prefer I read, some soft-core romance?"

"What you read is your business."

"That's for sure."

She was giving him her laser look, the unblinking blue gaze he once had loved so much, and now only admired.

"Well, I'll see you later," he said. "I'm going to watch some TV."

She did not respond.

Later, after she and Kathy had gone to bed, Baird stayed up and watched the late news, then started Jay Leno. Like water, though, his mind kept trickling to the lowest spot, the deepest rut. For the first time in his life he was beginning to wonder if his marriage was not only unhappy but doomed. In recent years he had become so accustomed to Ellen's coldness that he had barely noticed the recent difference in her. But there *was* a difference, and he could not ignore it any longer. In the past, her coldness had seemed only a manifestation of her unhappiness, another way of telling him how dissatisfied and miserable she was. But no matter how cold she had been, he had never felt that she no longer loved him. Always there had been moments, even days, when they would find each other again, as the lovers they once had been. And he had assumed that when she made it through these early years of menopause, things would return to normal and the two of them would be happy together again.

Now he was not so sure, for lately there was this new thing in her attitude toward him, as if she had reached the point where she not only had ceased to love him, but actually disliked him. And Baird did not understand. It made no sense, not for two people who had been so much in love, for so long a time. Still, he couldn't deny that it was there, no more than he could claim that it broke his heart, for Ellen had been unloving for so long now that he seemed to have lost the gift himself. At most, what he felt was a vague sense of dread: fear of change, fear of starting over. Yet when he thought of the alternative—the two of them living together alone after Kathy finally went out on her own—that was the scariest prospect of all.

Using the remote, he turned off the TV and sat there for a while in the family room, which he had added onto the house three years earlier in order to have a comfortable place to watch television, Ellen having insisted more and more that the den be used exclusively for reading and listening to music. Of course there was still the living room—the "museum," as Baird called it—but then and now it was a useless repository for Ellen's haphazard collection of antiques and oddities, including a pair of Empire settees so long-legged and uncomfortable that Baird could understand why Napoleon had never stayed at home for long. The other chairs were wooden rockers in which no one rocked and wooden straight-backed chairs in which no one sat. There was also a baby grand piano without strings, in effect a very expensive table for the display of family photographs.

And finally there was Ellen's collection of antique wicker doll buggies, each of which contained a potted fern of one kind or other. It was a room that the family merely passed through on their way to and from the den or family room. And it was Kathy's ace in the hole whenever her mother started railing about the "baby-girl shit" in her bedroom.

"Well, what about the living room?" Kathy would shoot back. "Ferns in baby buggies!"

Getting up, Baird went out onto the deck, which also was new, having been added to the house at the same time as the family room. In front of him was the best feature of the house and the reason for its recent swift appreciation: a view encompassing the lights of the university district and Laurelhurst, with Lake Washington beyond, wide and black, its far shore corruscating with the lights of the Eastside, which gradually grew dimmer as they rose into the foothills of the Cascades. The mountains themselves of course were not visible now, in the darkness.

Turning from the railing, he looked out at the street, gazing absently at a car parked just around the curve, on Alton, facing his house. For a few moments he looked straight at the car without even realizing what he was seeing. Then it struck him, that shape he knew only too well, the old car much too wide and high for a current model. Even in the dim glow of the streetlight he could see its cardboard window and primer-colored door—and now its driver too, leaning back, smoking, gazing up at Baird's house, the front corner room, *Kathy's* room.

Baird felt his heart begin to sprint. For a moment he thought of calling the police, but he judged that Slade was safely over the hundred-foot limit and anyway would probably drive on long before a police car could arrive. Still, Baird knew he *had* to do something, simply could not let the man continue to go unchallenged, so smugly convinced that he could do whatever the hell he wanted to whomever he wanted to do it.

Baird thought of jumping over the railing and running out to the street to confront him. But he knew that Slade, in his car, would probably have more than just a knife at his disposal—if not a gun, then at least a club of some kind. So he wheeled and ran back into the house, snatching his briefcase off the desk in the den. By the time he reached the front door he had the .25 automatic in hand and had let the case drop. Rushing out onto the front porch, he was just in time to see the old Impala coming around the corner, moving slowly, its ponytailed driver raising his hand in a mocking salute. Baird just stood there and watched as the car went rattling and smoking around the next corner.

After he went back into the house, he put the gun inside his briefcase and returned the case to the den. He closed and locked all the doors and windows downstairs, then went into the kitchen and poured himself a double vodka on ice. Sleep, he knew, would be a long time coming.

In the morning Baird told Kathy and Ellen about their late-night visitor, and Ellen seemed to take it harder than Kathy, evidently disappointed that Slade wasn't as innocuous as she had imagined, someone who would cut and run at the sight of a restraining order.

"I think it's time you went to Ralph and Dollie's," she said to Kathy. "For a couple of months anyway."

The three of them were at the breakfast table. Kathy had finished her juice and toast.

"No, I don't want to go there," she said, getting up from the table.

"It would be for your own good," Ellen persisted.

"I'm not going anywhere." Leaving the kitchen, Kathy went

upstairs and they heard her bedroom door bang shut.

"Well, I guess that's that," Ellen said. "She'd miss her daddy too much."

By four in the afternoon Baird had finished work for the day, and he decided that he wouldn't pick Kathy up as he'd done the last few days, waiting till four-forty-five and pulling up at Bond's Vine Street entrance, hoping she would already be there, waiting for him. When she wasn't, he would then have to circle the block, which could take three minutes or fifteen, depending on the traffic. And that left the girl much too vulnerable, he'd decided. In a worst-case scenario, he could imagine her having to wait there on the sidewalk for ten minutes or more *in Slade's company*, listening to his filth, fearing for her life.

So on this day Baird came a quarter hour early and parked in Bond's garage, then crossed over to the department store and went inside. As usual, he couldn't help being impressed with the work that had gone into making the first floor an enticing place to shop. Everywhere the designer's art was in evidence, with little gatherings of mannequins displaying this and that: beachwear, cocktail dresses, jeans, pullovers. And the counters were not just counters anymore, but minor showrooms in themselves, heavily decorated redoubts where attractive clerks sold everything from cosmetics to luggage.

At the center of them all, as far as Baird was concerned, was the costume-jewelry counter, where Kathy at the moment was hard at work, smiling warmly as she demonstrated a pair of large, yellow earrings for an elderly lady who was smiling herself, though a touch wistfully. Watching from a distance, Baird felt a rush of love and pride. He realized that the girl was only doing her job, trying to sell the earrings, but that didn't explain the sweetness of her smile or the fact that she truly appeared to be enjoying herself with the old woman. These days it seemed to Baird that most people like Kathy, those who were both young and beautiful, tended to share their bounty mostly with their peers, barely managing to even notice the dowdy rest of mankind. So he felt doubly proud of his daughter: proud that she had so much, and prouder still that she so obviously loved to share it.

In this buoyant mood, he looked away from her, aimlessly letting his gaze play across the immense room with its kaleidoscopic abundance of merchandise, the bright colors of summer already giving way to those of autumn. He saw clerks he'd met through Kathy, and there were floorwalkers and customers and a trio of swimsuited mannequins that looked so real and sexy that he thought of driftwood fires on the beach, passion in the sand. Almost smiling now, he let his eyes travel perhaps a centimeter farther—*and there he was again*, looking at Kathy from across the great room, near the Clive Street entrance, again a good, legal hundred feet away from her.

And in that vast welter of merchandise and mannequins and people—clerks and customers—Slade stood out like a panther in a sheep pen. He was just standing there, leaning nonchalantly against a pillar, and it was as if there were some kind of force field around him, a perimeter that others dared not breach. A floorwalker stood watching him from a distance; clerks glanced furtively at him; customers gave him a wide berth. And Baird could see that he loved it, that intimidating straight folk was probably the most fun he got out of life. On this day he was wearing another vest, this one a fringed buckskin type decorated with obscure Indian symbols drawn with a Magic Marker. Everything else was the same: the bare, muscular arms, the hard, hairy torso, the greasy ponytail, the Indian jewelry. But Baird figured it was his face more than anything else that made the force field work: the lifeless gray eyes and the mouth arched in its permanent sneer.

And suddenly this man was looking straight at Baird. The sneer broadened into a kind of smile, and Slade motioned with his head in Kathy's direction. Then his tongue curled out and he lewdly licked the air, twice, as if to make sure that Baird did not miss his intent. Immediately Baird started after him, moving as fast as he could without breaking into a run. But he had to go around the escalators and past a luggage display, which caused him to lose sight of Slade for a vital four or five seconds before he hit a walkway that led in Slade's direction. But even the walkway was not a straight shot, not since some fiendish young merchandising genius had hit upon the idea of laying out the store like a maze, the better to trap the unwary shopper.

Baird saw Slade go out the Clive Street entrance, moving casually, advertising his total lack of concern. And though Baird followed him through the same revolving doors just seconds later, when he hit the sidewalk the creep was nowhere to be seen, swallowed up in the horde of pedestrians moving past the store in both directions. Clive was a one-way street, tree-lined and busy, running sharply downhill past Bond's to the waterfront. In that direction, between two rows of buildings, Baird saw a large Japanese automobile freighter easing soundlessly toward shore, as if it were on a military mission. But he did not see Slade.

When he went back inside, he was aware that a number of people, customers as well as clerks, were watching him as he headed toward Kathy. She had come out from behind her counter, and though she was smiling at him, or trying to anyway, her eyes were bright with tears. At home, he would have taken her in his arms without a thought, and that was what he imagined she expected him to do now. But this was her place of work, and he didn't want her co-workers thinking of her as a daddy's girl. So he only put his arm around her, turning her, and walked her back to her counter.

"He just disappeared," he said. "Like he took some other life form. I probably should have checked out the dogs."

She smiled, but he could feel her trembling.

"I suppose Illinois is still out of the question."

She nodded, and it pained him to realize that she was afraid to speak, afraid to trust her voice.

"He was probably a hundred feet away," Baird told her.

The girl finally spoke. "Do you think he'll ever quit?"

Baird was wondering the same thing. "You bet I do," he said.

Because the next day was a Saturday, all three of them were at home. Kathy, as usual, had an opera playing on her stereo while she cleaned her bedroom and bathroom. Ellen meanwhile was rooting out every mote of dust and dirt in the museum. Later, once their individual holy of holies was immaculate, they would move on to the rest of the house, giving it a desultory cleaning at best. Baird told Ellen that he had some accounts to call on that afternoon and that he also had a shot at the Gordon Fisheries account, a shot that might entail his playing poker with the purchasing agent, among others. He told her that he would be late and that she shouldn't wait dinner for him.

She smiled wryly. "Are you having an affair?"

"Yes," he admitted. "Me and Sergeant Lucca. We just seem to hit it off."

Ellen grew serious. "You're not going to do something stupid, are you?"

"Like what?"

"Like confront our friend Slade. Like threaten him."

Baird looked at her, trying not to blink. "Don't be silly."

"I hope I am being silly. It's just that I know how you are about Kathy."

He put his hand on her shoulder. "Now I want you to listen to me," he said. "And I'm serious about this."

"About what?"

"About today. This afternoon and evening. You two are going to be alone here, and we already know this guy is crazy. So I want you to keep the doors locked. And it would be a good idea to get the gun out of the nightstand and keep it down here. Keep it handy."

Ellen was shaking her head in amusement. "What do you expect him to do—break down our door?"

Baird picked up his briefcase. "Just be careful, all right? You may think all this is a joke, but I'm not sure Jimbo Slade does."

Though he took his briefcase with him, Baird had no calls to make. He was wearing cotton slacks, an open, blue-striped shirt, and his brown-suede sportcoat, which even after a decade of casual wear, was still stiff and tough, probably made from the hide of an old bull. Which was the reason he had chosen it this day, because he knew he could carry the small automatic in one of its side pockets without the gun showing and without the coat drooping suspiciously.

When he got to Leo's, however, he left the gun in the car, still inside his briefcase. It was only the middle of the afternoon and he didn't expect to be in West Seattle until five or six. So there was time to kill, also a certain hard edge of sobriety to lose. Only Leo and few of the regulars were there, indifferently watching a Mariners game on television. Leo, the ex-football

player, had little patience with baseball, shaking his head in
boredom and disgust every time a side was retired with players
languishing on the bases.

"Worse than goddamn bowling," he said now. "I've seen
church services more exciting than this."

"Well, sure," old Wyatt said, "with Jimmy Swaggart smiting
his chest and bawling, *I have sinned against you, my Lord!*' You
can't beat that no how. But baseball, Leo—baseball's a thinking
man's game. Which of course is why you don't like it much."
Wyatt was a diehard Mariners fan.

"Thank God it's almost August," Leo said. "Time for the
M's to do their annual El Foldo." He pushed a vodka-tonic in
front of Baird. "What brings you here on a Saturday?"

"I come here on Saturday all the time."

"Sure you do."

Wyatt affirmed this. "Of course he does. Every Saturday,
like clockwork."

Leo regarded his small gathering of afternoon tipplers. "You
guys are trying to drive me crazy, right?"

"Now why would we do a thing like that?" Wyatt asked. "If
you don't remember, you don't remember. When a man begins
to fail, he's the last to know."

Leo frowned. "Hey, I know you. You're that Amtrak con-
ductor, right?"

Wyatt made a clucking sound. "Sad case. A real sad case."

Ralston was busy reading the morning paper, spread out on
the bar next to his beer. Shaking his head, he tapped the paper
with his index finger, which looked like three knuckles welded
together. "Another skeleton up in Snohomish. They say it's a
girl who disappeared about six years ago. Her old man, a cop,
committed suicide over it. And the guy they think done it, he's
already in prison. All they gotta do is try him for murder and
then hang him."

"Yeah, twenty years from now, if ever," Leo said. "First we
gotta pony up a couple million for his appeals."

Wyatt was in fervent agreement. "Welfare for lawyers, that's
all it is. Why not some welfare for dentists, for a change, huh?"

"Cuz everybody hates dentists," Ralston told him.

Another patron, Tibbs, was nodding sagely. "You ask me, I

say the Green River killer's still at work. He's just moved his operation up to the north end, that's all. Christ, they're finding bones up there every couple days, it seems. It's getting to be like a sport."

Baird said nothing. Of course it was a subject much on his mind these days: the relentless slaughter of females of every age and race and description. In fact the problem had become so pervasive in the area, so constantly a part of the evening news, that until recently Baird had barely taken notice of it, much as if a sportscaster *were* running through the day's scores. So he had no trouble seeing Tibbs' point. The killing of females did indeed seem to have become a kind of gruesome national blood sport, a form of recreation for the hordes of twisted males America seemed so adept at producing.

But Baird didn't care to add his two cents to the discussion. All he knew for sure was that as long as there was a breath of life left in him, his Kathy would not join that appalling cavalcade of victims.

Suddenly he became aware that the bar was silent, that the others were all looking at him.

"Well?" Leo said.

"Well, what?"

"I axed you where your lady-cop friend is today," said Wyatt, the only man in the place with a doctorate.

Since the black dentist had already been worked over many times for his pronunciation of "ask," Baird felt he couldn't use that as a diversionary movement. So he met him head-on.

"Wyatt, why are you such a nosy old bastard?"

"My patients want gossip."

"Patients!" Ralston scoffed. "Which one of the three you talkin about?"

"Let's not get off the subject—" the dentist said "—which is Baird's sexy new friend—with flat feet *and* a touch of color, I might add."

"What do you mean, color?" Leo said. "She's whiter than he is."

"Don't matter. I can tell. A touch of the tar brush, you fine people used to call it. And so it is. The lady is just too sexy to be white."

"The man's a racist," Ralston declared.

Wyatt ignored him. "I still want to know if we're gonna see her tonight or not."

"You better tell him," Leo said to Baird. "Otherwise he'll have his dentures in your ass all night long."

"*Dentures*, my foot!" Wyatt said. "I've got the teeth of a twenty-year-old."

"Then you better give 'em back—you're wearing 'em out." Leo was not above borrowing a good line.

Baird pushed his empty glass toward him. "There ain't gonna be any *all night long*," he said. "One more and I'm on my way."

"And just where would that be?" Wyatt asked.

Baird forced a smile. "Nothing very exciting, I'm afraid. Just business, you old gossip."

The dentist had a loud, cackling laugh, and he let it fly now. "*Old gossip*, my arse!" he said. "Just keeping up is all. And I'll just bet you gonna be doing business, Jackson. The kind of business I wouldn't mind doing a bit of myself tonight. Only I get the feeling the lady prefers her fellas more on the pale side."

"Well, that sure ain't you," Ralston said.

"Or maybe she prefers 'em on the under-eighty side," Tibbs put in, and again Wyatt cackled.

Smiling, Leo brought Baird his refill. "She ever comes in here again," he said, "you might as well put it in the paper."

Later Baird sat in his car looking down the street at the one-time motel where Slade rented a room. It was after seven in the evening, still hours away from nightfall, yet he felt as if he had been waiting days for the creep to show up. There were other low-rent apartment buildings on both sides of the street, eight- and twelve-unit affairs with insufficient off-street parking. As a result, Baird's Buick was only one of dozens of cars parked along the street, virtually bumper to bumper. So he did not feel particularly exposed or noticeable.

Fifty yards ahead, across the street, was the entrance to Slade's motel. Next to it was a weedy empty lot that gave Baird a clear view of room twelve. Since he'd arrived, no one had gone into or out of the room, nor was there any sign of Slade's car. So

Baird had grown less sanguine about his chances of running into Jimbo this way, confronting him and putting him on warning. But he had no idea of how else to go about it. He didn't know where Slade worked, and he didn't know what his hours were. Other than Baird's own house and Bond's Department Store, this was the one place he could be figured to turn up.

Still, Baird couldn't help feeling restless and stupid, sitting there hour after hour munching service-station corn chips and incessantly checking his right pocket to see if the gun was still there, still on safety. And every time he touched it, a breath of panic would blow through him. What on earth was he doing, parked in a strange neighborhood with a loaded gun in his pocket, waiting for some kind of showdown with a brutal young criminal? After all, wasn't he still just himself—nice, easygoing Jack Hanley Baird, middle-aged, middle-class family man and seller of paper supplies, the man who couldn't even shoot a deer when he had one in his gunsight, years before?

Even as he was thinking this, he saw the rattletrap Impala coming down the street toward him, dragging behind it a rooster tail of exhaust gases. The car swerved into the motel parking lot and skidded to a stop in the gravel, in front of room twelve. This time Slade didn't check his mailbox, just jumped out of the car and practically kicked down his door when it proved slow to open. As he slammed the door shut behind him, Baird started the Buick and pulled into the street, then into the motel's parking lot, moving slowly, reminding himself to take it easy and at least appear calm, since he didn't want Slade thinking he was in any danger.

He turned off the engine, pocketed the keys, and got out. He stepped up onto the foot-high porch that ran in front of the rooms and started toward Slade's door—when it suddenly flew open and the creep came hurrying out, head down, sliding a half-pint of whiskey into a pocket of his buckskin vest. At the point of running straight into Baird, he jumped back, looking startled and scared. But he quickly caught himself and like an actor assuming a role, was suddenly Mister Cool again, the pale eyes growing heavy with boredom as his upper lip arched in contempt.

"What the fuck is this?" he said. "What the fuck *you* want?"

"I want to talk to you."

Slade pulled the door closed and headed for his car. "Well, I don't wanna talk to you, Pops. I got your fuckin restrainin order and I ain't been within a fuckin hunnerd feet of your precious baby—so get lost."

He jumped into his car and slammed the door so hard one of the back cardboard "windows" slipped down. Baird tried to speak to him through the driver's-side window.

"You forget about her, you hear me! Don't come near our house! Don't—"

But Slade had started the car by then, and now he revved the engine so high that an explosion of dust and gravel choked off Baird's words. Coughing and rubbing his eyes, Baird stumbled over to his car and got in. Slade meanwhile had backed around, skidding in the gravel again and spinning his wheels in his haste to get away. Baird started the Buick and followed, blinking still as he backed around and accelerated.

He knew it wouldn't be too difficult following the old Chevy, something on the order of trailing a buffalo herd over dusty ground. Minutes later, crossing the freeway bridge that connected West Seattle to the main part of the city, he saw the Impala far up ahead, or at least the miasma that trailed it. So he pushed the Buick well above the speed limit and held it there until he had reeled Slade in to a more acceptable interval. Still, because of the traffic lights, he temporarily lost him in the downtown area, and found him again only because of the unusual figure he presented—the ponytail and buckskin vest and half-bare torso—striding across the parking lot of a strip club near the freeway. Baird was driving past at the time and caught him in his peripheral vision, turning to look just as the creep was entering the low-slung building. Baird circled back and parked. Before getting out, he checked his gun again, making sure the safety was on and that it was properly hidden, with the jacket pocket flap hanging out. Then he went inside.

Harold's was one of the best-known strip clubs in the metropolitan area. In perpetual conflict with the local bluenoses, the clubs had been reduced from serving liquor to beer and wine, and now no alcoholic beverages at all, just soft drinks and coffee. The bluenoses were also trying to abolish "table dances" and "couch dances," which had come to be the clubs' main attractions: nude dances performed for high-tipping individuals sitting at tiny cocktail tables or in the easy chairs and couches scattered along the perimeter of the room. In the couch dance, the girl would finally straddle the seated man and erotically gyrate just inches from his face and body. But he was not allowed to touch her, or at least that was what the signs said.

It had been three or four years since Baird last set foot in Harold's, but the place seemed the same as ever: dark, smoky, quaking with the heavy beat of rock music. A glitter-dome reflected multicolored lights off the walls and ceiling, while a lone dancer occupied the stage, largely ignored in the heat of the many table and couch dances proceeding at the same time.

In the dim light, Baird took the first empty table he could find, looking around for Slade as he sat down. And finally he located him along the back wall, sharing a couch with a lean young black man in an expensive three-piece suit, a white-on-white shirt, and a tie that seemed to glow in the dark. The black's nose also gleamed, and it took Baird a few seconds to realize that what he saw was not a bead of sweat but a tiny gold ring running through the man's left nostril. The two men apparently knew each other, for the black leaned over so Slade could say something directly into his ear, either for privacy or to be heard above the din. As they conversed, a dancer in a see-through leotard came over to Baird's table and asked him what he wanted to drink.

"A Coke," he said.

"A Coke it is." She smiled suggestively. "And how about a personal dance? Real close."

Baird shook his head. "I'm too shy."

Her smile withered. "Yeah, I'll bet."

As she walked away, she put a good deal of motion into the roll of her buttocks, as if to impress upon him what he was missing. Reluctantly, he returned his attention to Slade's couch, where another dancer was now serving drinks to the two men. Slade paid, tossing a number of bills on the coffee table in front of them. The girl took only one of the bills, made change, and left. Curiously, the black man picked up all the remaining bills, folded them neatly, and tucked them into an inside pocket of his suitcoat. Then, leaning over to speak to Slade again, he unobtrusively dropped something into Slade's open hand. Slade glanced down at the hand, closed it, then casually slipped it into a side pocket of his vest.

Given the appearance of the two men, and considering the furtiveness of the transaction, Baird assumed that he had just witnessed a drug deal: Slade buying either for resale or for his own use. As though to confirm this, Slade now looked about him, pretending a great casualness as his gaze swept from one end of the large, dark room almost to the other—stopping when his eyes met Baird's. Again there was that momentary rattled look, more surprise than fear, and once more his eyes and mouth flowed into their customary ruts: weariness above, contempt below.

He leaned toward his black friend and, nodding in Baird's direction, said something that elicited a bored smile from the black, no more than that. Slade put out his hand to be slapped, but the black dismissed the gesture with an almost foppish wave of his hand, as if to say that he was now above such juvenile ceremonies of camaraderie. Slade shrugged and got up. As in Bond's, he licked the air salaciously, close to the back of a couch-dancing girl. No one laughed or smiled, but he didn't seem to notice. His walk and expression conveyed the idea that he considered himself a man of great charm and popularity, a star moving through his fans toward the stage, where he was about to perform. But those who noticed him immediately looked away, much as the people at Bond's had done.

When he reached Baird's table, he spun a chair around and straddled it. "Well, if it ain't old Pops," he said. "Funny, I got this weird feeling I seen you someplace before."

Baird's mouth was dry and his heart seemed to be keeping time with the music, a steady *whomp*, *whomp*. "You didn't let me finish," he told him.

"Well, Jesus," Slade said, "I sure am fuckin sorry about that. But I'm here now, Pops, so why don't you just speak your piece and get it over with?"

"I intend to."

But the dancer in the leotard had come over to the table again. Before she could say anything, Slade waved her off.

"Forget the spiel, babe. I just bought a drink—left it over there where Henry's sittin. You know Henry, don'tcha? So why not be a good little girl and go fetch it for me? Who knows—I might even be nice to you later." Then he gave her a smile or sneer; Baird couldn't tell which. And judging by the girl's indifferent look, she wasn't sure either.

"Money-grubbing cunts," Slade said as she went for the drink. "In here, that's the only kind you get." He fished out a pack of cigarettes and offered one to Baird, who declined it. Slade sucked one out of the pack and lit it with a kitchen match that he ignited with his thumbnail. Then he snuffed the match between two fingers, as if he liked charring his skin.

"Okay, I'm listenin," he said.

"Stay away from my daughter," Baird told him. "And I mean more than a hundred feet. I mean out of her life. Out of her sight."

Grinning, Slade wagged his head. "Jesus, talk about overreacting. I see this girl I like, this beautiful doll, and I never even touch her. I walk her home from work a couple times. I visit her at her job and blow an innocent kiss or two. And what happens? Her daddy gets a restrainin order, and now I get the feelin he's threatenin me—am I right?"

"Could be." Baird kept looking at him, but Slade seemed more interested in the dancer up on the stage.

"Because you love your daughter, huh?" he said, sneering as he watched the girl. "Well, maybe I do too—you ever thought of that?"

Baird didn't answer. The waitress returned with Slade's drink, and Slade regarded her with the same amused sneer. When she was gone, he turned back to Baird.

"So, because I dig your daughter, you're gonna—what? You gonna have me beat up or somethin?"

"It could happen, I suppose," Baird said. "I've got this friend who knows some Samoan kids, gang members. You know how big they are, Samoans. Well, he says they'll cripple anybody you want for a couple hundred dollars."

Slade was still sneering. "Cripple, huh? But I could still get around, huh? I could still park a hunnerd-and-one feet from, like, say, your place?"

Listening to Slade, hearing himself, Baird could hardly believe this conversation was actually taking place. But he pushed on. "Yeah, I see your point," he said. "Things would just get heavier, that's all. I used to do a lot of hunting, and I've still got the guns—shotguns and rifles. Of course I'm probably not the kind of guy who could just shoot another man—not unless I went off my rocker. Which I don't think I'd ever do—unless something happened to my daughter."

"Jesus, that puts me in sort of a bind," Slade said. "Here's this girl I really dig, this girl I might even want to get close to. But if I try it, I get my head blown off. You think that's fair?"

"You bet I do."

Slade said nothing for a few moments, just sat there looking at Baird now. And Baird could see in his pale eyes that it was getting harder for him, carrying on the banter, acting as if none of this touched him. A muscle began to jump in his flat cheek and his sneer lost its edge. He looked over at the stage again, where the young nude dancer was pretending to copulate with a light post. Then he shook his head, as if in sad amazement at such a perfidious world.

"I just don't get it," he said. "I've never even touched your goddamn daughter."

Baird was happy to explain. "It's your record. You see, I know about the Ravenna woman. And I know about your stepmother, and the little girl when you were twelve."

Slade was not smiling now, not even sneering. "You been listenin to that cunt Jeffers, right? Well, she's a lyin bitch. If I did that woman in Ravenna, how come I ain't in jail? Cuz I didn't do it, that's why. Shit, man, I'm probably cleaner than you are."

Baird pushed back his chair and got up. "Well, you know where we stand. Stay away from my daughter."

"Or I get shot, right?"

"I've said my piece."

"That's for goddamn sure."

As Baird headed out the door into the vestibule, he was surprised to hear Slade right behind him. Wary, he kept the man in view as they went out the second door into the parking lot, where the club's many neon signs—the hundreds of flashing lights—made it seem as if they had stepped into a Fourth of July celebration. In front of them, coming from his own parked car, was a huge black man with a shaved head. As he passed by on his way into the club, the man looked the two of them over with such open curiosity that Baird turned and glanced back, only to find the man still watching them. Then he went on inside, and Baird suddenly remembered where he had seen him before: at the police station, in the detective's bull pen. He was the man Jeffers had spoken with when she'd wandered across the room.

Slade apparently didn't know the detective, and hadn't noticed his interest in them. "Listen," he said, "why don't the two of us talk some more, huh? Hit a few bars and have a few drinks together? I want to prove to you I ain't this crazy fuckin monster you think I am."

Again Baird had a hard time believing he had heard the man correctly. Until this moment, he'd been afraid Slade was about to pull a knife on him. "I've said all I care to say," he told him now.

Slade threw up his hands in a clumsy burlesque of exasperation. "Jesus, what a hardnose! I try to be friends and what good does it do me?"

Baird was at his car. "Get real," he said.

"The man whose daughter a guy can't even look at—or bang-bang, huh?" Slade laughed and shook his head. "Man, you are some piece of work, you really are."

As soon as he got behind the wheel, Baird started the car and drove off, leaving Slade standing there in the parking lot like a jilted lover. And it troubled Baird—scared him—the way Slade had reacted to the whole thing. If he had been in the creep's shoes, facing an antagonist who talked about hiring Samoan bone-crushers and threatening to shoot him, he would have readily agreed to the man's every wish. For certain he would not have tagged along with him out to the parking lot, suggesting that they carry on their conversation elsewhere. The more he thought about it, the more convinced he was that Slade had seen right through him from the beginning, had known all along that no matter what "old Pops" said about Samoans and shotguns, he simply wasn't to be taken seriously.

It filled Baird with a cold rage, the idea that this tyro degenerate, barely out of reform school, had judged him as so impotent that he felt free to toy with him, waltz him around like some pathetic maiden aunt. If that had indeed been the case—and Baird was convinced it was—he had a good idea what Slade's next move would be. How better to thumb your nose at "old Pops" than by driving straight out to his house and parking a safe and legal hundred feet away, virtually inviting him to break out the firearms?

Baird at the moment was on busy Olive Way, the most likely route Slade would take on his way to Fifteenth Avenue, which in turn would take him almost all the way to Baird's house. So he pulled over and parked. And he didn't have long to wait. Within minutes the old Impala came smoking up the steep grade. Baird waited until the car was well past him before he pulled out and followed. And a few minutes later, he was not surprised to see it turn onto Fifteenth. Two blocks farther on, however, Slade pulled into the parking lot of Gide's, one of the area's many gay bars. Slowing down, Baird waited until he saw Slade enter the place. Then he drove on.

FIVE

Overnight a cold front had moved in off the ocean, turning the Monday morning sky a sunless gray and dropping the temperature a dozen degrees. The air was uncommonly humid and still, but no rain fell; and whether for this reason or his encounter with Slade, Baird felt uneasy and irritable all day long. Given his mood, he wasted little time on chitchat with his customers and as a result had finished his route by the time he picked Kathy up at work.

Unlike him, she was upbeat and happy. "Guess what," she said. "I sold over a thousand today."

"Well, that's great," he said. "You can take us all out to dinner."

Kathy laughed. "Not a chance. I've already spent my commission on a mauve cocktail dress you would not believe."

"But you don't go out for cocktails."

"Maybe I will one of these days."

"You ever think of going back to school?"

"Sure."

"When?"

"Oh, I don't know. I'm in no hurry." She looked at him. "Why? Are you ashamed of me, selling jewelry?"

"Of course not. You ashamed of me, selling paper?"

"Yes!" Laughing then, she took hold of his arm and gave him a hug. "Never," she said. "In fact, whether I go back to school or not, what I plan to do is meet a nice old guy like you—only a lot richer—and stay at home and raise kids."

"Why an old guy?" Baird asked.

"Who knows?" She reached over and touched his crow's-feet. "Maybe because I like these cute little wrinkles you seniors get."

He smiled. "You sure know how to hurt a guy."

"Well, that's a woman's job," she said.

They were almost home by then, moving along Alton Street past the park, with the house dead ahead. As Baird slowed down, preparing to turn into his driveway, he saw Sergeant Lucca and Detective Jeffers waiting in a gray Ford LTD parked in front of the house. He pulled into the driveway and went around to the garage.

"What do you think they're here for?" Kathy asked.

"We'll soon find out," he said.

The two of them went in the back way. By the time Baird reached the front door, the detectives were already on the porch, ringing the bell. Baird opened the door.

"Good afternoon," he said. "What can I do for you?"

"We'd like to ask you a few questions." Lucca looked as if he'd eaten a rodent for lunch.

"Of course. Come on in."

Baird stood to the side as the two detectives came into the foyer. Jeffers, following Lucca, looked about with casual interest, not once making eye contact with Baird.

"God, I love these old houses," she said. "So much room. And brick too."

"We like it," Baird said.

As before, she was wearing designer jeans, a T-shirt, and the same tan-suede jacket. Lucca was in a shapeless brown suit. Even after Baird had closed the door, the two of them just stood there in the foyer, understandably unsure which direction to move in, with the dining room on one side and the museum on the other: a choice of straight-backed chairs or ferns in doll buggies.

"You remember Detective Jeffers," Lucca said.

Baird smiled slightly. "Of course."

Which caused her to give him a furtive look of reproval, apparently trying to warn him against making any reference to their conversation at Leo's.

"Hello," she said, nodding coolly.

They both said hello to Kathy, who was standing at the foot of the stairs, as if she were waiting to be excused.

"Let's sit in here." Baird went into the dining room. "Would you like coffee or a Coke? Anything?"

"This isn't a social call," Lucca said.

"Well, I'm going to sit." Jeffers pulled out a chair. "I think better sitting down."

Shrugging, Lucca followed her lead. Meanwhile Kathy was still waiting in the foyer.

"Kathy, why don't you go on up?" Baird said. "I'll fill you in later."

"Maybe she ought to hear this," Jeffers suggested. "It involves Slade."

Remembering the shave-headed detective outside the strip club, Baird had a pretty good idea what the detectives were there for, and he had no desire to be scolded in front of his daughter. So, as he headed around the table, moving behind the detectives, he gestured for her to leave, giving her a conspirator's wink at the same time. She smiled and went on up the stairs. Sitting, Baird reflected that his luck wasn't all bad, since Ellen was out for the evening, having dinner and seeing a movie with two of her women friends, divorcées she once had referred to as members of her "support group."

"What's this about?" he asked.

"You've got no idea?" Lucca said.

"Should I have?"

"Yeah, you should."

"Why don't you just tell me."

"Saturday night you were seen in the company of Jimbo Slade, the man you just had a restraining order slapped on. You care to explain that?"

"No problem. After Slade showed up here and at my daughter's place of work—"

"Within a hundred feet of her?" Lucca cut in.

Baird ignored the interruption. "When he did that, I decided to have a word with him. So I followed him to Harold's strip club and told him to stay away from Kathy altogether."

"Or what?"

"Or nothing."

Lucca laughed at that, a weary snort. "No threats or anything like that?"

"No, that would be a crime, wouldn't it? Threatening somebody?"

"Yes, it would be," Jeffers put in. "And it could also be pretty damn dangerous, Mister Baird. Especially with somebody like Slade."

Lucca sighed. He appeared troubled. "You know, if I had my druthers, I'd just tell you I really don't give a shit about this," he said. "I mean, if a man wants to play chicken with a psychopath, that should be his business, right? But we don't work that way. I'm afraid it's very much *our* business when you meddle in an open case."

"And what case is that?" Baird asked.

Smiling slightly, Lucca shook his head, as if he were both amused and stymied. Then suddenly he exploded. "We don't have to tell you that, for Christ sake! Do you really think you can meddle in official police business and then demand a fucking explanation when we tell you to back off?"

Baird was surprised. Jeffers looked shocked. Lucca's face had flushed deeply and his hands had tightened into fists. Looking down at them now, he slipped them under the table, as if he'd just discovered they were covered with warts. Jeffers tried to explain.

"It really gets to us," she said. "We do all we can to nail a slimeball like Slade, so we naturally expect a complainant to cooperate with us, to do what we ask—"

"Just what the hell are you two talking about?" Exasperated himself by now, Baird smiled in bewilderment. "I don't know what case you're referring to. I don't know how I've compromised your investigation. I don't know what the hell any of this is about."

"Sergeant Lucca told you that Slade was under suspicion for assault and rape," Jeffers said, looking confused herself by now, obviously caught in the middle, trying to back up her partner without at the same time revealing that she and Baird had already gone over these matters, alone. "And then you start making contact with the man. How are we to know what you tell him? We want his guard down, and here you could be alerting him that we're still on his case."

Lucca pushed back his chair, getting ready to leave. "Enough of this bullshit, okay?" he said. "Mister Baird, the fact of the matter is this—our chief and the people who put him where he is, they don't look kindly on vigilantes. That's why we have police, you understand? Now I know you say you didn't threaten Slade, but of course the three of us here know better. Why meet him if not to threaten him? So our concern is that you don't goad the bastard into an act of violence against your daughter, or for that matter, against you or your wife." He stopped there for a few seconds, as if he'd run out of breath. Baird had the feeling that if the two of them had been closer, the sergeant would have begun poking him in the chest with his finger.

"And just as important," Lucca went on, "we don't want *you* committing an act of violence against him. In fact, if you did—if you were that stupid—we'd go after you just as hard as we would him. A crime is a crime is a crime, as I once said. And that's why we're here, Mister Baird—to make sure none of these unlawful things take place. You understand?"

Baird pushed back his own chair and got up. "Perfectly," he said. "I never thought anything else."

As soon as the two detectives were gone, Kathy came hurrying down the stairs, her eyes wide with wonderment.

"You were with Slade?" she asked.

At the moment, Baird's full bladder was the only thing on his mind. "In a minute, okay?"

But in the bathroom, standing over the bowl, he sighed more in disappointment than in physical relief. He had hoped Kathy would not overhear his conversation with the detectives and learn about his having met with Slade. He tried hard to think what he could say to her, what magical words might lessen her fear and put her mind at ease. But when he came out of the bathroom, she was already gone. He called for her, but there was no answer. Going upstairs, he knocked on her door, then went on inside, where he found her sitting at her drawing board, coolly sketching out a dress of some sort.

He sat down on the bed. "Are you okay?" he asked.

"You're going to get yourself killed."

"No I'm not. I'm not a reckless man. You know that."

She swiveled on her chair, facing him now. "I know how he looks at me. He's a killer, Daddy. And if you were alone with him—"

"I was perfectly safe," he cut in. "I saw him in a public place."

"But *why?*"

"There were things I wanted to say to him."

"Like what?"

"For one, that his cause was hopeless. I told him that you'd never have anything to do with him, and that if he ever did anything to you, I'd make him pay."

"How?"

"By having him killed."

"By *what?*"

"I told him I've made contact with men who do that kind of work."

She said nothing for a few moments, just sat there looking at him in shock and confusion.

"And have you?" she asked finally. "Do you know such people?"

He shook his head. "No. But the important thing is that I make him believe it's true."

"But what about you? Who protects you?"

"The same men. I told Slade I'd already arranged for that. If anything happens to me, they'll come after him."

She was looking at Baird as if his face had undergone some unearthly transformation. "I just can't believe any of this—us talking about such things," she said. "It's so unreal."

"That's the word, all right. And it's even more unreal when you're sitting right there with the creep."

"I don't know how you could do it."

"Incentive," he said.

As she looked at him, her eyes began to fill. Getting up, she came over and sat next to him on the bed. She laid her head on his shoulder and hugged him.

"If anything ever happened to you—" she said.

Baird tried to reassure her. "Don't worry, baby. I'll be fine."

Before Ellen came home, Baird cautioned Kathy that her mother would be upset if she learned that the police had come to the house and that he had made contact with Slade. Of course she might learn these things eventually anyway, he said, but he couldn't see that it would serve any purpose to tell her now and ruin her evening, not to mention his own. Kathy listened politely, gave him a Mona Lisa smile, and resumed her communion with a Nieman-Marcus catalog. But when her mother finally did come home, the girl said nothing about the police or Slade.

Ellen seemed to have enjoyed her night out with the "guys," as the women called themselves now. She zestfully recounted how one of her guys had just ended a long-term relationship with her live-in boyfriend, virtually tossing the poor fellow out into the street. Then she told how much they had enjoyed seeing *A Room with a View* again. "The heroine's intended is such a perfect twit," she said. "An absolute hoot."

Later, in bed, Baird thought her good spirits might extend to him. But it was not to be. She was much too tired, she said. And then too, he thought, why on earth would she want to ruin such a fun night out with the guys?

The next day the heavy cloud cover finally gave up a bit of its moisture, the first rain in over a month and fairly rare for Seattle in August. Spurred by the change in the weather, Baird tried to make up for the previous day, taking his time with his customers and making sure that if they ran out of any paper products during the next two weeks, it would not be his fault.

He stopped to take Kathy home and then resumed his route, not finishing until after seven. At Leo's, he called home and told Ellen that he would be late, then went back to the bar, aware that Sally was watching him as if he were parading around with his pants around his ankles.

"What's so funny?" he asked her.

"Who said anything was funny?"

"You're sure acting like it."

Serving his vodka-tonic, she affected a look of sorrowful consternation. "The truth is, I'm quite sad."

"Is that a fact?"

"I'm afraid so. Trouble is, it's just so easy to misjudge someone, you know? You say to yourself, 'Now there's a real prince of a fellow. Straight as an arrow. The kind of guy who wouldn't play around if he owned his own escort service.' You know the kind I mean?"

Baird groaned and looked past her, at Leo. "What's she got on me anyway?"

Leo, drying a beer mug, shook his head. "Dunno, but it sounds serious."

"Oh, you bet it is," she said, taking a piece of note paper out of her apron pocket with a flourish. "Since I wrote it down, I will deign to read it. 'Jack B. Call 324-1822, signed Jeffers.'" She looked up at him, innocence incarnate. "You know anyone by that name, Jack? A woman, with a kind of dark, sexy voice."

"Sure," he said, taking the note. "Jeffers, right? Yeah, I've been screwing her a lot lately. In fact, any woman that might call me here, you can pretty well assume that I'm boning her on a regular basis."

Sally smiled. "Well, that's none of our business."

Down the bar, Wyatt Earp had a comment. "He's a lucky fellow, all right."

"What time did she call?" Baird asked.

"A little before five."

Baird took a long drink. "Well, I suppose I'd better hurry over to her place. She's probably hotter than a pistol by now."

Since Leo and the others all seemed to be enjoying this, Sally decided to stay with it, to go on beating her poor dead horse as long as she could.

"Well, a patron's sex life is his own business, I always say. Far be it from me to judge anyone who isn't running a tab."

Baird slid his empty glass toward Leo. "She's your wife," he said. "It's your duty to beat her on a regular basis."

"I know, I know." Leo shook his head. "But she's got wiles, Jack. Wiles you would not believe."

Sally picked up the phone behind the bar and placed it in

front of Baird, which gave everyone a good laugh.

"Oh yes I would," he said.

An hour later, Baird sat waiting at a small table on the landing behind Ivar's Salmon House restaurant. To his right, over a low chain-link fence, the waters of Lake Union lapped against the concrete of the landing. A mile to the south, across the lake, the tallest of the downtown skyscrapers were catching a few random rays of sunset, the cloud cover having finally begun to break up. In front of him were a few dozen tables, occupied mostly by tourists and university students, many of whom had food they had bought at the restaurant's outdoor fish bar, famous for its fried clams.

In the distance, beyond the landing, was Portage Bay and the ship canal, which connected Lake Washington with Puget Sound. As such, it was one of the busiest waterways in America, at times the bearer of a seemingly endless stream of pleasure craft going out to the Sound or returning from it. And finally there was the Interstate bridge, virtually overhead, eight lanes of traffic that produced a roar so constant one barely heard it after a time, somehow could sit back and enjoy the water and the boats and the seabirds in what seemed like peace and quiet.

Still, Baird considered it an odd place to meet Detective Jeffers. She had sounded serious on the phone, as if there were some urgency to their meeting, so he would have expected her to suggest some out-of-the-way bar or even a parking lot. But convenience had seemed more important to her than privacy. She said that her home, recently purchased, was in the Wallingford neighborhood, just up the hill from Ivar's. Baird had told her that he would be there in twenty minutes. Early, he had stopped at the fish bar to load up on fried oysters, french fries, cole slaw, and two coffees, which he then carried on a tray down to the landing.

He had just begun to eat when she arrived, again in jeans and boots, though with a UW Huskies sweatshirt in place of a T-shirt and jacket.

"I have an extra coffee," he said as she sat down. "And if you want some oysters, I can spare a few."

"Coffee would be fine," she told him. "Thank you."

As he passed her the cup she lit a cigarette and glanced out over the water. "I love it here at dusk," she said, smiling at him now. "In fact, I love this town. I wouldn't live anywhere else."

He smiled wryly. "These days I'm not too fond of it."

"That's understandable."

For a few moments neither of them said anything. Jeffers sat there looking at him with her smoky green eyes. She took another drag on her cigarette. Exhaling, she shook her head.

"I'm worried about you, you know."

"You don't have to be. I'm a cautious sort of guy."

"Oh sure. Tracking down a psycho like Slade and threatening him."

"Did Lucca send you here?"

That made her laugh. "No, I'm afraid not. But he's the main reason I wanted to see you—to explain about that ridiculous scene at your house yesterday."

"Ridiculous?" Baird said. "I don't know. At the end, he seemed to explain things pretty clearly."

"But he didn't give you any reasons—just orders. The case he mentioned, it's the same one I told you about—the bank clerk, Barbara Evans, the woman we think Slade raped. What we're working on is his alibi, this friend of his who claims Slade was with him at the time. The man is lying, and he knows we know he's lying, but he's scared to death of Slade. They were in juvenile detention together—both of them about sixteen at the time—and he claims that back then, Slade bragged about killing some bum out around Kent. Supposedly he just picked out a guy at random, some drunk sleeping in an alley, and brained him with a hammer, then threw him in a dumpster.

"The story's impossible to check, because bums are rarely reported missing and no body turned up. Which isn't surprising. With the trucks they have nowadays, nobody looks inside the dumpster—they just power-lift it and dump it in the back, compress it, and out it goes to the landfill. God knows how many bodies there are in those places. So this guy's story could be true. In any case, it's something for you to think about. Good reason not to push Slade too far."

Not yet finished with his oysters, Baird was glad that he had a good stomach. He also considered it a good thing that Jeffers had to lean close to be heard over the roar from the bridge. Otherwise he figured everyone around them would have been staring at her.

"You've got a point," he said.

"You just can't play games with this guy, Mister Baird. He's obviously a criminal psychopath. You can't predict his behavior. You may think you're getting to him—scaring him, winning him over, whatever it is you're trying to do—but you can't rely on it. He might just smile and put a knife in you."

Since Baird already knew this, or at least sensed it, the only words of hers that stuck in his mind were "Mister Baird." "I realize all that," he said. "And incidentally, my name is Jack. Friends, enemies, everybody calls me Jack."

"I knew your name."

"But you'd rather keep things formal?"

"Not at all—Jack." She smiled. "And my name is not Detective, it's Lee. My middle name actually. I can't tell you the first one—my father had this thing about poets."

"Let me guess," he said. "Edgar?"

She laughed. "Edgar?"

"Edgar Lee Masters. Spoon River stuff."

"No, I'm afraid not. But it would be an improvement."

"One more shot, okay?" he said. "Annabel?"

"My God!" She looked genuinely astonished. "You're kind of spooky."

" 'I and my Annabel Lee, in this kingdom by the sea.' Tennyson, right? I used to teach English in high school."

"Now that I didn't know."

"I liked the summers off."

Her smile faded. "He was a Jamaican. My mother is French Creole. When I was eleven, he was killed robbing a bank."

Baird looked closely at her. "Are you serious?"

"Afraid so."

"I'm sorry."

She turned and gazed out at the lake, where a large white sailboat was moving past, under power, headed for Lake Washington. "He was no damn good," she said.

"Well, he appears to have had good genes." Baird wanted to

bite his tongue. It was the kind of inane comment he liked to leave unsaid.

She made no reply, and the two of them slipped into an awkward silence. He had no idea what to say next, for he still couldn't quite understand the purpose of this supposedly urgent meeting. Granted, it was important for him to know about the dumpster killing, but Jeffers had already told him about the Discovery Park case and that Slade was still a suspect in that murder. Then too, she could have told him all this on the telephone. Of course there was still Sally's interpretation of things, but Baird knew better. A woman who looked like Lee Jeffers certainly wouldn't lack for amorous opportunities. And being a detective—apparently an ambitious one—she would know better than to get into an affair with a married man, especially one involved in a case she was working on. Now if he had been ten years younger and ten times richer, then maybe Sally would have been on the right track. But not now. He was confident of that.

"I appreciate your telling me about this," he said finally. "I mean about Slade. I'll be careful. I'll try not to see him again."

"Try?"

"Correction—I *won't* see him again."

The green eyes regarded him coolly, almost knowingly, as if she had been taking lessons from Ellen. "I wish I could believe that," she said, lighting another cigarette.

For some reason, Baird could not bring himself to reassure her.

Exhaling, she shook her head in puzzlement. "You know, one of the strangest aspects of this whole thing is Sergeant Lucca's attitude toward you. And that's one of the reasons I wanted to see you again—to explain things. I can imagine how much he pisses you off."

Baird shrugged. "Oh, I don't know. I just figured he's got a nasty disposition."

She gave a wry smile. "I'm afraid that's about it. He's a terrific detective. They say he's got a better record than the chief himself. But I'm afraid it's his whole life. He had a couple of brief marriages. No kids. He never dates, never takes time off. He must have *years* of vacation time built up. And . . . well, that's all there is. He seems to get colder and ruder every day he lives—not just to the public, but to us too, his fellow dicks. But I guess he's reserved a special place in hell for citizens who try to do our job for us."

"Cheeky bastards like me, you mean."

"He might say that. I wouldn't."

Baird was hoping he finally had heard the last about Sergeant Lucca, but Jeffers unfortunately had more for him. "It's weird, but the only people he's consistently decent to are the enemy—our suspects and perps. Them, he gives every consideration. His bible, I guess, is the Rights of the Accused. Which is one of the reasons the guys call him Bleeding Hart. Hart's his first name, you see."

In Baird's mind a caution light had come on. Why, he wondered, was she telling him all this if not to disarm him, make him think that he and she were on the same side, against Lucca. Forget him, she seemed to be saying. Trust me. Tell me your plans.

He smiled now, almost apologetically. "I hate to be rude myself, but I really don't give a damn about your sergeant. It's you I'd prefer to know about."

"Like what?"

"Well, like do you brush your teeth sideways or up and down?"

Jeffers laughed, showing her beautiful teeth. "Neither," she said. "I just run my tongue over them now and then."

"I'll have to try that." Catching her look, he amended his statement. "On my own teeth."

From that point on, their conversation was more casual, less about Slade and the case and more about themselves, especially about Detective Jeffers. After her father's death in New Orleans, her mother had moved to Los Angeles with Lee and Lee's two older brothers. At eighteen, Lee moved to Seattle on her own and gradually worked her way through the university, getting a bachelor's degree in Law Enforcement Administration. At twenty-five, she joined the Seattle police force and despite the benefits of affirmative action, was not promoted to detective until she was thirty-one, five years before.

She had been married twice: at eighteen to a local rich kid whose family managed to get the marriage annulled, and then, a decade later, to a narcotics detective who became such a heavy cocaine user himself that he eventually quit the force and became a dealer. Jeffers had divorced him by then and ever since, she said, had managed to stay "free and clear of men."

"For now, that's the way I like it," she went on. "If Mister Right ever comes along, I'll probably arrest him for loitering or something."

It was dark by now. Across the lake the downtown skyscrapers had a cold, unearthly beauty, which perversely came to life on the water, where their myriad lights shimmered gold and white, even gas-company blue. Close by, the ducks and seagulls were ending their long day of warfare, the ducks as usual winning in the water, while the gulls controlled the air. Baird picked the last morsel off his tray, a french fry, and tossed it to the ducks, one of which gobbled it on the fly.

"You ready to go?" he asked.

Jeffers nodded. "Yes. It's getting cool."

Baird followed her up the gangway and fell in beside her as they went around to the front of the restaurant, passing under the trees.

"I'll walk you to your car," he said.

She smiled at him. "Then you'll have quite a walk. I left it at home. I wanted the exercise."

"Then I'll drive you home."

"What about my exercise?"

"It's already dark," he said. "On foot in this town at night— you want to chance that?"

"Come to think of it—no. Police protection being what it is."

Baird smiled. When they came to his car, he unlocked the passenger door and closed it behind her, even though he knew it was an unnecessarily chivalrous gesture. Ellen, in similar circumstances, would probably have informed the man of his gaffe. But Lee Jeffers said nothing.

As Baird got in next to her, she ran her hand along the edge of the seat. "Real leather, huh? I love the smell."

"Well, this is my office," he explained. "I spend a lot of time in it. And then too, it's deductible."

"It still smells good."

Baird smiled at that, for some reason unperturbed that she had just stuck a pin in one of his gassier balloons.

After she gave him directions, he told her that he didn't smell the leather at all. "Just your perfume," he added.

"I don't wear perfume."

"Maybe your shampoo then."

"It's unscented."

He looked at her and found her smiling, evidently still having a little fun with him. And he wondered if she comprehended in the slightest the effect she had on him—as she undoubtedly would have had on most men—in such close quarters. Her legs in the tight jeans, her lustrous black hair, the curve of her breasts under the sweatshirt, her eyes so beautiful and expressive in the dashboard's glow—there seemed to be nothing else in the car, nothing else anywhere.

"We're here," she said. "The brown one on the right."

On each side of the street was a row of almost identical bungalows, one-time blue-collar homes now prized as yuppie starter houses, close to downtown, well-made, good investments.

"If it weren't for the house across the street," she said, "I'd have a view of the lake."

"Damned inconsiderate of them."

"I know."

Though she had her hand on the door, she didn't open it yet. And suddenly her expression was grave. "No more personal meetings with Slade, okay?"

"What if he keeps turning up, a hundred feet away?"

She shrugged. "There's no law against it. But if he does, call me, all right?"

"At the station?"

"Or here."

"Okay," he said. "And thank you."

She smiled at him. "Well, thank *you*. For the coffee. And the lift."

It was an awkward moment. Baird wanted very much to reach over and touch her in some way, shake her hand or maybe even kiss her on the cheek. But it was not his way, trying to get close to a woman other than Ellen. And even if he could have overcome that inhibition, he knew he would only have made the moment more awkward. So he didn't move. Jeffers opened the door and got out of the car.

"I'll wait till you get inside," he said.

She laughed again, just as she had that first night. "I'm armed, remember?"

Baird didn't give Ellen any explanation for his lateness other than to repeat what he'd said on the phone: that he had stopped off at Leo's. He was still afraid that they had not seen the last of Slade and that he might have to resume his campaign against him, "get in his face," as he considered it. And to do that without arousing Ellen's suspicions, he figured he would have to first set up a pattern of unexplained late nights. He knew this wasn't going to add to the peace and harmony of his home life, but he considered that a small price to pay for Kathy's safety.

There was no sign of Slade the next few days, however. And on Thursday night Ellen dragged Baird and Kathy to a local theater group's presentation of a play titled *Checking Off*, which the playbill described as a "stunning send-up of Chekhov's *Three Sisters.*" Since Baird was not even a fan of legitimate theater, believing the movies could almost always do it better, avant-garde theater was to him simply another word for agony, especially when it was presented on the cheap in a one-time Baptist Church that should have been claimed by fire generations past. Almost everything in the building was wood, and all of it creaked, especially the seats. Unhappily the wood also magnified sound, bouncing decibels back and forth like Ping Pong balls. Worst of all was the *kind* of sound it bounced: the local theatrical crowd in full throat, able finally to let it all out, the honk and squawk and screech of phony accents, all that gassy thespian enthusiasm they had to keep in check nine-to-five at the ad agency. And this being Capitol Hill, there was no shortage of men gesturing like Bette Davis, no dearth of large, crew-cut females in suits and ties, hulking over their pretty little dates, girls who looked like Dutch boys.

When Ellen had told Baird that she'd bought tickets for the play, he'd agreed to go along, hoping it would in some measure make up for his late-night transgressions. Unexpectedly, Kathy had agreed to go along too, which spared Baird the necessity of convincing her to join them, since he still didn't want her staying home alone. Always fashion-wise, she seemed to know just what the occasion called for: black jeans, a black-leather jacket, and a large, floppy tam with pink polka dots. Unlike her father, she did not look at all out of place.

When the play finally began around eight-thirty, not everyone noticed. For one thing, no lights had dimmed. Nor was there a proscenium arch, or even a stage as such—just a large, square platform like a prizefight ring, with corner posts and standing spotlights and television monitors and cameras and microphones and miles of electric cable lying about. There were also a couple of chairs and tables. When the crowd eventually realized that the master of ceremonies was speaking, it quieted down, though the emcee remained largely inaudible, mumbling into a microphone with a cut cord. A barefoot youth, he wore bib overalls with zebra-stripe holes running up and down the legs, also a top hat bearing the letters "M.C.," which Baird considered a really cute touch.

Then came the first fully audible sound: the electronically boosted voice of an actress in street clothes engaging a TV monitor in conversation. The actor appearing on the monitor was sitting offstage, in front of a TV camera.

Baird soon decided that the only way to get through the evening was to think about other things, such as the unsettling hour or so he had spent with Lee Jeffers. But every time he got a coherent thought going, a sudden noise from the stage—usually an electronic screech—would break through. Time and again he had to stifle the urge to lean toward Ellen or Kathy and offer a bit of commentary on the proceedings. And the effort must have shown, for when Kathy looked at him now, she suddenly began to sputter with laughter. Leaning her way, he confided that he was feeling queasy and might need to use her tam as a barf bag, which caused her to sputter all the more and finally to kick him in the leg.

Fortunately, Kathy was not the only one laughing. The cognoscenti naturally were howling at all the right places, demonstrating their deep knowledge of Chekhov, of just what it was that was being "sent up." One man in particular, a cackler on a par with Wyatt Earp, was carrying on as if he were at a Henny Youngman concert. When he reached what was hopefully a crescendo, Baird suggested to Kathy that she go tell him to put a sock in it, which resulted in more sputtering and another shot to the leg.

Ellen gave them both a stern look. Behind them, a man with minty breath and classy diction leaned close and suggested that if they did not like the show, perhaps they should leave.

Baird turned and smiled gratefully. "Now why didn't I think of that?" he said.

As the first act was ending, he told Ellen that he was leaving. "I'll wait in the car or get a drink somewhere. When it's over, I'll have the car out in front."

She looked at him as if he were an incorrigible child. "It doesn't matter that I want to stay," she said.

"No reason you can't stay," he told her. "I'll pick you and Kathy up afterward."

"No, you won't," Kathy interjected. "I want to leave too."

Ellen shrugged. "Of course. What else?"

Baird leaned close to his wife. "Come on, honey, you know this is the pits. It's excruciating. In a movie theater, you'd demand your money back."

She gestured indifference. "Go on, then. Go. I'll see you both later."

It wasn't easy, making their way through the entr'acte crowd, most of whom were battling their way toward the bar, shouting at each other in order to be heard. The wooden stairwell was deafening and smoke-filled, and when he and Kathy finally reached the cool night air of the street, Baird felt as if he had been swimming up through murky water and just now breached the surface. He noticed that they were not the only ones leaving, that they were in fact part of a sizable crowd heading for their cars.

"God, was that a waste!" Kathy said. "I can't imagine what they had in mind."

"Apparently not profit."

The car was parked in a lot across the street. When they reached it and got in, Kathy wondered out loud where they should go for a drink. "Henry's would be good," she concluded.

But Baird already saw Ellen coming toward them, crossing the busy street. "Probably nowhere," he said. "Here comes your mother."

His prediction proved true. Ellen said that she didn't want to stop anywhere for a drink or anything else. She just wanted to go straight home. As Baird pulled out of the lot, she explained why.

"I'd be afraid you two would just get up and leave me."

"Oh, come on," Kathy said.

"Next time I'll just buy a ticket for myself."

"Mother, you know that thing stunk."

"Stank," Ellen corrected. Smiling then, she suddenly began to laugh. "Oh God, but it stank!"

She had always had a lovely laugh, rich and easy, and for some reason on this night it opened Baird like a cleaver. To cover the tears unexpectedly welling in his eyes, he laughed too, as did Kathy, in the back seat. And soon the three of them were howling as if they would never stop. Ellen, gasping, managed to get out a few words.

"It . . . certainly wasn't . . . *Hamlet!*"

Even as he was laughing, Baird felt a twinge of uneasiness at his emotion. Here he was, a man prepared to do anything to keep his daughter from harm, a man who had spent most of his waking hours the last two days thinking about Lee Jeffers, and yet a man whose wife could still turn him into jelly with a single laugh. He wondered if he wasn't becoming a kind of Slade in reverse, a man crippled not by hatred but by love.

Turning onto Alton, Baird saw immediately that the house was not as they had left it. The lights left burning in the den and kitchen had been turned off, and upstairs, which had been left dark, there was now a light on—in Kathy's room. As he slowed down, Ellen saw it too.

"Maybe Kev's home," she said.

Their son had phoned Monday night, but he hadn't said anything about coming home.

"He doesn't turn lights off—he turns them on," Baird said.

He slowed the car to a crawl as they moved past the house.

"His car's not here," Ellen said. "The driveway's empty."

"Oh, Jesus!" Kathy cried. "It's *him!* I know it's *him!* He's in my room!"

"We don't know that," Baird said. "And we're not going to look. We'll let the police check it out."

He pulled into a neighbor's driveway, then backed around and parked, facing their house. Using the car phone, he called the police and explained the situation, told them that "a burglar or burglars" might still be in the house.

As they waited for the police, Kathy began to pound her fist helplessly against the front seat. "We can't stop him!" she said. "He's going to kill me and we can't stop him. Nobody can."

When the police arrived—two cars, with their lights flashing—Baird got out and waved the first one down. He told the officer at the wheel which house was his and why he thought there was trouble inside. For the moment he didn't mention Slade, figuring it would only complicate matters. He gave the officer a key to the front door and then watched as the man went on ahead and parked in front of the house. The second car pulled into the driveway and two officers got out. With guns drawn, they went around to the back while the first one went up to the front door, unlocked it, and went inside. Baird started walking toward the house. Inside he could see the beams of the officers' flashlights sweeping back and forth. Then the lights began to come on, one room at a time, first downstairs, then upstairs.

Meanwhile Ellen was calling out to Baird in a hushed voice, urging him to come back to the car. But he went on ahead, reaching the front porch just as the first officer came back out.

"They're gone," he said to Baird. "They broke in the back way. Looks like you lost a few things."

Baird signaled to Ellen and Kathy, who then got out of the car and came toward him. The other officers appeared in the driveway, having come from the back of the house. "We're gonna roll, Charley," the nearest one said.

The officer on the porch nodded. "Yeah, I'll take it from here. But you call in Burglary for me, okay?"

The two men got into their patrol car and backed into the

street. As they drove away, Ellen and Kathy joined Baird on the porch.

"There's one weird thing," the officer said.

"What's that?" Baird asked.

"I'll show you."

The three of them followed the officer into the living room. There, above Ellen's two Empire settees, Freddy Bear had been nailed to the fireplace mantel with a butcher knife run through his belly.

The officer shook his head in puzzlement. "It's just weird, a burglar taking the time to do a silly thing like that."

Kathy had started to run from the room, but Baird caught her and pulled her close. He could feel her trembling.

"I don't think it was a burglar," he said.

SIX

By the time the burglary detectives arrived, Baird had already tried to phone Lee Jeffers to tell her what had happened. But she was not at home, so he left a message on her machine. Both detectives were sergeants in their thirties, an Irishman and a Japanese seemingly more interested in their amiable Mutt-and-Jeff routine than in Baird's assertion that Slade was the burglar. The Japanese, Soto, did take the time to write down some of what Baird had to give him about Slade—his address and record and the fact that Sergeant Lucca and Detective Jeffers were already working on his case—but the Irishman, Reardon, obviously thought his partner was wasting his time. According to Reardon, it was a "prank bust-in," a non-professional job from start to finish, probably the work of neighborhood kids.

"A professional burglar," Reardon said, "would never waste time scrounging up a butcher knife so he could tack a teddy bear to the mantel."

Baird wanted to kick the man. "That's exactly what I'm saying," he told him. "Slade is not a burglar. This was meant to intimidate us and terrify our daughter."

The Irishman shook his beefy head. "Naa, this is strictly kid stuff. What did they get? What did they take? Purty much zilch. Hell, I bet it was some Jap kids that done it." He looked over at his partner. "What about it, Bobby? Any Jap kids in this neighborhood?"

"Jap kids, my ass," Soto said. "Only mick kids be dumb enough to take a Sears VCR and pass up a Nikon thirty-five millimeter."

Baird was glad the two of them were having such a fine time. He only wished there had been a rape or a killing so they could have truly enjoyed themselves. At the same time, he recognized that the break-in did have its bizarre aspects, even if the perpetrator—Slade—was interested only in terrorizing Kathy. He had broken in through the back door, for some reason jimmying it open, wrecking the jamb and springing the locks, when all he had to do was break the door's window, reach in, and unlock it. In the process, though, he had broken the glass anyway.

As far as Baird could tell, Slade had taken only the VCR, a pair of binoculars, and an old calendar watch of Baird's, passing up dozens of more valuable items, including cameras and silverware and—oddest of all—Baird's gun collection, if it could be called that. Basically just an assortment of rifles and shotguns accumulated over the years—nine guns in all, none of any particular value or rarity—they were kept in a glass-front oak cabinet that Baird had bought secondhand when he was in his thirties and still an occasional hunter. Considering what he had said to Slade in the strip club about the guns and what he would do with them, he figured the creep would have stolen them, or at least tried to neutralize them: take them out and break their stocks, smash the barrels against the fireplace, do what damage he could. But all he'd done was break the cabinet's glass front, leaving the guns untouched.

It occurred to Baird that this could have been a symbolic act on Slade's part, a taunting demonstration of just how empty he found Baird's threats. But then, Baird doubted that old Jimbo even knew what symbolism was. More likely, he simply had been in a hurry to get out of the house. Still, Baird didn't doubt that the creep had accomplished his objective: invading their home and leaving his grotesque message. Ellen immediately had wanted to take the teddy bear down from the mantel, but the police officer had said to leave it there for the detectives. And eventually Sergeant Soto did attend to it, gingerly pulling the butcher knife out of both the mantel and the bear's body and dropping it into a plastic bag so it could be tested later for finger-prints—the only such testing the police planned to do. No forensics expert was brought in to dust around the broken door or the gun cabinet or the mantel.

As Sergeant Reardon explained it: "This is small potatoes. We get a dozen of these a night, most of 'em by users. And even then we don't usually dust, not unless there was violence—and I don't mean against teddy bears neither. You were damn lucky, you know that? Japanese kids, they ain't very good burglars."

Soto grinned. "Unlike the Irish."

After the comical detectives had left—moving on to their next gig, as Baird thought of it—Ellen phoned Kevin in Bellingham to tell him about the break-in, but he was not at home either. Baird asked Kathy what she wanted done with Freddy Bear, and she said to get rid of him, so he took the bear outside and put it in the trash. Then he did what he could to secure the back door, reflecting ruefully that for years he had been intending to put better locks on the door or even replace the door itself. At least now he would have to see that something was done about it.

Later, after Kathy and Ellen had gone upstairs to bed, Kathy suddenly cried out, and Baird went bounding up the stairs, passing Ellen in the hallway. Together, they found the girl sitting on her bed, her face in her hands.

"What is it, baby?" Baird asked. "What's wrong?"

She gestured toward her dresser. "The bikini pictures. He took them too."

The "bikini pictures," as Ellen referred to them, were two five-by-seven blowups of snapshots taken at the Oregon beach a couple of summers before. One was of Kathy alone and the other was of the four of them standing in a row in their swim-suits, with the sea and Oregon's great surf rocks in the back-ground. In each photo Kathy was wearing the same revealing bikini and doing her best to mock its effect, posing with exaggerated sexiness, smiling haughtily while holding one hand behind her head and the other on her hip. As a result, Ellen had decreed that the pictures were not suitable for the baby grand.

So Kathy had kept the two framed photos on her dresser.

They were not there now, however.

Both Ellen and Baird tried to console the girl, but she was so terrified, Baird doubted that she even heard them.

"I keep *feeling* him here!" she said. "It's like he's still here. Like he's taken over our lives."

Baird tried to be strong for her, but he too felt Slade's presence everywhere in the house. It infuriated him, just the thought that the creep had sauntered through these rooms, touching this and that, probably bouncing on the same bed where Kathy now sat, maybe even stretching out, testing it against that fulfilling day when he could throw her onto it and draw out his switchblade.

Feeling shaky himself, Baird took her by the arms and brought her to her feet, hugged her. "Listen, honey, you sleep with Mom tonight, okay? I'll take the guest room."

Ellen demurred. "She'll have the same problem tomorrow night. It's something she's just going to have to deal with."

Surprisingly, the decision came from Kathy herself. Putting her arm around her mother, she ushered her toward the door.

"No, Daddy's right," she said. "I'll sleep with you tonight. And tomorrow I'll scrub everything in here. Then I'll be okay."

But going to bed did not mean going to sleep. Baird didn't even give it much of a try. Stacking the pillows under his head, he lay there in the dark listening to Kathy and Ellen across the hallway, in the master bedroom. Though he couldn't hear their words, he could tell from their voices that while Kathy wanted to talk, Ellen only wanted to sleep. He could hear his wife tossing and turning, responding to Kathy's words with sighs of exhaustion and exasperation. So Baird eventually got out of bed and went in to them. He suggested that Kathy take his place in the guest room, adding that he would sit up with her until she was asleep. She agreed almost too readily, not even saying good night to her mother before jumping out of bed and hurrying across the hall to the guest room. When Baird started to tuck her in, she reached up and took his hand, and he sat down on the edge of the bed.

"Are you really going to stay until I'm asleep?" she asked.

"Of course, baby. All night if you want."

Her eyes filled. "I can't stand the thought of him in my room."

"Me neither. But for now, just try to put him out of your mind, okay? He'll be my worry tonight."

She nodded. "All right."

He kissed her on the cheek. "I'll never let him hurt you, honey. You know that, don't you?"

"Yes."

"So go to sleep now. I'll stay right here. Then I'll be across the hall. I'll leave the doors open."

After she closed her eyes, Baird sat there for another five or ten minutes, watching her in the soft light. And when her breathing slowed, he kissed her again, on the shoulder in order not to wake her. Then he got up and started out of the room.

"Good night, Daddy," she said.

He smiled in the darkness. "Good night, sweetheart."

He went to the bathroom for a glass of water and ended up drinking two of them. It seemed he could not even think of Slade without his throat turning to parchment. When he got to bed, Ellen sighed and rolled toward him, waking briefly, though without opening her eyes.

"How's she doing?" she asked.

"Okay, considering."

"Well, this settles it. She's going to Illinois."

"I don't think she will."

"Maybe if you'd take her—drive her there—maybe then she'd go."

"We'll see," he said.

"But then what do I know?" With that, she rolled over again and immediately fell asleep.

Baird did not even try to follow her. He looked up at the shadows playing across the ceiling—the leaves of his neighbor's cottonwood rustling in the streetlight—and he felt an over-whelming helplessness. If he had ever needed proof that Slade was not going to back down, he knew he had it now. It just didn't make any sense to go on hoping for the best, not when you were dealing with a man who would break into a girl's home for no other reason than to terrorize her, in the process leaving his revolting little calling card, like a wild animal pissing on the perimeter of its turf.

Baird accepted it now that Slade was just going to keep on pushing, breaking whatever laws he chose to break, knowing that the police would not find anything they could use against him. And eventually, someday, somewhere, he would get Kathy alone, have her totally at his mercy. And Baird, like most fathers—like most pitiful, law-abiding, middle-class wimps—would do nothing but sit and hope and wring his hands, and in the end wind up despising himself for the rest of his days. In fact, all he had to do was turn on the television news and there he was: some poor bereft bastard sitting with his wife in their tacky living room, wiping his eyes and muttering to a reporter that he'd just never thought the fellow would go so far. Sometimes it was a son-in-law, sometimes a daughter's boyfriend; but just as often it would be an outsider, a random creep like Slade.

An hour passed before Baird finally gave up and got out of bed. He slipped into his bathrobe and went down to the kitchen, where he filled a glass with ice and vodka, adding a splash of tonic. Then he carried the drink back through the house and went out onto the deck and stood there in the darkness, sipping at the vodka, hoping to relax. To his right, down the street, was Lookout Park, deserted as far as he could see in the lights from the street. Beyond the park, in the brambly woodland down the hill, the darkness was solid, impenetrable. And Baird wondered if Slade was out there somewhere, crouched and silent, observing what he had wrought in the home of his intended.

Taking a deeper draft of the vodka, Baird recalled a time when he was only seven or eight years old, visiting his grandparents' Illinois farm. While aimlessly poking around the barnyard, he had come upon some sort of wooden cover lying on the ground, and as he reached down to stand it up, a cat was suddenly at his side, a sleek gray tom with jack-o'-lantern eyes. Baird went ahead and raised the lid, and in the next few seconds he learned unforgettably what the phrase "quick as a cat" meant. For the moment the lid came off the ground, there was an explosion of mice scampering in every direction—though not nearly fast enough to avoid the cat's murderous paws, which in the space of a few seconds maimed five or six of the tiny rodents.

Afterward, the cat casually went back over his catch, killing all but one, which he then lovingly played with for a good half hour, softly cuffing it this way and that, carrying it in his mouth and dropping it, repeatedly letting it limp away until it would reach some unknown forbidden point, whereupon the cat would playfully pounce on it again. And when the mouse finally died, the cat kept prodding it, as if trying to wake the poor creature. Failing that, he settled down and ate it.

Baird certainly didn't think of Slade as catlike, nor did the creep's eyes glow bright orange. But Baird would never forget the simple, mindless pleasure the cat found in torturing the mouse, and he couldn't help wondering if Slade wasn't similarly enjoying himself, watching helpless old "Pops" boozing out on the deck in the darkness.

Baird drank the last of the vodka and poured the remaining ice out over the railing. Then he drew back his arm and hurled the glass as far as he could down the hillside.

Before eight o'clock the next morning, Lee Jeffers came to the house. Baird was in the dining room, reading the paper and having toast and coffee. Ellen and Kathy were still upstairs, both having decided not to go to work that day, Kathy because she was exhausted and frightened, Ellen because she agreed that the girl shouldn't be left home alone.

Baird let Jeffers in and took her through the downstairs, showing her the back door and the gun cabinet, then the fireplace mantel, even though there was nothing for her to see there except a slit in the wood where the knife had gone in.

"You really think it was him?" she asked.

Baird looked at her. "You *don't?* Who else would it be?"

"I don't know. It just seems so silly. What did he accomplish?"

"Other than scaring the hell out of us, I'm not sure. You'll have to ask him."

She smiled wryly. "Oh, we will—don't worry."

Instead of her usual jeans and suede jacket, the detective was wearing a dark pantsuit with a white blouse and a purple scarf. She looked more businesslike but no less appealing than she had two nights before when he had driven her home. Leading her through the house, he touched her arm and the small of her back a couple of times. In the rear hallway, looking at the broken door, she turned suddenly, and they found themselves face-to-face, just inches apart. She looked flustered for a moment, then smiled and moved on.

"Not too bright," she said, "breaking the door that way. Not one of your better burglars."

"How about one of your better murderous sexual predators?"

She turned again and looked at him. "Reason enough to stay away from him, wouldn't you say?"

He didn't answer.

"Anyway, no more trying to go it alone, okay, Jack?"

They were coming into the foyer just then, as was Ellen, from upstairs. The two women said hello, and Baird explained to Ellen that he had just taken Jeffers through the house, showing her Slade's handiwork. Then he told Jeffers about the missing photographs, and she said that she would check with the burglary detectives during the day and that as soon as there were any developments in the case, she would call and let them know.

When she was gone, Baird went back into the dining room to pour himself a fresh cup of coffee. Ellen followed.

"What was that about going it alone?"

He shrugged. "I'm not sure. The night she went to Leo's— you remember, she called here first?"

"Yes. So?"

"She wanted us to know more about Slade—his juvenile record and so forth."

"I already know that."

"Well, during the course of the conversation, I think she somehow got the idea that if the police couldn't make Slade back off, I might give it a try myself."

"She *somehow* got the idea?"

"I guess from things I said."

"Well, you're not that reckless, I hope."

"Don't worry."

Ellen smiled now, not without irony. "A good-looking woman, that Jeffers, wouldn't you say?"

"I guess. In an exotic sort of way."

"Calls you Jack already. I didn't realize you knew her that well."

"That night at Leo's, she was there for almost an hour."

"That explains it, then."

Baird did not respond.

During the afternoon Baird called the police several times from his car but wasn't able to get in touch with either the burglary detectives or Lee Jeffers. Finally, at close to five o'clock, he called again from the Norsten office and got Jeffers on the phone. She had just heard from Soto in Burglary, she said. They had searched Slade's apartment and car and hadn't found any of the missing items. There were no fingerprints on the knife, and on top of that, Slade had an alibi for the time of the burglary.

"A stockbroker," she said to Baird. "Probably one of his johns. If the guy is still in the closet, somebody like Slade can get him to say almost anything."

"So he gets away with it," Baird said.

"*If* he did it, yes. We've got to have a case, you know."

"Oh, I know, I know. What I think I'll have to do is get Kathy and take her over to his place and let him have his fun. After all, we don't have a case."

Jeffers was silent for a few moments. "What you *should* do is get her out of town," she said finally. "Have her visit friends or relatives."

"She's afraid he'll find her wherever she goes."

"Jack, he's not the F.B.I."

Baird sensed that he had gone too far, said too much. So he tried to pull back. "I know. I guess I'm just getting paranoid. But don't worry about me, Lee. I'm okay. And Kathy's tougher than she looks. We'll muddle through this somehow. Maybe Slade will get AIDS and die."

Jeffers laughed. "You know, you're beginning to sound like a cop. *Sick.*"

That evening Ellen again broached the subject of Kathy leaving town for a while, and again Kathy was not receptive to the idea.

"What if Slade found out where I was and came after me?"

she asked. "Who would protect me? Uncle Ralph? He gets winded just getting up from the dinner table."

Ellen was losing her patience. "Just tell me how on earth Slade would know where you were? How could he possibly find out?"

Kathy ignored the question. "Or maybe Aunt Dollie," she went on. "God knows, if she sat down on him, my worries would be over."

Like her mother, Kathy was not very fond of Baird's brother and sister-in-law. When they were in their early thirties, Ralph and Dollie had "found Jesus" and ever since had been zealous Christian fundamentalists. They didn't drink or smoke or go to the movies, but they did have a hard time pushing away from the table. Otherwise, Baird considered them good, decent people, honest and hardworking. And he knew they would have loved having Kathy stay with them for a time, especially since their only child, Little Ralph, was now living in Hollywood, parking cars and writing godless screenplays. Still, Baird was relieved that Kathy felt as she did. He didn't like the idea of her being that far from him, not with Jimbo Slade on the same continent. Then too, Baird knew something that Ellen did not: that in the coming days, the initiative wasn't going to be exclusively with Slade.

"There are ways he could find out," Baird said. "He seems to be a resourceful sort."

"What *ways?*" Ellen snapped. "Name one."

"Phone records. Maybe he's got a friend at the phone company."

"And if he found out, he'd just drop everything and drive straight out to Illinois. Do you seriously believe that?"

Kathy answered for him. "I don't want to find out, Mother. *And I'm not going to.*"

Except for that little contretemps, it was a quiet, even peaceful, evening at the Bairds. In every room Slade's alien presence hung in the air like a foul odor, and probably because of this, the three of them stayed together for the most part. Usually Ellen would wait for Baird or Kathy to go into the family room and turn on the television before joining them, but on this night she led the way. And from eight o'clock on, the three of them were there together. Ellen had her knitting, Kathy chose the programs to be watched, and Baird stretched out on the couch, thinking about the next night, wondering whether he would even be able to find the creep and just what he would do if and when he did. He would have to play it by ear, that much he knew. But beyond that, what the "tune" itself would be, he had no idea.

As usual, Kathy had set herself up on the floor with a pile of pillows next to Baird's couch. She was wearing silk pajamas, and her shower-damp hair was tied up off her neck with a scarf. Occasionally she would lean into her father's hand like a cat wanting to be scratched, and he would lift a finger or two and comply. Then she would settle back again, content for the moment.

SEVEN

The next morning, a Saturday, a carpenter hired by Ellen showed up at nine o'clock to replace the door window, repair the jamb, and install new locks. Considering that burglars could still break into the house through almost any window they chose, Baird and Ellen had agreed not to replace the handsome old door with something opaque, modern, and probably ugly. Baird helped the carpenter for a while, taking the old door off its hinges and removing the rest of the broken window pane. Then he got out of the man's way and read the morning paper and *Time* magazine while watching the first two quarters of a pre-season football game: the Giants and the Bears playing with all the fury of Brown against Vassar. He drank two beers and ate half of a ham-on-rye sandwich, leaving the rest because his stomach was already working itself into a knot.

Finally, at three o'clock, he changed clothes, putting on a blue pinstripe shirt, gray slacks, and loafers. Since it was a fairly warm day, he decided he would have to carry his old suede jacket, at least until evening. Casually meeting Ellen's searching gaze, he explained that he had some business calls to make, then kissed her and Kathy good-bye and went out the door.

"You're not even dressed for work," Ellen called after him.

Still walking, he shrugged. "It's Saturday. And anyway, I'm a wild and crazy kinda guy."

If she laughed, he wasn't aware of it. He got into his car, backed into the street and headed west, going downhill to Lake Union, where he had two double vodka-tonics in one of the yuppie-heaven restaurants scattered along the east shore. Within the hour he was back in his car, feeling only slightly more relaxed, but ready at least to get things rolling.

He drove back to Fifteenth Avenue and turned into Volunteer Park, passing the spot where he'd had his first dispiriting glimpse of Jimbo Slade, coming out of the bus and hurrying after Kathy. He turned onto the blacktop drive that ran past the art museum, carefully checking the parked cars, looking for the old Impala hardtop. In front of the museum he had to stop to let a busload of Asian senior citizens pass, marching—as if against the flow of history—away from a sculpture resembling a mammoth tractor tire and toward the magnificent Ming dynasty camels that flanked the museum's entrance. Farther on, he circled the water tower and came back past the museum so he could follow the one-way lower drive that looped down past the park's men's room. Of the dozen or so cars parked along the lower drive, none was Slade's, so Baird returned to Fifteenth Avenue and headed south.

He didn't actually expect to find Slade in any of the spots where he'd previously seen him, but he figured it couldn't hurt to look, especially since all three places—the park, Gide's, and Harold's strip club—were on his way to Slade's apartment in West Seattle, where he expected to wind up again, parked down the street, twiddling his thumbs and going slowly crazy. So as he passed Gide's, all he did was slow down and glance at the cars parked along the street and in the small lot next to the gay bar. And as a result, he almost missed it, the Impala, parked at the very rear of the lot, near the alley. And even then, the only reason he spotted it was its distinctive bloated shape and greater size, not to mention its unique coloring: pale green, gray primer, and rust. Parking on the next street over, he decided to leave his sportcoat in the car, with the gun in the side pocket. The day was still warm and he doubted he would need any lethal protection where he was going.

Baird's experience of gay bars was limited. One of them in the university district was a customer of his, originally strictly phone-in. But now he stopped in once a month, wrote up their order for napkins and the like, and got out as fast as he could. The bartender seemed straight enough and the place was certainly clean, but Baird could never get used to the feeling of being looked at, sexually appraised, by other males. So it was not easy for him, entering Gide's on a bright Saturday afternoon.

The place was larger than Leo's and handsomely decorated, with real ferns and potted plants, not plastic ones. Also, unlike Leo's, it was packed wall-to-wall with patrons, most of them male, and almost all of them talking at the same time, some practically yelling to be heard over the din of voices and music. And it was not baseball playing on the TVs at either end of the bar, but hardcore pornography, avid mouths gobbling swollen penises. But the most striking difference from Leo's was in the patrons themselves, most of whom were physically connecting with each other: touching, nudging, kissing, fondling. And finally there was that difference Baird dreaded most: a number of men turning to look at him in a way Wyatt Earp and old Ralston never did.

It seemed to take forever before he finally found Slade in a corner booth in an alcove, sharing a pitcher of beer with a fortyish balding man in designer jeans and a silky short-sleeved shirt left hanging out, which seemed to be the uniform for the out-of-shape, as against the weight-lifter types, who preferred skintight black T-shirts. Slade himself had gone back to the leopard-skin vest, which Baird could see now was only printed leather. Otherwise he looked the same: ponytailed, bare-torsoed under the vest, his neck and ears and arms and fingers bright with junk Indian jewelry.

Seeing Baird, he started to sit up, then caught himself and lounged back, throwing a muscular arm across the back of the booth, in the bargain showing off his hairy armpit.

"Well, Jesus Joe Christ, if it ain't old Pops Baird hisself!" he said. "What is this? You come here to shoot me or what?"

"Only to talk. May I sit down?"

"Well, hell yes. Free country last time I looked."

As Baird sat, the other man smiled and thrust out his hand. "Lester Wall," he said. "I must say, I've never seen you in here before. One of Jimbo's little secrets, huh?"

Baird shook the man's hand. "Jack Baird. I've never been here before."

Slade laughed. "Just calm down, Lester. Old Pops ain't got a queer bone in his body, right, Pops?"

Baird looked at him. "Jack," he said.

"You got it, man." Slade looked at Lester. "Me and old Jack here, we're drinkin buddies from way back."

Lester wasn't buying. "Jimbo, you yourself don't even go *way back*. What are you, twenty-four?"

"Whatever. The important thing is how me and old Jack feel about each other."

Lester smiled uneasily. "Do I detect a degree of, well, *tension* here?"

"Naa," Slade assured him. "We just got a thing for the same chick, that's all. And Jack says if I don't mind my P's and Q's, he's gonna blow my ass off with a shotgun."

Lester laughed. "Hey, this sounds serious."

"Well, it isn't," Baird said. "Jimbo's just got a sick sense of humor. Truth is, I've got some extra money to spend, and he's gonna show me how."

"Now that *is* interesting," Lester said.

Slade was watching Baird intently, trying to divine just what he was doing there, without at the same time losing for an instant his look of cool indifference.

"Yeah, you could say that," he said.

At that point another man came up to the booth, having worked his way through the crowd. He was at least Baird's age, heavy, with wavy yellow-dyed hair, a scary smile, and very small, very even teeth. He was wearing pink sunglasses and an expensive off-white suit.

"Well now, what have we here, Jimbo?" he cried. "Have you been rummaging through the closet again?"

Slade sneered at him. "Get lost, you old fag."

The man clucked his tongue and looked at Lester. "Whores are so tedious," he said.

Slade brought his arm down from the back of the booth and sat up straight. "Get the fuck out of here," he said, not looking at the man. "And you too, Lester. Me and Jack, we got business to discuss."

The man shrugged, put his nose in the air, and left.

Lester gave Baird an apologetic smile. "Jimbo's manners still aren't the best, but we're working on him."

Wall left the booth then and joined some other friends nearby. Slade got a cigarette out of a pack on the table and lit it. Baird signaled to a waiter and ordered a vodka-tonic.

"Now what's this about money?" Slade asked. "I'm always interested in money."

"You mean, am I here to pay you off? Give you money to stop hassling us?"

Slade grinned. "*Hasslin?* Is that what I'm doin—hasslin you people?"

Baird hated having to listen to this kind of raillery from the creep, hated it even more that he had to participate in it. But he felt he had no choice.

"Yeah, that's what you're doing, all right," he said. "But don't get all excited about the money. I don't pay people off."

"And I ain't hasslin nobody. The court says I stay a hunnerd feet away from your daughter, and that's what I'm doin."

Baird said nothing for a few moments, wondering if the break-in had been a joke more than anything else, Slade demonstrating that he could violate Kathy's home and bedroom and still not come within one hundred feet of her.

"How about breaking and entering?" Baird said. "How about burglary?"

Slade frowned in puzzlement. "Burglary? What burglary?"

A waiter brought the vodka-tonic, and Baird paid cash for it. "The one at my house," he said. "The one where you smashed my gun cabinet and stuck a knife through my daughter's teddy bear."

Baird knew it sounded stupid and funny, so he wasn't surprised now as Slade laughed out loud, displaying a number of missing molars.

"*Teddy bear!*" he bawled. "Now you got me stabbin teddy bears?"

Baird took down a good part of his drink. "Look, I didn't come here to talk about that. I know the cops didn't find anything and you've got an alibi. So that's not why I'm here."

Blowing smoke out of his nose and mouth, Slade shook his head in comic exasperation. "Jesus, if only I had some idea what you're talkin about, Jack, it sure would be a help."

"Well, I might as well be up front," Baird said. "I know you'll get a good laugh out of it. But it's the truth nevertheless."

Slade pounded the table with mock impatience. "So let's hear it, Pops! Come on, this a workday for me."

"Well, it's simple enough. It's kind of like you said last week about hitting a few bars together and getting to know each other. I have this feeling that if you got to know me, and found out what kind of a girl Kathy is, you'd decide to leave us alone."

Slade was slouched back in the booth again, this time with both arms stretched out along the top, displaying his muscles as well as tattoos, among them a snake coiling around a dagger.

"Jesus, Jack," he said, "are you for fuckin real? Is this really you? Tell me it ain't so."

"Well, it's what you said, wasn't it? Hit some more bars together, get to know each other?"

Slade shrugged. "I don't know—it just don't sound like me, man. And then that part about your daughter—I think we're in trouble there. I mean, when I'm in love, Jack, I'm in love."

"You know a lot about love, do you?"

"I'd say about as much as the next guy. Just ask old Lester over there."

"No thanks."

As Slade refilled his glass of beer, Baird drained the last of his drink and signaled for another. Hoping he wouldn't vomit, he pressed on. "I just think there's some good in everybody. And when you get to know someone—really know them—it's not so easy to do them harm."

Slade was shaking his head and sputtering with laughter. And Baird had no trouble understanding why. Yet this whole approach, this orgy of naivete, was something he felt he had to get out of the way, much as the Seahawks' previous coach would almost always run the ball on first down: to reassure the other team, lull it into complacency. It was not a role Baird liked. Still, he played it out, sitting there and waiting for old Jimbo's laughter to subside.

"You don't agree with that?" he said finally.

Slade put out his cigarette. "Not so's you'd notice, Pops."

"Well, then too, there is another reason. A reason I find hard to talk about."

"Reason for what?"

"For being here. For getting to know each other."

Slade gave him a look, knowing and weary. "Don't tell me Fatso was right. You coming out of the old closet, Pops?"

"Not the way you think."

"How then?"

The waiter brought Baird's drink, and again Baird paid him. Before answering Slade, he drank deeply.

Slade sneered. "Must be quite a closet."

"You could say that. But I hate to talk about it here—all these people."

"Go on. No one's listenin, for fuck's sake. They're all on the make."

"All right then. You remember last time, I mentioned that woman in the Ravenna area, the one Detective Jeffers said you raped?"

Slade's pale eyes grew wintry. "Jeffers is a lyin cunt. I told you that."

"It doesn't matter," Baird said. "It's just that, well, I think about it a lot—I mean, you know, the way it must've happened and all. The way Jeffers described it. I—" His voice trailed off and he lowered his eyes, had no choice because of the way Slade was looking at him, sneering still, but also beginning to wonder.

Baird took another drink and plunged on, haltingly. "I mean, you know, every man thinks about such things. They may say they don't, but they do. I know they do . . . you know, wonder what it would be like to . . . you know. To—"

"To do it!" Slade snapped.

Baird looked away again. "Oh no, not me! Not me actually

doing it," he stammered. "But maybe to . . . to *see* it done. I guess I've always wondered what it would be like, that's all. I mean, I'm too chicken myself. But all my life I've thought . . . you know . . . how easy it would be. I mean, they stand there and sass you and give you all kinds of shit, like they were our equals, you know? Like we couldn't just reach out . . ."

And Baird at that point actually lifted his hand and extended it, saw it tremble for a moment in front of Slade. Then he caught himself and pulled it back.

"It would be so easy," he finished. "I can imagine it would be so very easy."

Slade was grinning now. "What do you take me for?"

"What do you mean?"

"I mean, you think I'd actually buy this shit? That we're some kind of brothers under the skin? That you're some kind of closet rapist or something?"

Baird was shaking his head. "No, I didn't say that. I know what I am. I'm a middle-class, straight-arrow family man. That's all I've ever been or ever will be. Hell, I don't even get parking tickets. And I'm not saying I know what you are, because I *don't* know. Like you said, your police record here is clean. I'm just saying that I do have this one little weakness in me—this *sickness*, I guess some people might call it. But I can't shake it. And I can't deny it's there. I think about such things and how it would be. And I guess, most of all, I . . . well, I think about seeing it, you know? *Watching it.* Especially if the woman was some bitch with a big mouth, you know? The kind who likes to tease you and get you interested and then pull it away and make you feel like a fool. I'll admit, I could just stand and watch it happen to someone like that. Just stand and watch, you know?"

Slade lit another cigarette. He was studying Baird carefully, sneering as he did so.

"So you'd like that, huh? Just to stand and watch?"

Again Baird lowered his eyes. He nodded. "Yes, it would be . . ."

"It would be *what?*"

"Satisfying," Baird said.

Slade did not respond for a time, and Baird had no doubt that the creep was still studying him, sneering at him. But Baird could not look back at him, for some reason could not meet his mocking gaze. Baird felt very warm. His body was slick with sweat. He drained his second drink and looked toward the bar, past the milling, frenetic clusters of yapping males, all seemingly indifferent to the big-screen TV and the images on it: a tangle of nude young men engaged in anal and oral intercourse. And it occurred to Baird that in an ironic way, this was the quintessential male environment, with sex as the end-all and be-all, sex as the very content of life. Here there were none of the conventions and civilizing restraints that women brought to the sexual table. And Baird didn't doubt that if women had been more like men, a bar like Leo's would have been much like this one, like Gide's, with booze and drugs and porno mere props for the feverish sexuality, the random touching, kissing, fondling, propositioning—and the making out too, the sucking and buggering probably taking place even then in the toilets and the back rooms.

At the moment, though, Baird was only trying to get the attention of the waiter, so he could order another drink, hoping that more alcohol would make all this a little easier, especially the fact that he was finding it so difficult to meet Slade's sneer, even though he knew why, and knew that it was a good thing. Still, he was sickened by it all. It was as if he had gone into his backyard to dig for night crawlers and instead had broken through a sewer line.

He caught the waiter's attention and signaled for another drink. Then he forced himself to look at Slade.

"You seem kind of thirsty," Slade said.

"Yeah, I guess I am."

"Baring the old soul—must be thirsty work."

"You've got a point."

Slade sat up and lit another cigarette. "What you said—this deal about gettin to know each other, doin a little boozin together—I got nothin against that. But it would cost me money, because I ain't just fuckin around here, Jack. I'm at work. Some of these old fags, like Lester, they give me money just to hang with me, you know?"

"No kidding." Baird was trying not to sneer himself.

"Yeah, I guess it makes them feel butch. Then too, I sell stuff, little goodies and such. So this deal you're talking about, it would cost me money."

Baird shrugged. "That's what I meant earlier, about having money to spend. The evening would be on me—food, liquor, whatever."

Blowing smoke at the ceiling, Slade frowned judiciously. "Yeah, but what about my income? Lost wages, so to speak."

"I'm not Lester," Baird said.

"Lucky you."

"I think so."

"So this would just be your treat, huh?"

"Right."

"And I call the shots?"

The waiter brought another vodka-tonic, and Baird paid him off, told him to keep the change. "We'll be leaving," he added.

Slade drank the last of his beer and belched. "What's the matter?" he said. "You don't like it here?"

Baird smiled coldly. "I hate it here."

In the hours that followed, Slade spent Baird's money with enthusiasm. They went into one of the state liquor stores and bought fifths of rum and Scotch and Russian vodka, as well as two half-pints of rum, for the bottles more than the contents, Slade said—containers that could be refilled and smuggled into places like strip clubs, where they would be needed to spike the soft drinks.

Next, with Baird driving, Slade directed them to a fried-chicken house in the central district, a seedy little restaurant run by an elderly black couple, both of them enormous and dour. And despite the number of drinks he'd already had, Baird had no trouble seeing what Slade evidently could not see: that the couple detested him, even though he called them Ma and Pa and slapped the man's hand and patted the old lady on the bottom and in general behaved as if he were their favorite white person in all the world. They mustered uneasy smiles in front of him, then shook their heads in bewilderment when he wasn't looking.

Though there were only three other patrons in the place, it

took almost forty-five minutes to be served: time in which Slade poured down rum and Coke, while Baird took his time with a tall vodka and 7UP. They were each served half a chicken with jo-jo potatoes, both deep-fat-fried and abundantly greasy, as were the green beans and biscuits, an anomaly Baird didn't even try to comprehend. Slade cleaned his plate and finished off Baird's chicken and biscuits, evidently feeling that the beans were not sufficiently greasy. All the while, the two men barely talked. Slade did ask him what kind of work he did, and Baird told him, even mentioned the company he worked for, hoping to build the creep's trust. Meanwhile Ma and Pa watched them as if they were undercover cops, and when Slade effusively complimented the couple on the food, they looked as if they thought he was making fun of them and their tiny establishment.

Afterward, Slade led Baird to two lowlife bars near the Pike Place Market. They were both dark, downstairs joints that served only beer and wine, which apparently was more than adequate for their few patrons, most of whom looked as if they had just washed ashore. In the second bar, there was even one old man with an eyepatch and a crutch, which Baird halfway expected him to start banging against the floor as he growled for a pint of grog. Not surprisingly, Slade acted as if he were one of the regulars there, and a favorite one at that, again an opinion no one else seemed to share.

He told Baird improbable stories about the various patrons, usually how he had outsmarted them or insulted them or punched them out. One he even claimed to have thrown down the concrete stairs that led up to the street.

"Broke a few of his bones," he said. "But what the fuck—he was askin for it. A man asks for somethin, I try to give it to him."

Throughout this litany of triumph, Baird sat and listened, by now drunk enough to not even try to hide his skepticism. And finally Slade seemed to notice. He said nothing for a few moments, then broke out his sneer again.

"Okay, Pops," he said, "I guess we been playin this game long enough. I'd say it's about time we laid our cards on the table."

"I thought I already had."

Slade shook his head. "Naa, I don't think so. I guess you must figure I got an I.Q. about forty, not to know what you're up to."

"And what is that?"

Slade slipped one of the refilled half-pints out of his vest pocket and emptied it into a glass of Coke. "Simple enough. I figure you're wearin a fuckin wire. I figure you're tryin to draw me out, get me to admit somethin on tape—somethin that cunt Jeffers can use against me in court."

Baird was not surprised to hear this, since it was an idea he had thought of himself, and might even have tried if he'd thought he could have gotten Jeffers and Lucca's approval and assistance. Still, he laughed at the idea now.

"Are you serious? What do you think I am, a part-time cop or something? You want to pat me down? You want me to strip in the men's room?"

Slade sneered. "Big thrill," he said.

Baird started to get up. "I'm serious."

Slade waved him back down. "Naaa—stay where you are. I'll take your word." He lit another cigarette and shook his head in futility. "But where the fuck does that leave us, then? Number one, you figure if I get to know you, then I won't do anything to your daughter—which I wouldn't of done anyway of course, cuz I don't do that kinda shit. Or number two, you're this weird kinda twisted fan who figures I might let him tag along and watch me do some cunt sometime—which of course I don't do."

Baird was shaking his head. "No, that's not what I said. I said I might have a *weakness* in that direction. But I didn't say I'd ever actually do it—you know, *watch*. I'm not *that* sick. Or maybe I should say I'm not that brave."

Slade drank the last of his rum-and-Coke. "So what're we doing here? What the fuck's going on?"

Baird shrugged. "I don't know. I guess I figured that you, with your background—you know, having been in juvenile hall with rapists and such—that you'd, well, *know* things. And maybe tell me about them. You know, satisfy my curiosity. Or . . . oh, I don't know. It's so goddamn hard to explain."

There was amusement in Slade's sneer now, almost a kind of

warmth. "Jesus, Pops, you really are a basket case, you know that? Down deep you're a fuckin weirdo case just like the rest of us. The shrinks out at Western, they'd just love to get their greedy little mitts on you. Old Mister Proper Middle-class Sicko Voyeur!" He laughed so loudly that even the old man with the eyepatch gave him a disapproving look.

Baird did not respond. He was not embarrassed so much as angry, internally raging at himself for what he was doing, for what he felt he had to do. Again he had broken out in a sweat, felt it sticking to his shirt and sliding down his spine.

Slade leaned toward him, suddenly his buddy, his co-conspirator. "Listen, Jack, there's somethin you just gotta see. *Someone*, I should say. And lemme tell ya, if there was ever a cunt a guy would wanta do—or watch someone else do—this is the one." Like a French waiter, he kissed his fingertips. "Primo, man. A fox of foxes. A pussy among pussies. And there's one other thing about her, somethin only you'd be able to appreciate. But I ain't gonna tell you yet. Wait till we get there. Then you'll see."

It was ten o'clock and already dark by the time they got there, a strip club located on the heavily traveled road that circled the northern end of Lake Washington, outside the city limits. The road was solid on both sides with retail businesses of every kind, a four-lane neon causeway difficult enough to negotiate when one was sober, trying to pick out the traffic lights from all the others, with shoppers' and diners' cars continually swinging onto the roadway and off. But this night, more inebriated than he had been in years, Baird had to concentrate all his energies on what he was doing. And even then it seemed as if he were driving through a tunnel with walls of light, rainbow-colored and spinning.

He vaguely remembered parking and filling the half-pints again. He remembered the sequential neon sign out in front, giving the club's name in separate gaudy syllables: "Oo-la-la." And he remembered paying the cover charge for both of them. Then they were sitting on a love seat in one corner of the room, which looked a good deal like Harold's, except that it was larger and more dimly lit, even the stage. He was aware of Slade spiking his drink and popping some kind of pill: speed, he imagined, judging by the man's hyper manner.

When a girl came up and offered to do a couch dance for them, Slade asked her where "Satin" was, and the girl said that Satin was on her break. Slade then nudged Baird and told him to get out his money.

"Give her a five," he said, and Baird did.

"Now, tell Satin there's an extra twenty-five for her here," Slade said to the girl. "Fifty altogether. But she's gotta come now—and really pour it on. You tell her that, okay?"

The girl gave a limp smile, nodded, and walked off.

"Money-grubbin cunts," Slade said. "All of 'em."

Baird was very tired. He watched the girls with indifference and long since had stopped listening to Slade. He almost spilled his glass of 7UP, trying to pour vodka into it from his own refilled half-pint. Slade laughed and slapped Baird's knee.

"Hey, you drunk old sicko!" he said. "You ready for this?"

Baird had no idea what he was talking about. And then suddenly there was another girl standing in front of them, a bored-looking girl who plucked the fifty from Baird's hand as if she were removing something dirty from a child. Smiling then, she took off her bra and began to dance for him and Slade, gracefully undulating right over them, her body crawling with the colored moving lights from the glitter-dome. And by then Baird's heart had stopped, or sunk, he wasn't sure which, because he saw now what Slade had meant back in the downtown bar.

The girl had long, wavy dark hair and a beautiful, delicately featured face, with haunting eyes and a lovely mouth and dazzling smile. And her body, though small, was so perfectly shaped—so tight and lissome in the waist and legs, yet so lushly full through the breasts and buttocks—that she seemed to have been formed by something other than nature, some hand of consummate genius. As Baird stared at her in a kind of anguish, Slade gave him an elbow in the ribs.

"Well, what about it, Pops?" he said. "You see what I mean?"

"Yes."

"You bet your ass you do. A fuckin dead ringer, right? She could be your daughter, right?"

Baird did not answer.

"Just like in the photos," Slade said. "Absolute primo perfection."

And Baird did not even care what Slade—intentionally or otherwise—had just admitted, for he had never doubted that old Jimbo was the one who had violated his home. More to the point, Baird could not take his eyes off the girl.

"See? What'd I tell ya?" Slade gloated.

"Yes, I see."

Slade laughed happily. "Just think of the possibilities," he said. "All them juicy possibilities."

Driving the same road home, Baird found the tunnel even smaller, a tight circle of clarity surrounded by darkness and noise and confusion. There, in the center of the circle, he felt, if not cold sober, at least sober enough to know how drunk he was. So he drove with manic caution, all the while trying hard to concentrate on the ravings of his passenger, who was happily, boisterously, stupidly drunk.

"Jesus, Jesus, Jesus, but that Satin, huh, man? Christ, what a fuckin piece, what a fuckin primo-perfect piece of fuckin ass, right, Jacko? A guy see that, he's just got to have it, man, no two fuckin ways about it. He's just gotta have it. And that's what I'm gonna do, Jacko. I'm gonna dip into that like real soon."

"Satin, huh?" Baird said. "You gonna do her?"

Slade seemed to catch himself then, realize what he was admitting to. "Naa, not *do* her, man!" he said, looking offended. "I don't *do* any women. I ain't like that. All I mean is I'm gonna *have* her, you know? Like on a date. All nice and legal."

"My mistake."

"I know some guys, though—one in particular. For the right money, he'd do any cunt you say, anywhere, anytime. And you could watch."

"No kidding?"

"What I say, huh? You gone deaf or something?"

"Just wanted to be sure, that's all."

"Yeah, and I know why!" Slade whooped with laughter.

"Cuz you'd be all for it, you fuckin old sicko!"

Slade was slouched back against the passenger door, drinking Scotch straight from the bottle. The rum was gone altogether, the vodka half gone, the empty half-pints tossed away in the parking lot, missiles for Slade's amusement. Though the night was cool, he had rolled his window down and kept sticking his head out, as if he wanted to feel his ponytail flapping in the breeze, right along with his tongue.

"Well, how about it, man? You want a deal like that or not?"

Baird shook his head. "No, I couldn't do that. It would be wrong. Just like the guy doing her would be wrong."

Slade howled at that, dancing his feet against the carpeted floor. "*Wrong!*" he bawled. "How the fuck you figure that, an educated old fucker like you? It's just nature, man—that's all it is. Satin and your daughter and every cunt that ever lived, they got this thing we need, right? And we didn't ask to need it, did we? Fuck no, it's just the way it is. Like food and water, it's somethin we just gotta have. So when a guy asks for it, and they say no, what're you fuckin supposed to do? Just say okay and then go starve to death? Fuck no! And anyway, if a guy just up and takes it—what's the big deal? The cunt's havin sex the same as the guy. She don't lose nothin. Fact, if anybody does any losin, it's us, you know? Cuz we shoot our load, right?"

Baird glanced at him, wondering if he was serious. But old Jimbo's eyes were half-closed and his face was slack, as if he were about to fall asleep. Baird looked back at the road, the circle of light, just in time to see something bright red pass overhead.

Slade giggled. "Jesus, man, you just ran a red light! You're a fuckin menace, that's what you are! A fuckin old sicko voyeur menace!"

Shaken, Baird wanted to pull over and phone Ellen or Leo to come and get them, see them safely home. But of course he couldn't do that, not with the passenger he had. And anyway, it wouldn't happen again, he assured himself. He had been frightened awake. The circle of light was larger now, more like a tunnel again. Then too, there was still work to do.

"You seriously believe all that?" he asked.

"All what?"

"About rape."

Slade yawned, then tasted himself, smacking his lips like a dog with candy. "Your fuckin A," he said finally. "It's the truth, ain't it? *Rape!* Shit, all rape is, is a guy takin what nature forces him to take. And if the cunt gets a little banged up in the process, that's her goddamn fault for resistin. After all, what's happenin to her ain't no different than what's happenin to the guy—they both havin sex, right? So what's the big deal?"

They had just driven over the Montlake bridge, leaving the university district, so Baird was acutely aware that time was running out. He wasn't sure exactly what else he needed from Jimbo Slade, but he went after it anyway.

"This Satin," he said. "You're going to use her as a kind of surrogate for my daughter?"

"A what?"

"Surrogate. A substitute."

Slade shook his head. "Hey, I keep tellin ya—I don't do nobody. Not Satin, and not your precious little girl either. Understand?"

"That's good to hear. Because I want her safe. I want them both safe."

"Yeah, like hell you do. I know what you want, Jacko. You want me to do Satin so bad you can probably taste it right now. And you know why you want it? So you can watch and play your little game—pretend you're me and Satin is your kid. Am I right? Ain't that what you're really hot for? Daddy's little girl finally sittin right where she belongs—*on your twisted old cock!*"

"Now who's the sicko?" The moment Baird said it, he wanted to howl with laughter. Even as drunk as he was, he could appreciate the surreal absurdity of the moment: old Jimbo's twisted buddy Jack calling him a sicko.

Slade suddenly pushed up the armrest and slid across the seat, as if he were about to blow in Baird's ear. Instead, he took hold of the lapels of Baird's jacket and, giving him a playful shaking, laughed drunkenly in his face.

"Jacko, I am so fuckin hot for that cunt," he said. "If we wasn't so fuckin wasted, we could go back tonight and do her— I mean, take her out—you know, everything all legal. But I'm really hammered, man. I'm wasted. And tomorrow I got things I have to do—money to make, shit like that. But some other night, Jacko. Some other night we go to the Oolala again, okay? Late. Satin gets off at one. And I know where she lives. I've followed her other nights."

"Satin?" Baird said.

"Well, fuck yes, *Satin!* Who else? You comin with, or not?"

Baird strained to free himself from the weight of the alcohol. He knew he had to choose the right words, do the right thing, but his brain felt as heavy as his eyes, which kept falling shut.

"I don't want you to do this," he said. "It's wrong."

Slade looked at him in disgust. "Man, you don't listen. I never said *I* would do anything. All I'm sayin is we go and check her out. We scope her comin home—cuz who knows, there could be some bad-ass rapist fiend just waitin for her, ready to do his little thing—*while we watch!* While *you* watch!"

"It would be wrong," Baird said. "Legally and morally wrong."

Slade's grin became an open sneer. "Well, who gives a fuck what you say? In this world, I do what I fuckin want!"

"Don't do it for me."

"Hey, I wouldn't do shit for you, man. I'm just askin in case some other guy might want to do her, and for a little extra scratch would let us watch. You be for that or not?"

Baird felt like a bottom fisherman, patiently paying out his steel line. "If I didn't go along," he said, "would he do her anyway?"

"What d'ya think—he'd be doing her just for you? You got a high opinion of yourself, you know that?"

They were driving along a residential street, moving uphill toward Fifteenth Avenue. For another block, Baird said nothing, then he nodded. "If it's gonna happen anyway—okay, I'll be there."

But Slade suddenly decided to waffle. "Well, who knows what's gonna happen—not me, man. I'm just sayin, 'What if.' "

"And I'm just saying, 'Okay, then, I'll be there.' "

"Big surprise." Slade gave him a playful punch on the shoulder and slid back across the leather seat, again slouching against the passenger door. "How else you gonna be a sicko voyeur unless you came along?"

"Good point," Baird said.

When they reached Gide's parking lot, Baird went all the way to the rear, turning into the alley before stopping.

"Well, it's been real," Slade said, sitting up and holding out his hands for a brotherly slap. Feeling like a fool, Baird sat there for a few seconds before forcing himself finally to lift his hands and lamely let them fall on Slade's. The creep laughed and punched him in the arm again.

"Jesus, Jacko—you'd make one lousy nigger, you know that?"

"You're probably right."

"Hey, old Jimbo's always right. So, some other night soon, okay?" His sneer was almost a grin again. "You bring your wallet, and we have us a real party, Jacko. Us and maybe Satin too. Who knows?"

With that, he laughed again and got out of Baird's car. Raising his arm in a kind of sidelong Nazi salute, he walked toward the old Impala, whose gray-primered roof shone silver in the moonlight. Baird immediately put his foot on the gas and sped away, roaring down the alley as if he were fleeing for his life.

EIGHT

Baird knew he was still too drunk to drive any farther than he had to, yet he soon found himself going on past his own neighborhood and heading downhill, toward Lake Union. He hadn't forgotten the red light passing overhead, the belated terror of realizing that he had just sailed through a busy intersection against the traffic signal. But even that was not enough to keep him from plunging on now, like a twig in white water.

He pretended to himself that he was thinking of driving over to Leo's, but it was an hour past closing time and he wasn't headed in that direction anyway. Instead he turned west under the interstate and made his way through the narrow streets of the Wallingford district until he came to her house. And there he stopped, right in the middle of the street, since there were no vacant parking places on either side. Like most of the houses in the block, the brown bungalow was dark, without even an outside light burning. And for a few delirious moments Baird considered getting out of the car and stumbling up onto her porch and pounding on the door.

"It's me!" he would yell at her.

The door would open and she would hold out her arms and

he would take her right there, on the floor, with the door open behind them and his car still parked in the middle of the street, lights on and the motor running. Thinking about it, he laughed out loud, for some reason almost proud to be so drunk and hopeless, lurking outside Detective Jeffers' house like any other sex fiend, like any other Jimbo Slade. But then he remembered that that wasn't the reason he had come here. It wasn't "Love me!" he wanted to yell at her, but "Save me!" And abruptly his eyes were swimming and he thought the steering wheel was going to break in his hands. Desperate to get away now, he tromped on the accelerator and the Buick's tires screeched.

A short time later, driving past Lookout Park, he pulled over to the curb and got out. He saw no one else in the park, and at the end of the street only the usual lights were burning at his place and the houses of his neighbors. He walked across the park's narrow strip of lawn and headed downhill through the trees and brambles. In an open space carpeted with needles, he fell to his knees and put his finger down his throat, wishing that he could get rid of it all, not just the greasy chicken dinner and the foul residues of vodka and Scotch but also the feelings of shame and disgust that seemed to have congealed in his stomach. Instead all he got up was a skein of phlegm, rank and viscous. He wiped his mouth with a leaf, then got to his feet, urinated, and stumbled back up the hill.

Within minutes he was home, slipping in through the front door because he had forgotten to put the new back-door key on his ring. In the downstairs bathroom he drank some Pepto Bismol and washed it down with water. Then he walked quietly through the museum and fell onto the couch in the family room, not bothering to remove his jacket or even his shoes. In the museum he heard the grandfather clock strike three times. Then he let go, dropping like a stone into dark water.

It wasn't until after Baird left that Slade discovered how hopelessly drunk he was. At first he was unable to find his car keys, fishing in every pocket for what seemed like an hour before he finally located the goddamn things. But then the fucking keyhole wouldn't hold still for him. And worst of all, when he did manage to get the door open, he tried to lean on it as he was getting into the car and the goddamn thing swung open and he fell on his ass, right there in the empty parking lot. For a while he just lay there on the asphalt, laughing at himself and kicking out at the fucking car, driving the heels of his cool rattlesnake boots into the rusty old fender.

It took so long getting to his feet that he began picturing himself in a prizefight ring, on the canvas, looking up at his fellow jailbird, old Iron Mike, standing over him in his black shoes and no socks, his face expressionless and his huge arms hanging ready, like a couple of smoking cannons. And Slade laughed.

"I'm gonna git you, motherfucker!" he bawled, making it to his feet finally, only this time falling into the car instead of next to it.

He didn't try to put the key into the ignition or even bother to close the car door. He just stretched out on the bench seat and immediately fell asleep. When he awoke, it was still dark, but he had no idea how long he had been asleep, for hours or only minutes. Checking Baird's calendar watch, he saw that it was almost four in the morning; but even that was of little help, since he didn't know what time it had been when he'd fallen asleep. About all he knew was that he was feeling like shit, not quite so drunk now, but queasy and parched, with a booming headache and a full bladder.

Under the seat he found a pint of rum, not quite empty. He drained the bottle, then drove the few blocks to Volunteer Park and the water fountain there. He drank deeply, doused his head in the fountain's stream, and filled the empty rum bottle in case he needed more water on the way home. Still unsteady on his feet, he took a piss right there at the fountain, in fact *on* the fountain. In front of him the fenced-in reservoir glowed in the moonlight, as did the Sound far in the distance, beyond the Space Needle, near which the college girl had laughed at him—just as he had been laughed at earlier this night.

It was a thought he carried with him back to the car. And as he drove, he began to feel it again, the anger he thought he had all but drowned in the night's booze. It was an anger with a face: the smug mug of his new "buddy," Jacko Baird. Christ, but it galled him that the man thought him so stupid he wouldn't catch on to what was really going down, what the whole long fucking night together was really about—nothing more or less than the same old shit Jacko had dished out at Harold's the week before: his smug conviction that Slade simply wasn't good enough for his precious fucking daughter. And all the bullshit talk about the two of them getting to know each other and Jacko secretly wanting to watch while some poor cunt was getting hers—it was just a lot of noise to cover up what he was really saying: "You ain't good enough, Jimbo. And you're stupid enough to con. So let's be 'pals.'"

Yeah, in your fucking dreams, Slade thought now. Somehow, somewhere, sometime, he was going to look down at that smug mug, its skin going purple and eyes bulging, begging for just one more breath, and he was going to say, "What's the matter, Pops, you don't want me to be your pal no more?"

That would be so goddamn sweet, so totally satisfying, Slade could almost feel it, a high better than coke or coming. And then the smug bastard would be out of the way and the two of them, Slade and Kathy, would finally be able to get together without any interference. For now, though, all he had was his anger, the old feeling of sickness and rage at being so grossly underestimated, at being judged not good enough, not smart enough or straight enough for the Bairds of this world. He was so lost in the feeling—and still sufficiently drunk—that he almost ran down two old farts in the crosswalk on Fifteenth, in front of the hospital. In the rearview mirror he saw them yelling and gesturing at him, and that only deepened his anger and resentment.

He wasn't sure why he didn't drive down the hill to the freeway and head for West Seattle. It seemed almost as though there was something else he had to do, one last duty to perform before he could go home and sleep. Maybe it was just to keep on driving, he thought, keep himself busy so he wouldn't have to think about Baird and what the smug bastard thought of him. He considered stopping off at an after-hours joint and getting another pint of rum, but settled for half a meth, figuring it would at least ease his headache. But as his heart rate jumped, so did the pain.

Though it was still dark out, he could see a faint smudge of light in the sky, the first rays of the morning sun striking Mount Rainier far to the south, otherwise invisible in the haze. The smudge looked like a rip in the sky.

Working his way south, he came upon a young couple fighting next to a car parked in the street. The man, a skinny spade with dreadlocks, was indifferently slapping the girl, who was Asian—a hooker, Slade figured, since it was his experience that only a fallen chink would be found dead with a nigger. Slowing down as he passed them, he saw that the girl was small and pretty, so he circled the block. And when he came to the same spot again, he was surprised to find the car and the spade already gone. The girl, though, was walking along the sidewalk, and Slade saw in the light of the streetlamps that she was crying.

Pulling over, he threw open the car door and called to her. "Hey, purty girl, can I give you a lift somewhere?"

Baird woke briefly at first light. Feeling dizzy and nauseated, he made his way to the downstairs bathroom, where he urinated and washed down a couple of aspirins with two glasses of water. Then he went back to the family room and again dropped off. It seemed only seconds later that it was bright daylight outside and Ellen was standing over him, dressed in jeans and a shirt.

"God, you stink," she said. "Why don't you go up to bed?"

"Yes, why not?"

Looking bored, she watched him get to his feet and head upstairs. After visiting the bathroom again, he went to his bedroom, his and Ellen's. Just as he was closing the door he saw Kathy watching him from across the hall. She looked frightened and concerned, but he didn't want to talk to her; he didn't want her seeing him in the shape he was in. So he closed the door and crawled gratefully into the unmade bed. But as he began to fall asleep again, her face stayed with him, the lovely eyes looking grave and troubled.

In time, though, it was not Kathy he saw but the dancer Satin as she undulated nude an arm's length away, her skin crawling with what appeared to be incandescent worms. And soon she was straddling him and moving her hips, easing herself onto him while his hands reached hungrily for her breasts. Then there were other hands pulling at the girl, trying to take her from him. Baird grew desperate, moving faster and faster, hoping for release. But the hands pulled harder, and suddenly she was gone.

Baird felt a crushing sense of loss and disappointment. He wanted to kill someone.

He slept till one in the afternoon. After showering and getting dressed, in jeans and a pullover, he went downstairs and had coffee in the kitchen. Kathy came in and asked if he wanted something to eat and he told her that he would get it himself. She asked if scrambled eggs and bacon would be all right, and he said yes, that would be fine. She said nothing more then, not until she served him, generously adding toast and orange juice to his order.

"You must be hungry," she said.

He reached over and pushed out a chair for her, inviting her to sit with him, but she shook her head.

"No, I don't want to sit," she said, giving him a look of reproval.

"You're mad at me."

"No. We were just worried, that's all. Mom said you always call when you're going to be real late. And we didn't know if you were all right."

"I'm sorry you were worried, baby. But everything was all right. I was with Leo and his wife and some friends of theirs. And I guess I had a bit too much to drink, and didn't realize how late it was."

Kathy was standing at the sink, her arms folded, still trying to show her disapproval of him. It was not an easy role for her.

"Would you do me a favor?" he asked.

"Maybe."

"Come over here."

She came grudgingly. He put an arm around her waist and gave her a hug. "I'm sorry, sweetheart," he said. "I didn't mean to worry you. But everything's all right. Honest. So take it easy, okay?"

Her smile lit the room. "Why not?" she said.

Later, he heard her upstairs, talking to her mother, assuring her that everything was all right. But Ellen wasn't interested.

"If your father wants to carry on like some college fraternity lout, let him. I could care less."

Later still, Baird had stretched out on a chaise on the deck,

taking the afternoon sun. After a while Kathy came out and took
the chair next to him, without lying back. When he squinted at
her, trying to see her in the sun's glare, he could see that she was
still troubled. She spoke hesitantly, almost guiltily.

"Daddy, I know you said everything was all right, but I've
been thinking."

"And—?"

"And I've been wondering if you weren't just trying to protect me—keep me from worrying—by saying that. I've been
wondering if maybe you weren't out with *him* instead."

"Slade?"

"Yes."

"But why, honey? What would I be doing with him?"

"I don't know. The same things, I guess. Following him.
Threatening him."

"But I already tried that. And we both know how well it
worked. Poor old Freddy Bear."

"I guess that's my problem, Daddy. Two days after that, you
leave Mom and me alone at night. That isn't like you."

"The police have Slade under surveillance," he said. "So I
wasn't worried about him. I'm sorry if I upset you, though. It
makes me feel like shit."

"Oh, Daddy."

He reached up and touched her face, and her hand covered
his, holding it there.

"Maybe Mom's right," she said. "Maybe you should take me
to Uncle Ralph's."

"No, I feel better with you here. We can protect you here."

"Are you sure?"

Baird looked at her, still somewhat unsettled by her eerie resemblance to the stripper, Satin. It was curious, he thought, how
the one could stir him only with lust, while the other, virtually
her double, could fill his heart with a look. At the moment,
though, it was his eyes that filled.

"Yes, I'm sure," he said.

Seeing his tears, she got down on her knees and hugged him.
"I love you so much, Daddy," she said.

Baird kissed the top of her head. He lifted her face and kissed
her on the cheek. Then they both realized that Ellen was stand-

ing in the doorway, watching. Kathy got to her feet and smiled at her mother.

"Everything's okay now," she said. "He's not the bad boy we thought."

After she went back into the house, Ellen took her place in the chaise next to Baird, lying back and closing her eyes against the sun.

"Well, it's nice to see there's at least some love in this house," she said.

Baird looked over at her. "I love you too," he said.

"Do you, Jack?"

"I wasn't with a woman last night."

"Did I ask?"

"I've been depressed lately, that's all. And I drank too much."

"No kidding."

"Mid-life crisis, I guess."

"Yes, that must be it." Her voice was cool, emotionless.

Unlike the uniformed police and the regular detective units, the Metro Squad did not work in force on Sundays, since their cases were already on the books—were not hot, in other words—and therefore could be investigated more easily at the discretion of the detectives. On this Sunday, though, both Sergeant Lucca and Lee Jeffers were on duty when Detective Bob Harrelson, in Homicide, called about a body found in a dumpster off South Rainier. He had been the principal on the Discovery Park rape-murder and had been downright accommodating when Lee horned in on the case, thinking it might tie in with the Evans' rape.

Lee had wanted to roll on this call alone, since it was her case, or at least might turn out to be part of it, and because she had developed a comfortable rapport with Harrelson, who was about fifty, a beefy, hard-drinking extrovert who liked to kid her about her partner.

"Old Bleeding Hart," he had told her. "Worked five years with the bastard, and I don't think I ever saw him laugh."

So Lee wasn't enthusiastic about showing up with Lucca. But there wasn't much she could do about it. The sergeant, listening to her take the call, got up from his desk and announced that he would drive.

On the way there, he criticized her work again, saying that she was trying too hard to link the three cases, and now possibly four.

"They really ain't got nothin in common," he told her. "Least of all, Jimbo Slade."

"So what are you doing here then? Why tag along?"

"Someone's got to keep you in line."

She gave him her killer smile. "I'm so fortunate to have you."

"And don't ever forget it," he said.

As they pulled into the alley off Rainier, he reached out the window and put the yellow flasher on the LTD's roof and turned it on, siren and all. The crowd, mostly young blacks in a festive mood, parted reluctantly, some play-kicking the car with their inflatable Nikes, while others mugged for the new arrivals, throttling themselves bug-eyed and drawing fingers across their throats, preparing the detectives for what was awaiting them up ahead.

In addition to police cars and an ambulance, two TV trucks were already on the scene, their reporters and cameramen ignoring the yellow tape, penetrating even closer to the dumpster than the paramedics, who stood waiting patiently with their gurney while the detectives, Bob Harrelson among them, went about doing their work: measuring, photographing, taking notes. After Lucca parked, Lee led the way under the tape. Harrelson, seeing Lucca, made a big show of greeting him, even throwing up his hands.

"Well, as I live and breathe, if it ain't the Conscience of the Department, me old buddy Bleeding Hart Lucca."

Lucca barely glanced at him. "Fuck you, Harrelson," he said.

Lee tried to pretend everything was sweetness and light. "What's up?" she asked.

Harrelson shrugged. "Problems. The ambulance jockeys are sayin its our job to get the victim out of there, and we're sayin it's their job. As you'll see, it's not your average dumpster—all chicken bones, ribs, fat, spoiled greens—you name it."

Lee smiled. "I'd argue too."

But Lucca wasn't amused. "What bullshit," he grumbled,

and went over to the paramedics. He showed them his shield and said, "Sergeant Lucca, Metro Squad," then unloaded on them, explaining that they had their goddamn jobs only because their goddamn ambulance was licensed by the goddamn city and state, and that those licenses could be revoked at any time for malfeasance or nonfeasance of duty.

"In other words," he bawled, "I'd advise you to get on the fucking stick! *Now!*"

As if he had to show them the way, he went straight over to the dumpster, where Lee already had reluctantly joined Harrelson. The container alone would have been bad enough, with its flies and stench, its colorful mosaic of maggoty offal. But there in the midst of all that lay the victim, a small, very pretty Asian girl, nude except for a pair of black-felt boots. And the contrast, the revolting horror of it, made Lee glad she had skipped breakfast.

"We're not sure what she died of yet," Harrelson said.

"Where's the M.E.?" Lee asked.

"On his way."

"Well, he's sure not gonna want to get in there with her," Lucca said, gesturing to the paramedics. "So get her out."

During the next hour, the detectives learned a good deal more about the victim, an eighteen-year-old Vietnamese named May Tan. The medical examiner estimated that she had been dead no more than six hours and that the likely cause of death was a stab wound in the back, puncturing her heart. She had been beaten severely about the face and had been sodomized both orally and anally, with visible signs of dried semen on her— evidence that would have elated the detectives even a week earlier, before a state appellate judge ruled that DNA-type testing was not sufficiently well established scientifically to be admitted as evidence against a defendant. Of course that still left blood-typing, and though it sometimes contributed to the case against a defendant, it was rarely sufficient to make for a conviction in and of itself.

May Tan had worked for a small escort service run by one Tommy Dice, twenty-eight, an ex-con with a considerable rap sheet, including convictions for robbery, assault, drug dealing, and pimping. The uniforms, after locating Dice, had brought him to the scene, Harrelson having hoped that someone in the crowd might have seen him with the victim, perhaps even dumping her in the alley. But no one came forward.

The detectives, with Dice, then moved from the alley into the chicken-and-ribs restaurant responsible for the revolting dumpster. It was a dark, dismal joint with uncomfortable old wooden booths and steel-tube tables and chairs. Though the place was still closed at this early hour, the owners—an elderly black couple—had come down from their upstairs apartment to let the detectives in. Heavy and glum, the pair shuffled around in slippers, shaking their heads. No, they hadn't seen anything or heard anything, and no, they didn't know the girl or Tommy Dice.

Finally, with Lee and Lucca looking on, Harrelson sat Dice down in one of the booths and slid in across from him, his burly torso barely making it between the table and bench. He offered Dice a stick of Doublemint gum, which was refused, then took one for himself and sat there grinding away and looking over at Dice as if they were great good friends instead of polar opposites: Harrelson middle-aged, white, overweight, wearing a rumpled tan suit, seemingly as jolly as Old St. Nick, while Dice was probably still in his twenties, slim, blue-black, hair fried into dreadlocks, his clothes gaudy and expensive, shirt a dazzling blue satin, pants billowy white linen. And there was gold too, yards of it draped around his muscular neck.

Like most big-city cops, Lee knew Dice's type only too well: the supercool professional black criminal. This one in fact looked so cool, so bored, he appeared to be in danger of dropping off. Except for the blue-black color, he reminded Lee of Marty, her second husband. On the force, in Narcotics, Marty had been a wild man—angry, hyper, sleepless—waging his own personal war against the Great American Plague. But once he went over to the enemy, it was as if he had found Jesus, something that totally transformed him. And it wasn't just the coke he was using, for he had begun doing that while he was still a cop. Rather, Lee believed it was simply that he had found his calling, that of the outlaw. Further, she believed it was almost endemic in black men, an alienation from the American establishment so severe that many could not live with themselves except outside its cool embrace. And Dice at the moment was doing little to change her opinion, giving Harrelson nothing, making the detective pull his story out of him bit by bit, as if he were extracting the man's teeth.

Yeah, he knew the victim. No, not as a prostitute, just as a friend. Yeah, that was right, just a friend he drove around with. He would take her this place or that and just wait in the car for her while she went inside to visit friends.

Harrelson was grinning. "And last night did you take her around to visit friends?"

"I guess so."

"And when was the last time you saw her?"

"I don't know. Twelve or one, something like that."

"Where?"

"On Rainier. An apartment a few blocks north of here. She went up to see some guy—Arnold Dunlap, or something like that. And I guess she came out early. I mean after being there only a couple minutes. And I guess we fought about that."

"Why?"

"I don't know. Maybe I got tired of waiting."

"But you said she came out early."

Dice shrugged, his eyes still half-closed. "I don't know—I guess I was a little hammered. I was drinkin Scotch."

"Did you hit her?"

"Naa. We just talked, you know? I mean, I talked and she yelled. Then I split. I drove off and left her there."

Dice quite naturally did not want to admit to being a pimp, even though it would have helped him in this instance, since he could have been more explicit about what they had fought over—most likely money, whether or not she had held out on him. But Harrelson made do with what he had. He wrote down the name and address of the girl's last john, said that's where he was going next, then turned to Lee and Lucca.

"Okay, he's yours. What d'ya want to know?"

Dice didn't look up at either of them.

"You know a small-time dealer named Jimbo Slade?" Lee asked. "A white guy with a ponytail. Wears just vests—likes to show off his pecs."

Dice shrugged. "Maybe I seen him around. I ain't sure."

"You didn't see him last night?"

Dice shook his head.

"Was he one of May Tan's 'friends'?"

"Beats me."

"You know, if you did see him last night," Lee said, "it might help get you off the hook."

At that, Lucca exploded. "You can't tell him that, for Christ sake! You're inviting him to perjure himself."

Harrelson clucked his tongue. "Heaven forfend," he said.

But Dice was interested. "What hook?" he wanted to know.

Waving his arms, Lucca moved between him and Lee. "That's enough. We're finished." He looked at his partner as if she had just thrown up on him. "And your case is finished, Detective. You've got four separate crimes here, and all the tugging and twisting, and now the coaching of a possible suspect—it ends right here. Your Jimbo Slade is no longer a suspect of any kind, at least not in the Metro Squad. Is that clear?"

Lee felt like a little girl again, one who had just been slapped in public. For one searing moment she thought of bringing her booted foot right up into Lucca's groin. Her face burned. She looked at Harrelson, who was smiling, shaking his head in comic reproval.

"You've done it now, Lee," he said. "You have offended the Bill of Rights, the ACLU, and His Holiness, your partner, all in one fell swoop."

Lucca was as calm as Dice. "Again, Harrelson—fuck you."

Finally Lee found her voice. "Well, we'll see what case is closed and what case isn't."

Lucca concurred. "Bet on it."

Harrelson called one of the uniformed officers over to the booth and told him to take Dice downtown and hold him for questioning.

"I'll be in later to take his statement," he said.

Dice got up and went along with the uniformed officers. He was still cool and unruffled, his drowsy eyes proclaiming that whatever The Man threw at him, he could take it.

Lee envied him that.

NINE

The next five days were almost peaceful. There was no sign of Slade. He didn't make any appearances at the department store, he didn't park outside the house at night, he didn't even burglarize the place. As a result, Baird began to feel pretty good about things. He couldn't help wondering if his campaign of "getting in Slade's face" was beginning to pay off.

On Monday evening, just two days after his late-night bar crawl with old Jimbo, Baird offered to take Ellen and Kathy out to dinner and a movie, but Ellen declined without bothering to give a reason. When Kathy kept after her, urging her to reconsider, Ellen remained adamant. She suggested that the two of them, father and daughter, go on alone. But Baird didn't care to step into that trap, giving his wife one more reason to feel left out and embittered. Even that failed to improve her mood, however, so for the rest of the week Baird was not inclined to hurry home in the evenings, often not dropping off his orders at the warehouse until eight or nine o'clock. Each evening he spent an hour or so at Leo's, shooting the breeze and pricing his orders and even chancing a steak sandwich on two occasions.

The peaceful days came to an end on Friday. By noon of that

day, Kathy was feeling ill enough to leave work, her menstrual period having begun that morning. She tried to phone Baird in his car, then Ellen at the university library, but was unable to reach either of them and instead took a taxi home. And she evidently found it a frightening experience, being alone in the middle of the day in the large old house, where Slade so recently had roamed at will. Upstairs, she undressed and locked herself in the bathroom to take a long, hot shower before getting into bed.

It was while she was showering that Baird came home himself, stopping off to pick up a catalog for one of his customers. As soon as he came through the front door, he heard the shower running upstairs. Thinking it was Ellen who had come home early, he called to her and started up the stairs. At that same moment, the shower was turned off. Then there was an interval of a few seconds before the screaming began, Kathy having heard *something* while she was showering, and now *someone* on the stairs. It was a gulping scream, staccato and shrill, full of terror. Baird ran up the last few stairs and pounded on the door.

"Kathy!" he cried. "Kathy, it's me!"

But she went right on screaming, as if once she had begun to let it all out, there was no stopping it. Desperate finally, Baird took a step backwards and kicked the door, breaking the lock. And the moment she saw him, she seemed to implode, sinking down onto the bathroom rug as if her body were a burst balloon. She was naked still, wet, and beginning now to sob. Baird put her terry robe around her and picked her up and carried her into her room. Holding her on his lap, he sat down on the bed, hugging and kissing her, trying to console her.

"It's just me, baby," he kept saying. "You're all right. You're safe. It's only me."

Minutes passed before she could stop sobbing long enough to speak.

"I thought it was *him*, Daddy!"

"I know, baby. I know."

In time, he got a towel out of the bathroom and dried her hair. He left the room again while she got into her pajamas. Then he came back, tucked her into bed, and sat with her while she explained about feeling sick at work and trying to phone him and finally taking a taxi home. He stroked her head and told her to sleep or at least to rest. But almost an hour passed before she let go of his hand and closed her eyes.

That evening Baird told Kathy and her mother that he still had customers to call on and that he would probably be late coming home. Then he drove to West Seattle, stopping on the way to pick up a burger, fries, and a cup of coffee. He expected to have to wait past midnight for Slade to show, if indeed the creep showed at all. But when Baird got there, pulling into the gravel parking lot of the rundown, one-time motel, he saw the old Impala in front of number twelve. Getting out of the car, he stepped up onto the low porch and knocked. Inside, a radio or record-player was blaring the music of a heavy-metal band. When the door finally opened, Slade stood there red-eyed and sleepy-faced, wearing only a pair of old jeans, zebra-striped with holes, the kind the hip people had worn a few years earlier.

"Jesus Christ, if it ain't my old pal Jacko," he said. "What can I do for ya, man?"

Baird smiled thinly. "You could invite me in."

"Well, hell yes—goes without sayin.'"

Inside, Baird felt almost physically assaulted by the rock music. Closing the door, Slade padded over to the radio, a boom box, and turned it down.

"Iron Maiden," he said. "They're my boys."

The one-time motel room was still only that, a box about a dozen feet square, with a pulled-out daybed, a table, a few chairs, and a connecting bathroom as well as a small refrigerator and a two-burner stove. There were holes in the rug and the place reeked of marijuana smoke. The dingy walls were covered with taped-up pictures of *Playboy* and *Penthouse* centerfolds, along with a number of black-and-white pages from hardcore rags—pictures of men and women performing sex acts in various groupings.

Flopping back on the daybed, Slade gestured for Baird to take one of the chairs. "Take a load off," he advised.

Baird sat down.

"You want a beer? Or a little weed? You want some weed, Jacko?"

"No, thanks. I'm okay."

"So . . . ?" Slade threw out his hands. "So what d'ya want?"

Baird squirmed. "Well, you remember what we talked about last weekend? That guy you know. The one who—for a consideration—might, you know . . ."

"Let you watch?"

Baird sighed. "Well, yeah. I've been thinking about it."

"No shit."

"But what I said still goes—I wouldn't want anyone hurt because of me. I mean, because I paid."

Slade was sneering by now. "Of course not."

"And only if it was gonna happen anyway. I mean, I wouldn't want this guy to do the thing on my account. I wouldn't want to be responsible for it, you know?"

"Sure. You want your fun, but you don't want to get your fuckin hands dirty."

"Something like that."

Yawning, Slade stood up and got a beer out of the refrigerator. He popped the can and slurped the foam off the top, then straddled the other kitchen chair. "So all that talk last Saturday," he said, "that wasn't all bullshit, huh? You really are a—"

"A sicko?" Baird cut in.

Jimbo was grinning. "Hey, I was just feelin ya out, that's all. Shit, every fucker likes to watch. Just like they like to do it too—if they can, that is. It's no big deal. I don't dis you for it, like the brothers say. Shit, I don't mind watchin myself now and then." He paused for a few moments, his pale eyes narrowing. "Fact is, I used to watch my old lady—my mother—all the time, with Uncle This and Uncle That. What a pig she was."

Baird was feeling so tense he wouldn't have been surprised if he pulled a muscle, just sitting there. And he was sure it showed, this tension. It didn't worry him, however. He figured he would seem more natural that way, more believable to Slade.

"This guy," he said. "You know if he's made any plans?"

"You mean, has he got some cunt already picked out?"

Baird nodded.

Slade grinned. "Normally, no way. I mean, guys don't advertise it when they're gonna commit a felony, right? But in this case, I happened to be with the cat just last night. And you know where? At the Oolala, same as us. And guess what? Guess who really turns him on—just like me and you and every other fucker with a cock."

"Satin," Baird said.

"You got it. But listen—don't get the wrong idea. This guy ain't some nut-case rapist. He dates women, he sleeps with 'em—hell, he even lived with one for a while. It's just he's got a real hard-on against ones like Satin—females who think no guy's good enough for 'em, not unless he's got a couple million in the bank. Anyway, this friend of mine, he kinda likes to teach 'em a lesson, you know? Teach 'em who's boss."

Baird was wishing he had accepted Slade's offer of a beer. His throat was parched and he was beginning to get a headache.

"And he actually said it?" he asked. "I mean, that he's gonna do it? And soon?"

Slade took a long pull on the can and belched. He shook his head. "Now come on, Jacko, let's not get ahead of ourself here. We don't know this guy would even consider lettin you in on the deal. I mean, you ain't exactly his type of cat, right? Mister Clean and all that. All I'm sayin is, I'll take your money, I'll go to him, I'll propose the deal, and we'll see what happens."

"The money," Baird said. "How much you think he'd want?"

Slade shrugged. "Who knows? For starters, let's say a hunnerd up front, just to see if he's interested. Then bring three or four more Monday night, in case he says okay."

"Monday?"

"Yeah. He said that was gonna be the night." Slade gave a laugh of sorts. "He said he was gonna do her right there on the stage, but he was only jokin."

"Let's hope so."

"But he'll be there. That's what he said anyway."

"How do I know he won't just take my money and walk?"

"You don't, Jacko. In this kind of deal, you take your chances. There ain't no guarantees."

"I guess that figures." Baird reached for his wallet, got out two fifties and gave them to Slade, who stuffed them into his pants pocket as if they were Kleenex.

"Remember," Baird said. "I really don't want this to happen. I don't want Satin hurt. I'll probably try to talk the guy out of it."

"Sure you will."

"No, I mean it. I don't want to be the cause of anyone getting hurt."

"Then what the fuck you doin here?"

"I don't know. I guess I'm kind of mixed up."

Slade sneered. "Yeah? Well, I ain't. I know what you want, Jacko, even if you don't. And remember this—you know about somethin ahead of time, you can't go waltzin to the police later. Cuz you're an accessory, you understand that? And if you're there, at the scene, you're just as guilty as the main man. You talk and you could wind up in the slam same as him. You got that?"

Baird nodded. "Don't worry. I'd never go to the police. Not if I was involved."

Getting up, Slade drained his can of beer, crumpled it, and tossed it into a waste can. He yawned again and ran his fingers over his washboard stomach, not scratching it so much as fondling it.

"I hope not, Jacko," he said. "Cuz that would be stupid, you know? Real stupid."

Baird got up now too. "I realize that. Don't worry about it."

Slade laughed again. "Hey, man," he said, "I don't worry about nothin."

Slade turned off the lights in the room and went to the window to watch Baird drive off. Grinning, he reflected that he even hated the man's fucking car, a four-door Buick Le Sabre, a family man's car, a square's car. Slade could imagine old Jacko making regular payments on the goddamn thing, sending them off month after month like all the other nine-to-five jerks in the world. It irritated him that Baird probably pitied him his shitty wheels and crummy little room, never dreaming that he already had enough money—cash money—to buy a like-new Corvette and rent a decent apartment somewhere, maybe even with a view. But he was still on parole, and he didn't want his nosy goddamn case officer thinking he was eating higher on the hog than a dishwasher was supposed to. Also, the brothers got a good laugh out of his car, and he figured that as long as they were laughing at him, they wouldn't be shooting at him. He felt safer that way.

All this, though, barely registered in his mind, was at most a whispered aside compared to the rebel yell of hatred and resentment he felt, watching Baird drive away. He wanted to whirl and plunge his fist into the wall as hard as he could. But that would have been stupid, he knew. Even though the wall was plasterboard and he probably could have punched right through it, he also could have wound up hurting his hand in the process, in which case, the police—Jeffers and Lucca—would have tried to make something of it, evidence that he had beaten the jogger, or now, the gook hooker.

That was a good part of his beef against Baird. He blamed him for what had happened to the girl. If it hadn't been for him, Slade wouldn't have been that drunk or angry, and wouldn't have lost it the way he did, going off like a goddamn rocket when the cunt refused to get in the car with him. Even now he kept seeing her as she bent down and looked in at him, her sexy mouth curling slightly downward as she shook her head in rejection, as if he were not Jimbo Slade but someone altogether different, some fat, ugly, old pervert.

"No tank you," she had said, her almond eyes still full of tears from her fight with the dude.

Immediately he had slammed the gear into park and slid across the seat, scrambling out the passenger door after her, scaring her so badly she tripped and fell on the sidewalk. He hit her just once at that point, to keep her from screaming. Then he dragged her back to the car and threw her in. Driving on, he was surprised to see the chicken joint again, just a few blocks from where he'd picked up the girl. Turning at the next corner, he'd pulled into the alley behind the restaurant and parked there, probably because there were no houses around, just a few commercial buildings and vacant lots.

Still drunk, he'd had a hard time getting in her, and he guessed he made her pay for that too, more than he should have, as it turned out. But he figured it really wasn't his fault. It was Baird who had made him that angry, playing his goddamn games all night long, treating him as if he were some kind of retardo, too blind and stupid to know when he was being conned. Slade was positive that things wouldn't have gone that bad for the girl if only Baird hadn't been so arrogant, if only the bastard had come right out with it and admitted that what he really cared about wasn't voyeurism but the same old thing as before: keeping Jimbo Slade away from his precious fucking daughter.

Slade still couldn't figure out what the man was planning, though. The likeliest scenario, he imagined, was that the bastard would actually go along with him and watch him do some girl, like Satin, and then plant something at the scene: say, a bottle with Slade's fingerprints on it, something like that. Then he'd make an anonymous phone call to the police, and Jeffers and Lucca would come calling.

Slade could just picture the cocksucker sitting around that big old dump of his, planning the gig. And it made him grin, because he knew that whatever the plan was, old Jacko was in for the surprise of his life—that much Slade could guarantee. He would have to play it by ear of course, depending on how the thing developed. But there was one particular ending that was gradually coming clearer in his mind. In it, he could see Satin regaining consciousness in her little red sportscar, remembering nothing but being hit from behind, and slowly beginning to realize that she was in a bad way—naked, battered, raped—and covered with blood that was not her own. Then, like being goosed with an electric cattle prod, she would discover Mr. Jack Baird slumped next to her in the front seat, his pants down around his ankles—and a knife stuck in his chest. A knife, as it would turn out, with her fingerprints all over it. -

He knew the idea was a bit too neat, too cute. In real life, things didn't always work out the way you planned them. Yet there was really nothing complicated about the plan. It was just a matter of waiting to see if things fell into place, then making his move. He had always been good at that.

In any case, old Jacko was soon going to find out that he was in over his head. This was not some wimpy, white, middle-class game he was playing. It was not golf or tennis or tiddledywinks or whatever the hell the smug bastard normally played. No, this game was different. This game was for keeps. This game was for all the marbles. This was a man's game.

The rest of that weekend Baird spent a good deal of time lying out on the deck alone, at war with himself. One moment he would feel that he had it all together, knew exactly what he had to do and was convinced that he could make it work, that it would all come out right in the end, with Slade in jail and the rest of them—himself, Kathy, Satin—all still in one piece, un-hurt, safe, *free*. Then, as if he were an upended hourglass, it would start draining out of him, all his confidence and determi-nation, and he would see himself winding up in jail, or worse. He would see himself dead. After a time, though, he would hear again the sound of Kathy screaming and again would feel himself shaking like an alder leaf in a gale. And the hourglass would turn.

When Monday finally came, he continued to think about it all so steadily—worry about it so much—that he imagined ev-erybody thought he was sick. He tried to concentrate on any number of other things, but never quite managed it. He was like a man overboard in the middle of the ocean, trying hard to think about everything except water.

In the early afternoon it occurred to him that he hadn't fired the .25 automatic since the day after he'd bought it from Cham-bers, three years earlier. Here he was, relying on it for protection against Slade, and he didn't even know if the gun would jam or if the bullets were still good. Also, he had forgotten to take his suede jacket with him when he left the house that morning. So instead of stopping for lunch, he bought a frozen, dressed turkey in a supermarket and drove home with it, knowing that Ellen and Kathy would be at work.

Down in the basement, he carried the turkey into the old coal bin, now a storage room. He set the plastic-wrapped turkey on a box and took the gun out of his briefcase. As he recalled, there were seven bullets in the clip, one of which he now pumped into the chamber. Stepping back, he aimed at the bird and fired twice. The plump white corpse trembled slightly but took the slugs neatly, in two small, dark holes.

Satisfied, Baird put the bird back in the paper sack and took it, the gun, and his briefcase upstairs. At the gun cabinet, he got two more .25-caliber bullets out of the single small box he kept there in a drawer. He inserted the bullets in the gun clip, slipped the clip back into the handle, put the safety on, and returned the gun to his briefcase. Then he got his suede jacket out of the hall closet and carried it, along with his briefcase and the bird, out to the car. On his way back to his route, he detoured down an alley and tossed the turkey into a dumpster.

Later, after he had dropped off his orders at the warehouse, he stopped at Leo's to fortify himself for the ordeal ahead. Sally, apparently bored, came after him as soon as he sat down.

"I sure love those old styles," she said, referring to his suede jacket. "It takes a man with real self-confidence to wear them."

"The pockets are leather," Baird said.

"So?"

"So you can carry more. For instance, if I were to render that certain intimate service you crave, and you paid me off in Krugerrands, the pocket could hold them all without breaking through."

Sally laughed. "Krugerrands! Dream on, Jackson."

"I'll have a double," he said.

Leo, wiping down the bar, came toward them. "Jesus, doubles now, huh? I might get rich yet."

"Not on me, you won't. This is just an aberration."

"Too bad." Leo made the drink and served it. "Hey, Jack, whatever happened with that guy who was hassling your daughter?" he asked.

"No problem," Baird said. "I shot him."

The big man laughed. "See? You didn't need me after all."

TEN

After leaving Leo's, Baird stopped at one other bar on the way to the Oolala. In addition to another double vodka-tonic, he ordered a ham-on-rye sandwich, more to slow the effects of the alcohol than because he was hungry. Earlier in the day he had loaded up on half-pints of rum and vodka, just as Slade had instructed Friday night when Baird was leaving the man's motel-room apartment.

"Booze and cash," Slade had said. "You forget either of 'em, the deal's off."

Driving on now, Baird felt cold sober compared to his condition the last time he had visited the Oolala. Normally, three doubles would have been his limit, but on this night they served only to keep him from jumping out of his skin. He drove with the windows down, for it was still typical late-August weather, clear and dry, with the nighttime temperature in the sixties. The road, Bothell Way, was jammed with beer-high kids cruising in convertibles and pickups and lowriders, tossing empty cans and loaded insults as they jockeyed with each other. When Baird finally reached the parking lot of the Oolala, he was relieved to see that Slade's car was not yet there. And this troubled him, shamed him, to realize how strongly he hoped Slade would *never* show up, even if it meant the threat to Kathy would go on as before.

A half hour passed before old Jimbo finally pulled into the lot, his car belching blue smoke. Baird checked the gun in his pocket, making sure the pocket flap was in place. Then he got the bag of half-pints and walked over to the Impala. Slade was still inside, patting his ponytail into place. As he got out, Baird saw that the man wasn't wearing one of his two vests for a change, but a long-sleeved black-vinyl jacket with chrome studs and pins and silver piping, the kind of jacket an impoverished Elvis might have worn. Predictably, he had left it unzipped, the better to display his hairy chest and rippling stomach.

"New threads," he said. "What d'ya think?"

"Real cool."

"You know it, man."

"The kind of thing Satin won't recall."

"It ain't me she's gonna see, remember?"

"Ah yes, this friend of yours. You give him the hundred?"

"Of course. You got the extra three?"

Baird nodded. "Yeah. But where is he?"

"He'll meet us inside. *If* he comes, remember?" Slade reached for the bag. "Well, let's see what Santa brought us." He picked out two bottles, pocketing a half-pint of rum and handing a vodka to Baird. Then he placed the bag behind the driver's seat of his car and locked the door, despite the cardboard windows in the back.

Inside the Oolala, Baird again paid the cover charge for both of them. This time Slade chose a couch in the far corner of the room, apparently feeling a need for greater privacy. "There won't be no Satin tonight," he said. "Not dancing for us anyway."

"Gonna play it cautious, huh?"

"No, I just ain't gonna play it dumb."

"You scared?"

"What the fuck's there to be scared about? We ain't knocking over a bank, you know. We just gonna be a coupla spectators, that's all. We just gonna tag along. And most likely, all we gonna see is a girl sayin yes and puttin out nice and peaceful. This guy, the cunts really go for him."

"He sounds like a real winner."

Slade looked at Baird. "Hey, what's with you anyway? Why so fuckin sarcastic tonight? You backin out?"

"I'm against doing it, that's all. I don't want to see the girl hurt."

"So you told me."

"You don't believe me."

"Fuck no. Unless I miss my guess, once my buddy's finished, you gonna dive right in there for seconds. You gonna have the fuckin time of your life."

"You think so, huh?"

"I *know* so."

Looking around the strip club, Baird could almost have believed that he and Slade had never left the place nearly ten days before. Everything seemed exactly the same. In the dimness, the patrons looked no different, just as the dancers and the music and the lightshow had not changed. The girl who took their order for soft drinks was one of those who had waited on them the last time, a redhead with creamy white skin and rigid silicone breasts. Evidently remembering the two men, she asked if they wanted Satin again, and Slade jumped all over her.

"If we wanted Satin, we would've fuckin asked," he told her.

She smiled anyway. "Then I'm your girl. I'll put it right in your face."

"You ain't nobody's girl," he told her. "You're too fuckin ugly."

She gave him the finger and sauntered off, unexcited, evidently used to dealing with creeps.

"You sure told her," Baird said.

Slade shrugged. "Fuck her."

In time, Slade did agree to have one of the girls dance for them, a light-skinned negress who reminded Baird vaguely of Lee Jeffers, a younger version, sinewy as a miler, with a beautiful mouth and eyes full of contempt. As before, Baird found it difficult to sit and watch a nude woman dancing so close to him. Three different times he saw Satin dancing, once on the stage and the other times for men sitting alone, one at a table and another in an easy chair across the room. And at a distance, Baird had no problem watching her, in fact could barely take his eyes off the girl, with her beautiful face and body, and the way she

moved to the music, in rhythms that seemed to come from inside
Baird himself, imperatives he did not even know he had.

Now and then his mind would cough up shreds of his
drunken dreams of two nights before, lights from the glitter-
dome crawling like glowworms over ivory skin, and he would
drink again, would shakily pour more vodka into his soft drink.
And he would wonder what on earth had happened to his life.
How was it that he came to be here, committed to this mad en-
terprise?

Oddly, Slade did not seem any more enthusiastic about
things than Baird was. As the evening wore on, he grew steadily
more sullen and testy. He popped a couple of pills. He went to
the bathroom every twenty minutes or so. And he was drinking
much more than Baird. Little more than an hour had passed
before he went out to his car to get another half-pint of rum.
Even though the bouncers were obviously keeping an eye on
him, he took no pains to conceal that he was spiking his drinks. It
was almost as if he wanted to be kicked out of the place. And
there seemed to be nothing that pleased him, least of all their
intended victim. Watching Satin dance, he sneered and shook
his head.

"Look at that cunt," he said to Baird. "She thinks she's such
hot stuff. But when you come down to it, she's just another cunt,
good for nothin but layin down and spreadin 'em. You think
she's so special cuz she looks like your kid, but I got news for
ya—they're both cunts."

Baird broke into a sweat. Sitting there on the couch, he felt
almost too close to turn and look at Slade. And anyway, he knew
what he would have seen: the sneer and the cold, pale eyes. How
great it would have felt to loop his fist into the center of all that
ugliness, smash it like a melon. Instead, he unbunched his fists
and breathed deeply, telling himself to save his rage, use it later,
use it when it would count.

Slade drained his glass and reached for Baird's wrist, checking his watch.

"Christ, not even midnight yet," he groused.

"Yeah, and where's your friend?"

"I told ya he might not come. But there's another place—he
could be there."

"Where?"

Slade didn't answer. "Come on, I'm outa here," he said.

Baird obediently got up and followed him out to the parking lot. There, the cool, unsmoky air hit his lungs like an irritant, making him cough. Slade tossed his empty half-pint over a row of parked cars, and it shattered against something solid.

"Fuckin strip clubs!" Slade bawled. "It's all tickle and tease. If this country was honest like in Thailand and them places, the cunts would just come over and unzip your fly and suck you off. Be a lot less fuckin crime then."

Crime. Baird didn't know what to say. He had never heard Slade mention the word before, had doubted that the man even knew what it was. At the moment, though, old Jimbo was heading for Baird's car.

"No, not mine," Baird said. "This is your show. If a witness describes a car, it's got to be yours, not mine."

"I thought we was in this together."

"Like I said—I'll go along, but I won't participate. If it was up to me, nothing would happen. No one would get hurt."

Actually, Baird knew that it would not have mattered even if they took his car, since he planned to call the police in on them at the end. But he was afraid that if he agreed to use the Buick, Slade might have become suspicious, knowing it was a stupid thing for Baird to do.

Walking toward his car now, Slade shook his head in disgust. "Some buddy you are," he said. "Fuckin creep is more like it."

Baird almost laughed out loud, knowing that old Jimbo's charge was not without merit. Things had come full circle. He was now the creep's creep.

Slade drove them to a small, quiet beer tavern located a block from the lake. The half-dozen patrons, like the bartender, all looked older than Baird, working stiffs content to drink their beer in silence as they sat watching a fight rerun on television. Slade led the way to the last booth in the room, where he could continue to hit his half-pints out of sight. He ordered a pitcher of beer and made steady inroads into that too. And in time he fished a small vial out of his pocket, then produced his switchblade and flicked it open. Dipping the point into the vial, he brought up a tiny mound of white powder, which he then snorted up his nose.

"I'd offer you some," he told Baird, "but you don't need it. You don't need nothin to be a sicko voyeur."

"Thanks anyway."

They had been in the bar about a half hour when Slade finally made the announcement.

"I don't think my friend's comin. I'm afraid you lost your hunnerd bucks."

"Big surprise," Baird said.

"What d'ya mean by that?"

"I never expected him to show."

Jimbo looked more puzzled than angry. "Why the hell not?"

"Because I figured you and him were one and the same."

"You mean I made him up?"

"That's what I mean, all right."

"And why the fuck would I do that?"

"Because you're the one who wants to do Satin. Only you want me to pay you to do it."

Slade did not respond for a time. He sat there frowning and glaring at Baird, then took a long pull on another half-pint of rum, recapped it, and put it away. Finally he grinned, sneered.

"You're full of shit, you know that, Jacko? But I gotta admit—it *is* an idea. I could use the cash. I really could. Only I wouldn't be 'doing' her—I'd just pick her up and con her into it, that's all."

"Because the cunts really go for you, right?" Baird said.

And for a moment he had no idea what Slade would do next. At first the man looked merely confused. Then Baird could see the anger building in him. In the flat of his cheek a muscle began to pulse like a tiny heart.

"You *tryin* to piss me off, Jacko?"

"No."

"Well, you're doing it anyway. And I've had just about enough bullshit outa you."

Baird shrugged. "I'm sorry. The thing is, I just don't know where I stand. Are you going ahead with Satin, or do I pick up my marbles and go home?"

"I thought you didn't want the thing to happen. And above

all, I thought you didn't want to pay to have it happen."

"I don't. It's entirely up to you. If you're going ahead with it anyway, then I'll pay to be there. To watch it. But I don't want her hurt. I don't want anyone hurt."

Slade shook his head. "Jesus, you're makin me dizzy, you know that? I can't follow you." He reached across the table. "Gimme the money, and we'll see what happens."

"That's not good enough."

Slade groaned. "All right, then—yeah, I'm gonna do her, with you or without you, I don't care which." His fingers beckoned for the money. "So pony up. Or take off. One or the other."

Still Baird held back. "Just so we understand each other. I'm not paying you to do this thing. If I don't pay, you go ahead anyway."

Slade still had his hand out. "Yeah, yeah—what'd I just say?"

"All right, then."

Baird got out the money and gave it to him, and Slade settled back in the booth. Neither of them said anything for a time, and Baird was surprised at how rapidly his drinking partner's mood began to change. Once Slade admitted to his mission—to what he had intended all along—Baird had expected to see more of the cockiness and drunken fervency so in evidence on the drive home the previous week. But instead Slade was becoming increasingly sullen and somber, more like a condemned man than a man about to condemn someone else, sentence her to life in the harshest of prisons. It was almost as if he had been unfairly chosen for the task at hand and deeply resented it. And finally he explained. As if he were confiding secrets of state, he leaned across the table and spoke in an urgent whisper.

He had never known his father. His mother was a whore. One of his earliest memories was of himself peering over the foot of her bed, watching in terror as some fat slob pounded away on her, grunting and gasping as if he were trying to kill her. But then poor old Mom had turned her head and winked at Slade—*winked at him!*—and he knew from that moment on just who the enemy was.

"*Cunts*, my friend! Mother, sister, stranger, whatever— they're all cunts! And no matter what you ever fuckin do to 'em, you never really get even. There's just no way!"

Then it was the foster homes, so many of them that a social worker once joked that Slade should change his name to Foster.

"I fixed that fucker," he said. "I made sure which car was his and then I put a screwdriver to it, keyed it real good on both sides."

Next, he went on about reform schools, or "juvy," as he called them.

"I made 'em all. And one thing I learned—you either fight the brothers or you bend over for them, one or the other. I fought 'em. Hell, I even crippled one, smashed his foot with a hammer."

Baird took a pull on his tiny bottle of vodka. "Why tell me all this now? How can you think of anything but Satin?"

"I *am* thinkin about her. I'm just tellin ya—it won't be just me doing her. It's all them years, all the bastards who've been hammerin on me since Day One."

"That's a cop-out," Baird said. "It's your choice. You do it, it'll be because you choose to do it."

"Bullshit. It's like that foster mother the cunt Jeffers says I did. The old hag started hittin me with a broom cuz I skipped school. So I took the broom away and hit her back. And when she falls, her dress hikes up, and it dawns on me—what better way to let her know who's boss? Old hag probably dug it. Best fuckin day of her fuckin life."

Slade settled back in the booth, breathing hard now for some reason. He drank more beer and lit a cigarette, and all the while, Baird sat there looking at him. Finally Slade bridled.

"What the fuck you lookin at?"

"One last time, Slade—don't do it. Satin may not look it, but I bet she's had a rough time the same as you. Why add to her problems? Give her a break, okay?"

"Cold feet, huh?"

"Whatever. And I don't want to watch either. I really don't."

"Who gives a shit?" Sneering, Slade again checked Baird's watch. "Almost twelve-thirty. Time to recon—ain't that what they say in the army?"

"I wouldn't know."

Slade laughed. "Boy, you really have slipped through, you

bastard. No bumps and bruises on old Jack Baird, right? Just smooth sailin all the way."

"I wouldn't say that."

Slade looked at him with deep resentment. "Yeah? Well, I would. Someone like you—you make a killin just by gittin born, you know that?"

Baird did not answer.

"No foster mothers for old Jack Baird, right?"

"That's right—no foster mothers."

"No sir, just Mommy and Daddy and Little Jack. And growin up in one place, I bet, livin in the same fuckin house, probably with your own cozy little room. Then college and a purty wife, a purty kid, a good job. A killin, Jacko—that's what you made. Just by gittin born."

"If you say so," Baird said.

The strip-club road followed the shore around the north end of Lake Washington and then ran straight east through the town of Bothell to Route 405, the north-south Interstate that served the east side. The land between the lake and the freeway at that point was still semi-rural, an odd mixture of horse farms, country estates, and an occasional raw, new apartment building, most of which looked grossly out of place, like a garden in Manhattan.

According to Slade, it was in one of these that Satin lived, a two-story, ten-unit, barracks-like building set back a couple of hundred feet from the blacktop road. On either side of the entrance there was about a half-acre of woods, mostly fir trees and ferns, which effectively obscured the building from the road. Beyond the wooded entrance was the parking lot, newly blacktopped, with each space delineated in bright yellow paint. The building itself faced away from the parking lot, with balconies on one side and the entrances to the individual apartments on the other. In between the lot and the building there was a flagstone walkway bordered by bushy evergreens as tall as a man.

Slade made a circle in the parking lot, then drove back out through the wooded entrance and turned south on the blacktop. A quarter-mile farther on, he pulled into another driveway and backed around, then headed back north. When he reached the wooded entrance again, he turned in and went straight across the parking lot this time, pulling into a space near the end of the evergreen walk.

"The cunt's apartment is on the second floor," he said. "I followed her here twice already. I don't know why she takes off at one—the other strippers don't. Maybe she gets sleepy, huh?"

"I wouldn't know."

"When we see her lights coming, I'll jump out and you get down in the fuckin seat. Don't let her see you. She'll park in one of the open spaces. And when she starts down the sidewalk, I'll be there to say hello. I'll bring her back to the car, maybe put her in the trunk—I don't know yet. And we'll do her someplace else. There's lotsa nice woodsy spots around here."

Baird was grateful for all the vodka he'd had. As it was, he had to steel his body to keep from shaking. On top of that, he felt feverish, hot one moment and cold the next. And he felt the same in spirit, alternately fighting to control his rage and fear. Listening to Slade detail how he would go about ravaging the girl, Baird wanted to take out his gun immediately and beat him over the head with it, no matter the consequences. But a moment later he would feel paralyzed with fear, mostly for Satin and his own family, knowing what might befall them if he screwed up.

Waiting there in the car, he tried to think ahead to when it would all be over. He tried to concentrate on what he would say to the police. He tried to imagine how it would play.

Yes, I was with him—but not as a friend. He's been stalking my daughter, and I thought that if I got to know him—went out drinking with him—he might leave her alone. And then tonight when it dawned on me what he was up to—that he wasn't here to talk to this girl, as he claimed, but to attack her—that's when I jumped out and stopped him, and had her call nine-one-one.

"And you just happened to have a gun handy?"

"For my protection. I knew his record."

That was what he hoped for. That was the way the thing was supposed to come out.

Again Slade grabbed Baird's wrist and checked the time. "Only fuckin one o'clock," he said. "Could be another half hour before she shows."

He jumped out of the car and went to the back, twice unlocking the trunk and slamming it shut, evidently having decided to dump the girl in there for the drive to the "nice woodsy spot" where he and Baird would then entertain themselves at their leisure.

He got back into the driver's seat. Though he left the door slightly ajar, no interior lights came on, either because they were burned out or because he had disconnected them. Breathing deeply, he took another pill and washed it down with rum, the last of another half-pint, which he then dropped over the seat onto the floor. He shook his head ruefully.

"You know, it's so goddamn weird. I don't feel a fuckin bit horny now. Not like last week at all. Christ, I was really sailin along then. Now I'm down. I'm depressed. I hate every fuckin thing in the world. Especially her. And you. I feel dead."

"Why don't we leave, then?"

Sneering, Slade again shook his head. "You just don't give up, do you? There's no fuckin way we're quittin now. When I'm like this and suddenly let it all go, I get like a goddamn tiger. I get so hard I could open cans with it. And the cunt, she could be a fuckin gorilla, I'd still beat the piss outa her. When old Jimbo's like this, he's one mean dude, lemme tell ya."

Baird felt a wave of nausea. Had he been alone, he might have thrown up. As it was, though, he just sat there in the passenger seat watching as Slade got out his switchblade and began to clean his fingernails. He could hear music playing softly in the building, Barbra Streisand and a male performer singing a duet, most likely about love.

At that hour, there were not many cars on the blacktop road. Every time one appeared, its headlights coming over a hill from one direction or around a curve from the other, Slade would open his door and start to get out. Then, as the lights disappeared behind the wooded entrance and kept going, he would curse and get back in.

Finally, at close to one-thirty, another pair of lights came over the hill. But this time the car slowed down as it reached the woods, and Baird saw its headlights flickering as the car came toward them through the trees. By then, Slade was already outside. He pushed the door closed and moved in a swift crouch past the front of the car and onto the evergreen-bordered walk-way.

Baird's mouth went dry and his heart began to wallop his chest. Hunching down in the front seat, he peered out the win-dow and saw a small red sportscar pull into an empty space three cars away. As the car's door opened, he saw the girl's face in the light, heavy-eyed and glum, not as striking without her makeup. She got out, closed the car door, then hitched a large handbag onto her shoulder and started forward, moving between two evergreens onto the sidewalk. At that same moment, Baird opened the Impala's door and saw the girl turn in alarm, having heard the sound. It was then that Slade struck, stepping from behind another evergreen and clapping one hand over her mouth while furiously looping the other, a fist, into her face and head, over and over.

Immediately Baird scrambled out of the car, terrified that Slade was going to beat the girl to death before he got to him. Fumbling the gun out of his pocket, he reached the walkway just as Slade punched the girl out of his own grasp, sneering in utter hatred and joy as she dropped hard onto the flagstones, her bloody face already ballooning. Slade then reached down and seized her by the hair, either to pull her up for more punishment or to drag her to the car. But before he could do either, Baird lunged forward and struck him in the head with the gun, again and again, until he too crumpled onto the walkway and did not move.

Baird then took *him* by the hair, clamping his ponytail in one hand and the lapel of his vinyl Elvis jacket in the other, and dragged him roughly back to the car. He fished Slade's keys out of his pocket, opened the trunk and dumped him in. Closing the trunk, he hurried back to where the girl was, still lying on her back on the flagstone walk. She had begun to moan and was holding a trembling hand out in front of her face, as if she feared to touch it.

"You'll be all right, honey," he told her. "You'll make it. Just hang on."

Running back to the car, he got in and jammed his hand against the car horn, glad that it was one of the old-fashioned klaxons, made to wake the dead and blow beetles off the road. Someone inside the building began to yell at him, and he raised the gun out the window and shot it into the air. Then he started the car, backed around, and drove out of the parking lot. At the road, he turned left, heading south, for he knew where he wanted to go now. As he drove, he tried not to think about it all, what had happened so far and what was yet to happen. But the one thing he could not put out of his mind was Satin's eyes as Slade held her mouth shut and began to punch her: the eyes of a horse in a fire, the very look Slade had told Kathy he liked most in a woman.

Driving slowly, Baird kept moving south and west. He went through a residential neighborhood on his way to Holly Point Drive, which snaked through a small state park for over a mile before coming to the lake, where it then ran south along the lakeshore bluff. The park section was unlit and so heavily wooded with old-growth firs that the sky overhead seemed like a road itself, a narrow path of starlight.

Even during the day, it was a lightly traveled road; now, at night, it was virtually deserted. Seeing no headlights in either direction, Baird pulled onto the shoulder and stopped. For the last few minutes he had heard sounds of bumping and pounding in the trunk, so he knew Slade had regained consciousness. Taking the car keys in one hand and his gun in the other, he got out and went around to the rear of the car. He looked in both directions again, making sure there still were not any other cars on the road. Then he inserted the key in the trunk's lock and turned it. And as the lid popped open, Slade came lunging up out of the blackness, swinging his switchblade in a broad arc. Baird saw the blade glint in the starlight and jumped back just as the knife's point nicked his coat, then rang against the steel of the trunk lid.

"*Fucker!*" Slade bawled.

Baird shot him. He fired at him three times, hitting him twice in the chest and once in the head. He watched him slump back into the trunk. Then he slammed the lid closed, and it locked.

About a mile farther on, Baird came to a turnoff, a narrow, semi-private gravel road that ran even closer to the lake, starting along the top of the bluff and snaking downhill, connecting the five or six houses that wealthy owners had been able to build on the steep, wooded hillside. When the road came to a dead end at the last house, Baird turned around and drove back to the blacktop. He tried two other such gravel roads before he found one he could use. Halfway down, the third road went into a sharp S-curve, dropping toward what must have been the last house on the lane.

In the middle of the curve Baird stopped the car and turned off the lights. From that spot he couldn't see either the house above or the house below. Trembling by now, he got out and went over to the outer edge of the narrow road. Even though there was a good seventy-foot drop to the water below, there was no guardrail. In the days when he had still owned a boat, he occasionally had fished this part of the lake, and he knew there was no beach under the bluff, just the vast green wall plunging straight into the water. He remembered that it was fairly deep right up to the shore, his depth-sounder usually having registered thirty feet or more.

So he wasted no time. Leaning into the car, he put on the emergency brake, pushed the gearshift into drive, then released the brake and stepped out of the way. And the old Impala went obediently to its grave, rumbling and smoking over the edge of the road and rolling downhill for about twenty feet, smashing saplings and bumping over rocks before it finally took to the air and dropped the rest of the way down to the water, where it made a large splash. As the car sank from sight, Baird took the gun out of his pocket and threw it as far out into the lake as he could. He saw the blip it made in the choppy black surface, but he heard nothing, not with the wind blowing as it was.

He turned and walked back up the S-curve a short distance, then cut through the woods above the road, figuring that anyone he might have awakened in the houses would not be able to see him in the trees. Though he wanted to get out of the area as fast as he could, he was too exhausted to walk fast. And anyway, he knew there was still a long night ahead of him. He knew he was a long way from home.

ELEVEN

I t was almost four in the morning when Baird finally got home. After dumping Slade's car, he had spent the next hour on foot, walking along Holly Point Road at first, then picking his way through the thick woods of the state park until he reached an all-night convenience store located on the road that bordered the park. There he telephoned for a taxi and had the driver take him to a motel a few blocks from the Oolala. After the cab had pulled away, he walked back up the road to the strip club and got his car, which by then was the only one in the parking lot.

As he drove home, he tried not to think about anything except what he was doing, crawling along under the speed limit, even though the road was practically deserted. He knew he would have plenty of time later—half a lifetime—to think about it: what had happened, what he had done. But this was not the time for it, he kept telling himself. Better now to pretend the thing did not even exist, was not right there beside him like a rabid hyena chained in the passenger seat, snapping and snarling.

When he finally arrived at his house, he paused in the kitchen only long enough to drain the last few ounces in a bottle of vodka. Then he went upstairs and slipped into his and Ellen's bathroom, off the master bedroom. He pilfered two of her tranquilizers and downed them along with a couple of aspirin tablets, then slinked back out of the bedroom, being careful not to glance over at the bed for fear he would find her lying there wide awake, watching his every move. He quietly closed the door behind him and went into the guest room across the hall. There he got out of his clothes and fell into bed as if it were a final resting place, a bier from which he never expected to rise. At the same time, neither did he expect to sleep. He figured he was much too exhausted for that, too violated, too lost.

Eyes wide open, he lay there staring at the shadows playing across the ceiling. But what he saw was his hand raising the tiny, black automatic and bringing it down on Slade's head over and over, and then minutes later holding it out and squeezing the trigger, firing the gun endlessly into the dark pit of the trunk. He watched the car fall toward the lake, and he saw the splash it made before it sank from sight, and he wondered who he was now, *what* he was—certainly not good old Jack Baird anymore. He was afraid he had killed that man just as surely as he had murdered Jimbo Slade.

Despite his expectations to the contrary, he eventually did fall asleep. But he was awakened by Ellen at eight o'clock, on her way out, about to drive herself and Kathy to work.

"You going to work today?" she asked. "Or are you giving that up too?"

Baird was still in a sweat of terror, coming down out of a nightmare. He nodded vaguely. "Sure," he said. "Of course."

"Of course," she repeated. "How silly of me."

Through the open door he saw Kathy looking in at him as if he were in a hospital room, a room she shrank from entering. He closed his eyes and settled back into the pillow and stayed there until he heard Ellen's car drive off. Then he began the excruciating process of putting himself back together, showering and shaving, treating a touch of diarrhea, and washing a couple of multivitamins down with a shake of milk and honey and raw eggs.

He dressed hurriedly and drove to work, surprised to see that his hands were no longer trembling. He checked his call-in orders, submitted to the usual raillery from the warehouse workers ("Well, if it ain't the late Jack Baird!"), and even did a little josh-ing himself with one of the secretaries, sixty-eight-year-old Emma Bergen, leaning over her desk and breathing in her per-fume, observing that if he smelled that good, he'd probably play with himself. Laughing happily, she gave him an elbow in the hip and he limped away, complaining that the good ones always played hard to get.

Then he set out upon his workday, knowing he would get through it only by forcing himself to think about anything and everything *except* what had happened the night before. With this goal in mind, he was almost grateful that he felt so ill and ex-hausted, because it was something he had to think about, or at least deal with, minute by minute throughout the day. Several customers commented on his appearance, one even suggesting that he ought to go home and go to bed. But he persevered and in the end even made a good day of it, writing up a couple of large corporate orders and selling a new drive-in chain its first order of printed paper cups, one hundred thousand in all.

When he went for Kathy at four o'clock, he called ahead to tell her that he would pick her up outside, on Clive Street. After they drove away together, she asked him if he wasn't still worried about Slade.

"Well, of course I am," he said. "Why else would I pick you up?"

She shrugged. "I don't know. I guess just because you didn't come inside. And then last night."

"What about last night?"

"You know—leaving us alone all night."

"It wasn't all night."

She gave him a sad, searching look. "What's wrong, Daddy? Mother's really upset. I don't think she said two words all night."

"What else is new?"

"Is there anything I ought to know?"

Baird shook his head. "No, there's no problem, baby. It's happened before. I just go through periods when I like to stay out after work and have a few drinks with the guys. It's no big deal."

As he said this, he kept staring straight ahead, not wanting to see the look in her eyes. It was not something he was used to, lying to his wife and children, or to anyone else, for that matter.

Baird's final customer of the day was the Mooney Hotel Bar, located in the university district. It was a handsome basement bar, with plush carpeting, a lot of dark wood, brass, and leather as well as a large-screen TV customarily turned to a sports channel, with the sound kept low. Baird had already written up the bartender's order and was sitting at the bar, drinking a double vodka-tonic and trying to appear casual as he leafed through the evening newspaper. Finally, on the second page of the local news section, he found the item he was looking for, three column inches under the heading, "Dancer Victim in Mystery Assault."

The story said that twenty-year-old Terri Dean had been assaulted outside her Bothell apartment by two men early that morning as she was returning home from work at the Oolala night club, where she performed as an exotic dancer under the stage name of Satin. Miss Dean had suffered multiple facial and head contusions and had been taken to Kirkland's Evergreen Hospital for observation. She was unable to describe her assailants other than that one of them was a white man about forty years of age. Miss Dean told the police that she was not able to see the other man, who had seized her from behind and repeatedly battered her about the face and head. The dancer said she had no idea why she had been assaulted. The police reported that she was neither robbed nor raped.

Baird's hand had started to tremble again as he was holding the paper, so he folded it and pushed it away. Picking up his drink, he tried hard to look relaxed, but he found himself gripping the glass so tightly he was afraid that Sammy, the Asian bartender, would notice. He pivoted on his stool then, gazing at the TV screen at the far end of the room.

It was after five and the local news was on. The two middle-aged anchors—a handsome, balding man and a beaming blond woman—were tossing the ball back and forth, finishing each other's sentences as if neither of them had enough breath for an entire news item. Then the picture cut away to a reporter standing on the very flagstone walk where Satin had been attacked and Baird had clubbed Slade senseless. In the background was the apartment building, as well as a half-dozen onlookers: a young mother, her two clinging children, and three teenage boys mugging for the camera. The reporter was a black man in his twenties, coatless, with a loosened tie and rolled-up sleeves, obviously a hard worker.

"It was right here that exotic dancer 'Satin'—Terri Dean in real life—was assaulted at about two o'clock this morning," he reported as the picture briefly cut away, first to a couple of anonymous topless dancers in a dim strip club, their breasts fuzzed out, then to a still photo of Satin in a string bikini. "Now, this normally wouldn't be that big a story," he went on. "Terri Dean, shown here in a publicity photo, wasn't robbed or raped. But according to police, there are some very strange aspects to the case. Miss Dean described one of the assailants as a good-looking businessman type around forty. And this man, she says, leaned down at the end, while she was still lying on the ground, and said to her, 'You'll be all right, honey.' And finally, as they were leaving, the two men honked their car horn and fired their guns, presumably in the air, as if they wanted to call attention to what they had done." The reporter smiled wryly. "Weird, huh? Back to you, Barry."

The male anchor came back on, shrugging philosophically. "Well, a day in the life," he said. "Thanks, Harvey."

The female anchor smiled joyously. "Well, maybe Jeff has better news for us. What about it, Jeff? Is this weather going to hold?"

The picture cut to the weatherman, who seemed embarrassed by it all. Baird looked away. He drained his glass and waggled the ice in it, signaling Sammy for a refill. And seemingly without even thinking, he added to his order.

"And a pack of Marlboros," he said. "No, make it two, Sammy. And a book of matches."

Sammy served him. "I didn't know you smoked, Jack."

Still trying to appear casual, Baird opened one of the packs and lit up. "Off and on," he said, not bothering to mention that he had been "off" for five years now, ever since his forty-second birthday.

He dragged the smoke into his lungs, trying not to cough.

And he wondered what the devil he was doing. Certainly he didn't expect the nicotine to synergize with the vodka and somehow stem the rising tide of panic in him. At the most, he imagined it was simply that the old habits and restraints—the elements of a sane and sensible life—suddenly did not matter. As far as Jack Baird was concerned, war had broken out, the earth had quaked, his belly was full of cancer. Smiling grimly to himself, he even reduced it all to an epigram: *Killers smoke*.

Why, he wondered, would TV even cover such a story? Satin had not been raped or robbed. No one had shot her. And the reporter's explanation, that the story had some unusual aspects, simply didn't wash. Baird wondered if there had been a dearth of bodies discovered that day. Perhaps no skeletons had been found along the Green River or maybe the Crips had not opened fire on the Bloods or just possibly no sullen young father had beaten his infant son to death. But then Baird knew he was being a bit naive. More than likely, Satin was on TV simply because she was what she was, young and beautiful and a stripper to boot, a victim whose story allowed the news director to squeeze a few seconds of tits-and-ass in between the sports and the weather. It was probably no more complicated than that.

Yet it unnerved him, seeing not just Satin but the rest of it too, right there on television in daylight: the flagstone walk and the evergreens, the very place where fifteen hours earlier he had altered his life forever. He felt exposed and vulnerable. It struck him as preposterous that he could sit at the bar among the innocent and not be seen for what he was. He kept feeling that Sergeant Lucca and Lee Jeffers were going to come walking through the door at any moment, handcuffs at the ready.

Seconds after putting out his first cigarette, he lit another. And he signaled Sammy for a refill.

"Love that quinine water," he said.

After leaving the Mooney bar, Baird wanted to go straight to Leo's, not for more drinks so much as for the comfort of being among friends, the false sense of security he might have found there. But he wasn't ready to face Leo and Sally and Wyatt Earp any more than he was ready for Ellen. He had the unreasoning fear that if he looked any of them straight in the eye, they would know immediately what he had done, as if the mark of Cain were stamped right on his pupils.

And anyway, he knew that more than anything else, he had to be by himself now. He had to think. He had to go through the whole thing as if it were a filthy closet and sort it all out. He had to get some inkling of where he stood and what might lie ahead of him, what he had to do and how he had to change in order to deal with it. And he knew he couldn't do that at Leo's any more than he could have done it at home. So he drove south and east through the university's arboretum until he reached one of the parks along the Lake Washington shore. There he pulled in and parked at the far end of the lot, a good distance from the half-dozen other cars there. In front of him a heavily shaded lawn sloped down to the rocky shore, beyond which the lake stretched two miles across, to a broad green strip dominated by the high-rise buildings in Bellevue and limned by the distant Cascades, still snowcapped, spectral in the light smog. Baird gazed blindly at the scene. It could have changed into a brick wall and he would not have noticed, so intent was he on that spot ten miles to the north, on the other side of the lake: the bluff overlooking Slade's grave. It was a spot he could not see, however, due to the northern floating bridge, which blocked his view of it.

He inclined his seat and lay back. Despite the three doubles he'd had, he felt clear in his mind. More than anything else, he wanted to get a handle on his feelings, divine just how much was guilt and how much simple fear of being found out. From the moment he'd stopped firing the gun and closed the trunk lid on Slade, he'd accepted it that for the rest of his life he would have to carry a heavy burden of guilt, simply because he had killed another human being, whether rightly or wrongly.

Yet guilt didn't seem to be what he was feeling now, not yet anyway. He judged that most of all, it was fear he felt, the insistent worry that someone might have seen him during the shooting or as he was getting rid of the body and the car. He kept remembering the force with which the old Impala had struck the water, and in his mind he kept seeing the trunk lid pop open and Slade's body lift from the wreckage and practically swim back up to the surface in order to point a finger at him.

But Baird was feeling something else too, something that

surprised him greatly: a sense of power and exhilaration not unlike that he'd found in the back seat of his father's car at sixteen,
holding a half-naked Sue Ann Johnson in his arms as he ejacu-
lated into her tight little vagina. At first, with Slade, he had
thought it was only relief he was feeling, an overwhelming sense
of deliverance from the threat old Jimbo had posed to Kathy and
himself. By now, though, he was beginning to realize that there
was something else going on, a new and different kind of drug
singing in his veins.

He got out a cigarette, lit it, dragged. And finally he got
around to it, asking himself the hardest question of all: why he
had not carried out his original plan and called in the police once
Slade had been subdued. As he'd expected, the incident had
proved to be intensely chaotic. Since his was the only face the
girl saw, it stood to reason that she would point to him as her
attacker, not Slade. And Baird was the one carrying a gun, the
one who had beaten the other man senseless. So he very easily
could have been arrested right along with Slade, no matter what
he told the police at the scene.

But then he'd known that all along, had anticipated that it
might go that way at first. In the end, though, things would have
come out right—he had convinced himself of that too, hadn't
he? He had no police record. He had been a solid citizen all his
life. And once he called in Lee Jeffers to back up his story about
Slade, certainly the local police would have believed him, would
have understood that all he was trying to do was catch Slade in
the act, so the state would finally have a solid case against him
and be able to put him behind bars, where he belonged.

Yet Baird had not paused a single second once he'd clubbed
Slade to the ground. Seemingly without giving the matter any
thought at all, he'd simply dragged him to the car and locked
him in the trunk and driven straight to the place where he'd then
shot him dead. And disposing of the body, the car, and the
gun—he wondered if it all wouldn't seem a trifle too neat, too
planned, as if it had been in the back of his mind all along, his
true mission, perhaps hidden even from himself until the moment was at hand.

It was a reasonable interpretation. Yet he was certain it was
wrong. The truth, he believed, was simply that as Slade had at-

tacked the girl, it was not her Baird had seen but Kathy—lying on her back on the flagstones, her trembling hands raised to protect her already bloody, swelling face.

He wanted desperately to go on thinking about it all. He felt he had to get it straight in his mind before he could get on with his life. But he wasn't able to keep his eyes open.

It was after ten when he finally woke. He was surprised that he hadn't been mugged, lounging there in the dark with the windows open. At the moment, though, his main concern was his bladder, which felt as if a stake had been driven into it. As he relieved himself in a nearby clump of bushes, it crossed his mind that if he were arrested at that moment, caught in midstream, so to speak, the newspapers could have a field day. "Murderer Caught Pissing in Park." Or "Vigilante Suspect in Hosing of Mum Bush." Then he caught himself, puzzled at his state of mind, at how untroubled he seemed. He felt oddly casual and confident, even reckless, as if all the flak of daily life could no longer reach him, not at the altitude where he was cruising now.

Getting back in the car, he cautioned himself that his mood was undoubtedly temporary, like the high of a five-martini evening. He had little doubt that very soon the real thing would come crashing down upon him, like no hangover in his life. Again he thought of going home or to Leo's, but he decided that he still wasn't ready for either of them, not the noisy raillery of the bar any more than one of Ellen's silent inquisitions, with the lasers bearing in upon him. And anyway, he knew that he was going to have to keep late hours for the next couple of weeks in case Slade's body was found and the police managed to pinpoint the time of death. It wouldn't do for him to have been out late, away from home, on that one night alone.

Ravenous by now, he drove downtown to Bramante's Ristorante, the kind of place where the mob would have hung out, if Seattle had had a mob. Though it was a tomblike place, dark and sinister, the restaurant served delicious Italian beef sandwiches and green salads that stuck to the ribs. Taking one of the candle-lit booths, Baird as usual found that he could barely see the menu, let alone the waiter, a wizened old man who bore an eerie resemblance to the old-time comedian, Jimmy Durante.

When Baird ordered a vodka martini, the old man countered, "How bouta tabla red? It'sa reala good."

Baird was agreeable. "Sure. Why not?"

The carafe of red wine did nothing to lessen Baird's buoyant mood. A jukebox in the back was softly playing Dean Martin's version of "That's Amore," a record that had begun playing on the radio once when Baird and Ellen were making love, their climax and the singer's "that's amore!" taking place at precisely the same time. However, it was not sweet nostalgia but lust that Baird felt now, listening to the song. And in his mind it wasn't Ellen he saw but Satin and her perfect little body, which in turn led him to think of Lee Jeffers and what she might have looked like nude under a pink spotlight or undulating above his and Slade's couch, moving to that most elemental of rhythms.

Baird was feeling even better by the time he left the restaurant. He walked into the dark parking lot as if he owned it. He squealed the Buick's tires and drove well over the speed limit as he maneuvered around Lake Union and moved uphill into the Wallingford district. When he reached Lee Jeffers' street, he again found both sides lined with parked cars, virtually bumper to bumper. Not to be thwarted, he pulled into the detective's narrow driveway and parked behind her car, blocking most of the sidewalk.

Going up the bungalow's porch stairs, he heard a Volkswagen Beetle drive slowly past, its tiny motor sounding so much like Ellen's that he wondered—not very seriously—if he should consider it a sign from on high, a warning to slink back to the marriage bed. The thought amused him sufficiently that he was still grinning when the porch light came on. He thought of pushing his eye tight against the peephole but was too late, as the door opened now, still chained. Through the crack he saw the detective looking out at him, fetching in a blue floor-length robe.

"What's this?" she asked. "You trying to get arrested?"

"Not that I'm aware of. And I'm not here about Slade either. Haven't seen the bastard in days."

"What do you want then? You know it's almost midnight?"

Baird frowned. "What do I want? Well, let me think. Oh, yes. My life's falling apart and I was sitting at this bar and I asked myself who would I rather talk with than anyone else on earth. And you came to mind."

"I'm not a shrink, Mister Baird."

"Jack—remember?"

"Jack, then."

"I know. But I don't want counseling anyway."

"What then?"

Baird thought about it. "Emanations," he said. "As I recall, you give off emanations that can make a man feel unreasonably happy."

"No kidding." She wasn't smiling. "I'll tell you what—a cup of strong black coffee for the road, and that's it, understood?"

Baird nodded solemnly. "Understood."

Inside the house, she closed the door behind him and walked on ahead toward the kitchen, which was on the right, just past the dining area. On the other side there appeared to be two bedrooms and a bath, with a stairway at the rear leading up to the attic and down to the basement. But Baird barely glanced at his surroundings, not with Lee Jeffers' muscular buttocks just ahead of him, rolling hypnotically under the velour of her robe, which was cinched tightly about her small waist. Her black hair was tousled, with a few loose curls falling over her face, giving her the slave-girl look then popular in Hollywood.

As she went about making coffee, Baird sat down at the kitchen table.

"You go out drinking by yourself very often?" she asked.

"My wife doesn't understand me," he said, trying not to smile.

Jeffers gave him a wry look. "And you think I will?"

"Why not? I'm an open book."

"Maybe I don't feel like reading."

"Ah, what disappointment."

"Life can be rough."

Though her manner was that of a grownup with a child, Baird did not take offense. He imagined she thought him drunker than he was. "Listen, I appreciate you making coffee, Lee," he said. "But the truth is, I don't really want any. I don't want to upset my stomach. Maybe something with a little vodka or gin in it. Something for the road."

Shrugging, Jeffers turned off the burner under the teakettle. "I shouldn't have any either. I do have to sleep tonight."

"Me too."

She smiled coolly. "Not here, you won't."

"Oh hell, I know that. I'm not so high I'm having delusions of grandeur."

She filled a glass with ice, poured in Diet 7UP and added a shot of vodka from a bottle she kept above the broom closet, as if it were floor wax.

"You do know how to sweet-talk a lady, don't you, Jack?" she said, handing him the glass.

"No, that was just an honest observation. Any rational man would think of you as the jackpot—you must know that. The winning lotto ticket. We may play the game, but we don't really expect to win."

"There you go again."

"The sweet-talker, huh?"

"For sure. You know, you surprise me. The other times we've met, you came across as Jack Baird, family man. I liked him better."

"So did I. But lately he seems to have lost the touch." He gestured for her to join him at the table. "Why don't you have a drink with me? I'll get it."

"No thanks."

She went back into the living room then, and he got up and followed. Not by accident, she sat down in a wingback chair near the front door. Baird knew that the second he finished his drink, she would be on her feet, opening the door and ushering him out. Nevertheless, he sank back on the sofa as if he were there to stay.

"Well, how do you like my house?" she asked.

"Very nice. Very comfortable. I like it here."

"Just don't get to liking it too much. Soon as you finish that drink, you're out of here. Sleep, remember?"

"Of course." The drink tasted like pop. As he sipped at it, he contemplated her reaction had he suddenly blurted the truth to her:

"*I killed Slade last night.*"

"*Oh, really?*"

Again he thought of her in the Oolala, without the blue robe. And once more he asked himself when it would happen, when he would begin to feel it. Looking at her, he wondered if he was having a breakdown.

"The emanations," he said. "I still feel them. And I think they're helping me."

She gave him a rueful look. "No kidding."

"Yeah. I feel stronger now. Happier too."

"All that."

"Remarkable, isn't it?"

"Very remarkable."

He finished his drink and placed it on the coffee table. Immediately she got up and moved to the door. He followed, smiling, meeting her somewhat quizzical look. At the door, just as she was reaching for the knob, he took her in his arms and tried to kiss her, but she turned her head away. He forced her up against the door then and pulled her face back so he could push his mouth into hers—when her knee suddenly swung up into his groin and her forearm, hard as a two-by-four, smacked into his face, cutting dead his sharp cry of pain. He staggered back and fell to the floor, gasping and holding his testicles.

"You stupid asshole," she said. "You're the last person I would've expected that from. What in God's name got into you tonight anyway? Are you on something?"

Baird was trying to catch his breath. "Jesus, did you have to do *that*?"

"You didn't give me a lot of choice."

"Goddamn, it *hurts!*"

"Oh come on, I barely touched you," she said. "You'll be all right. Are you gonna leave now, or do I call the uniforms in?"

"No, I'm leaving—don't worry about that. Just give me a few minutes, okay?" He crawled to the couch and leaned back against it, still breathing hard. "Jesus, I'm cramping like the devil," he said. "I hope I don't puke."

"You do and you'll clean it up."

"What a tough guy."

"That's for sure." She was still standing near the door, her arms folded under her breasts. "What did you expect, that I'd melt in your arms? Let you carry me off to bed?"

Baird shook his head wearily. "God only knows. I didn't plan any of it. It was just an impulse. I guess I'm drunker than I thought."

"I guess."

He looked up at her. The pain was beginning to ebb now, and he got it into his head that he might be able to explain himself to her. Even before he went on, he knew that it would be the alcohol speaking. But he couldn't stop himself.

"It was just an impulse," he said again. "A wild hair. You're a very beautiful woman, Lee, and for some reason that seems to be all-important to me lately. I don't know why, but it is."

"Maybe you ought to reorder your priorities."

"Yeah, I suppose so. But sometimes I think we get the feeling—men, I mean, as we get older—I think we get the feeling that beauty somehow will save us. I mean, that if we can have that certain beautiful girl just once—take her in our arms, you know, naked, and kiss her and hold her . . ." He knew he was talking gibberish, that he was only making a greater fool of himself, but her look, rueful and puzzled, led him to continue. "And push it in all the way, and come, really come—fill her belly with it—that somehow that will save us. Make us whole. Make us young again. I don't know why. I know it doesn't make any sense. But there it is. It's like sometimes we're starving, and only beauty will fill us."

Though Jeffers still looked cold and angry, her eyes inexplicably had filled. "That's stupid," she said. "It makes no sense at all."

Baird started to get to his feet, then gave up and sat down on the sofa, hunching forward over the pain. He could barely remember what he had said. More than anything else, he was aware now of how drunk he was, how vulnerable. He was afraid that if he didn't hold his tongue, he would confess everything, and for no other reason than his sudden terror of silence.

"Listen, if you want to sleep it off here, on the sofa, you can," Jeffers said. "You're in no shape to drive anyway."

Baird thought about it. "Maybe for a little while."

"I'll get a blanket," she said. "And when you're ready to leave, just pull the door closed. It will lock. You won't have to wake me."

With his legs still drawn up, Baird edged down onto the sofa, laying his head on a pillow at one end. Jeffers went down the hallway and opened a linen closet. She got out an afghan and brought it back to the living room. As she spread the cover over him, she smiled sadly.

"Look, I'm sorry—I probably reacted too hard. I didn't think," she said.

"No, it was my fault."

"Well, try to get some sleep, okay?"

Leaving a night-light on, she went into the nearest bedroom and closed the door, though not tightly, letting it just touch the jamb.

Baird did not fall asleep. The pain in his lower abdomen gradually disappeared, and after thirty minutes or so he got up and went down the hallway to the bathroom. In the mirror he saw a skein of dried blood running down his chin and neck from a split in his lip. He washed the blood off and drank a glass of water and urinated. Then, coming back up the hallway, he paused at her bedroom door. He knew that all he had to do was touch it slightly and it would open. And normally that was about all he would have done—*thought* about touching the door and going in. On this night, though, his hand came up and the door moved a few inches. And because of the night-light, he was able to see her clearly through the opening, lying on her side in a double bed under a sheet. Her right breast was exposed. The curve of her hip was steep and beautiful.

Quietly he pushed the door all the way open and went over to the bed. It occurred to him that as a policewoman, a detective, she might have a gun under her pillow and that within a few seconds he could be lying on the floor with a bullet in his chest.

But it was not to be. Instead she opened her eyes and calmly watched him as he reached down and peeled the sheet off her body, which even in the darkness looked a golden olive color, burnished, ineffably lovely.

Baird got out of his clothes and moved onto the bed. He ran his mouth along her thighs and then kissed her belly and her breasts. His erection hooked against her pubis and she reached down and guided him in. Their mouths joined and he began to move in her. Neither of them said a word.

When he got home, he found some of his clothes in a pile in the upstairs hallway, outside the guest room. Inside, there were more of them thrown on the floor and the bed and piled high on a chair. Ellen had even tossed in his things from their bathroom: his shaver and toothbrush and other toiletries. Seeing the mess, he felt no anger, because he knew he had it coming. But it puzzled him somewhat, since as far as Ellen knew, he had only been out drinking. He was too tired to think about it, though. All he could manage was to clear the things off the bed and get out of his clothes before collapsing again, giving himself over to his nightmares.

In the morning neither Ellen nor Kathy bothered to wake him, and as a result he slept till almost ten o'clock. He thought of phoning the warehouse and telling them he was sick, but as usual talked himself out of it, because the prospect of picking up the day's accounts later, adding to his already busy days, was not a pleasant one. However, he did phone in that he was having car trouble and wouldn't be in for another hour. Then he called Ellen at the library and asked her to pick up Kathy for him at four, since he was getting such a late start. In answer, he heard an offhand "As you wish." Then the phone went dead.

He spent a few minutes hanging up his clothes, again had a shake for breakfast, and set out on the second day of his new life. He scanned the morning paper and listened to the news on the radio, but there was nothing more about Satin, and—better yet—nothing about a body having been fished out of Lake Washington. However, this aspect of his new life—Jack Baird the killer, the man awaiting his heavy appointment with guilt and remorse—was not the one that filled his mind as he moved through the day. But Lee Jeffers was.

Even when he was with a customer, the images would flood in upon him. He would see her lying calmly in the dimness as his hand peeled the sheet off her body, and he would see her stretched out on her side, her hair cascading over his stomach, partially obscuring her face as she took him in her mouth. And later, when he was on top of her again, holding her head like a chalice in his hands, he remembered how her tongue had laved his cracked lip. Sometimes, as he caught himself thinking about her, he would wonder if he was losing his mind. It had been less than forty-eight hours since he had killed a man, yet here he was, mooning over a woman, and not just any woman either but one who would arrest him in a minute if she learned his terrible secret.

Around noon he phoned her at the police station, but she was not in. The operator took down his car phone number and Lee phoned him about an hour later, agreeing to see him again that day, though not at her house. She suggested the history-museum parking lot, which struck him as an odd choice until he got there at the specified time, six o'clock, and saw her solitary car parked along the perimeter of the huge lot, facing the ship canal just beyond a row of poplars.

Pulling in next to her, he got out of his car and entered hers, sliding onto the passenger seat. And though he detected a touch of coolness in her look and smile, he kissed her anyway, on the cheek. As usual, she was wearing jeans and boots, though this time with a man's chambray workshirt and a leather vest.

"I see you survived," she said.

"At the very least."

Smiling, he put his hand on her waist and started to move closer, in order to kiss her more properly, but she pulled back.

"Let's just talk, okay?" she said.

"I was going to kiss you, that's all."

"I think it would be better if we slowed down a bit and talked this over."

He looked at her. "I take it you're having regrets."

"No, not regrets. I just wanted you to know that as far as I'm concerned, last night was—well, just what it was, nothing more or less."

"Meaning?"

"That it was great. That I know we really like each other."

"But—"

"Yes—but. I knew you'd been drinking. And I know you're married, and that you've got a kid who really needs you now, with our friend Slade still in the picture. So I don't expect anything more. I don't think there ought to be anything more."

"Do I have any say in this?"

"Of course. But it won't change what I'm saying. Also, there are professional considerations. I don't want to get involved with a man now, especially not a married man."

"You finished?"

"For now."

"In other words, we had a one-night stand and should leave it at that."

She had been gazing down at her hands, and now she looked up at him, her dark eyes both assertive and defensive. "You could say that."

"No, I don't think I could," Baird said. "You see, I've got a problem, Lee. I've been thinking about you all day long. And I don't mean just about your body and the good sex we had. There was something else that happened last night, and I'm not sure it's something I can just forget about. I might want to, I might even need to—but I'm not sure I can." He sat there looking at her, wondering what he would say next, just as he imagined she was. Then he plunged on.

"I guess what I'm trying to say is . . . I'm afraid I've fallen in love with you."

"Oh, come on, Jack," she said. "We're not kids. We don't have to fall in love just because we went to bed."

Baird tried to smile. "Maybe I do."

She turned and looked out through the trees at the water, where a young couple was canoeing slowly past. And there was a sudden softening in her eyes, the beginning of a smile on her lips. Baird leaned over and kissed her on the neck. He undid one of her shirt buttons and ran his mouth lower, into her cleavage. Then he felt her hands on his head and her lips kissing him on the ear and in his hair.

"Damn you," she said.

TWELVE

That evening Baird moved slowly as he got out of the Buick and went up the back porch stairs of his home. It was still early, not yet eight o'clock, so he knew they would both be there, the two persons he loved most in the world, yet at the moment wanted least to see. Though they probably would not even have believed him if he'd told them all that had happened, the whole terrible truth, they at least were aware that he had been out till almost sunup on three of the last four nights. And in his family that was extraordinary behavior, reason enough for a wife and daughter to wonder if the fabric of their lives was not beginning to unravel.

Baird would not have been greatly surprised if the two of them, watching the clock during these last long nights, had conjured up someone very like Lee Jeffers, someone young enough and sexy enough to bedazzle a middle-aged family man like him. So he figured he had reason to feel dread.

As he opened the back door and went on inside, he felt as if he were entering a stranger's home. This one looked much too sunny and comfortable, not at all the sort of place where a philandering murderer would reside. Mercifully, no one was in the kitchen. Grateful for this small favor, Baird opened the liquor cabinet and put away the two large bottles of vodka he had bought earlier that day. He drank a glass of water, then went on through the dining room, heading for the stairs. But even before he reached them, Ellen came breezing past, practically running for the front door.

"Where you going?" he asked.

"Out," she said, not bothering to look at him.

The screen door banged shut behind her and she hurried down the front stairs, heading for her VW, which was parked at the curb.

"Well, have a nice time!" he called.

Without answering, she got into the little car and drove away. Baird turned back to the stairway just as Kathy rounded the landing and came skipping down, barefoot, wearing denim shorts and a colorful crew shirt.

"Hi, honey," he said. "Where's your mother going?"

"Somewhere with Susan. A movie, I think."

"You didn't want to go?"

"I wasn't asked."

"That wasn't very nice of them."

"I wouldn't have gone anyway."

Baird smiled. "Well, that takes care of that."

The girl did not respond. Looking indifferent, she went past him and into the museum, probably heading for the den.

"I'll see you later," he said, again to no response.

After changing into khaki slacks and a pullover, he returned to the kitchen and made himself a meal of sorts—a ham sandwich, potato chips, iced tea—which he then carried through the house to the den. He did so without enthusiasm, for a change not even wanting to talk with Kathy. But he felt he had no choice. It simply wasn't in him to go on living there with his wife and daughter as if they were all strangers, carefully avoiding each other, the air crackling with tension and resentment. If nothing else, he wanted at least to keep open the lines of communication, even if all he got for his trouble was static.

He found her sitting on the floor, reading a copy of *Vogue* and listening to the stereo, a soprano aria he had heard often enough but still couldn't place. He turned the volume down, sat, and took a bite of his sandwich. Kathy meanwhile was pretending that she was still alone.

"I don't know why you buy that," he said. "It's all ads."

"For the nudes. They turn me on."

"No kidding."

She still wasn't looking at him. "Sure. Sex is what makes the world go around, isn't it?"

"True enough."

"And variety's the spice of life. Isn't that right, Daddy?"

"I wouldn't know."

"Oh, really?"

Baird sighed. "Look, honey, I know what you're getting at. But it's like I told you in the car yesterday. I'm just going through a rough period, that's all. I've been staying out late because I've been drinking—I admit it. But that's all."

For a time she did not respond, just sat there on the floor raptly studying her magazine, turning each page as if it were made of papyrus. And Baird could not help asking himself whether Lee Jeffers was worth it, whether the excitement he found in her bed and company could possibly justify the loss of his daughter's love and respect, not to mention that of his wife. It was a question whose answer he already knew of course, and had always known.

"That's not what Mother thinks," Kathy said finally, still not looking up.

Baird had a pretty good idea what Ellen was thinking, but didn't want to hear it, especially from his daughter. "Is that why she tore out of here tonight?" he asked. "So we couldn't talk?"

"No, Susan called her."

"Good timing."

"It doesn't matter anyway," Kathy said. "Even if she was here, I don't think she'd be talking to you."

"Is that a fact?"

"Don't you want to know why? You say you've been out drinking these nights. But that isn't what Mom thinks."

"No?"

Kathy shook her head. "No. She says you're just doing what all men do. She says men use us until we get old and ugly, and then they throw us away and get someone young." The girl looked up at him now, her eyes cold and matter-of-fact. "And that's what you're doing now, Mom says. You're throwing her away. You're throwing *us* away."

"That's not true, baby."

"Really?" It was not a question. Closing the magazine, Kathy tossed it on the couch and got to her feet and started for the door. Baird reached out to stop her, but she avoided his grasp and hurried on, her bare feet padding across the museum floor. As he got up to follow her, he felt the ham sandwich lurch in his stomach like something alive. Afraid he might vomit, he made himself stand there for a time, breathing deeply, trying to relax. Then he went looking for Kathy again—why, he wasn't sure, since she already had made it abundantly clear that she didn't want his company.

When he reached her bedroom door, he was not surprised to find it closed. He knocked and waited. When nothing happened, he went in anyway and found her lying across her bed, looking down over the far edge of it.

"Please talk to me," he said.

She spoke to the floor. "Why? What difference would it make? You have your life, Mother has hers, I have mine."

"We have a life together."

"*Did*, don't you mean?"

"Why?" he asked. "What's so different now?" He was beginning to wonder if she—and her mother—knew about Lee Jeffers.

"It just is, that's all."

"Why?"

She rolled over, propping her head on one hand. "Why? Because you're not a drinker—that's what Mom says. She says you never have been. That you've never liked getting drunk, especially not night after night."

"I'm afraid my liver doesn't agree."

"Look, I'd like to be alone now," she said. "There are things I want to do."

Baird sat down on the edge of her bed. He took her hand in his, and when she started to pull it away, he tightened his grip. She gave him a look, almost a look of fear, and it was then that he felt the thing beginning, as if something vital had given way in him, something like a dam. He uttered a kind of moan, and Kathy looked stricken. Her eyes filled and she reached out for him, but he pulled back at her touch and felt himself slipping down off the bed onto his knees. And in a heavy, desolate sobbing, it began to come out of him, all that had been building behind the dam. Immediately Kathy was with him on the floor, taking him in her arms like a mother with a child.

"Oh no, Daddy—don't!" she pleaded. "Please don't cry!"

But he could not stop, and for a time their voices formed an eerie counterpoint, his racking sobs answering her soft pleas. When he finally ran down, she hugged and kissed him.

"What is it, Daddy? What's happened? Tell me!"

He managed to shake his head. "Nothing, baby. Just life. Only life."

She took his face in her hands. "Tell me. Please."

Baird gently pulled away and stood up. "Really, it's nothing," he said. "I guess I always thought I could make your mother happier. And now I know better. Maybe that's been working on me—I don't know."

"But that's been true for a long time, and you've never been like this. Please, Daddy—tell me."

He reached down and pulled her to her feet. He hugged her and gave her a kiss on the forehead. "Look, I'm really sorry about all this," he said. "I feel so damn stupid. I don't know what came over me. But you don't have to worry, honey. I'm okay, I really am. And I love you—you know that. I would never do anything to hurt you."

She stood there looking up at him, her eyes full of anguish and confusion. "What does that mean?"

In answer, all he could do was shake his head. And finally she sighed and turned away. She moved onto her bed and lay facedown on it again, giving him her back, obviously angry that he would not confide in her.

"You'll be all right?" he asked.

"Of course. Why wouldn't I be?"

He smiled lamely. "Well, I guess I'll go down and read the paper. If you want to join me—"

"I'll be all right here," she said.

* * *

For the rest of the evening, Kathy stayed in her room. Baird turned on the television in the family room and glanced through the evening paper. And even though he had promised himself not to have any alcohol that day, he soon went to the kitchen and came back with a vodka-tonic. He thought a good deal about what he should do when Ellen returned. On the one hand, he knew that he couldn't very well go through his normal routine, shuffling into her path, giving her a peck on the cheek and asking how the movie was before going on up to bed with her. If he tried that, he was afraid her response would be something on the order of Lee Jeffers' reaction to his first kiss, though hopefully not nearly so effective. On the other hand, if he continued to just sit there watching TV, Ellen would come home and go up to bed without his even seeing her or saying good night, and that would only widen the chasm between them.

He was still worrying about the problem when she drove in at ten-thirty. He hurriedly put out a cigarette and jumped up, then caught himself and slowed down, ambling back through the museum so he could casually bump into her on her way upstairs.

Instead, he frightened her, actually made her jump as he came out of the darkened foyer into her path. "Christ, you gave me a fright!" she said.

"Sorry."

She sniffed the air. "What in God's name—are you smoking again?"

He shrugged. "You've got a good nose."

She sidled past him as if he were a leper. "Jesus, you really are falling apart, aren't you?"

"So it would seem."

As she headed upstairs, he added a halfhearted "Good night," getting nothing in return. For a short while he continued to stand there in the foyer, feeling as if he'd been run over by a truck. Then he got out a fresh glass and made himself a stouter drink, even though his last one was still unfinished.

Back in the family room, he sat down in front of the TV again, though it might as well have been turned off for all the attention he paid it. His tête-à-tête with Ellen had left him feeling more than ever that he was losing control of his life. He had known all along that it wasn't going to work, wandering back to greet her as if everything were still all right between them, or at least manageable. Yet he'd gone ahead anyway, like a perfect fool. And now, when he tried to figure out why, the only answer he could come up with was that he still wanted a sane and secure home life—*needed* his wife and daughter's love—the better to carry out his new career as a philanderer. Which of course was total hypocrisy.

For that matter, he knew that his behavior with Lee Jeffers was not above reproach either, not after having made his little declaration of love that afternoon. It was true, he did find her extraordinarily appealing, but then he imagined that most men would feel the same way, especially after having sex with her. But as for loving her, he was afraid he had overstated his case a bit there. What he really loved were the feelings she gave him: the sense of danger and excitement, the intense sexual gratification, and above all, the temporary amnesia he got when he was with her. For those moments at least, he had been able to forget his mental picture of Slade floating inside the trunk of the old Impala, swaying there in the aqueous dark like some monstrous sea plant. Lying in Lee's arms, his tongue in her mouth and his cock in her belly, Baird had briefly forgotten that chilling image. And he wanted to go on forgetting it.

But as things stood now, he didn't feel overly guilty about his declaration of love, largely because Lee had not seemed to take it too seriously either. Even after uttering her "Damn you," as if he'd stolen her heart, she obviously still had that busy muscle very much under control. They had gone on to neck a little more, cautiously, watching for patrol cars, and she had told him that though she had changed her mind and did want to go on seeing him, they would have to be discreet about it. Then she had repeated herself, reminding him that she had a very demanding job and that having an open affair with a married man would not help her career in the slightest. He was to phone her now and then if he liked, and he could come to her house some evening the following week.

From this Baird gathered that he wasn't going to be enjoying as many temporary bouts of amnesia as he had hoped. And that was probably a good thing, he reflected, because the affair with

Jeffers, like his crumbling home life, was not the most pressing thing on his mind at the moment. Overriding everything else, he had to get a grip on himself. He had to "chill out," as Slade once advised him. Over and over he told himself that if he'd had guts enough to kill the man, then he ought to have guts enough to live with that fact. Not to do so would be more than ironic. It would be pathetic.

It was a thought he liked so much that he drank to it now, draining the fresh glass too. And he was relieved to see that there was nothing on the eleven-o'clock news about either Satin or any bodies found floating in Lake Washington. He was about to go back for another drink when two other news stories caught his attention: the first about a young father who had hacked his two infant sons to death with a hatchet; the second about a baby's severed hand found in a suburban pond.

The father, an African alien, had been angry at his wife. He told the police that since it was he who had given the boys life, he had the God-given right to take it. The police described the murder scene as the grisliest they had ever seen. A beefy, gray-haired detective wept openly. Even the reporter seemed cowed. But it was the severed hand—the idea of it—that stuck in Baird's mind. Showing remarkable restraint, the TV station did not actually show the hand, though its cameras did bore in on the place of discovery, the shore of the pond, bordered by a woodsy rail fence in front of which six or seven adolescent boys were horsing around, playing to the camera, having a great old time, so unconcerned one would have thought their little waterhole had turned up a baseball mitt instead of a human hand.

Baird switched off the TV. He took the glasses back to the kitchen and made himself another drink, this one with only a splash of tonic. He took it out onto the deck and sat in the darkness sipping the vodka and looking down over the trees in the park at the lake in the distance, its obsidian surface glittering with lights from the homes of the Eastside rich. And it occurred to him that it was probably a good thing he was not able to see the northern quarter of the lake too, with its steep bluffs and dark secrets. Otherwise he might have had to spend the rest of his life sitting right where he was, watching that distant shoreline through his binoculars and wondering just when the body would finally reappear, like a severed hand.

Baird slept poorly that night. Alcohol often had that effect on him, making him drop off immediately only to wake a few hours later with a parched throat and a full bladder. This night, though, his sleep was even worse than lying awake, a sleep of dreams that had him sweating and tossing and even whimpering at times, making sounds that eventually woke him, spilling him so abruptly out of the dream that he was able to remember pieces of it: sitting underwater, watching as bright, shiny fish circled him until he reached out finally and caught one, only to discover that it was not really a fish but a child's arm, a thin, walleyed arm wriggling fiercely in his grip. Dropping it in horror, he swam for safety, diving deeper, down to a kind of trapdoor in the lake bottom, an opening through which he could see a number of infants sitting in a classroom, row after row of them, some without arms or legs, all of them hacked and mutilated but smiling at him nevertheless, even giggling as bright chains of bubbles rose from their round little mouths.

When the alarm buzzed at seven o'clock, Baird turned it off and went back to sleep. And when he woke again, it was after ten and he was alone in the house. On the bed table there was a note written by Kathy.

> Daddy—
> I called Norsten for you and told them you had the flu or something and wouldn't be coming in. I said you were finally asleep and would call in later. Mother will pick me up at work. Take care. Love,
>
> Kathy.

In the shape he was in, the note brought tears to Baird's eyes. Even though he had never doubted his daughter's love—never doubted that she would come around in time—the girl's gesture touched him unreasonably. Except for that, he wouldn't have minded if a pair of jailers and a chaplain suddenly came through the door with his last meal. Later, as he showered, shaved, and dressed, he kept seeing bits and pieces of his dreams: the swimming arms, the fins with fingers, the hacked little bodies, the budlike mouths emitting streams of bubbles.

He wasn't sure why his subconscious had locked onto the slaughtered-infant thing, except for its obvious horror. But the hand in the pond, the fish, the bubbles—he knew all too well what they were about. And he decided that he could take it no longer: the fear of being caught, the anxiety of not knowing once and for all if Slade and his car and his switchblade were still where they belonged, under the bluff, under the water. Baird knew that it was probably the stupidest thing he could do, the classic mistake of the typical hapless criminal, but he decided he would do it anyway. He would return to the scene of the crime.

He thought of getting a rental car, but reasoned that if anyone would see him there and remember his license-plate number—in the event Slade's body was eventually discovered—that person could just as easily remember the plate of a rental car, which could then be traced to Baird the same as his own car. So he went in the Buick, driving slowly across the Evergreen Point Bridge, with the windows down and the air-conditioning off even though the temperature was in the low nineties, an extremely hot day for Seattle, which normally was cooled by northern breezes throughout the summer. This day, though, the air was dead still, and Baird could see the resulting smog stretching so far to the south that Mount Rainier looked like a great ghostly sail becalmed in a sea of rust. But the lake, as always, appeared cool and lovely, deep blue and flecked with dozens of boats ten miles in either direction. He followed its shore north through Kirkland and Juanita, an uninterrupted suburban sprawl, and very pricey along the waterfront, with even condos running into seven figures now.

In time he reached Holly Point Road and finally the gravel lane itself. The houses it served were all on the lake side, all at least a hundred feet apart and at descending levels as the lane wound down along the sloping top of the bluff. They were expensive homes, the first two with closed garages and no sign of anyone on the premises, the next two with late-model station wagons parked in blacktop driveways, amidst kids' bicycles and toys. Baird came to the S-curve and pulled to a stop at a point from which he could not see any of the houses, neither the one above him—the fourth in line—nor the one below, except for the topmost portion of its red tile roof.

Getting out of the car, he lit a cigarette and walked cautiously to the front edge of the road, trying to appear like someone in the real estate business, someone looking for waterfront property. Across the lake, close to the opposite shore, a long white ketch was dead in the water, its sails hanging limp. Even as Baird watched, two speedboats roared past it, heading south. Seconds later the tall sails began to rock in complaint and Baird continued to watch the boat until it was again still in the water. Then he forced himself to look downward, over the edge of the bluff. And there it was, an almost undetectable rectangle of light, probably a dozen feet under water and twenty feet from shore: the gray-primered roof of the Impala.

It was not easy to make it out. In fact it was almost impossible to see because of the way the noontime sun played on the water. Yet he was positive he saw it. Certainly he was not so frightened that he would invent the damned thing, convince himself that it was there when it really wasn't. It occurred to him that he might have been able to see it not *in spite* of the sun playing on the water but *because* of it, because the sun's angle was such that its rays bounced off the car's silvery roof and ran straight up to him, as they would do for anyone standing in the right place at the right time.

He turned away from the edge and walked back to his car, feeling as if he might vomit. He closed his eyes and waited for a short while, then opened them and went back to the edge. He took off his sunglasses as he looked down at the water again—and this time he could not see the car at all. It simply was not there. The sunlight spangling on the water was no brighter than before, and certainly the sun's angle could not have changed appreciably in the few moments that had elapsed. Yet the ghostly, rectangular underwater shape had disappeared.

Baird dragged deeply on his cigarette and flipped it out over the water, watched as it fell in a trajectory almost identical to that of the car. He put his sunglasses back on and again stared down at the water. For a few seconds he thought he was able to make out the silvery shape again, but then it disappeared. So now he was not sure of anything: whether he had seen the shape in the first place, or whether he was not seeing it now. Feeling stupid and scared, he went back to his car again, this time edging dejectedly behind the wheel. He lit another cigarette, started the engine and moved slowly downhill, going all the way around the curve. Ahead of him he saw the last house on the lane, a white-stucco Mediterranean affair with three separate levels built into the slope of the bluff. The house was large and luxurious, with a three-car garage fronted by a blacktop pad that was not quite wide enough for Baird to U-turn on. So he pulled up to the garage and backed around, braking, about to start back up the lane just as an elderly black woman in a maid's uniform came out of a gate next to the garage. Baird almost stopped to explain that he was out looking for properties, but then he realized how reckless that would be, giving the woman a good look at him and letting her hear his voice. So he put his foot on the accelerator and got out of there.

At four-thirty that afternoon, Baird had been sitting at Leo's bar for almost an hour, nursing a vodka-tonic and promising himself not to get drunk again, at least not that night. Since Wyatt Earp was the only other regular in the place, the usual joshing and raillery had been minimal. Eventually even Sally had given up on Baird, leaving him to his vodka and worries. Finally, though, she again wandered over to him.

"I think your blessed solitude is about over," she said.

"Really?"

Her response was to tip her head in the direction of the front door. Looking there, Baird saw Lee coming in with Sergeant Lucca, trailing him slightly, either in deference to his senior grade or because she didn't want anyone thinking she was his date, which Baird could understand. As before, the man walked like a weary duck. He was wearing shiny polyester pants belted below his pot gut, a loosened tie, and a sportcoat that hung on him like an old shawl. He held his mouth slightly pursed, in contempt and suspicion. Behind the horn-rims, his eyes were red and sleepy.

He came straight to Baird. "We'd like to have a word with

you." He motioned with his head toward the pool-table area, but Lee had a different idea.

"Let's sit down and have a Coke," she said. "I'm parched."

Lucca grimaced but turned back and joined her in one of the bar booths. "Okay, two Cokes," he said, looking over at Sally. "With glasses and ice." Then he turned back to Baird. "Come on. Sit."

It was more an order than a suggestion, the sort of order one gave to a dog. But Baird did not quibble. His heart was already pounding hard, and in his head he was screaming at himself. Was it even *possible* that the car and body could have been found and identified in the few hours since he'd left the scene? He would have felt no different if Lucca had pressed a gun to his head and spun the chamber.

As he sat down, Lee smiled at him. "I told Sergeant Lucca I bumped into you here once," she said by way of explanation.

Watching Lucca light a cigarette, Baird wanted to do the same but was afraid his hand would tremble and the detective would notice.

Exhaling, Lucca put an end to Baird's anxiety. "Slade's missing. Bastard seems to have disappeared."

"Well, that's good news," Baird said as Sally served the Cokes, for a change without commentary.

Lucca took a long drink, practically draining his glass. Then he got back to business.

"We've had this light surveillance on Slade," he said. "Usually in the evening, just a short tail after he leaves his kitchen job."

"But all of a sudden he's gone," Lee added. "His car too. We figure he didn't leave town, though. His stuff's still in his rented room and he hasn't collected his pay on the kitchen job."

"So where is he?" Baird asked.

Lucca regarded him coldly. "We were hoping you could tell us."

Baird tried to look baffled. "*Me?* How would I know? I'm not the one who's been tailing him."

"Well, it's kind of hard to be sure," Lucca went on. "I mean, you did try to play policeman for a while there, didn't you?"

Baird shrugged. "You warned me off, remember?"

"And you always do what you're told, is that it?"

Baird looked at Lee. "What is this? Have I missed something? Am I the criminal here?"

"No, of course not." Lee smiled uneasily. "We just—"

Lucca cut her off. "Look, no one's accusing you of anything. We just know Slade isn't easily discouraged. So we figured he'd keep on stalking your daughter, and you might have seen him at it—you know, parked on your street or maybe at your daughter's work. Maybe she's seen him."

Baird shook his head. "No, he hasn't been around. We've been lucky. But why this sudden interest?"

Finishing his Coke, Lucca took some ice in his mouth and began to chew on it. "Maybe you've noticed in the paper—there's been a couple of new rape cases, one of them a rape-murder. My partner here thinks they might have been Slade's handiwork."

"It wouldn't surprise me," Baird said.

"And one other reason," Lee put in. "You remember Sergeant Lucca told you about that other young woman Slade stalked—the bank loan officer who subsequently was raped? Well, we thought the hospital had lost the rapist's hair and semen samples, but now they've found them. So we need to do some testing on Slade."

"So naturally you can't find him."

"That's the way it goes," Lucca said.

Baird was trying hard to look casual, even indifferent. "Well, as far as I'm concerned, I hope he stays lost. If I ever see him again, it'll be too soon."

Lucca put out his cigarette and got to his feet, grunting and sighing in a kind of private language of disaffection, wordlessly telling everybody just what he thought of them. "Well, I guess we've wasted enough time here," he said, adding, "Oh yeah, thanks for the Coke." He was looking not at Baird but out at the street, squinting against the brightness.

Lee gave Baird a fleeting smile, as if to say, "Yes, the man's a slob—but what can I do?" Following Lucca out of the booth, she touched Baird's wrist and ran a finger down his hand so lightly he shivered. He watched as she trailed the sergeant out the door. Then he looked over at the bar, straight into Sally's mocking eyes. As he got up and slipped back onto his stool, she shook her head in comic reproval. He pushed his empty glass toward her.

"One more," he said. "A double."

"Need to cool off, huh?"

Later, at a seafood bar, Baird picked up some fried oysters, jo-jo potatoes, and cole slaw and drove to Shilshole Bay, where he parked in the long lot facing the water. As he ate the food and drank a cup of coffee, he gazed out at the still-crowded beach and the boats on the Sound. In time, across the water, the sun edged behind the jagged line of the Olympics, setting the range briefly afire. When the light was gone altogether, he started the car and drove to Lee Jeffers' house. This time she heard him coming and opened the door even before he reached it. Inside, he stood there for a few moments looking at her in the soft light from a single table lamp. Again, despite the warmth of the evening, she was wearing the floor-length blue robe, tightly belted.

"Has it been a week already?" she said.

He took her in his arms. "More, I think. Much more."

As he kissed her, he undid the sash on her robe and his hands moved on her skin, running down her flanks onto her buttocks. She slipped the robe off her shoulders and he lifted her onto his body. She pushed her mouth into his and he felt her legs tightening around him. He carried her that way to the sofa and lowered her onto it. While he struggled out of his clothes, he moved down her body, kissing her breasts and belly and pubis. Naked, he moved on top of her and entered her, and she rolled them off the sofa onto the soft shag carpet, and then rolled again, wanting him on top. And he felt her passion as strongly as his own, a rage suddenly shared.

Still, even as he dug his toes into the shag and his fingers into her buttocks, even as his body pounded into hers and his breath came in ragged gasps, he felt as if a part of him were standing off to the side, clucking and shaking its head, wondering if he would ever again be himself, ever again know exactly who he was.

THIRTEEN

A s the weeks went by, Baird got the feeling that he was undergoing a life change as sweeping as puberty. An easygoing man all his life, he now was almost constantly full of anger and belligerence, which he concealed under a veneer of casualness that bordered on the reckless. He smoked two packs of cigarettes a day, he had at least a half-dozen vodkas each night, and if he could believe Ellen, he even moved differently.

"Lately you walk like a lout," she told him. "Like you might kick anything that gets in your way."

At work he began skipping his small accounts, the mom-and-pop stores and bars like Leo's, which took up at least half his working hours yet produced no more than fifteen percent of his income. He knew it was an article of faith for old man Norsten that the salesmen service *all* their accounts, since they all lined his pockets. So Baird accepted it that he and the old man would eventually cross swords over the problem. But like so many other things now, it seemed a matter of total unimportance.

It was at night in the Norsten parking lot that Baird learned just how reckless he had become. He had stopped at Leo's for drinks and supper while he priced the last of his orders, so it was almost eleven when he pulled into the lot and parked, about to go inside and deliver the orders to the night crew. He had opened the Buick's door and placed one foot outside, on the blacktop, while reaching to the right, inside his briefcase, for the loose stack of invoices—when suddenly there was a gun quivering in his face and behind it a thin young black man with bulging, bloodshot eyes and a missing front tooth.

"Money!" he hissed, spraying Baird with spit. "You watch and ring! And you car!"

"All right, all right," Baird said. Holding the orders in his right hand, and with his left hand raised, he got out of the car.

"Money! Gimme money!" the kid sputtered.

Instead Baird gave him the invoices, tossing them into his face, at the same time grasping the barrel of his gun and forcing it away from them.

"Motherfuck!" the youth yelled, swiping at the cascade of paper as if it were a swarm of bees.

Baird kicked him in the knee and the kid dropped the gun and lurched sideways, his hands reaching for the asphalt in a kind of cartwheel movement to keep from falling. Then he ran, gimping rapidly across the parking lot and into the alley, where he disappeared. Baird sagged back against the car, his mouth powdery and his heart pounding. Yet he smiled, more in bafflement than anything else. Why would he do such a thing? Why would he take such a chance? He had no idea.

Nor was he sure why he picked up the gun, a lightweight .22 revolver, and put it in his briefcase. Then he retrieved the scattered invoices and took them into the warehouse. When the night foreman commented on how dirty and wrinkled some of the sheets were, Baird said that he had dropped them.

The foreman shook his head. "You better get ahold of yourself, Jacko. You're losing it for sure."

"Could be," Baird said.

If he was in fact "losing it," he knew most of the loss was taking place at home. For some reason, he found it increasingly impossible to even try to cover up his affair with Lee Jeffers. He began to see her almost every night, seldom leaving her place before midnight. And on three occasions he stayed the night with her, going home only when he was sure Ellen and Kathy had left for work. So he was not surprised when his daughter stopped speaking to him altogether and began to use the bus again. Occasionally he still drove to Bond's to pick her up, but the last time he tried it, she walked right past his parked car, pretending she didn't see him or hear the car horn.

Unlike her daughter, Ellen would occasionally speak to him, usually in sarcasm.

"Well, there he is—Mister Nightlife himself."

Often, at the sight of him, she would shake her head as if in sorrow at what a pitiful figure he had become. Once she suggested that he ought to ask his "new bimbo" to take it a little easier on him, evidently because he was looking so awful. Sometimes she would mention her coming studies at law school, as if she'd already been accepted by the university, which as yet was not the case. And every now and then she would bring up her plans to sell the house, as if the divorce court had already awarded her sole possession of it.

"Once I get rid of this monstrosity," she said, "I'll breathe a lot easier."

On that occasion Baird wasn't sure whether she was referring to him or to the house. One day, in desperation, Kathy tried to get the two of them to sit down with her and discuss "our problems."

"It's not as if we don't have enough of them," she said.

But Ellen would have none of it. "Actions speak louder than words," she said.

Baird knew that he and Ellen eventually were going to have to talk like rational human beings and try to decide whether or not their marriage was over, and if it was, what they were going to do about it. But he hadn't reached that point himself yet, and he was relieved that Ellen evidently felt the same way. At the moment, they were like a couple in the midst of an automobile accident, not even sure yet that they would survive. So other matters, such as who was to blame and who would lose and who would win—those things would have to wait.

One of the most uncomfortable times for Baird was the Labor Day weekend, when Kevin came home for four days, a vacation not from college so much as from his job as night manager at a Bellingham motel. While the boy looked like a clone of Baird, he had his mother's temperament, the same toughness and impatience and ambition. Kathy evidently had expected him to join her in trying to bring about a rapprochement between their parents, and when he declined, informing her that he was not in the marriage-counseling business, she lumped him in with his father as a person to whom one did not speak.

Though Baird and Kevin had always been close, on this weekend he found the boy maddeningly difficult to talk with. Their few times together were spent mostly in silence, usually watching television. Only once, when the two of them drove down to Ivar's deck for oysters and beer, did they touch upon the forbidden subject.

"You know, I'm not all that surprised," Kevin said. "I mean, well, Mom's been kind of unhappy for years, right? I mean frustrated, you know? I figure she just wants to be something other than a housewife, you know? Not her fault, and not yours either—that's the way I see it."

Baird sat there looking at his son, a tall, lean kid with a nice strong smile and eyes no less blue than the sky beyond his sun-bleached hair. He was wearing denim shorts and a school sweatshirt, and he looked as if he had the world aced, as if he knew for a certainty that there was nothing ahead of him but success. Baird wondered how the boy would have reacted if his old man had told him what was really on his mind.

"I just can't think about Mom and the family now, Kev, because there's this guy I killed and dumped in the lake, in the trunk of his car, over near Juanita. If you look hard you can see the jalopy right there underwater, where the fish are really tiny arms and legs swimming around and the best way not to think about it all is to stay half drunk and keep fucking a sexy young detective who's looking for the guy I shot. You got all that?"

But of course he said nothing of the kind. Instead he lit a cigarette and blew the smoke out toward the water. Kevin wagged his head.

"Now *that* I can't figure—you smoking again," he said. "That ain't too smart, you know?"

Baird smiled bleakly. "Yeah, I know."

* * *

Six hours after Kevin left for Bellingham, Baird again found himself at Lee's house, sitting with her in an old-fashioned porch swing on the covered redwood deck at the back of her house. It was after ten at night. They had dined on cold salmon and fruit salad, and their lovemaking afterward had not been any warmer. Midway, she had gone dead under him, finally pushing him off and complaining that there was never any sense of fun in their lovemaking, that he went after her as if he were trying to beat her to death.

"Your cock isn't a weapon, you know," she told him. "And you squeeze me so fucking hard I think my bones are going to break."

"It's called passion," he said, without conviction.

Frustrated, he finally had followed her out of bed, putting on a light summer robe left by her second husband, the narcotics-detective-turned-dealer. After mixing another drink for himself, he went out onto the deck while she busied herself in the kitchen, at what task he had no idea, since their dinner had come straight out of the refrigerator, ready to eat.

The deck was Lee's pride and joy, built by herself and two other cops over the course of a weekend. It was exceedingly large for such a small house, taking up half the tiny backyard, which was boxed in by a tall, thick hedge. There were a number of redwood tubs on the deck, some hanging, some resting on the floor, each filled with either flowers or ferns. And there were wind chimes and a string of delicately colored Japanese lanterns, all of which reinforced Baird's growing suspicion that though Lee talked tough and had a macho job and liked to dress like a man, she was thoroughly feminine at heart. And this worried him, in that it made her even more appealing to him. Against his better judgment, he had begun to think of her in the long term, as someone he would live with, or even marry. And he knew that was preposterous: the cop and the killer.

Finally she had come out and joined him on the swing, and now they sat there together, mostly in silence. In her hand was an open bottle of beer; in the little things at least, she was thoroughly macho.

"The nights are cool anyway," she said. "It's getting like goddamn California here."

"You won't say that in November."

"You're right about that."

For a time they said nothing more, just sat there gazing out at the darkness. Baird put his arm around her, and she let it stay.

"Damn Slade," she said. "He still hasn't turned up. I guess maybe he did leave town after all. Which only figures. We finally got reason to haul him in, naturally he disappears."

It was one of the few times she had mentioned the creep during the past weeks. As far as Baird knew, the police still wanted Slade only because of the recovered hair and semen samples, so he could be tested for a match.

"Don't worry, he'll turn up," Baird said. "He'll get arrested in Timbuktu or someplace and you'll get to fly there and bring him back."

"Lucky me," she said.

"Lucky Slade." Baird kissed her on the neck and she reached up and stroked the back of his head, letting him know that she was over her huff. He slipped his hand inside her robe, on her breast, and kissed her on the mouth. And she invaded his robe too, her hand warm.

"Old Faithful," she said.

"That's me."

She smiled mischievously. "You think the neighbors can see us out here?"

"Through *that* hedge? Not a chance."

She moved off the swing and onto her knees, pushing his robe farther apart and taking him in her hand again, then in her mouth. In the dimness, it looked to Baird as if an animal with curly black fur was burrowing into his lap. He sighed and called up the faith of his childhood.

"Oh God. Oh Jesus, that's nice. You're too good to me."

She stopped and smiled up at him, covering him at the same time. "And don't you forget it."

She stood up and took him by the hand and led him back inside to the bedroom again, and this time he was more gentle and tried to be more playful too, though he wasn't sure he succeeded.

When they were finished, they both lit cigarettes and lay there in the half-dark, silent and separate, as if someone had cleaved the bed with an ax.

"Is she ever awake when you come home?" Lee asked. "What does she say?"

"Ellen?"

"No, your cat."

"No, she doesn't say anything."

"Just accepts it, huh?"

"I wouldn't say that."

"But no showdowns? No 'I'm mad as hell and I'm not going to take it anymore'?"

"Not in so many words."

Lee laughed softly, ruefully. "I guess I should be grateful for that. It lets us go on as we are, without having to make any difficult decisions."

"Like what?"

"Don't play stupid. You know what I mean."

"Yeah, I guess I do."

"And you don't want to make that kind of decision any more than I do."

"Not right now, anyway."

"Right. How could we?" She blew smoke at the ceiling. "God, listen to me. I must sound more like Ellen every day. Each of us wanting our little piece of you—when there just ain't that much left over."

"Left over from what?"

"Not from what—from *who*. From your beautiful little Kathy, that's who. How can mere mortals like me and Ellen compete with all that?"

"Jesus, you're really reaching tonight." Baird got the remote off the bed table and turned on the television, which sat on a table just beyond the foot of the bed. "It's eleven," he said. "Let's watch the news."

"What do you mean, *reaching?* I've seen the two of you together, remember? And even that first time, I thought poor Mrs. Baird, with a gorgeous thing like that still at home, clinging to the old man, and the old man clinging right back. And why not? I almost got the hots for the kid myself."

Baird looked at her. "What the hell is all this about anyway? Jesus, a few minutes ago we were . . ." At a loss, he shook his head and turned back to the television.

But Lee was not quite finished. She gave a sharp laugh and said, "You know what? I'll bet Ellen was rooting for Slade!"

At that, Baird wanted to get up and leave or maybe even shove her out of bed, but what he was seeing on television not only riveted his attention, it almost stopped his heart. For there it all was, just as he had feared it inevitably would be: the steep green bluff and the battered old Chevy coming up out of the lake like some kind of local Loch Ness monster, spouting water from every orifice. Around it were scuba divers, both in the water and in tiny yellow rafts, giving it one last check and then pushing off as the tow-truck cable came taut and the Impala bumped backwards onto the shore and began to climb the hillside, trailing seaweed.

There were two cameras covering the scene, one from the road at the top of the bluff and the other from a hovering helicopter, both in daylight. Baird heard the voice-over as if a judge were passing sentence on him.

"The car was discovered late this afternoon by two Kirkland teenagers gig-fishing along the shoreline. And this was the scene just a few hours ago, when the sheriff's police hauled the vehicle out of the water and up the hillside."

Lee had sat up and pulled the sheet around her. Baird felt that she was looking not only at the TV now but at him too, probably sensing the change in him. He wanted to turn the infernal thing off, but he knew that wouldn't change anything, that she would learn the truth soon enough whatever he did.

The picture went live now, cutting to a young Asian reporter standing on the lane in the floodlit darkness, with Slade's car in the background, already in position to be towed away by the huge truck that had winched it up the hillside.

"And, Gary," said the reporter, "it was only after they got the car up here and opened the trunk that they found the man's body. Lieutenant Moore, with the county police, said that a positive I.D. on the victim is not possible at this time because of the condition of the body. However, the lieutenant did confirm that the victim had been shot once in the head—anywhere else, we'll have to wait on the autopsy."

Now the anchor got into the act. "Do they have any idea, Mark, how long the car—and the victim—were in the water?"

"The lieutenant said three or four weeks, though they won't know for sure until they get the medical examiner's report."

"Thanks, Mark." The anchor shook his handsome head. "And the beat goes on," he said, turning to his pretty co-anchor just as the camera moved to her.

She smiled winsomely. "Well, moving on to some happier news . . ."

Baird turned off the TV and put the remote back on the table. He got out of bed and started to put his clothes on, still not looking at Lee. When she spoke, her voice was soft, even wondering.

"Slade had a car like that, didn't he? Early seventies Chevy Impala, isn't that what he had?"

"Could be—I don't know. An old heap anyway. Why?"

"Why? Because he's been missing for weeks, that's why. And that car, I remember it from the day I served him. How many twenty-year-old Impalas would have an orange door like that? And the rest of it—like camouflage."

Baird tried to sound weary, indifferent. "Rust and paint primer, most likely."

"Well, what do you think?"

"About what?"

"About what? Slade, for God's sake! It could be him, you know."

Baird forced a laugh. "Are you serious?"

"Well, a lot more than you are, it seems."

"Lee, for Christ sake—the car could be anybody's. What's the big deal?"

"Bullshit. It's Slade's car. I know it is."

Baird had sat back on the bed to put on his shoes. "Okay, then. It's Slade's car. And the body, that must be his too, huh?"

"It could be."

"And it could *not* be too."

"And you're just not interested, one way or the other?"

"I'm not a cop, remember?"

She got out of bed and came around to his side, putting on her robe. "Jesus, but you're the cool one," she said.

"Yes, I'm the cool one," he agreed.

She got a cigarette out of a pack in her robe and lit it, not once taking her eyes off him. "I just can't figure you," she said. "I'd think you'd be damn excited. This psycho who was stalking your kid—suddenly he could be dead and you don't give a shit?"

"When I know it's him, then I'll give a shit."

Because she was standing in the doorway, he had to sidle past her. She followed him into the living room.

"You're just going to take off?" she asked. "You don't want to talk about this? I could make phone calls, you know. I could find out if it's him."

"Feel free." He kissed her on the forehead and started for the front door.

"Jack, you're scaring me," she said.

He stopped and turned, forcing a smile. "*Me* scare you? That'll be the day."

"No, you are. You really are. I tell you I can call and find out, and you don't care. I find that scary."

"It's because I'm out on my feet, Lee. My ass is dragging. And it'd probably take you hours to find out anyway—to find out it *isn't* Slade."

"I would still think you'd want to know. If it is him, you'll be a suspect—have you thought about that?"

"Me and forty other guys. The man is a whore and a rapist and a drug dealer. Anybody wanting to kill him would have to stand in line. You know that."

She had followed him to the front door. "Just do me one favor, all right?"

"Okay—what?"

"Just tell me you didn't do it. That's all I'm asking."

Baird groaned. "Oh, come on, Lee—for Christ sake."

"Please, Jack. Just look at me and tell me you didn't do it."

"What is this, some kind of kid's game?"

She didn't answer.

"Come on, Lee. Be serious."

"You bastard," she cried. "Tell me! *Say it.*"

"I'll tell you what I will say. *Fuck you.* How's that? Just fuck you, Detective Jeffers."

She was staring at him now as if he had sprouted horns. Looking awed, even cowed, she stepped back from him. "I don't know you, do I?" she said. "I don't know you at all."

He leaned against the doorjamb and sighed. "Jesus, Lee. Let's see . . . how do I put this? Number one, if the stiff turns out to be Slade, I'm not the one who killed him. Number two, I don't kill people. I wouldn't even know how. And number three—good night!"

With that, he turned and left, letting the screen door slam behind him. He went down the stairs and was just starting down the front walk when she got in the last word, yelling it at him.

"Liar!"

Even though he was driving in the direction of his home, Baird knew he could not go there, not yet anyway. Ellen often watched the late news, and Kathy sometimes had her bedroom TV on as she got ready for bed. Though the KIRO report hadn't identified Slade as the victim, Baird knew there was a chance that one of the other stations might have done so, simply on the basis of the car license or I.D. on the body.

But as he drove on, he realized that it hardly mattered whether or not his wife and daughter had seen the news story. The fact was, he simply could not bring himself to go home now, and maybe not ever. He felt literally heavy with fear, almost as if he were carrying Slade's body on his shoulder. His pulse was fast. It seemed impossible to draw a normal breath. Even steering the car seemed a kind of feat. And all the while a voice in his head kept passing sentence upon him: *You will be arrested. You will be tried. You will go to prison.*

He drove east through the arboretum and pulled into the same park he had visited on the night after the killing, trying to sort through his feelings. This time he went on through the parking lot and over a small hill before stopping and getting out. Opening his briefcase, he took out the black kid's .22 revolver, then walked the short distance to the lakeshore, which at that point was protected by a breakwater made of basalt boulders, some as large as refrigerators. Scattered haphazardly along the shoreline, they made for numerous convenient niches on which one could fish or sunbathe or just brood. The niche Baird chose was walled off on three sides and even partially covered on top. Though it wasn't quite dry, he sat down anyway, drawing up his feet and slipping the gun into his belt. He leaned back against the rough stone and lit a cigarette, glad that he at least was smoking again. The sweet pang hitting his lungs seemed just about the only unalloyed pleasure he had left.

He was amazed that Lee had picked up on Slade's car so readily. She apparently had seen the old Impala only once and certainly hadn't ridden in it or spent time in it with Jimbo himself, as Baird had. He knew that the police were trained to know the makes and models of cars, but he was still impressed by how quickly she had identified the old heap. Her quick expertise only reinforced his suspicion that he was coming to the end of his rope. He was not sure what she had meant by calling him a liar, whether she actually believed he had done it or was only testing him, looking for his reaction. But then he knew it really didn't matter. If she didn't believe him guilty now, she would soon enough.

Worst of all, he figured she probably had already phoned Lucca to share the news, which meant that the dour sergeant would soon be coming after Baird like a hungry bloodhound. Judging by the TV story, it was the sheriff's police that had jurisdiction, not the Seattle police or the Kirkland department. But Baird knew that would not deter Lucca. One way or another, the sergeant was going to make himself part of the investigation.

Considering how long the body had been in the water, Baird judged that they might have trouble pinpointing the time of death, maybe even the *week* of death. And he hoped that would make it difficult to build an airtight case against him. Still, he knew it was not inconceivable that they would accumulate enough evidence to bring him in for questioning, with the media probably reporting on his every move. Whether he eventually went to prison or not, his life would be ruined. He would lose his job and his house. His friends would either drop him or treat him like someone else, some disgusting vigilante hero.

And of course he would lose Ellen, or more accurately, would *complete* the job of losing her. Wondering how she would react—with pity or scorn—he decided it would be the latter, since she could reasonably conclude that he had thrown their lives away because of his unreasonable love of Kathy. For that matter, Baird didn't expect much sympathy or understanding from his son either. He imagined that Kevin would think his father had done the terrible deed with no thought of how it would affect his son's life and career, which unhappily was quite true.

And that left Kathy. Baird hated even to think about how his daughter would react, learning that her doting old man had murdered for her, had shot a man dead rather than risk her safety. Would she feel revulsion? Would she turn away from him? Baird had no idea. And he imagined that frightened him most of all, the possibility that in trying to save her, he might have lost her.

He recognized that it was probably this thought that had brought him here, to sit in this canopy of black rocks with a stranger's gun in his lap. In time he took a last drag on the cigarette and flipped it out into the water. He listened to the waves lapping peacefully about him, and he looked out at the lights of the Eastside shimmering on the lake's surface, all running straight at him, there at the hub of the universe.

He took the gun out of his belt and looked at it, and it occurred to him that a more religious person might have concluded that the young black man had come to the Norsten parking lot not to rob Baird but to deliver the weapon, give him the means of his release. One of God's little jokes.

For a minute or so he just sat there staring at it, wondering if he would eventually turn it and actually point it at himself, maybe even raise it to his temple. But it remained where it was, shaking in his hand.

Finally he got to his feet. And just as he had done on the other side of the lake, he drew back his arm and threw the weapon as far as he could. This time he heard it splash.

FOURTEEN

B y the time Baird got home that night, Ellen and Kathy were both in bed, and he had no intention of waking them and telling them that Slade had been found murdered. He slept off and on during the night and did not get out of bed in the morning until the house was quiet, the women gone. In the kitchen he found the morning paper spread out on the table, opened to the first page of the local news section. Using a green felt-tip pen, Ellen or Kathy had circled the lead story as well as the photograph next to it, which showed Slade's car being winched out of the lake. The headline and subhead read:

CAR AND BODY OF LOCAL MURDER VICTIM RECOVERED
FROM LAKE WASHINGTON.
Shooting victim found locked in trunk of his car.

The story identified the victim as James R. Slade, twenty-four, an ex-convict wanted by the police for questioning in regard to the murder of eighteen-year-old May Tang, a prostitute. A spokesman for the county police reported what Baird already knew, that they would have to wait for an autopsy to determine how and when the man died.

The heavy green line circled the article twice, as if it had been scrawled in anger. Next to it, covering half the page, was a large, forceful exclamation point, all of which suggested that it was Ellen's work, not Kathy's. But then its authorship was beside the point. What mattered was that, come nightfall, he was going to have to face them both and play the Great Innocent again. Though he hated the very idea of it, he didn't expect it to be difficult, since he himself could barely believe that he had actually killed someone.

Yet he put his performance off as long as he could, calling on all his customers that day and stopping at Bramante's at eight o'clock for a few drinks and a roast-beef sandwich. It was too dark in the ristorante to see anyone very well, which was exactly what he wanted, peace and quiet while he ate. He couldn't remember if he had told anyone at Leo's the name of the man stalking Kathy, which was another reason he had chosen not to go there, not wanting to spend the evening discussing Jimbo's gruesome departure and what a remarkable stroke of luck this was for good old Jack Baird.

After paying his bill, he scooted out of the soft plastic booth, felt his way toward the front door, and started for home. When he got there, he found Ellen and Kathy in the family room, watching a network movie on television. Kathy, fresh from the shower, had her wet hair tied in a towel turban and was wearing a light yellow robe cinched even tighter at the waist than Lee Jeffers could have tolerated. She was sitting on the carpeted floor, painting her toenails. Ellen was in her usual chair, her legs tucked under her while she toiled away on a new cable-knit sweater. She was wearing her white jogging suit, evidently having just come home from a power walk.

Baird started to light a cigarette, then thought better of it. "Well, I saw the morning paper," he said. "I can't say I was saddened by the news."

Since Kathy was still ignoring him most of the time, he was surprised to see her look up at him now, with a rueful smile. "Me either, Daddy. I suppose I should be ashamed to admit it, but I'm glad he's dead. I can hardly believe it, though. He seemed so—I don't know—*indestructible*."

"Apparently he wasn't."

Ellen spared him a glance. "You're home early," she said. "Your playmates all busy tonight?"

Baird ignored the question. "You been out jogging?"

"Walking. I told you I don't jog anymore. Old knees. Old everything. But then I guess you already decided that."

"Great to be home." He sat down on the couch, starving for a cigarette.

"Who do you think did it?" Kathy asked.

"Slade? I don't know. He was involved in drugs, I understand. Maybe he owed money. Something like that."

"Detective Jeffers tell you that?" Ellen asked.

Baird shrugged. "Her or Lucca. I don't remember."

"Lucca didn't seem like the sharing type."

"You never know."

"That's for sure."

Baird sat there watching his wife's fingers manipulating the knitting needles, the effortless speed so at odds with the woman herself, who as usual sat perfectly still, perfectly relaxed, her handsome face almost expressionless. He moved a pillow to the end of the couch and stretched out.

"Maybe there'll be something about Slade on the news," he said. "You know, the police have been looking for him for some time. The woman that was raped in Ravenna—the hospital finally found the hair and semen samples from the rapist. Misplaced them somewhere. So the police were going to bring him in and test him for a match."

On the floor, Kathy shivered. "Just the thought of him makes my skin crawl."

"Well, you don't have to worry about him anymore," Ellen said. "Just a thousand other creeps."

"That's a pleasant thought," Baird said.

"It's an unpleasant reality," she shot back.

Kathy unwound the towel on her head and began to dry her hair with it. "Well, it wasn't necessary, Mother," she said. "It's not as though we didn't already know it."

Hear, hear, Baird thought. It seemed forever since anyone had sided with him about anything. And it buoyed him as the newscast began now and he had no idea what it would reveal—in fact would not have been greatly surprised to see his own picture suddenly appear on the screen while a sonorous voice-over told the world that Jack H. Baird, local paper salesman and budding philanderer, was the main suspect in the case.

But there was other, fresher mayhem to report: a drive-by shooting in West Seattle; a gang fight in Tacoma, leaving two dead; and forest fires burning all along the West Coast, due to the long, dry summer. But finally there he was: old Jimbo Slade, standing before a height chart and holding up his mug-shot number, probably in California, after the assault on his benefactor. The voice-over said that the body found in the trunk of the car hauled from Lake Washington the previous day had been identified as that of James R. Slade, a twenty-four-year-old ex-convict employed as a dishwasher in a Seattle restaurant. On the screen, Baird saw the Impala coming out of the water again. Then the camera cut to the same Asian reporter from the previous night; only now he was standing in daylight on the curving lane with the same chunky, elderly black maid from whom Baird had sped away. For the moment, he stopped breathing.

"Barry, this is Alma Jessup. She works as a live-in maid in the house just below here, around the curve. She remembers hearing something on the night of August twenty-fourth, a Monday." He thrust the mike at her.

"Yes, I sure did hear something that night!" the old woman yelled into the mike. "I remember cuz my employers, the Feldmans—real nice people, by the way—they give me a little birfday party the night before. And my birfday is August twenty-three. Anyway, I woke up close to two a.m., and I hear this car on the road—you know, gravel crunching, cuz the car is moving kind of slow like. And then it stops and I hear the door open and close, then nothin for a second or two. Then there's a kind of bumpin sound and finally a splash. Well, I thought someone just threw somethin away, you know—an old TV or somethin like that—and I wasn't gonna lose no sleep over it. So I went back to bed. But I guess I was wrong."

The reporter turned to the camera. "So, Barry, if what Mrs.

Jessup heard was in fact the real thing, that places the murderer here on the night of August twenty-fourth—actually two A.M. on the twenty-fifth—which was just about three weeks ago, very close to the medical examiner's estimate of time of death. And incidentally, the autopsy also revealed that Slade had been shot twice in the chest as well as once in the head. And he was shot while he was in the trunk. The police found shells from the gun, though not the gun itself. So progress is being made."

In the studio, the female anchor had a question. "Do the police have any suspects yet, Mark?"

Mark smiled. "Jean, if they do, they're not telling me."

"All right, and thanks, Mark," Barry contributed. "Good report."

Baird felt strange lying there on the couch as if nothing unusual had happened. The old black woman had probably just put a noose around his neck and thrown open the trapdoor. By establishing the time of the killing so exactly, she had made it necessary for him to invent an alibi. Though he had never considered himself much of a racist, at the moment he wouldn't have minded burning a cross on the old woman's lawn.

"God, it gives me the creeps, seeing him," Kathy was saying. "Even on TV. That same look. So repulsive." She shook her head in revulsion.

"A crazy man," Baird said. "I guess he hated women."

He reached out and touched Kathy's neck, and she scooted closer, inclining her head toward him, just as in the old days. And he was moved. It had been so long since she had let him come close—in fact not once since he'd broken down in her bedroom. He edged his fingers up into her hair.

"Well, as your mother said," he told her, "you don't have to worry about him anymore."

"And thank God for that." She got to her feet. "I guess it's bedtime for me."

Standing with her legs locked, she bent down like a ballerina and kissed Baird on the forehead. He knew he should have been content with that, but he found himself reaching out and holding her there a second longer while he raised up and kissed her on the cheek.

She smiled warmly. "Good night, Daddy."

"Good night, honey."

She went behind Ellen's chair then and brushed her lips against her mother's cheek.

Ellen did not respond.

"Well, good night, you guys," the girl said, on her way out of the room. "It's good to see you together for a change."

When she was gone, Ellen gave a sharp laugh, like a bark. "*Ha!*"

"I take it you don't agree," Baird said.

She wrinkled her nose. "Doesn't matter. Not now. But I will say this—I seem to be coming up in the world. I think I actually felt her lips touch my cheek."

"Does it ever dawn on you to kiss her back?"

"What? And make her jump? I've learned the hard way."

"For what it's worth, I agree with her. It's nice to be back home. Here. With you."

Ellen put down her knitting and turned to look at him, as if she'd heard a mysterious sound in the house. "*Back home?*"

"That's what I said."

"One night. What am I supposed to do, run over there and throw my arms around you? The wanderer has returned?"

"Whatever was bugging me, keeping me out drinking, I think it's passed."

She smiled in contempt. "No kidding."

"That's how I see it."

"That it's passed, huh? In other words, your little detective has kicked you out and now you expect to come back home and pick up where you left off—boring me stupid?"

For the moment, Baird had lost his voice. Until now, Ellen had never explicitly referred to Lee Jeffers as his lover.

"I don't know what I expect," he said.

"Good, because you're not going to get it." She was putting her knitting away now, getting ready to go upstairs to bed. And suddenly she smiled again, almost sweetly. "Your lady cop—let me guess what happened. She thought you were in love with her, when in fact you were only toying with the idea, trying it on, like a new coat."

"I don't know what you're talking about," he said.

Her only response to that was to give him a pitying look. Then she got up and left, her slippers scratching across the floor of the museum. She did not say good night.

Alone, Baird lit a cigarette and turned off the television. And despite an earlier decision not to drink any more that evening, at least not after having left Bramante's, he decided that a few more vodkas couldn't possibly hurt anything.

Lee Jeffers had been hating her job ever since that Sunday morning in the chicken-and-ribs joint, when Lucca had scolded her like a naughty child in front of Harrelson and the others. And it hadn't lessened her resentment any, knowing that she had been in the wrong, had opened the door wide for Lucca to come bullying his way in, so goddamn eager to cut her down to size. She still didn't understand what had possessed her, making that stupid remark to the pimp about getting him "off the hook." The only explanation that made any sense was that she was so frustrated by Slade—so convinced of his guilt and so helpless to prove it—that she had temporarily lost her head. But what galled her the most was the swiftness of Lucca's response, as if he had been waiting patiently all these months for just such an opportunity to jump all over her.

"See, fellas?" he'd seemed to say. "Affirmative action in practice. What a joke."

And now there was the killing of Slade himself, an apparent professional hit. She was still embarrassed by her initial reaction the previous night, seeing the thing on television and going off half-cocked simply because Baird had seemed so calm about it, so indifferent to it. Now though, after having had more time to reflect, she realized how ridiculous it was to think he could have had anything to do with it: this nice, funny new friend of hers, this lover who got her off better than anyone since Marty. She couldn't believe she had actually called him a liar when he left. Because of that, she was doubly anxious to see him again and apologize, get down on her knees if she had to—though that, she reflected, would inevitably lead to other things. It was a thought that had her smiling as she reached her desk now, over an hour late, which meant she had missed Lucca's daily sardonic briefing—a gift she owed to the bandit plumber, who had arrived late at her house, the racks on the sides of his old truck gleaming with acres of copper pipe.

Most of the detectives were already on the street, working their cases. A few were busy at their phones or catching up on paperwork, which was something Lee herself had no choice but to do. As she worked, she saw Lucca enter the bull pen from the corridor, being unusually attentive to a small, trim man wearing an expensive tan summer suit with a pink shirt, a wheat-colored tie and a pink-and-red kerchief stuffed just so in his jacket pocket, a touch of the raffish. His thinning hair looked tinted and his tiny shoes gleamed with polish. He moved tentatively, smiling nervously at Lucca, as if he wasn't sure what to expect from him, kindness or abuse.

Across the room, at his desk, Joe Daniels winked at Lee and waggled his beefy hand, assuring her that he knew a faggot when he saw one. In response, Lee gave him a listless shrug, unimpressed that her friend had caught something a blind person could not have missed, there being a sudden effluvium of expensive perfume in the stale air. Puzzled, she watched Lucca usher the man into the office of the lieutenant, who was on vacation. Through the blinds on the office window, she could see the two of them together, Lucca surprisingly not taking the lieutenant's desk but facing the man in one of two guest chairs, as if they were equals. The little man spoke with shy animation, using his hands, and Lucca kept nodding, as if he could not have been happier with what he was hearing.

Watching them, Lee would have bet all her new copper piping that the man had something to do with Slade's murder. Though it was technically a county case, she knew Lucca would worm his way into it one way or the other, and for himself too, not just for the Metro Squad. There was simply no way the sergeant would leave such a plum for her to pick, even though it normally would have been hers, considering that she was already working on Slade's case, albeit with Slade as a suspect, not a victim.

It worried her that Lucca might put Baird at the top of his list of suspects, simply because he had no one else and because he disliked him so much. If that happened, she knew she would

have to walk an exceedingly fine line—on one side, praying that
the sergeant wouldn't find out about her relationship with Baird,
and on the other, hoping that they wouldn't uncover anything
incriminating against him. Then too, she would have to stop
seeing him, and that was going to hurt, much more than she
would have expected a few weeks earlier. But she couldn't help
herself; she really liked the man, married or not. Even when he
was like last night, so tightly wound, she loved his company. He
made her feel good. He made her happy.

Trying to think about something else, she looked over at the
lieutenant's office again. Lucca was just getting up, holding a
small tape recorder. He said something to the little man, then
went out to the lieutenant's secretary, Donna Warren, and gave
her the recorder, probably so she could type up the man's statement. Then he went over to the coffee stand and poured two
cups, carefully sugaring and stirring one of them. Returning to
the lieutenant's office, he handed the sugared cup to the little
man, who gave it a tentative sip, then smiled at Lucca, who
seemed relieved that he had pleased his new friend. While
Donna typed, the two men went on talking.

After he escorted the little man out, Lucca came back to his desk.
Spinning the chair around, he straddled it, then slid over to
Lee's desk, grinning like a wino with a full quart. For him, this
was a performance so uncharacteristic that Lee wondered if he
was having a breakdown.

"Guess who that was," he said.

She barely looked up from her paperwork. "Tinker Bell?"

"You shouldn't be so homophobic, Detective. No, that was
Lester J. Wall, one of the most successful interior designers in
the city—and a very close friend of the late Jimbo Slade."

"One of his johns, you mean."

"Not according to him. Anyway, he has just made a statement to the effect that our friend Jack Baird was with Slade again
about a week before the murder."

"So?"

"So hear me out, for Jesus Christ sake." Lucca was not grinning now. "Wall claims Baird came into Gide's—you know, the
gay bar up on Capitol Hill—he came in and joined him and

Slade at a table. Slade introduced him as Jack Baird and said they were both hot for the same girl and that Baird had threatened to blow his ass off with a shotgun. And Wall says he could see it was serious. He says it was obvious that there was bad blood between them, even though Slade pretended to be joking about it all. Baird said he had some extra money to spend and he wanted Slade to show him how and where. And later Wall saw them leave together."

Lee leaned back in her chair, chewing thoughtfully on a pencil. It gave her real pleasure to seem unimpressed in the face of her partner's rare bout of enthusiasm.

"I still don't see the significance. It's still a whole week in between, before the killing. What are you saying, that Slade and Baird were together for the whole week?"

Lucca's face had begun to redden. "Don't be so fucking obtuse, okay? First, Joe Daniels sees him with Slade at Harold's strip joint—remember? Next, we go to his house and warn him to stay away from Slade. Then there's the burglary at his house. And now, a week before the murder, the man is back at it again, trying to scare Slade off."

"And when that doesn't work, he just goes ahead and smokes him, is that it?"

"Why not? Who else we got?"

Lee smiled in disbelief. "Oh, come on, Sergeant—you know what the man is like. He's a straight arrow. A family man. A nice guy."

"Mister Niceguy, huh?"

"Exactly. The kind of man that might go wacko one day and blow away his boss or wife—now, that's feasible. That's what solid citizens do. But what they don't do is plan and execute a hit like this. At most, they'd try to hire someone else to do it—and get caught in the process."

Lucca had begun to smile again, a very patronizing smile. "You like the guy, don't you?"

Lee was defensive. "Oh, I don't know. I imagine most people do. He seems harmless."

"Not to me, he don't. I had him pegged right off, the way he came in here that first day, ready to bite my head off. And then schmoozing us at his house the way he did. He's got it in him, all right. Just the fact that he'd play footsie with a heavy hitter like Slade, that's not your average Mister Niceguy."

"So what do we do?" Lee asked. "Arrest him? Bring him in and beat it out of him? Execute him maybe?"

"Don't be a smartass. I'm not saying he did it. I'm just saying he's a suspect, that's all. And we're gonna start watching him."

"I thought it was a county case."

"It is. But they're nowhere. I checked with Dixon over there, and they ain't got a clue. Anyway, we're all on the same side, last time I checked."

"You going to tell them about your designer friend?"

The smile came again, this time tilted toward the impish. "Not so's you notice. Not yet anyway."

Lee knew he was after something, was not just keeping her informed. So she asked the usual question. "What do you want me to do?"

He didn't respond for a few moments, just sat there sucking on his teeth and staring into space, as if he didn't already know what her orders would be. Then he nodded thoughtfully, agreeing with himself.

"Yeah, I think maybe you should see a little more of our friend Baird."

"Just what do you have in mind? Pillow talk?"

"You said it—not me."

"What are we now—the KGB?"

"Oh, don't be so dramatic. All I said was get close to the guy. But now that I think about it . . ." He gestured at her body. "Hey, you might as well put all that equipment to good use. That is, other than motivating the brass to play favorites."

"*That's* what I've been doing?"

"If the shoe fits, Detective."

"Well, it doesn't!"

Lucca shrugged, as if it were a matter of vast indifference to him. "Getting back," he said. "I want you to contact the guy. Make up some excuse and get closer to him, find out what he's doing, how he's holding up."

"And if he's innocent?"

"Then you get the pleasure of his company. After all, he's such a nice guy, right?"

FIFTEEN

The following Saturday Baird was preparing to watch a football game on television—the Huskies playing Stanford—when he saw Sergeant Lucca pull up and park in front of the house. Kathy had gone clothes shopping with a girlfriend of hers, a fellow clerk at Bond's, but Ellen was at home, upstairs, cleaning the bathrooms. Since Baird didn't want her hearing whatever it was the detective had to say, he went out on the porch to intercept him. Evidently off duty, Lucca was tieless and wearing a zippered windbreaker. If he was carrying a gun, Baird could not see it. He came shuffling up the walk as if he had been on the road for months.

"Good afternoon," Baird said. "You always work Saturdays?"

The detective shrugged. "You know the old saying—no rest for the wicked."

"Will this take long?"

"Just a few questions, that's all."

Baird went down the porch stairs, effectively blocking the sergeant's advance. "My wife's vacuuming," he said. "It'll be a little noisy in there. Why don't we just walk up the street, toward the park?"

Lucca smirked. "Sort of arm in arm?"

"Not very likely."

"We could sit in my car."

"Let's not."

"Okay, then. Lead on."

With Lucca duckwalking beside him, Baird led the way up the street, toward Lookout Park. The trees were already changing color, and the day itself was cool and gray, with a so-far unkept promise of rain in the air. Baird was not uncomfortable, however, since he was wearing a sweatshirt in addition to his usual Saturday jeans and loafers. Then too, he had his terror to keep him warm, his all-but-insupportable curiosity as to what the sergeant was about to say.

"I was going to watch the game," Baird said.

"What game?"

Baird looked to see if the man was serious. "The Huskies, you've heard of them? That great big school down there?" He nodded in the direction of the mile-distant Husky stadium, which sat at the edge of the lake like a split cathedral.

"Oh, *football*," Lucca said. "I don't follow it. I'm not much of a sports fan."

"Well, it takes all kinds."

"Don't it, though?"

They walked in silence for a short distance. Then Lucca wagged his head, as if in wonderment. "Big surprise about Slade, wasn't it?"

"Yes, it was."

"I checked with the guys in Narcotics, and they say there's nothing on the street about it. No rumors or anything. But then he wasn't really a dealer, just a small-timer. Buy enough for himself and his johns mostly, maybe a couple other people. Not really a dealer."

"Very interesting."

"Well, it is to me. Of course, it's my business."

They had come to the "lookout" portion of the park, a flat area with trees and benches and a broad vista to the east, which Lucca remarked on now.

"Jesus, what a view, huh? You can see just about everything except the north end of the lake. That's where they whacked him, you know. Or at least dumped him. North of Juanita, under one of them high bluffs."

The sergeant looked at him, but Baird said nothing.

"It must've taken a weight off your shoulders, not having to worry about him anymore."

Baird sat down on one of the benches and Lucca joined him, dropping onto the seat with a grunt, as if the effort exhausted him.

"TV said the sheriff's police were handling the case," Baird said.

"Oh, I wouldn't worry about that if I was you. Our squad, Metro, we got kind of a special purview. The tough cases, we seem to get them all, sooner or later."

"Then why don't we get to it?" Baird said, lighting a cigarette.

Lucca made a great show of following Baird's lead, getting out his own pack and extracting a cigarette and lighting it as if he were just learning how.

"Get to it?" he said. "Well, I guess you've got a point there. No reason not to. You'll remember that a member of our squad saw you that one night with Slade—you remember Daniels, don't you, the big black guy with the shaved head?"

"So?"

"So now one of Slade's gay friends, a Lester Wall by name, he comes in and volunteers a bit of information. It seems he misses his old pal Jimbo. And he says that on a Saturday, the fifteenth of August, a man with your name and fitting your description comes into Gide's little fern bar and without any invitation sits right down with him and Slade. And that eventually this guy and Slade, they leave together, for parts unknown."

Lucca looked over at Baird, openly curious as to what effect this information was having. But Baird said nothing, tried not to show anything. The sergeant dragged deeply on his cigarette, then went on with his story, not exhaling so much as letting the smoke gradually seep out of him, as if his lungs had caught fire.

"Now this fellow Lester, he claims Slade said—right there in front of you—that you had threatened to shoot him with a shotgun if he didn't stay away from your daughter. Well, I could hardly believe my ears. I mean, it's hard to figure, a smart, upstanding man like yourself saying a thing like that in front of a witness. Very indiscreet, Mister Baird—especially with Slade getting himself killed just nine days later."

Baird didn't miss it, that Lucca had the time element right. But he let it pass, for the moment. "No, I didn't say that in front of a witness. Slade *said* I said it—there's a difference."

"So there is. My mistake."

"How do you know when he was killed? That old black lady on TV?"

"Naw, witnesses are liable to say anything. And the more they say it, the more they believe it. Fortunately, we've got something that backs up the old lady, something real solid. And it's ironic as hell. You remember that burglary you had, the one you said Slade did?"

"Of course."

"And you remember the items you said were missing. One of them was a gold Lord Elgin calendar watch, right? With a broken wrist band, right? Well, guess what they found in one of Slade's pockets. Just guess."

He was smiling at Baird now, or at least twisting his mouth into a tortured approximation of a smile. When Baird did not respond, the sergeant laughed.

"Don't want to guess, huh? Well, I can understand that. I guess if I was in your shoes, I wouldn't want to say anything more than I had to either."

Baird dropped his cigarette onto the grass and stepped on it. "So the creep had my watch," he said. "So what? That just proves he was the one who burglarized my house."

"The watch wasn't waterproof. It stopped on Tuesday, August twenty-five, at one-fifty-four in the morning."

"So?"

"So where were you at that hour, Mister Baird?"

Baird tried hard to look both incredulous and amused. "Where was I? What the devil are you saying? I'm a suspect?"

"You can hardly believe it, right?"

"Yes—*right.*" Baird shook his head in disgust. "Jesus, this is too much, just too fucking much. But all right—you want to know where I was? I was home in bed. With my wife."

"And she'll verify that?"

"Of course."

"Of course." Lucca leaned forward on the bench and dropped his cigarette between his knees, onto the grass. He puckered his mouth, gathering spit, then dropped a gob of it onto the still-lit stub. It was as if he wanted to be as obnoxious as possible in front of Baird, making it abundantly clear that their relationship was not an equal one, that he could do almost anything he pleased and Baird would do well to just sit and take it.

"I'll tell you why I'm here," he said now. "The case is already starting to break for us—some new developments I can't tell you about yet. But they got me pretty well convinced that it was you who wasted that piece of shit. And I'm also convinced that the longer the investigation goes on, the tighter the noose is gonna get for you. So I wanted to give you some advice." He looked at Baird, his expression almost kindly now. "You listening to me?"

"How could I help it?"

"Good. This is my advice. Don't hang tough on this. Don't play it out. You come forward now—that is, you come to me, voluntarily—and I can virtually guarantee you won't be charged with first-degree murder. The threat Slade posed to your daughter, the things he probably said to you about what he was gonna do and all, you probably got a good case for temporary insanity. Hell, you might even walk. It could be. But that's only if you turn yourself in."

Baird said nothing for a time. About a hundred feet ahead of them, near the point where the hill fell away and the brush thickened, a young man stood holding a frisbee while the dog he had been throwing it to, a Labrador, sat at his feet, quivering with anticipation. Closer, on another bench, an elderly couple sat in silence, looking down at the lake, where a large construction barge had forced the bridge to raise, stopping traffic in both directions. Even in daylight the brake lights of the cars sparkled like a string of rubies.

Baird stood up. "Well, I've got a football game to watch."

"What's your answer?" Lucca asked, getting up from the bench too.

"Answer to what?"

"Don't play games, Mister Baird."

Baird started for home, not bothering to wait for the sergeant to catch up. "My answer," he said, "is that I think you better stop working Saturdays. In fact, maybe you ought to think about taking a few weeks off and rest up. Do you a world of good."

"That's not the answer I was looking for," Lucca said.

Baird shook his head in mock sympathy. "Jesus, I'm really sorry about that."

When he came in the front door, Ellen was waiting for him, looking every inch a cleaning woman, from the bandana tied over her hair to the jeans she wore, so threadbare they looked almost fashionable.

"What did he want?" she asked.

"Nothing important. A few questions about Slade, that's all."

"Like what?"

They were in the foyer, and he had no intention of standing there and being grilled as if he were a child.

"The Huskies are on," he said. "I've already missed a quarter."

She followed him through the museum to the family room, where he picked up the remote and turned the game on. Before he could slip into his recliner, she took the remote from him and pressed the mute button.

"I asked you a question," she said.

He looked forlornly at the silent screen. The purple-and-gold had just scored a touchdown. "Sergeant Lucca seems to be suffering a nervous breakdown," he said. "He's got it in his head that because I saw Slade a couple of times—had a few drinks with him—I must be the one who killed him."

Ellen looked at him in disbelief. "You *what?*"

"On two occasions I tracked Slade down and had a few drinks with him, tried to feel him out, see if he'd back off. I didn't tell you because I knew you'd worry about it."

"You were actually with him? You *drank* with him?"

"It seemed like a good idea at the time."

"Did you threaten him?"

"Of course. That was the whole idea."

"And when did all this take place?"

Baird got out a cigarette and lit it.

"Please don't do that. Not in the house."

He ignored her. "When? The first time, oh, over a month ago. The second time, right after the break-in."

"And when does Lucca think you did the deed?"

"You remember my calendar watch was one of the items missing after the burglary? Well, it turned up on Slade's body, stopped at one-fifty-four A.M., Tuesday, the twenty-fifth."

"How does that tie you in?"

"It doesn't. As far as I can see, it just proves he stole it."

"And Lucca's serious about this? He actually thinks you could have done it?"

"I don't know—maybe he's just playing games. Who knows?"

"Did you set him straight?"

Baird looked at the TV again. A beer commercial was playing, showing the usual beautiful young people cavorting at a beach. "Well, I reminded him that I was a paper salesman, not a hit man."

Ellen took her bandana off and her hair spilled out, Titian red, newly colored. "He can't be serious, can he?" she asked.

"As I said—I don't know."

It was then that Baird began to see something in her eyes, a kind of light way back, perhaps the first glimmering of doubt. "Jack, I know you didn't do it. I know you *couldn't* have done it," she said.

"That makes two of us."

"But why would Sergeant Lucca even *think* you could have done it? I mean, it's preposterous."

"That it is."

"And even if it was in you, you wouldn't have had any reason. The man never even touched Kathy."

Baird said nothing and Ellen kept looking at him, just as Lee Jeffers had done, only with the weird unblinking intensity that was hers alone.

"I know you didn't do it," she repeated.

"Of course I didn't do it," he said.

But she kept staring at him, and Baird knew that if he looked away, he would look guilty. So he played her goddamn child's game and stared right back, coldly. And that new thing in her eyes, the small dim light, seemed to brighten. Finally she put her hand over her mouth and stepped back, as if she'd been struck.

"You didn't do it!" she whispered.

He made a face, weariness and disgust. "Ellen, don't be an ass."

"Of course," she gasped. "For *her*. You would do *anything* for her."

Baird took the remote from her and turned the sound up high. He dropped into his recliner and put his feet up. Then he looked up at her, with contempt and disbelief.

"Get real, will you?" he said. "For Jesus Christ sake, you're as bad as Lucca. You think I could actually kill someone?"

Without answering, she turned and left the room. He heard her tennis shoes on the museum floor, practically running.

Fuck her, he thought. Fuck them all.

He doubted that Ellen would tell Kathy what she had just learned, or at least thought she had learned. Still, he knew it was considerably beyond him at the moment to see the look on his daughter's face if Ellen did tell her and she came running to him for denial. He could more easily have shot Slade all over again. So he turned off the television and got out of the house before Kathy returned. Normally he would have put on a shirt and sportcoat, even to go to Leo's, but on this day he made do with the sweatshirt and jeans. Also, he hadn't shaved yet, which was a habit of his on Saturdays.

So he fully expected Sally to comment on his shabby appearance. But it turned out that she was so angry at Leo about something that she had nothing left over for her patrons. She did not serve Baird's vodka so much as plunk it down in front of him, letting the liquor run over, unmopped. He made no complaint, however, happy to put up with the poor service so long as its corollary was silence. He wanted just to sit there at the bar and watch the ballgame and drink enough to keep from screaming.

On a hike up in the Cascades he and Ellen once had come upon a couple of teenagers trying to climb a hill so steep it was a virtual cliff. Halfway up, one of them lost his grip and began to slide back down, frantically grasping at small outcroppings of rocks and scrub bushes and clumps of bear grass. But nothing held, and he continued his hapless slide until he finally reached the bottom, bloody and bruised and scared, trying not to cry.

That was how Baird felt now, only worse—as if he were sliding to his death and every rock and bush he grasped at, every hope, came away in his hand. As terrified as he was, he felt that he could not even think clearly, at least not cold sober. So he drank with considerable thirst, smoking and munching popcorn and watching the ballgame on television. Occasionally Leo would park in front of him, commenting on the game, pointing out wherein this year's Huskies were not quite the equal of the previous year's team. Happily, he seemed oblivious to Baird's mood, apparently seeing nothing unusual in an old friend holding onto his glass for dear life.

Sally, always more perceptive, would occasionally give Baird a look of rueful curiosity, as if to say that she knew something was wrong in his life but that she couldn't be bothered at the moment, not with big Leo still chained in her doghouse. Finally, though, serving him a fourth or fifth drink, she came around the bar and sat next to him.

"You want to tell Mama all about it?" she said.

"Would it help?"

"Always."

"I've grown old and stupid."

"Well, who hasn't? The question, Jack, is *how* you've grown old and stupid."

"In strange and wondrous ways," he said.

She smiled. "Why do I doubt that?"

"Because you're so smart?"

"That's for sure."

When she left him, he went back to his vodka and the television, where a second game was already in progress: Notre Dame and whoever, nationally televised. After the first quarter he went to the men's room and then came back to his stool and pushed his empty glass at Leo once again. And again Leo dutifully filled it. Baird lit a cigarette and absently looked toward the front of the bar, where someone had just come in. For some reason, he was not surprised to see that it was Lee Jeffers, quite alone this time and looking predictably sexy in stonewashed black jeans and a black-velour vest over a green blouse. Hanging from a strap over her shoulder was a small handbag, probably the repository of a gun—a gun she might use to arrest him with, he reflected. He picked up his drink and stood.

"We've got to talk," she said.

"Okay." He started toward the restaurant side.

"No, not here. Some other place. Outside."

Baird turned and looked at her. "No one will hear us over there. It's private."

Giving a shrug, she followed him then, on the way telling Sally that she would not require anything. One other couple was on that side, having either a very late lunch or an early dinner. Baird led Lee to a corner booth at the front, as far from the couple as he could get. He took the wall side, so he could see into the bar, above the row of plastic ferns that ran along the top of the dividing wall. If Lucca or one of the other members of the Metro Squad suddenly wandered into the bar as backup for Lee, Baird wanted to know it, for he was still sober enough to suspect that she was there as a cop, not as a lover, or at least an ex-lover. For all he knew, she might have been "wearing a wire," as they described it on TV cop shows.

Sitting, they both immediately lit cigarettes.

"I phoned your house a while ago," she said. "But your wife answered. Like a jerk, I hung up."

"She must've loved that."

"I can imagine." Lee started to say something, then broke it off, shaking her head and smiling, her eyes unexpectedly moist. "God, it's good to see you again," she said.

The words lifted him, opened him. Afraid his own eyes might fill, he looked down at her hands on the tabletop and enclosed them in his own. "I didn't know where we stood, Lee. I mean, after what happened. After what you said."

"Oh, listen, I'm so sorry about that. You just threw me, that's all. You were so cool."

"Numb is more like it. I was just numb."

"I know. I know you couldn't have done it."

He did not respond to that. He was wondering what her reaction would be if and when the truth came out. More than ever before, he realized how much he wanted her in his life.

Glancing at the bar, she gently pulled her hands free. "We still have to be careful, Jack. We can't go back the way we were, at least not yet."

"No, I suppose not."

She took a deep breath then, as if she were under considerable pressure herself. "Listen, Lucca called me this morning. He said there's been a break of some kind in Slade's case, and that it looked bad for you. He wanted me to come in, but I begged off. I told him I had a date. I didn't mention it was with you."

"Yeah, he told me about this 'big break' too," Baird said. "He stopped by around noon today. Tried to talk me into giving myself up—I guess because of this new development, whatever the hell it is. I told him I didn't even care what it was, because I hadn't done anything."

Exhaling smoke, Lee sighed. "The very next morning he was on your case. Some little fag designer came in and said you were with Slade again the week before the murder. But by then I think Lucca already had you picked out as the perp anyway—sorry, the perpetrator. Later he asked me to start seeing you on my own and find out what I could. He practically ordered me to sleep with you."

Baird smiled. "He's a little late."

"Exactly. And that's the main reason I'm here, Jack. Do you have any idea what kind of a fix I'm in because of this? Because of *us?* Here I am, sleeping with a guy who suddenly turns out to be my boss's hot new murder suspect. The boss calls up and says, 'Come on, let's go to work,' and I beg off, whining about it being Saturday and bullshit like that, because I can't very well tell him the truth, can I? 'Oh, I'm sorry, Sarge, but I've been fucking Jack Baird for about a month now, and that sorta compromises me, don'tcha think?' "

Baird wasn't very sympathetic. "That's real tragic, Lee—considering my own predicament. You won't mind if I worry about me first?"

"I know, I know." She looked embarrassed. "It's just that I don't know how to play this thing. I have to know what you're going to do—or already did. Like today—did you say anything about us to Lucca?"

"No."

"Do you plan to?"

Baird thought about it. "No, I don't see any reason why I should. I can't see what difference it would make, unless you turn out to be my alibi. But Lucca says Slade was killed on the night of the twenty-fourth, and our first night together was after that, wasn't it? I can't remember dates lately. Too much vodka, you think?"

She didn't respond for a few moments, just sat there looking at him, her eyes filled with doubt and anxiety. "Jack, it could ruin my career," she said finally. "They probably wouldn't take my shield or anything that drastic. There's no law against having an affair. But this would ruin me with Lucca. I'd be out on my ass as far as the Metro Squad is concerned. And career-wise, that'd be the kiss of death. They'd have me out tracking down parking violators."

"Would that be so bad?"

"Don't be funny."

"Sorry," he said.

"I just have to know what to expect, that's all," she went on. "Otherwise I won't know how to play it with Lucca. If it's going to come out about us anyway, I should tell him up front and minimize the fallout. But if it isn't going to come out, then I'd just as soon pull back and go through the motions, you know? On your case, I mean. The investigation."

Baird didn't know what to say. If the last few months had taught him anything, it was that a man could lose control of his life in a matter of seconds, in no more time than it took to fire a gun. He had no idea what the future held, whether Lucca was just fishing or truly had him by the throat, in which case Baird knew he would have to do what he could to save himself. But he couldn't see that there was anything to be gained by telling the sergeant about his affair with Lee. And anyway, as he was beginning to realize, he cared for her more deeply than he had thought.

"Don't worry about it," he said. "I won't tell Lucca or anyone else. It's our business."

She reached over and laced her fingers into his, suddenly indifferent to their audience at the bar. "I do miss you, Jack. What's it been? Eight, nine days?"

"At least."

"But for now—"

"I know. We have to go on not seeing each other."

"I'm afraid we don't have much choice, at least until this case is resolved."

"Unless we see each other in an official way."

"I hope not. I really do."

"I don't know," Baird said. "If it's the only way I'll get to see you . . ."

She smiled ruefully. "Don't even think it. No, this will end. One of Slade's johns or a fellow dealer—somewhere, some low-life is going to start bragging, and we'll be in business."

"That would be nice."

"It will happen. Don't worry."

Again she started to pull her hand away from his, but this time he didn't let go of it. She seemed puzzled for a moment, but then, seeing his look, she smiled at him, a sad, lovely smile.

"I really have to go now," she said.

Baird nodded. "I know, Lee. But I just wanted to say . . . I love you." The words seemed to surprise her even more than they did him.

Gathering up her purse and sliding out of the booth, she had an odd, anguished look. "I guess I'd better be on my way," she said.

Baird got up as she left. "Take care," he said.

Given his nature, he couldn't help watching her, the way she moved in the tight black jeans. Most of the men on the other side craned to look at her too as she made the turn and came back along the bar, heading for the door. Nearing it, she smiled at Baird across the plastic garden, a smile that made him want to run after her.

The rest of that day Baird continued to feel as if he were slipping helplessly down some sandy slope to hell and there was nothing he could do about it. After he left Leo's he picked up some fast food at McDonald's and drove to Northlake Way to eat it, parking outside the small marina where he had kept his last boat, the Reinell. The parking lot was nothing more than a single row of angled parking spaces facing a chain-link fence, beyond which were the docks and boats and the lake, with the downtown sky-line in the distance, some of the high-rises already lighting up for the night.

As he sat eating and listening to the radio, a yuppie couple docked their sailboat and eventually came walking up the main pier to the fence. After they passed through the gate, heading for their Beamer, the man detoured over to Baird.

"Hey, friend," he said, "this isn't a public parking lot. We're a private yacht club now. You can't park here."

He was in his thirties, a slim blond man with a no-nonsense haircut and rimless glasses. He was dressed all in white, which was a serious gaffe for a true Northwest mariner.

Baird smiled. "Are you a yachtsman?"

"I'm a member here, yes."

"I thought maybe you sold Eskimo Pies."

The young woman called for the man to hurry up, but he stood his ground. "Very funny," he said to Baird. "But you still can't park here. I just might call the tow people from my car."

"The *tow* people?"

"That's right."

"Your boat's too small," Baird said.

The man frowned. "Too small for *what?*"

"To be a yacht. It has to be thirty feet to be a yacht."

At that, the man turned and went back to his car, throwing his hand down and out, as if he were brushing bugs away. But Baird was not quite finished.

"Maybe a popsicle," he said. "You got any popsicles for sale?"

After the couple roared away, Baird finished his meal and tossed the wastepaper over the fence, something he would never have done in the past. And it occurred to him that he was proba-bly beginning to understand the criminal mind. Once a man began to think of himself as a lawbreaker, perhaps all laws be-came suspect.

It was dark when he left the marina, driving back around the west side of the lake again, as if it were time to go to work instead of home to bed. But he was afraid that Kathy would still be up, and the thought of talking to her now—answering her ques-tions, lying to her yet again—seemed at the moment a greater trial than anything Lucca could throw at him.

He drove downtown and bought a ticket at the only remaining porn theater in the city, figuring that the place would not be crowded and that he would not see anyone he knew. He took a back seat and watched a few minutes of pedophilia, a sexy-looking young woman sucking the big toe of an aging male porn star, a sexual practice Baird never had been able to understand. He would just as soon have had his elbow sucked; he couldn't imagine that it would have felt much different.

He closed his eyes for a few moments, and shortly—actually a half hour later—he was shaken awake by the usher, a little old man with wispy hair and a single visible tooth, which made him look a bit like Oliver Dragon, a lovable, obstreperous hand puppet on a TV show from Baird's childhood. The man wasn't as funny as Ollie, however. Spraying the area with spit and vapors of muscatel, he told Baird to either watch the movie or leave the theater.

Baird left. And by now he was feeling as if the whole world automatically knew him for what he was, could see it as clearly as if he had a Day-Glo "M" stitched to his lapel. Why else would he suddenly be banished from parking places and tossed out of theaters? He never had been before, and in truth, it unnerved him, made him wonder if he wasn't giving off an aura as unmistakable as that of the old wino usher. A jury wouldn't even have to deliberate his case. "Guilty," they would say. "Just look at the man."

It was a thought that forcefully reminded Baird of how essentially sober he still was, not nearly as paralyzed as he needed to be later at home in case Kathy had stayed up and was waiting for him. So he stopped at Bramante's for a few peaceful drinks in the gloaming and then went down the street to a fashionable yuppie bar, where he divined the essential difference between people, the two basic categories being those who looked at your eyes first and those who looked at your clothes. Since he was still wearing old jeans and a baggy sweatshirt, he understood that he was underdressed for the bar, that he should have been wearing either an expensive jogging suit or gray Dockers and the subtle, smoky colors of an Irish-wool sweater. Then too it would have helped if he'd known something about computers or hadn't found himself pushed up against a young couple quarreling over the rights of the homeless.

He had two more drinks there, then made his way to what he thought was just an average cocktail lounge, located next to a motorcycle-repair shop, that being the reason for all the Harleys parked along the curb. Once inside, though, he thought he had stumbled upon a reunion of the Goths and Vizigoths, thirty or forty men running the gamut from emaciated orange-haired types to ones more like Leo, only bearded and tattooed, with great hairy bellies spilling over studded belts. They wore heavy boots and vests of sheepskin and black leather, decorated with signs and totems and other undecipherable symbols. Some were playing pool. A half dozen were at the bar. For the most part, though, they were just lounging around, yelling and drinking beer out of bottles. When Baird came in and walked to the bar, they fell silent and watched, as if he had just arrived from another planet.

The bartender came over to him, and Baird forced a laugh. "Hey, this is a beer bar, ain't it?" he said. "My mistake. I been drinkin vodka all night and I figure I better stick with it, ya know?"

But as he started to leave, the bartender snapped the cap off a bottle of Australian beer and set it in front of him.

"Here, this won't hurt ya," the man said. "Put some lead in your pencil."

"Well, that's what I need, all right," Baird agreed, sitting down finally and taking a pull on the bottle.

Reluctantly he acknowledged the bikers on either side of him, both of whom were carefully looking him over. He gave them a nod and a smile of sorts and got back to his beer. The one on his left, a young man, looked uncomfortably like Slade, even down to the greasy ponytail. The other, a man probably in his fifties, looked more like Father Time, his sad, gaunt face framed by a cowl of long white hair and a wispy beard. His eyes watered and he kept clearing his throat. And something about him, either his old sheepskin vest or his open armpits, gave off the tangy odor of a wet dog.

Over the next hour these two told Baird their stories, the one picking up his own sad tale every time the other paused to drink or make a run for the toilet. They kept touching him for emphasis, and there were times when they each had a possessive hand on his shoulder. As they went on and on, he thought of the Three Stooges and how Moe would have handled them: hitting them simultaneously in the nose, then beckoning them close for the sharing of a secret and banging their heads together. But he was not Moe. So he drank and he smoked and he listened, probably because their stories were not all that common.

The old biker was none other than the man on the grassy knoll, the long-sought second gunman in the assassination of President Kennedy. He was tortured by guilt and wanted desperately to turn himself in but was afraid that the media would make a great circus out of it. All the famous men in the conspiracy—Oswald, Ruby, Giancana, Garrison—were to him Lee and Jack and Sam and "Gare." While the young man wasn't in the same league, he was nevertheless "one of the very finest" stage actors in America, as even his enemies would attest. He'd had supporting roles in two local off-Broadway productions and had "blown everybody away." But there was a cabal of local theatre critics, every one of them a flaming queer, and they simply couldn't stand the thought of a great young straight actor coming out of Seattle. So they had singled him out for special attention, had crucified him, butchered him, vilified him, Now he couldn't even get a non-speaking part. The queers ran everything. Even the governor of the state was queer, did Baird realize that?

In the mirror behind the bar, Baird saw himself in his Husky sweatshirt, a middle-aged collegian caught between the Ancient Mariner and a prematurely embittered thespian. And though he knew he looked trapped and pitiful, he also knew he at least wasn't face-to-face with Kathy, wasn't standing helpless before her, about to drown in her wounded, beautiful eyes. *Daddy, is it true?*

Then too there was the simple matter of physiology: the amount of alcohol in his blood. Since even lighting a cigarette had become a challenge, the task of getting up and going home seemed insurmountable. Once, heading for the men's room, he staggered into one of the Vizigoths and almost bowled the poor man over. Instead of being angry, the hairy beast righted him and even steered him through the door toward the urinal, which Baird was almost positive he hit.

Eventually, though—while he could still stagger—he took his leave. He bade good-bye to his new friends, neither of whom knew a thing about him, or apparently cared to know. The old man cautioned him that his story was strictly "off the record," and Baird promised not to tell a living soul. Then he went on outside, where the cool fresh air washed over him like a breaker, almost knocking him off his feet. The parked motorcycles glittered like jewelry, and he thought that if only he knew how to start one, he would have gone for a ride—probably off a cliff or into a tree. Smiling, feeling almost happy, he wandered down the street to where his car was parked and patiently wrestled the key into the door lock. When he finally started for home, he drove very slowly, not sure he ever wanted to get there.

Behind his garage, Baird vomited so forcefully he set the neighborhood dogs to barking. Entering the house, he neglected to lock the door behind him and knocked over a chair in the kitchen and bumped against the dining-room doorway. In the downstairs bathroom, he stripped and stepped into the shower, briefly scalding himself before he was able to regulate the water mixture. He kept turning it colder until it felt like ice pelting him, and then he left it that way, for what reason he could not imagine, since he knew that only time would make him sober.

When he was finished, he found his winter robe hanging behind the door, an anomalous stroke of luck he gave no thought to, putting it on while he was still dripping wet. He walked on through the museum to the family room and stretched out on the couch, pulling an afghan over himself. Hours later, he dreamed he woke in the dark and that Kathy was there with him, stroking his forehead and his hair. Then he came fully awake and realized that it was not a dream and that she was actually there, sitting on the edge of the couch in her pink-silk pajamas, her eyes moist in the darkness, full of anguish. He started to get up, but she put her hand on his shoulder and he settled back.

"I couldn't sleep," she said. "I heard you down here."

He groaned. "Go back to bed, honey. I'm really drunk. Christ, I must stink."

"Daddy, you were kind of crying—"

"Oh, Jesus." He put his arm over his face.

She lightly pushed it off and, leaning down, kissed him on the cheek, even as he tried to pull away.

"I'm still drunk, baby," he said. "Please leave me. *Please.*"

She began to cry. "You were calling my name, Daddy. Well, I'm here now. And I need you too, just like always. I love you. I don't care what you did or didn't do. It makes no difference. Whenever I've needed you, you were always there. So if you need me now, please let me help. Let me stay with you a while."

Even in the darkness he could see her eyes streaming. He reached up and touched her face, caressed the wetness.

"Mom told you," he said.

She nodded. "What that disgusting Lucca thinks, yes. And whether he's right or wrong, I don't care, Daddy. I love you either way, just the same. It makes no difference."

He took her in his arms then and she began to cry on his shoulder, just as he had with her, up in her room. He kissed her hair and patted her.

"I'm so sorry, baby," he got out. "I've made such a total mess of everything."

"No, you haven't. It's going to be all right. I just know it's going to be all right."

As drunk as he was, he still knew that he had never loved her more than he did at that moment. He hugged her tightly, and a wave of nausea swept through him. Bile rose in his throat and he choked it down. The room began to spin and it seemed impossible to keep his eyes open. He became terrified that if he did not hold Kathy tightly enough, she would drift away from him, like one of the mutilated underwater babies in his dreams. His eyes fell shut again, and he heard a kind of sob or moan. Then he was gone.

Later Baird would vaguely remember looking up and seeing Ellen standing just inside the doorway, or at least a shape like hers, a silhouette in the darkness. And it seemed to him that he was alone then, or perhaps, as drunk as he was, he had merely forgotten that Kathy was there with him. At dawn, though, as the first light began to seep like fog into the room, he awoke with a start, suddenly aware that the girl was indeed still there with him on the couch, lying asleep in his arms, her back pressed up against him. And he also realized that because he was wearing only a robe, and because he was in the usual condition of a man waking in the morning, the only thing between his flesh and his daughter's was her silk pajamas.

He moved quickly, covering himself and shaking her awake at the same time. "I guess we fell asleep," he said. "You go on back to bed, honey."

A heavy sleeper, Kathy got up slowly and did not move at first, just stood there beside the couch in a daze. Getting up himself, Baird kissed her on the cheek and patted her bottom, sending her on her way. He followed her to the front stairs and watched until she was safe in her room. Then he went into the downstairs bathroom and huddled over the stool, retching violently. Though all he brought up was phlegm, its passing nevertheless made him shudder with relief. He urinated and took three aspirins and drank water and Pepto Bismol. Then he went up to his own room and got into bed. He slept through most of Sunday.

SIXTEEN

The following Tuesday Sergeant Lucca and Lee Jeffers, accompanied by two other detectives, showed up at Baird's house at seven in the morning. They rang the bell and banged on the door. Not yet dressed and wearing only a bathrobe, Baird went downstairs and let them in. Lucca served him with a search warrant.

"The boys here are gonna comb your house," the sergeant said, indicating the tall black with the shaved head and a second detective Baird had not seen before, a stocky young man with curly brown hair and a pugnacious Irish mug. Lee, wearing a raincoat, lagged behind Lucca like a bashful child.

"And you, Mister Baird," the sergeant went on, "we're gonna have to take you downtown. We need to have a few questions answered."

"I'm under arrest?"

"No," Lucca said. "Not yet."

Ellen, already dressed, had followed Baird down to the foyer. But Kathy was fresh from the shower and wearing only a robe. She stopped midway on the stairs.

"I can have a few minutes to get ready?" Baird asked.

"Sure. And if you're hungry, we can pick up some doughnuts on the way."

"We'd like to follow in our car and wait for him," Ellen said.

"That won't be necessary," Lucca told her. "He'll be with us the whole time, and we'll bring him home when we're finished. Anyway, you better stay and watch these guys. They could make a mess."

Baird suggested to Lucca that they all could wait in the living room while he got ready. He liked the idea of the four of them trying to sit on Ellen's Empire settees. The minutes would seem like hours. But nobody moved. The four detectives stood there looking at him as if he were speaking in tongues.

"Shouldn't you give Tom a call?" Ellen said to Baird, referring to their neighbor, Tom Dagleish. Though he was basically a divorce lawyer, he had handled the Bairds' occasional legal needs.

"Yeah, I suppose so," Baird said.

"Your lawyer?" Lucca asked. "Sure, go ahead. If it makes you feel safer. But remember, you're not under arrest yet. You give us the information we want—clear up a few little points—and you could be free as the wind. On the other hand, you clam up and take the fifth, and a lot of people—including the D.A.—they're gonna think you got something to hide. Then you *will* be arrested. I guarantee it."

"Your concern is touching." Though Baird said it to Lucca, he was looking at Lee, who was obviously not very comfortable in Baird's house, at least not with Ellen so near.

Baird went back upstairs. While he dressed, he tried to figure what Lucca was after, the reason for the search warrant. The gun, of course. Bloody clothing. Maybe a credit card slip from the Oolala on the night of the murder, if the sergeant had progressed that far, which Baird doubted. And since they would find none of those things, he was not too worried about the search warrant.

The interrogation, however, was a different matter. Of course he was not buying Lucca's characterization of it as "just a few questions." In the same vein, the sergeant would probably have described death by hanging as "a period of discomfort."

Baird had little doubt that the interrogation would be a mine-field, with Lucca encouraging him to step lively. But Baird also believed he had a distinct advantage: he knew exactly what had happened, and there was no solid evidence against him—no gun, no fingerprints, no witnesses, no items left in Slade's car—nothing but motive and opportunity. And this last he took care of now, as Ellen looked in on him while he finished getting ready.

"Monday, the night of the twenty-fourth," he said. "As I re-member it, I came home around ten that night and we went to bed a little after eleven. That's right, isn't it?"

Her expression was beautiful in its complexity, saying so many things at once, most of which he could not have begun to translate into words. He could not even tell if she was going to go along with him, not until she spoke.

"Sure," she said. "That's how I remember it."

As he moved past her, he bent to kiss her, and she turned away. But Kathy, at the head of the stairs, flew into his arms. He kissed her on the cheek and she held him tightly for a few mo-ments, her eyes filling.

"I'll be all right," he told her. He looked over at Ellen. "I love you both," he said.

Then he went down the stairs, toward Lucca and Lee, who were still waiting in the foyer.

They drove the two miles to the Public Safety Building in total silence, no one saying anything, not even about the heavy traffic. They parked in a garage under the building, then took an elevator to the fifth floor, where Baird was booked and finger-printed and photographed. When he complained about this, saying that he had thought he was not under arrest, Lucca ex-plained that it was routine with possible suspects. If Baird sud-denly died of a coronary, the case would still have to be solved and his fingerprints might well figure in that solution.

"And might well not," Baird said.

After that, he was put in a holding cell, a room with large windows looking out on the bull pen.

"It'll just be a few minutes," Lucca told him, probably enjoy-ing his little deception. For in reality Baird waited over an hour in the small, stuffy room. Other arrestees came and went, most of them surly young black men who, for all he knew, could have been robbers or pimps or drug dealers, or even killers like himself. They stretched and yawned and cracked their knuckles, but said virtually nothing.

It was Lee who came and got him. On the way to wherever they were going, she finally spoke. "Remember our deal. You don't mention our affair, and I'll help you all I can."

He didn't recall her having put the second part in exactly those words, but he nodded anyway. "So be it," he said.

Lucca was waiting for them in an interrogation room, smoking and pacing, his heavy, dour face looking almost animated for a change. The room was essentially the same as those Baird had seen on TV and in the movies: bare except for a table and chairs, with a large mirror set into one wall, probably a one-way window through which others could observe the interrogation as well as listen in, though Baird saw no sign of a microphone. Up in a corner of the room, the lens of a TV camera pointed down. On the table there was a small tape recorder next to a pair of plastic ashtrays. Lee sat down at the end of the table, Baird took the chair that Lucca indicated, and Lucca sat down across from him.

"You don't mind if we tape this, do you?" he asked, turning on the recorder.

Baird shook his head. "No problem."

Lucca went ahead, telling the recorder the time and date and identifying himself and Lee, then naming Baird as the person being interrogated in regard to the James Slade homicide. He offered Baird a cigarette, took one himself, and lit them both.

"Well now, what say we get started, Jack?" he said, adding, "It's okay if I call you Jack?"

"Sure. Let's be pals."

"All right, then—Jack. First, Jack, you're here of your own free will, right?"

Baird gave a wry laugh. "Oh sure," he said.

"No, really," Lucca insisted. "You're free to go if you want."

"All right, then. Yes, I'm here of my own free will."

"And you understand that you have a right to counsel and that you don't have to answer any questions we may put to you today?"

"Yes, I understand that."

"And you waive these rights?"

"For now."

"Good enough." Lucca dragged on his cigarette and considerately exhaled away from Baird. "Okay then, Jack. The first meeting you had with Slade—the first one we know about anyway—when was that?"

"Early July sometime."

"Detective Daniels in our squad—he's the one saw you outside of Harold's strip joint—he puts it June thirty, a Saturday."

"He could be right. I don't remember exactly."

"You just ran into Slade there, or what?"

"I parked outside his apartment," Baird said. "Then I followed him to Harold's. Inside, he came over to my table. I didn't go to his."

"Well, he must've been curious, right? Somebody following him around. How'd he know who you were?"

"I think you know that as well as I do. After the restraining order we got on him, he kept parking outside our house. I imagine he saw me there."

"And what did you hope to accomplish at the strip club, meeting him like that, face-to-face?"

Thinking, Baird dragged on his cigarette, exhaled, stubbed it out. "At first I thought that maybe if he got to know me as a person—you know, as just another human being—I figured it might have some effect, maybe make him stop harassing us and terrorizing my daughter. I knew by then that the police weren't going to do anything about him, so I figured it was worth a try."

"But it didn't work?"

"No. It amused him, I guess."

"So what happened then? Did you threaten him?"

Baird knew that he'd denied this in the past, threatening Slade. But he also knew that Lucca now had the testimony of Slade's gay friend, Lester Wall, to the contrary.

"Sure," he said. "Why not? I lied to him about having a contact with a Samoan gang. I told him that if he didn't lay off, he could get hurt."

"Did he believe you?"

"I don't know. He didn't act like it."

"So what did you do, up the ante?"

"In what way?"

Lucca smiled. "Like, did you mention guns?"

Again Baird had to consider Lester Wall's testimony. "Could be—but in an oblique way, that's all."

"*Oblique?*" The word seemed to amuse Lucca.

"Meaning I didn't threaten to shoot him. I just told him I used to be a hunter and that I still had some rifles and shotguns."

This information seemed to please the sergeant considerably. He smiled and nodded, as if a slow student had come up with a correct answer. "Just that you owned rifles and shotguns, huh? Not that you might use one on him."

"That's right. I left it vague."

"But a clear threat nevertheless."

"I said vague, not clear."

"Okay. Vague it is. But still a threat."

"I guess it could be construed as such."

"I guess." Lucca put out his cigarette and promptly lit another. Waving the match out, he looked at Lee. "Is there anything you want to add?"

She shook her head. "No. Not so far."

Cocking his head at his partner, Lucca smirked at Baird. "My strong right arm," he said. "Lately it keeps falling asleep."

"You want me to take over, just say the word," Lee snapped.

"Only kidding, Detective."

Baird was still surprised at the immense difference in Lucca, this man who normally looked so wary and dyspeptic, as if a good belch was all he had to look forward to. Now his eyes fairly gleamed behind the thick glasses, his slack mouth worked voraciously, and he could not keep his hands still. They drummed, scratched, and picked at things: a shred of tobacco, even a speck of something stuck to the tabletop—dried paint or fly dung, he didn't seem to care.

Meanwhile Lee sat back in her chair, her arms folded, as if she were a disinterested spectator. Whenever Baird would look at her, her eyes would skitter away.

"Now, where were we?" Lucca said. "Oh yeah, we're up to your second meeting with Slade. When was that?"

Baird gave him the date and told him how the meeting had

come about, as pure happenstance, simply because he had spied Slade's car while he was driving past Gide's.

"Just a spur-of-the-moment thing, huh?" Lucca said.

"That's right. A couple of days earlier he had burglarized our house. He took my daughter's favorite teddy bear—you know, from her childhood, a sentimental thing—and he stuck it to the fireplace mantel with one of our kitchen knives. You people couldn't prove it was him, though. You couldn't find anything."

"So you decided to take matters into your own hands."

"I decided to warn him again."

"And when you found him inside, was he alone?"

"No, he was with one of his gay friends. A Lester somebody."

"Lester Wall?"

"Could be. I don't remember."

"And eventually the two of you—you and Slade—you left together, is that right?"

"That's right."

"Where'd you go?"

"Drinking. And we had dinner."

"Drinking and dinner, huh?" Lucca pushed back his chair and got up, smiling, shaking his head. "Now that is passing weird, you know? Just straight-out weird. Imagine, here you are, this straight arrow in your forties, a businessman, no criminal record at all, clean as a hound's tooth. And you go out drinking and dining with this twenty-four-year-old ex-con with a rap sheet as long as my arm—a drug-dealing male prostitute, a rapist and possible murderer, a guy you say just burglarized your house and kept terrorizing your daughter. *And you go out drinking and dining with him?*"

Baird shrugged. "Same reason I said before. I thought that maybe if he got to know me, and if I could get through to him, make him understand that my daughter was off limits, that if he ever touched a hair of her head . . ."

When Baird failed to finish the thought, Lucca prompted him. "You would what?"

"I would kill him."

The sergeant said nothing for a few moments, letting the words hang in the air like the stench of cordite after a bombing.

He was standing behind his chair, staring raptly down at Baird. When he finally spoke, his voice was soft, almost apologetic.

"And did you kill him, Jack?"

"Of course not. He never touched my daughter."

"I see."

Again Lucca offered Baird a cigarette, and again Baird took it. The sergeant lit a match. Baird leaned into the flame.

"After Gide's," Lucca said, "where did the two of you go?"

"First, a chicken-and-ribs place south on Rainier. Slade liked fat, I gathered. The drumsticks must have weighed five pounds apiece. We went to a couple of downtown bars next, then I dropped him back at Gide's, so he could pick up his car. That must've been around nine or ten."

Lucca turned his chair around and sat down, straddling it. He put his hands on the chair back and lowered his chin onto his hands, looking up at Baird like a whimsical child. Baird wanted to reach out and take him by the nose, pull him yelling and kicking across the table.

"You didn't go anywhere else?" the sergeant asked.

"No."

"Like, say, you didn't go to a strip joint called the Oolala?"

Baird did not respond, just sat there trying not to show anything. It was like trying to hide the fact that one had been kicked hard in the face.

"The Oolala," Lucca repeated. "You never went there?"

"No," Baird said. "I've never even heard of it."

Lucca smiled. "Well, geez, that's kind of weird too. There's a stripper there who remembers table-dancing that night for Slade and a second guy who fits your description to a T. What do you make of that?"

"A case of mistaken identity."

"You weren't there, huh?"

"No."

The sergeant sat up straight now, still smiling slightly, crookedly, a man definitely enjoying himself. "Then you won't mind giving her a look-see, I take it? In a lineup."

Baird thought of refusing. He knew it was time to pull back and call his attorney, but he also knew that ultimately he was going to have to stand in Lucca's lineup, no matter how strenuously he or his lawyer might object. Even more than that, though, he needed to know who was going to view the lineup, one of the other dancers or Satin herself. He needed to know if he was going to suffer a bloody nose or a bullet in the heart.

"Sure," he said. "Why not?"

Lucca grinned. "You're a real plunger, right?"

"Could be."

"Well, that's great. I like a plunger. Fact is, I'm kind of one myself. I believe in something, I go all out. Like after our little talk Saturday, I didn't watch no football game, I can tell you that. I went home and laid down and I looked up at the ceiling for it must've been two hours. And I kept thinking: *How in the sweet name of Jesus did it happen?* How do we get from you two sitting together at Gide's, talking and drinking like friends, and finally leaving together to go have dinner and do some more drinking—how do we get from that to Jimbo Slade winding up in the trunk of his car at the bottom of Lake Washington, with three bullet holes in him? How the devil do we get from Gide's gay little fern bar to that bluff over in Juanita?" He shook his head dolefully. "And nothing comes. I just couldn't figure it. If Jimbo thinks you're gonna waste him, he ain't gonna go barhopping with you then, is he? No way. So I kept at it, kept staring up at that dirty ceiling of mine, and finally I have to settle for the obvious.

"I tell myself, well, this fella Baird, he obviously snookered the guy in some way, no bolt out of the blue or anything like that, just the simplest, most logical explanation possible. And what I finally figured was that somehow you got Slade thinking the two of you had something in common—a bond of some kind. But what in Jesus' name could it have been, huh? Because what Jimbo Slade seems to dig most is not just scaring women shitless, and not just fucking them against their will. No, what he digs is slashing and beating and sodomizing till they're half dead, like the girl who worked at Seafirst. And that sure ain't your scene, is it, Jack?

"But I say to myself, hey, this Baird ain't just your average paper salesman, you know? I figure this Baird, maybe he's even cool enough to snooker Slade into believing he's got some off-beat tastes of his own—like, say, *watching*. Because Jimbo wouldn't believe—in fact no one would believe, even *I* wouldn't believe—you'd go the whole route with him. You know, share the blood lust and all that."

The sergeant paused there, apparently to let it all sink in. His eyes, magnified, looked bright, even feverish. He stood up and lit another cigarette. Dragging, he looked down at Lee, who continued to sit at the table as if she were the accused no less than Baird.

"What's that, Detective?" he asked. "Did I take the words right out of your mouth?"

Lee looked embarrassed. "Word for word," she said.

Lucca shook his head ruefully and turned back to his primary quarry. "So I say to myself: If that was it—if that was how you gained the man's confidence—if that was why he was letting you hang with him, thinking of you now as some kind of audience, a one-man fan club, then my next step is to check our hit list for that night—the night he bought it, according to the old maid and your stolen watch. So I check the list to see what unlucky females were assaulted that night, especially on the Eastside— and what do I come up with? This loony-tunes attack on a stripper named Satin. Two guys. One she never sees who starts beating her to a pulp. And the other who seems to make the first one disappear, then leans down and says, 'Honey, you gonna be all right. Just hang on.' "

Baird wanted to cross his arms on the table and lay his head down. He felt a great weariness in his mind and heart, so much so that he considered giving in and confessing everything to this inhumanly dogged and prescient policeman. He wanted to tell him yes, that he was guilty and proud of it and that he was ready now to sign a confession and accept his punishment. But in the end it was his weariness that saved him. He just sat there, staring at the sergeant, saying nothing.

"I figure it this way," Lucca said. "That you kept giving him rope, and he kept taking it. And finally, when he had enough, when you had your proof—when you saw he was every bit as sick and vicious as you figured he was—you whacked him."

Baird shrugged. "It's an interesting theory."

"Ain't it, though? And ain't it neat we can test it right here today, with that sexy little stripper, Satin? You ready for her, Jack?"

"Why not?" Baird said again. He couldn't think of anything else to say.

They took Baird downstairs to a room adjoining the lineup room. He waited there in the company of a uniformed officer for forty minutes while Lucca assembled the other members of the lineup, who straggled in one and two at a time, most of them detectives. The last two were still putting on ties and tucking in their blue shirts, presumably uniformed officers changing into street clothes.

There were seven men in all, and once they were together, Baird could see that they didn't constitute a fair lineup. Only one of them was Baird's age and height, but he was twenty pounds heavier and had thinning gray hair. The others appeared to be in their thirties or late twenties, possibly because Lucca had wanted men with a full head of hair and no paunch, like Baird. But whatever the sergeant's reasons, the result was the same: a lineup in which no one but Baird could possibly have met Satin's description. Yet he was reluctant to complain about it, reasoning that if Satin did identify him and if the lineup was indeed unfairly constituted, his lawyer might be able to convince the judge to throw out the girl's testimony, if the case were ever to come to trial. Whereas, if Baird complained now, Lucca might simply disband the present group of men and round up another, fairer group—one more difficult for a lawyer to protest later.

So he said nothing. And finally they were told to enter the lineup room. He was fourth in line as the group filed onto the narrow stage and turned to face a bank of bright lights. He was relieved to see the snout of another TV camera up in a corner of the room, for it meant that there would be an incontrovertible record of the lineup. Lucca or a prosecuting attorney could not very easily change the lineup's makeup out of whole cloth later on, in the event it was challenged in court.

Like the other men, Baird just stood there, staring into the brightness. In time, over on intercom, Lucca told one of the other men to stand in profile. Then he told Baird to do the same.

Finally he dismissed everyone but Baird, and the other men filed out. When they were gone, the sergeant appeared in the doorway and asked Baird to follow him, which he did. They went through a second door into the viewing room, where Satin stood waiting, looking both vulgar and stunning in orange sunglasses and a skintight, lime-green pantsuit with a bolero jacket. Lee was standing off to the side, her attitude still that of a spectator more than a participant.

When Baird entered the room, Satin had involuntarily moved back a step. Now, to compensate, to show that she was cool and unafraid, she struck a sexy, casual pose, moving her weight onto one leg and running her fingers back into her long, thick hair. Like a referee, Lucca moved between the two of them, though not so far that he blocked their view of each other.

"All right now, Jack," he said, "I want you to say a certain line to Miss Dean. And in your natural voice, okay?"

"Why not?"

Lucca then gave him the words to say, and Baird repeated them, in a monotone. "Honey, you're going to be all right. Just hang on."

Lucca grimaced. "*That*'s your natural voice? Come on, Jack, give me a break."

"So I'll do it again," Baird said.

"And *natural* this time, okay?"

Baird recited the words again, again in a monotone, only this time raising his voice slightly. Looking disgusted, Lucca told Lee to take Baird into the other room, which she did, leaving the door partially open behind them. As a result, Baird was able to watch as Lucca pressed Satin for an answer. The girl shrugged and shook her head, and Lucca turned first one way and then the other, as if he were trying to avoid a pesky fly. When he spoke to her again, he got the same response.

Lee had been watching too. "Looks like you could be off the hook," she said.

In the other room, Lucca opened a second door for Satin, who left hurriedly, without saying anything more, without even looking at the sergeant, whose face had turned an angry, splotchy red.

"I've never seen that girl before," Baird said to Lee.

The detective regarded him coolly. "Is that a fact?" she said.

Baird knew that boxers often had no memory of being knocked out, so he wasn't surprised that Satin had not been able to identify him. As he understood it, trauma often wiped the slate clean in both directions, before and after, how long depending on the severity of the trauma. Still, the girl somehow had managed to remember the words he'd spoken to her after Slade's attack, as she lay on her back on the sidewalk. Though it was an anomaly he could not explain—why she would remember his words but not his person—he was thoroughly willing to live with it.

Oddly, when he first saw her in the viewing room, he thought he had detected something like recognition in her eyes behind the orange shades, just a millisecond of connection, maybe even compassion, and then it was gone. In any case, he almost loved the girl for disappointing Lucca so greatly. And in the days that followed the interrogation, he thought of her often. In his wilder moments, he even considered going to the Oolala and paying her to dance just for him.

Fortunately, his wild moments were few and far between. His day at police headquarters, and especially his forty minutes in the holding cell, had affected him strongly. Within minutes of being dropped off at his house by Sergeant Lucca, he was on the phone to his lawyer neighbor, Tom Dagleish. Dagleish then phoned a local criminal lawyer, Abe Steiner, whom Baird met with the next morning. Steiner at first was anything but impressive: an old, small, potbellied man with about a dozen black-dyed hairs running from one temple to the other, like cracks in his liver-spotted pate. He wheezed and coughed and squirmed uncomfortably in his sumptuous leather desk chair. And he tied down the finances first, saying that he charged one-fifty an hour and that he would need a two-thousand-dollar retainer just to look into the case. Also, if Baird was indicted and the case went to trial, he could expect to pay upward of sixty-thousand dollars for the attorney's services.

Baird reminded Steiner that he was only being investigated at this point. Getting out his checkbook and beginning to write, he suggested that he pay an initial retainer of one thousand dollars and five thousand more if and when he was indicted. And if the case went to trial, he would continue to pay in increments of five thousand, with a forty-thousand-dollar ceiling.

"I couldn't do more than that," he said. "I'm not a lawyer or doctor, just a paper salesman."

Steiner made a face, as if he'd bitten into a lemon. "I bet you don't give your paper away," he said.

"It's not *my* paper, Mister Steiner. I don't own it."

Shrugging and shaking his head, looking sorely put upon, the attorney finally agreed. "All right, all right—one thousand now and forty tops. I hate to bargain."

"Me too."

Steiner squirmed and sat back, steepling his hands. "So what did you do, Mister Baird? Who was it they say you killed? Just tell me your story."

Baird spent the next hour in the lawyer's office, giving him a detailed account of Slade's harassment of Kathy and of his own attempts to discourage the man. Steiner kept firing questions at him, all to the point, no less incisive than Lucca's had been. And essentially Baird gave him the same story he'd given the sergeant, the only difference being that he admitted he had accompanied Slade to the Oolala on a Saturday in August—though still omitting the vital fact that he also had been there with Slade the night of the killing, nine days later.

He conceded to Steiner that he probably should have admitted this to Lucca—the first visit to the strip club—since there were other dancers and employees who might possibly remember his having been there together with Slade, and that if Lucca questioned them, the truth would probably come out.

Steiner made his lemon face again. "Unimportant, unimportant. A suspect naturally wants to look as innocent as he can, and he fudges here and there. So the two of you were there together—so what? That don't put you with him the night of the murder, or the alleged night, I should say. How can they know? A stopped watch? What bullshit. It could've stopped anywhere, anytime—they don't know any more than we do. And the autopsy—a body that long in the water, they're lucky if they pick the right *week* the guy bought it, for Christ sake. It's a lotta bullshit. They got nothin on you but motive."

"That's good to hear."

Steiner shrugged, as if to say it was nothing, that any fool could have told Baird the same thing.

"Just to be sure I understand Lucca's case," he said, "lemme lay it out for you, make sure I've got it straight. Slade had a history of sex crimes and was the chief suspect in the Ravenna rape. Then he starts stalkin your daughter and even burglarizes your house. When the police don't do nothin about him, you go it alone. You follow him, you meet him, you threaten him, and finally you develop this kind of weird rapport with the guy—the object being to give him enough rope to hang himself. He winds up dead. Lucca shows his mug shot to the dancer, Satin, who was assaulted the alleged night of the murder, just a couple miles away. And she says, yeah, she danced for him and another guy the Saturday before the killin. So Lucca brings you in, expectin her to I.D. you as the guy with Slade at the Oolala, and then a couple days later as one of her two assailants. Right so far?"

"Close enough."

"But she don't, so he's got to release you. But you figure he'll keep digging until he finds someone else at the strip club who *will* be able to I.D. you there on that Saturday night."

"I'm afraid so."

"Okay, let's say he does," Steiner said. "So what? What does he gain? It still don't put you together with Slade on the night of the killin. And it sure as hell don't put you on that bluff at two in the morning, givin Slade the old heave-ho. And one more thing—even if this Satin had identified you as one of her assailants, what good does that do Lucca? She didn't see the second guy. She don't know him from Adam. He could've been Slade, or he could've been Tiny Tim—she don't know. So she can't put you two together, as I see it."

"At least not there."

"And not at the strip club either. She didn't remember you, right?"

"So I gathered."

Steiner made his sour face again. "So they got zilch, my friend. They got nothin. And we don't want to give them nothin. So you don't play footsie with Sergeant Lucca anymore. He picks you up or calls you in, you don't say word one. You call me and I talk to him, understood?"

"Understood."

"Good. Meanwhile I'll wander over there later and see what they think they got. If it's no more than you say, then you're home free. They ain't got a prayer."

Leaving Steiner's office, Baird wanted to feel as optimistic as the little lawyer apparently did. But of course he knew things that Steiner did not. He would have thought that the worst of these was that he knew he was guilty. But that barely crossed his mind. What worried him most was the chance that someone else at the Oolala would remember him—and identify him—as being with Slade on the night of the killing. And he knew that even Steiner would not consider that to be zilch.

Things at home seemed to be improving. Kathy at least appeared to be in better spirits, again sitting close to her father in the evenings as they watched television with Ellen, who knitted steadily, saying almost nothing. Neither woman pressed him about the case, either because they were totally convinced he was innocent or because they were afraid that certain questions might elicit answers they did not want to hear.

After the interrogation, Baird had expected something to appear in the newspapers about the case, at least that the police had brought in a suspect for questioning. But there was nothing, and he imagined the reason for this was that Lucca at the time was running his own private investigation. The sheriff's police, who had jurisdiction, probably hadn't even been told about Baird, and wouldn't be, not until Lucca had the case all wrapped in a neat little bundle so he could take it over to the county building and drop it in their laps, show them and the media how the pros got things done. Whatever the reason, Baird was grateful not to be reading about himself in the papers.

At work he kept silent about the whole affair, knowing that old man Norsten was a stickler for appearances. When one of the other salesmen got a divorce, Norsten insisted that he keep his disgrace as secret as possible, certainly not let his customers know what a miserable failure he was. So Baird felt safe in assuming that the old man would not have enjoyed keeping a murder suspect on the payroll.

More and more, though, Baird felt a need to talk to someone about the case, especially about his own depressing predicament. Leo seemed a logical choice: a close friend with sufficient self-confidence that he wouldn't feel the need to make points with his patrons by spilling secrets. So one slow afternoon, when Leo asked him what had turned him into a doubles drinker, Baird told him the whole story, omitting only the end of it, the fact that he was guilty. He even told Leo about his second night at the Oolala, something he had not shared even with his lawyer. And he confessed that his marriage was on the rocks and that he'd had an affair with one of the detectives on the case, the sexy young woman who had come into the bar to see him on a couple of occasions.

"In short, Leo," he told him, "I feel like I jumped off the Space Needle some time ago and haven't quite reached the ground."

Shaking his head in amazement, Leo made and served him a triple vodka with a dash of tonic. "On the house, man," he said. "Jesus Christ, this is unbelievable."

"Ain't it, though?"

"But the marriage thing, and the black chick—I did know about that."

"What do you mean, you knew about that? I didn't tell anybody about that."

"Sally told me."

Baird laughed wearily. "Sally—Jesus. She ought to work for the *Inquirer*."

"You got a point."

"But don't tell her about this, okay? This is just between us."

"Right."

Yeah, right, Baird thought a few days later, when everybody in the bar began to treat him like a wounded war hero. Serving him, Sally reached out and fervently squeezed his hand.

"It's going to be all right, Jack," she said. "You're going to make it, honey, you hear? And if you need an alibi—any day, any hour—just say the word. You got it."

Forcing a smile, Baird thanked her. He also threw Leo a look that the big man pretended not to see. And he noticed in the days that followed that it was almost impossible for him to pay for a drink. If one of the regulars didn't pick it up, Leo would say it was on the house. Whenever Baird spoke, the others hushed. And when he said something funny, they howled. When Wyatt Earp or Ralston climbed down from their stools and headed for the men's room, which was exceedingly often, they seemed unable to pass Baird without a laying on of hands, a back pat or friendly shoulder poke, as if to assure him that all was well, they were in his corner.

Though he was touched by all this concern and loyalty, he also was made uncomfortable by it. He did not like being made a star, especially for such a dubious achievement. And he couldn't help worrying about what was said in his absence. He could almost hear Leo and Wyatt and Ralston, all the earnest arguments about whether or not he had actually done the deed. Worst of all, he could imagine the numerous non-regulars listening in, fascinated, eager to spread the news to the guys at work or in the bar down the street.

On a Friday night, ten days after Lucca's interrogation, Baird was sitting out on his deck in a winter jacket, smoking cigarettes and nursing a brandy while he gazed out at the lake and the lights of the city. It was a view he knew he would greatly miss if he ever had to move elsewhere, such as prison. After a day spent dealing with small hassles and large worries, he found that the view often brought things into a more tolerable perspective. It made him feel not quite so overwhelmed. And that was a good thing, especially on this night, when Ellen came out and joined him, bundled in a hooded ski jacket. The temperature was hovering around fifty degrees, too cold to sit in any real comfort. So Baird figured that his wife's visit would be brief and casual. But he was wrong.

"It's chilly out here," she said, slipping into the chaise next to his.

"Want some brandy?"

"No thank you." She said nothing more for a short time, then hit him with it. "Jack, I've filed for divorce."

"Just like that?" He was surprised at his self-control.

"No, I've been thinking about it for a long time. And it's not because of your fling, or your drinking, or this Slade thing. In fact, it really hasn't got anything to do with you. I'm lucky to have you, that's what my friends are always telling me. Such a handsome man, they say, and so nice and charming. And I agree. Until lately you've been a terrific husband. But it just doesn't matter anymore. I'm simply tired of marriage. I'm tired of being a mother. I want to live alone. I *yearn* to live alone."

Baird took a gulp of the brandy, then one last drag on his cigarette before flipping it out into the wet grass. "Well, there's not much I can say to that," he said. "I knew you were unhappy. I've known that for a long time. But it never dawned on me that living here was such a trial for you. It's hard to figure—a wife and mother *yearning* she didn't have anyone."

"I didn't say that. I just said I want to live alone."

"It's the same thing, isn't it? But then I guess it really doesn't matter. You want your freedom, of course you can have it—not that it's mine to give or take away. I know I've really put you through hell this summer, and I'm sorry about that."

"Jack, you're not listening. This isn't about us. It isn't about you or anything you've done. It's me, that's all. I want a different kind of life."

"Who'd you see—Dagleish?"

"Yes."

"What kind of life?"

"I've been accepted into law school at the university. Pre-law actually. I figure that I can be practicing by fifty. I want to do legal-aid work for the homeless."

"Sounds real profitable."

"I'm not going into it for the money."

"Dagleish gonna take me to the cleaners?"

"No, I explained that this house is about all we have. A fifty-fifty split, I figure I can live with that."

"So we'll have to sell it?"

"I've already talked to a realtor."

Baird lit another cigarette. For some reason, the thought of her contacting a realtor on her own irritated him every bit as much as her having seen a lawyer. "Busy hands are happy hands," he said.

"You ought to know."

He smiled bleakly. "You've got a point."

"No, it isn't that. Even if it *was* you who took care of that creep, that's not why I want a divorce. I just want a new life."

"I know. You just told me."

"I want to make sure you understand."

Suddenly Baird's eyes had filled. "There is one little problem, though," he said.

"What's that?"

"I still love you."

"And I still love you," she said, with so little feeling he wanted to punch her.

"That much, huh?"

She didn't seem to hear. "But I still feel frustrated and unfulfilled. And I have to change that."

"What about Kathy? Have you told her?"

"Not yet. But she's a big girl now. She's a woman. It's time she went off on her own anyway."

"And Kevin?"

"He's coming down tomorrow morning. I thought we might have a kind of family meeting. I'll tell them about this, and you can fill us all in on the case—where you stand and what you think will happen. I'm sure they're as worried as I am."

"I've told you everything," he said.

"I know, but I'm still worried." She got up from her chair and leaned over him, to kiss him on the forehead. But he tipped his head back and pulled her farther down, to kiss her on the mouth. She pulled back, but he held her there a moment longer, trying to push his mouth into hers. All she would allow, however, was a chaste, sisterly touching of their lips.

"Don't stay too long," she advised. "It's chilly out here."

As she went inside, he smiled sadly. "It sure is," he said.

Ellen held her "family meeting" the next day at lunch. She told Kevin and Kathy not to make any plans for that time, not to go running off anywhere, because there were important matters that had to be discussed. Though both of them seemed impressed by their mother's serious manner, that didn't keep them from making short work of the lunch itself, which consisted of ham sandwiches and a tossed salad. First, Ellen asked Baird to tell them about the "Slade thing," as she called it, so they could have some idea of what to expect. Baird told them about his meeting with Steiner and what the lawyer had concluded.

"He said all they have is motivation, the possibility that we felt threatened by Slade and that I might have decided to end that threat. But the fact is, I didn't kill the man—probably couldn't have even if I'd wanted to—and I wasn't with him. So I'm not worried. Next week they'll probably move on to some other suspect."

Kevin expressed amazement that the police would even bother to investigate his father. "Two minutes with you, you'd think they'd have the sense to see you're not the type. I can't believe they're so stupid. My God, I've got plenty of motivation to kill my accounting prof, but that doesn't mean I'm going to do it."

Baird expected Ellen to point out that the professor had not turned up dead, but she let it pass. Instead, she refolded her napkin, took a drink of water, then quietly dropped her trio of bombs: that she had filed for divorce and had put the house up for sale and would soon be starting law school. Kathy did not respond at all, either because these were developments she had expected or because her mother had already told her of them. But Kevin reacted strongly, becoming angry and tearful. He told Ellen and Baird he realized that their marriage was not a perfectly happy one in recent years—but then whose was, he wanted to know. He accused his mother of expecting too much and of not "standing by Dad in his hour of need." More immediately, he expressed concern about his college funds, whether Baird and Ellen would continue to pay for his tuition and books and half of his living expenses.

"You know, MBA's don't come cheap," he reminded them.

Ellen told him not to worry. "The money will keep coming," she said. "Especially if we're able to sell the house soon. But keep in mind, Kathy still has her schooling ahead of her. And she's thinking of starting Cornish next semester."

This was the first Baird had heard of any such plan, and it pleased him greatly. "Is this true?" he asked, taking hold of Kathy's hand.

She smiled and shrugged. "I guess so. It's about time, wouldn't you say? It's what I'm interested in—fashion design. I'd still work part-time, though."

Baird was grinning. "Well, that's great news, honey. I'm very pleased."

Other than that happy moment, it was a sad little luncheon, much like the last get-together of the employees of a bankrupt company. Ellen was management, cool and efficient, consigning the rest of them to futures they had not sought and did not want. Baird and Kathy were the resigned majority, Kevin the disgruntled minority.

"Where do we go for Thanksgiving?" he asked. "McDonald's?"

The next day he went back to school, and on Monday, Ellen and Kathy went back to work, as did Baird. He coasted through that day and the next three like a drugged man, trying hard not to think about anything except the selling of paper products. Each night he drank heavily and each morning he rose late, after the women had already departed for work.

It was on Friday morning that Sergeant Lucca came calling again, this time with handcuffs and an arrest warrant.

SEVENTEEN

T hough Baird was arrested under a warrant issued to the sheriff's police, Sergeant Lucca acted as if he were in charge of the operation. The man nominally in command, Detective Sergeant Holcomb with the sheriff's police, did not seem to mind. Clean-cut, thirtyish, immaculate in a banker's gray wool suit, he deferred to Lucca with the eagerness of one who knew his authority was unearned.

They let Baird call Steiner from the house, then took him straight to the county jail, where he was booked, fingerprinted, strip-searched, outfitted in a baggy orange jumpsuit, and finally photographed against a height chart, front and profile, just like Slade. Just like a killer, Baird thought.

The jail itself was only a few years old, immensely expensive and already overcrowded, a place of carpeted floors and cells formed of glass instead of iron bars—unbreakable glass that a number of prisoners already had broken through to freedom.

For over an hour Baird languished in a holding cell with a dozen other prisoners. Then two jailers came for him, manacled him, and took him to a small room, where Lucca and Holcomb sat waiting at a conference table. As the jailers left, Lucca told

Baird to sit down at the table, which Baird did, holding up his manacled hands in the process.

"Is this really necessary?" he asked.

"Rules," Lucca said.

"Where's my lawyer?"

"Soon. First we want to give you one last chance, Jack. We've got you cold now. A dancer and bouncer at the Oolala will testify that you were with Slade the night of the murder and that you left together around eleven-thirty. And Miss Dean— the sexy Satin—has helpfully changed her tune and now admits she saw you with Slade at the club that night and that later you were one of her assailants, the one who saved her from the other—obviously Slade. So in a word, Jack, your goose is cooked. You're going to jail for murder-one. If you're smart, you'll go for a plea. We're going to let your lawyer in now and you two can talk it over in private. Then—if you've got any smarts at all—we'll call in a D.A. and wrap this up. Okay?"

Baird said nothing. The two detectives got up and left the room and seconds later Steiner came in, breathing hard.

"The bastards!" the little lawyer bawled, banging his brief-case down on the table. "They got no right talking to you without me here! Fuckin Lucca thinks *he*'s the law! Well, I'm gonna show him a thing or two."

"I didn't say anything," Baird said. "Lucca just told me what they have now, the new stuff. He suggested we go for a plea."

"Is that what you want?"

"No."

"Good. Then we don't. Their case is still all circumstantial. They can't place you at the scene, they don't have the murder weapon, they don't have a fingerprint, they don't have shit. And the stripper changing her testimony—I'll eat her alive. They ain't got a prayer."

"So we go for it," Baird said.

"We plead innocent—right?"

"Right. What else?"

Grinning, Steiner pounded Baird on the back. "Good boy!" he exulted. "That's what I wanted to hear. We gonna make Lucca look like the fuckin jerk he is."

* * *

Baird was arraigned at three o'clock that afternoon, manacled again, feeling as if he were about to faint from humiliation and rage as he sat next to the wheezing Steiner, listening to the judge read the charges against him: murder in the first degree of one James R. Slade, twenty-four, of 628 Thurman Avenue in West Seattle, and second-degree assault and battery upon the person of Miss Terri Dean, twenty, of 1700 104th Street in Juanita.

Ellen and Kathy were in the first row behind Baird. Across the aisle, Lee Jeffers was sitting with Lucca and Sergeant Holcomb just behind the prosecuting attorney, who was a tall, heavy young man with a brute's face and a surprisingly soft and appealing voice. His name was Jimmy O'Neil.

"A real Irish putz," Steiner said to Baird. "You're lucky you ain't got him representin you."

The judge, Josephine Swanson, was about Baird's age, a small, thin woman with iron-gray hair and a look of imperious indifference. As a dime-store clerk, she would have been intimidating. On the bench, she was thoroughly scary—though not to Steiner.

"Old Jolly Josephine," he said. "I'll have her eatin outa my hand."

The courtroom itself was small and quiet, with carpeting and theater seats and walls that soaked up the sound so effectively the judge had to speak into a microphone.

"How do you plead?" she asked.

"Not guilty!" Steiner cried, loud enough to carry into the corridors outside.

"And you, Mister Baird—you agree with your counsel?" the judge asked.

Baird nodded. "Yes. I am innocent."

The proceeding then went on to the matter of bail, with the prosecuting attorney calmly asking that it be set at a half-million dollars, given the gravity of the charges. Steiner, who seemed to have only the one gear—indignant outrage—pounded the table for emphasis as he extolled his client's spotless reputation as a family man and model citizen, as a long-time resident of the city and responsible homeowner. He asked the judge to set bail at one hundred thousand dollars and then thanked her when she compromised at a quarter million. Baird did not feel like thanking anyone.

"What does it mean, that I've got to come up with twenty-five thousand cash? I haven't got it."

Steiner was getting his papers together. "So you get a second mortgage, that's all. And while you're at it, you better make it for a hundred thou, so you can keep me working and feed your family too. You'll probably lose your job."

"That's a comforting thought."

"It's life. Listen, let's just hope we keep Judge Swanson. Bitch is in a permanent coma."

Though the judge may have been bored by the case, the media were not. In the corridor, as a couple of uniformed police led Baird and Steiner back to the jail, reporters and TV people formed a virtual phalanx for them, hurrying along backwards, filming them and throwing questions at Baird, who walked in silence, his head up, indifferent to the cameras and the manacles on his wrists. Whatever the reporters' questions were, he didn't even hear them. All he could think of was the look on Kathy's face as he was being led out of the courtroom: the anguish and disbelief and terror all coming through her tears. Next to her, Ellen looked merely rueful and angry, probably hating him for bringing all this down upon them. Across the aisle, Lucca observed Baird's departure like a proud parent, as if a son of his were graduating magna cum laude. Lee, however, did not even glance Baird's way.

Back in the jail, Steiner and a court clerk led Baird through the necessary maze of paperwork before he could be freed, which he finally was at five-thirty that afternoon.

In the evening, after the last TV van and reporter had given up and driven away, Baird put on a light jacket, got his .38 pistol out of the bed table, and left the house, planning to go for a long walk through Volunteer Park, even though it was already dark and the park was officially closed for the night. He had gone only half a block when Kathy came running up behind him and took him by the hand.

"Want some company?" she asked.

"I'm headed for the park," he told her. "You know, it's not the safest place at night."

"So now you've got me to protect you," she said.

"I guess I can't argue with that."

"It wouldn't do you any good anyway."

For the first few blocks they retraced the route Kathy took from the bus each day, the same route Slade had once walked with her, crooning about death and orgasms while Baird followed in his car. The stretch along Fifteenth Avenue was fairly well lit, more so in front of the condo buildings than the private homes. But once they crossed the avenue and entered the park, they walked in darkness. The blacktop drive glistened from an earlier rain, and many of the leafy trees, half barren now and backlit by the park's old-style streetlamps, shone like silver spiderwebs in the dampness.

Baird and Kathy went past the spot where he had parked that first day, waiting for her bus to come. Then they went down the hill through the towering firs, past the area where the men's room was, the home-away-from-home for the city's more reckless gays. Even now, at night, there were a number of cars parked along the drive. And more than once, Baird's hand slipped into his jacket pocket, to make sure the gun was still there, though he couldn't imagine how he would actually come to use it, a man already charged with murder. But it was nighttime in a dangerous park in a dangerous city, and the gun at least gave him a sense of security.

He and Kathy stayed on the blacktop, coming back up the steep hill to the water tower, where they turned north, heading along the street between the reservoir and the old art museum. Occasionally she would let go of his hand and they would walk on for a few minutes, then he would feel her fingers reaching for him and he would take her hand again. He knew that it was at least uncommon for a girl her age, a woman actually, to walk hand in hand with her father. But considering where they were and how dark it was—and especially where they had been that afternoon—he judged it a harmless and natural thing. And anyway he loved the feeling of her hand in his. It comforted him. It took him back to that lovely time when he was in his early thirties and she was just a child, a time when he was not about to be tried for murder.

Just past the art museum, Kathy led him onto a gravel path that cut across the park, through the trees. And a short distance farther on, she detoured to a nearby bench and sat down.

"I want to talk, Daddy," she said. "I'm going crazy."

Sitting next to her, he sighed in concurrence. "I know, baby. So am I."

It had begun to rain again, so lightly Baird could hardly feel it. But he could see it on his daughter's face, a sheen that accented her perfect features. In the light of the distant streetlamps, her eyelashes appeared tipped with diamonds.

"I know I'm old enough to be on my own," she said. "I know I should be able to live without my father. But I don't know that I can, Daddy. The thought of you in prison—I'm not sure I can live with that."

Her eyes filled and her mouth arched in anguish. Baird took her in his arms. He patted her and kissed her on the forehead and cheek, which tasted lightly of salt.

"You won't have to, honey," he assured her. "Steiner knows what he's doing. And he says the whole case is circumstantial. They have no real evidence. I didn't kill the creep, so how could they prove I did?"

"Then why would they go to all this trouble? Why would the district attorney bother to indict you?"

Baird had already answered these questions at home, explaining as much as he could to her and her mother and brother. But he knew that she needed to hear it again and again.

"It's because I was with him that night, just hours before he was killed. And they have witnesses that I was there. But I'd say the main reason is Sergeant Lucca. The man simply picked me for the crime—his partner told me that. I guess that's the way he works. He decides who did what, then builds his case."

"But why?"

"I don't know. I wish I did."

"A person can be convicted on just circumstantial evidence, can't they?"

"I guess it happens."

"So you really don't know, Daddy. You *could* be convicted. You *could* go to prison."

"But I won't."

She laid her head on his shoulder and hugged him, crying softly. "I don't know if I could make it," she said again. "I love you so much. I know Mother thinks I'm a case of arrested development or even worse, some kind of sicko, an Electra or something. But I just love you, Daddy, that's all. You've always been so good to me, and never judged me, and never tried to hurt my feelings the way she does. And you've loved me, always. I always knew that, no matter what. I always knew my daddy loved me."

She was sobbing now. And Baird was not dry-eyed either. Unable to speak for a time, he hugged her and kissed her head, nuzzling her thick, damp hair.

"That's for sure," he said finally. "I've always loved you, baby. And I always will. And I won't leave you. I won't go to prison."

"You promise?"

"Yes, honey, I promise."

It occurred to him that if anyone had seen the two of them sitting there in the middle of the park in the drizzly darkness, hugging and crying, that person would probably have thought them lovers. But he didn't care. He knew that he loved Kathy only as a father loved a daughter. It was true, he probably cared more for her than he did for anyone else, including his wife and son. And she probably loved him just as much. But he could not see anything wrong in that. In fact, he had little doubt that it was the best thing in his life, something of real value, something to keep him going no matter what lay ahead.

So he did not take it lightly, the promise he had just made to her. At the same time, he knew that in order to keep that promise, he was going to have to do more than wring his hands and hope for the best.

At home, he changed into dry clothes and again left the house. He drove through the university district to Lake City Avenue and went north along the lake, stopping at a number of bars on the way. In each of them he had at least two double vodka tonics, drinking them quickly while he smoked or nibbled on peanuts or whatever other snack the bar provided. No one seemed to recognize him from the television news earlier, which was a considerable relief. He imagined that the bartenders and their patrons simply couldn't make a connection between him as he was now, combed and shaved and wearing a dark-blue blazer and gray flannel slacks, and the poor manacled wretch on TV, lost in a baggy orange jumpsuit.

Nevertheless, when the eleven-o'clock news was about to come on, he drained his glass and hurried out of the last bar, making do after that with a bottle of Reisling bought at a supermarket and drunk in his car, while he was parked outside the Oolala, keeping his eye on Satin's little red Geo Storm.

At twelve-forty-five, when he saw her come out of the building and walk toward the car, he started the Buick and headed for her apartment building, driving as fast as he dared. He still had the .38 pistol with him, though hidden under the seat now in case he was stopped for drunken driving, which he knew was not exactly a long shot for a man who had developed the habit of drinking doubles. Why he had brought the gun after the walk through the park, he wasn't sure. He didn't feel that he was in any particular danger now, and he certainly had no intention of using it on Satin. Yet there it was, stashed directly under him. Smiling in alcoholic whimsy, he wondered if he had brought the thing along just in case he happened to run into Sergeant Lucca somewhere—say, on a lonely bluff above the lake.

When he reached Satin's apartment house, he found the parking lot much better lit than it had been on the night of the killing. Also, the evergreens that had bordered the walkway had been replaced with ornamental shrubs too small for anyone to hide behind. He went around to the south side of the building, where the entrances to the individual apartments were. At the front there was a recessed bank of mailboxes, each with a tiny space for the tenant's name. T. Dean, he saw, was in Number Twenty-three, on the second floor. He knew that she would be frightened when she first saw him, so he tried to make himself appear as innocuous as possible, sitting down on the bottom stair, ready at any moment to rest his head on his arms, in the manner of a common street drunk—not exactly a stretch for him, he reflected.

Within a few minutes he heard a car turn in and saw the beam of its headlights darting through the trees. He heard it pull into a parking space, then its door opening and closing, followed by the sound of spiked heels on the walkway. When she came around the corner of the building, he didn't even look up, not until she spoke.

"What are you doing here? What do you want? You're not supposed to be here! Sergeant Lucca said—"

"I know, I know," Baird said. She was standing next to the mailboxes, holding her right hand inside her purse, and he wondered if he was about to be shot or maced. "I'm not here to hurt you," he went on. "I just want to talk to you. I want to know why you changed your testimony."

"Because I decided to tell the truth, that's why. Now you know, you can leave."

She was wearing a tan cable-knit sweater and a short, tight brown-leather skirt. Her abundant hair was hanging loose.

"I just want to talk with you," he said again, getting heavily to his feet. "You know, if I'm who you say I am, then I probably saved your life."

For a few more seconds she continued to stand there motionless, floodlit, undecided. Then she withdrew her hand from the purse, and he was relieved to see that it wasn't holding a gun but a key ring attached to a fuzzy pink ball. She moved past him on the stairs.

"All right, come on up," she said. "But only for a few minutes, all right?"

"Yes. Thank you."

Inside, she flipped on a wall switch and a pair of dim, heavily shaded lamps came on, barely lighting the apartment, which was quite small, just a living-dining area, a kitchenette, bedroom and bathroom. In the dimness, Baird had the feeling that he had stumbled into Bramante's by mistake. When Satin switched on a stereo, though, it was not Dean Martin he heard but a heavy-metal band, mercifully turned low. She went into the kitchenette and got a Coke out of the refrigerator.

"You want anything to drink?" she asked, reaching for a lone bottle of rum.

"Rum and ice would be fine," he said.

She made his drink first, then her own, rum and Coke mixed half and half. "I usually don't have the hard stuff," she said. "My mother was a lush."

"That's too bad."

"Yeah. Tell me about it." She got two white pills out of a prescription bottle and washed them down.

"Tranks," she said. "Ever since the assault, I've been real tense."

"That's understandable."

After she had given him his drink, Baird went into the living area and stood there waiting for her.

"Well, sit down," she said. "Who do you think I am—Princess Diana?"

He took her advice, sitting in a cushioned wicker chair. She kicked off her shoes, a pair of brown pumps, and dropped onto the sofa.

"What do you think of the place?" she asked. "I decorated it myself."

Baird had no doubt of that. In addition to the white wicker living-room set, there was a large, velour-framed wall mirror hanging above a pair of green polka-dot beanbag chairs. In the dining area there was a smoked-glass table with chairs made of black plastic and gold-colored metal tubing. There were gauzy pink throw rugs and a half-dozen enlarged wall photos framed in velour of different colors. It was the photos themselves, however, that dominated the place, all of them of Satin, all in color, and all astonishingly beautiful. Two were of her face and one was a shot of just her eyes, but the other three were full-figure pictures of her dancing nude. They were so compelling that Baird had a hard time paying attention to the girl herself, who was sitting right in front of him. And this seemed to please her. She smiled and laughed.

"Everybody says I'm a real narcist," she said, dropping a syllable. "I mean, having all these pictures of me here, and in my working clothes. But I say why not? It's what I do. And I work hard to stay in shape, and I know I'm not always going to look this way."

Baird was trying hard to conceal how drunk he was. Even on the stairs, he had moved with great care, knowing that if he tripped or made a fool of himself in some other way, she would not want to talk with him. So he spoke carefully now, trying not to slur his words.

"Even old, you'll still be beautiful."

"Oh, come on."

"No, I mean it. Your eyes won't change, and your face—your bone structure—will still be the same. You'll look older, but still beautiful."

Though she was smiling, she looked embarrassed too, and he wondered if she was blushing. In the dimness, it was hard to tell.

"But then, you didn't let me in just to hear compliments," he said. "So I might as well get to it. It's like I said outside, Terri—I'd really appreciate it if you could explain it to me, why you changed your testimony."

Her smile faded. "I already told you—because it's true. Sergeant Lucca told me about lying in court and what could happen to me. Perjury, it's called. I could've went to prison."

"You didn't know that before?"

"Not like he told me. And anyway, it's true, isn't it? You *were* one of them."

"If that's so, why did you lie at first?"

She sipped at her drink. "I don't know. It just seemed easier, that's all."

"And now it's not?"

"It sure isn't. I'm telling you, that Lucca can scare the hell out of you. Not only the perjury thing, but he also said he'd get on my case full time. He said he'd keep hassling me—haul me in for prostitution and like that. And I never hooked in my whole life."

"He can't do that. It's illegal. It's intimidating a witness."

"All he wanted, he said, was the truth."

"That 'truth,' Terri, might put me in prison for the rest of my life. You realize that?"

She looked uneasy. "You know, you really shouldn't be here. I think maybe it's time for you to go."

"Oh, come on, honey," he said, forgetting himself. "There's no reason to be afraid. I'd never hurt you. I'm not Slade, you know."

" 'Honey.' " She smiled shyly. "That's what you called me that night."

"It's a habit, I guess. I have a daughter about your age."

Baird was finding it hard to concentrate. He had to keep reminding himself that he had come here for a specific purpose: that if he couldn't persuade her to go back to her original position, unable to identify him, then he at least had to convince her—*remind* her—that she had not even glimpsed the other assailant and therefore could not identify him as Slade. Steiner had told Baird more than once that if Lucca or the D.A. got to the girl, somehow convinced her that she had seen both Baird *and* Slade together just ten or fifteen minutes before the murder was alleged to have taken place—that, Steiner said, would be the ball game. Baird would be convicted.

"So you will identify me in court," he said now. "As one of the two men."

"Well, it's *true*, isn't it?"

"But it's also true that you didn't see the other man."

"That's what I keep telling Lucca. But he says I did see him, that I had to see him."

"But you didn't, Terri. You never saw the man behind you. And if you say you did, that would be perjury."

"I know, I know." She shook her head in confusion.

"You would be lying, and I would probably go to prison for that lie."

"I don't want that," she said. "I won't lie for Lucca—I promise."

"You mean that?"

"Yes," she said. "Yes, I really mean it."

Baird felt as if a boulder had been rolled off his chest. "Thank you," he said. "You're a good girl, Terri. Not just beautiful, but good."

She shrugged in embarrassment. Smiling slightly, she sipped at her drink again, and for a time, neither of them said anything. Like a shy child, she stared down at her hands, folded in her lap. Then finally she spoke.

"You know, my father never called me honey or anything like that. Not even my name much."

"That was his loss," Baird said.

"In high school, if I came home late, he'd call me a harlot. Or a painted woman, he'd say, like we were living in Bible times. He was real religious, especially after my mom ran off. He never smiled. And he never called me honey."

"Maybe he wanted to," Baird suggested. "Some people just shut off their feelings. They become like cripples."

The stereo had switched to an album of songs by Carly Simon. And Baird caught himself looking at the nude photos again. The girl caught him too, and he smiled in embarrassment.

"It's hard not to look," he confessed. "They're not your average living-room pictures."

"You know, it's funny," she said. "I remember couch-dancing for you and that Slade. And you wouldn't look at me then. You kept turning away."

"Well, it's not that easy. I mean, when you're right there, so close."

"Why?"

Baird wasn't sure how to answer her, or even that he wanted to. "Maybe because I felt a little naked myself," he tried.

She looked puzzled. "How do you mean?"

"Well, look at you," he said, indicating the pictures. "You must know that every man who sees you wants you. And there I was, a man old enough to be your father. I guess I felt that if I looked right at you, you'd see what a dirty old man I was."

"I'd never think that."

"Well, I did," he said. "And listen, it wasn't easy—I mean, not looking at you."

"You really think I'm beautiful?" she asked.

"Of course I do."

"Most guys, they say I'm sexy or that I'd be a good piece of ass. Stuff like that. They make you feel like meat."

"You don't look like meat, believe me."

She smiled again. "You're real nice, you know that?"

"Sergeant Lucca doesn't think so."

"Screw him." The girl put her drink down on the coffee table and sat back on the sofa, clasping her hands in her lap again, all the while looking over at Baird in a way he couldn't read. For a few moments he thought she was amused by him, but then her eyes suddenly filled.

"Lucca says your daughter looks like me."

"It's true. She does."

"You love her a lot?"

"Yes."

"Lucca says that's why you killed Slade—to protect her."

"He's entitled to his opinion."

"Would you kill to save her life, though?"

Baird raised his glass and drank, wishing—not very logically—that he was more sober, more in control of his tongue. "I think most fathers would," he said.

Satin shook her head. "Not mine. He wouldn't lift a finger."

"You don't know that."

"Yes, I do."

She was still sitting there with her hands in her lap, and her eyes were streaming now. Getting a handkerchief out of his jacket, Baird went around the coffee table to give it to her, but she didn't seem to notice it. He sat down next to her then, still holding the kerchief. Finally she took it.

"When my mom left, I did everything I could," she said. "I did the cooking and cleaning, and I did my best to keep my grades up. But he never thanked me. He hardly ever spoke. Only when I'd come home late. Then he'd holler and yell all that Bible stuff. And I'd wonder what I'd ever done to make him hate me so."

She began to cry, and Baird patted her on the shoulder.

"You should try to forget him," he said. "You've got your whole life ahead of you."

"But I don't like my life that much. I don't like what I do, most of it anyway. The dancing is okay, and the money, but the guys make you feel like a whore."

Baird took another swallow of rum, and it was like the water drop that bursts the dam. Suddenly he felt hopelessly drunk, stupid, tongue-tied. In fact he felt much the same as he had that second night with Slade, when it had seemed as if he were driving through a tunnel. He had the feeling that his consciousness, like his vision, was beginning to fray and blur.

"Hell with those guys," he said. "You're a good girl, Terri. A good, beautiful girl."

She shook her head. "No, I'm not."

"Sure you are—and remember, I'm bigger than you." As he patted her arm, she moved closer to him.

"Would you hold me?" she asked.

He put his arm around her, all the while continuing to pat her as if she were a child. But he could feel her body even through his jacket, and the smell of her—light perfume and secret sweats—hit him as hard as the rum. She tilted her face up to him, the tears still welling out of her eyes. And she absently crossed her legs in such a way that her tiny skirt climbed almost to her panties. As tired as he was, he closed his eyes for a few seconds and it seemed as if he were in the park again, feeling the light rain on his face and seeing it on hers, the diamond-tipped eyelashes.

"Why would he hate me so much?" she asked.

"I don't know, honey. I can't imagine."

"I'm so unhappy."

She turned her face in against his neck and he unthinkingly began to kiss her on the forehead and in her hair. She raised her head then, her eyes half-closed, and he kissed her lightly on the lips. Her tongue moved into his mouth and he pushed his hand under her sweater, onto her breasts, which were bra-less, full and firm. Later he would have a hard time remembering how things had developed after that. He would remember feeling that he was still only consoling the girl, holding and patting her. Yet there were the other things too, scraps of memory blowing through his mind. He remembered seeing her pull her sweater over her head, and he remembered the taste of her breasts and the feel of her hand pushing into his pants and closing on him. It seemed that only moments later they were both naked on the sofa and he was taking her in his arms, and he had the impression that a wind was blowing and that her body was slick from the rain.

Then he heard her voice, a soft cry of pleasure, nothing more. Yet it struck him like ice water in the face, for he realized suddenly exactly where he was and with whom he was, and worse, *what* he was. He pulled away then and staggered to his feet, barking his shin on the coffee table. He lurched across the living-dining area and made it into the bathroom, where he fell to his knees in front of the stool, retching violently, wanting to vomit, *needing* to vomit. But nothing came.

When he finally emerged, Satin gave him a commiserating smile. She had put on a terry-cloth robe and was sitting in the wicker chair.

"What a lousy time to get sick," she said.

She had picked up his clothes and laid them on the coffee table, which meant that he had to dress in front of her. He did it quickly and clumsily.

"If you want to call me sometime . . ." she suggested. "I guess you could say we have some unfinished business."

He wondered how the girl could even stand to look at him.

"I don't know—there's the trial," he said.

"After, then."

"Yes. After."

She got up as he started for the door, but he didn't wait for her. Mumbling good-bye, he left the apartment and hurried down the stairs. By the time he reached his car he was blinded by tears and the car keys were shaking in his hand.

EIGHTEEN

On the following Wednesday, at nine in the morning, Baird again found himself sitting in the same cozy courtroom, this time for the preliminary hearing, which Steiner claimed he was going to turn into the *final* hearing, convincing the judge to drop all charges against Baird. Should he fail, though, he assured his client that the trial itself was going to be "big, really big," because even the present hearing had filled the courtroom and left scores of would-be spectators lined up in the corridor, hoping to get in.

The media also were in full attendance, even the TV people, since Steiner had persuaded Baird to go along with the prosecutor and Judge Swanson, neither of whom objected to having cameras in the courtroom.

"We ain't got nothin to hide," Steiner said to Baird, the bad grammar a continuing affectation that miraculously disappeared whenever the little lawyer addressed the court or a TV camera. "We keep our chin up, and we look bright and interested," he went on. "Cuz we ain't killed nobody. But we're curious, like everyone else. We want justice."

It was obvious to Baird that the person who wanted TV coverage the most was Steiner himself, who seemed to grow a foot every time a camera was turned his way. In the end, though, Baird approved the coverage only because he didn't care one way or the other.

Among the crowd, he saw a number of his friends and co-workers, including an entire row of regulars from Leo's, with the man himself and Sally sitting nearest the aisle. Not far from them were Satin and another dancer and one of the bouncers from the Oolala. Again Lucca and Lee Jeffers and Sergeant Holcomb were sitting in the row behind the prosecutor's table. Lee looked noticeably uncomfortable, perhaps because she was wearing a dress. Lucca, though, had the expression of a man who had just sat down to a lobster dinner. All he lacked was a bib.

Ellen and Kathy and Kevin were right behind Baird. And there would have been other family members too—brothers and sisters, aunts and uncles, from Illinois and points east—but Ellen had convinced them not to come until the trial itself, and even then, only if they insisted. He was innocent, she had told them. He would be acquitted.

Baird was wearing a gray business suit, white shirt, and blue knit tie, certainly an improvement over the orange jumpsuit and manacles he had worn at the arraignment. On that score alone he knew he should have felt better than he had on the earlier occasion. But he did not. In fact, ever since he'd left Satin's he had felt a pessimism and depression like no other in his life. He had come to realize as never before how thoroughly and un-speakably he had betrayed his wife and daughter, loving the one not enough—and the other too much, and in a way he had never suspected, never dreamed of.

It was a failure—an *evil*—that seemed to strike at the very heart of his life, making him suspect almost everything about himself, everything he was, everything he had done. He had even begun to wonder about the killing of Slade. All during the past week he kept asking himself why he had not stayed with his original plan and called in the police once he had subdued the man and rescued Satin, and his answers no longer satisfied him. Yes, the creep eventually would have gotten out of prison, and yes, he undoubtedly would have come after Baird and Kathy, and yes, he would have posed a perennial threat to other women. But still—to just stand there in the starry night and pump bullets into the man's chest and head—did an adulterous pervert really have that right?

Baird was not so sure anymore, not about that or anything else. So it had been a difficult week, with everyone but Ellen asking him what was wrong, why he was so quiet, why he wanted to be alone so much of the time. Steiner had even warned him that he had better shape up and stop brooding or they would surely lose the case. As usual, Kathy was the worst. Over and over she would come to him for reassurance and love, only to get a pained smile and a pat on the shoulder. And even when her eyes would fill and she would beg him to tell her what was wrong, all he could do was shake his head and walk away.

These feelings of guilt and remorse were not so overwhelming, however, that they sapped his will to live or made the prospect of imprisonment any more appealing. He followed the proceedings with the consuming interest of a man on trial for his life, which of course he was.

At the moment, the prosecuting attorney was holding forth, and on this day Baird did not find Jimmy O'Neil's voice at all appealing as the large young man verbally reconstructed Baird's crime brick by brick, like a mason building a wall. He told the judge about Slade's juvenile crimes and how much of his childhood he had spent in various juvenile facilities; he explained about Slade's time in Hollywood, living with a gay art director whom he ultimately robbed and crippled by beating the man with his own Oscar statuette, a crime that resulted in Slade's one incarceration as an adult: two years in Soledad prison.

O'Neil told about the rape of Barbara Evans in the Ravenna area and why the detectives on the case held Slade to be the chief suspect. The prosecutor then moved on to Baird's case and the similarities in the way Slade had stalked both Evans and Kathy, saying many of the same obscene things to both women. Then O'Neil called Sergeant Lucca to the stand.

The detective made his way to the witness chair just as Baird had known he would, shuffling forward, looking tired and bored, the old pro wearily going to work. Indifferently he tried to button the jacket of his single-breasted blue suit, then gave it up as he took the oath and sat down. O'Neil had him identify himself, then began the questioning, asking about his first contact with the defendant. Lucca told about Baird coming to the squad room in late June with his wife and daughter and making the complaint against Slade.

"And when you told the defendant that all the police could do was help him get a restraining order against Slade, was he grateful for this help?"

"No, not at all," Lucca said. "He was disappointed and angry. I got the feeling he expected us to arrest and incarcerate Slade, just based on his complaint."

Steiner objected strenuously, and Judge Swanson sustained.

"Withdrawn," O'Neil said, like the others content to play their silly game, pretending something said and heard could be rendered unsaid, unheard. He then asked Lucca whether he or any other members of the Metro Squad had had any other contacts with the defendant, and Lucca told him about Detective Joe Daniels seeing Baird and Slade coming out of Harold's Club together on the thirtieth of June.

"Did this worry you, Sergeant?" the prosecutor asked. "Did you do anything about it?"

"Yes," Lucca said. "I went out of my way to do so. I went to the defendant's house and warned him against trying anything on his own against Slade. I told him he was playing with fire."

"And as far as you know, was that the last contact the defendant had with Slade?"

"No, it was not."

Lucca went on then, telling about the burglary at Baird's house, giving special emphasis to the mutilated teddy bear and Baird's stolen watch. O'Neil brought out that Baird had insisted to the police that Slade was the burglar. The prosecutor said that Detective Jeffers would testify to this at the trial. Lucca then testified about Lester Wall coming in voluntarily after Slade's body was found. The sergeant said that Wall had told him about the meeting at Gide's bar, recounting how Slade had said to Wall—in front of Baird—that Baird had threatened to shoot him if he didn't stop pursuing Baird's daughter. Lester Wall, O'Neil said, would also be a witness at the trial.

Steiner at that point leaned toward Baird and wheezed in his ear, "What a putz this O'Neil is. I'm gonna make mince meat out of him."

"We are now at the heart of the state's case," the putz said, "the point at which things move from motivation to action. Why the defendant, this college graduate, this forty-seven-year-old family man, would be running around drinking and taking in strip joints with a drug-dealing ex-con, a possible rapist and murderer—that's the sixty-four-thousand-dollar question, Your Honor. And the answer is this: the defendant wanted Slade's guard down. He wanted to give Slade enough rope to hang himself. Only in this case, it was the defendant who did the hanging."

Judge Swanson tapped her gavel lightly. "Just the evidence, Counselor, all right?"

"Of course, Your Honor." The prosecutor returned to Lucca. "Now, Sergeant, once you learned of James Slade's death—once his body was recovered—how were you able to link his murder to the defendant? In other words, what is it that led to the arrest of Jack Baird?"

Baird knew that this was a special moment in Lucca's life, one of those rare occasions when a man is able to demonstrate before the world what it is that sets him apart from his peers. But as Baird expected, the man did not preen at all, did not sit up straighter or speak louder or clearer. Still, Baird had no trouble seeing his joy.

"Well, I knew where the body was found and the approximate time of death, because of the defendant's watch—found on the body—and the statement given by the maid, Mrs. Jessup, who heard Slade's car being dumped in the lake. But there was no real connection with Mister Baird until I started looking into crimes committed at that same time and in that same area—with particular attention to the sort of thing Slade might have been involved in. That's when I came upon the assault on Miss Terri Dean—a very odd assault, I might add."

Judge Swanson interrupted at that point to remind the prosecutor that this was only a preliminary hearing, and that he was going into too much detail, that only the salient facts were needed. The burly O'Neil thanked the judge for her advice, then went on as before, carefully drawing out of Lucca the full story of his investigation: the continuing sequence of fortuitous hunches and discoveries. When they finished, O'Neil smiled gratefully and thanked the sergeant, who then got up and duck-walked back to his seat, his coat still open, his expression unchanged. Once he was seated, Baird forced himself not to look over at him, half expecting to see the man burping contently, raising his bib and daubing at his mouth, wiping away the melted butter and bits of flesh.

The prosecutor meanwhile had turned to the judge in triumph. "In short, Your Honor, thanks largely to Sergeant Lucca's diligent work on this case, we now have three witnesses who will testify that the defendant and James Slade were together at the Oolala nightclub on Lake City Avenue on Saturday night, the fifteenth of August. Two of the witnesses are dancers, and one is a bouncer at the club, a man who knew Slade's reputation as an ex-con and drug dealer. The bouncer and one of the dancers also will testify that the defendant was at the club with Slade nine days later, on Monday night, the twenty-fourth of August—in other words, on *the night of the murder!*"

"Objection!" Steiner bawled. "The day and hour of the victim's death are not known, Your Honor. All the prosecution has on that score is woolly speculation."

The judge sighed. "Again, Counselor, this is not a trial."

"The *alleged* night of the murder," the prosecutor amended. "The defendant and Slade were seen leaving together at around eleven-thirty that night. Two hours later, the dancer known as Satin—Miss Terri Dean—was assaulted outside her Bothell apartment by two men, one of whom then apparently attacked the other. Miss Dean will testify that the defendant, Jack Baird, was one of these men. And keep in mind that Miss Dean's apartment is only a few minutes' drive from the spot where Slade's body—shot three times—was dumped in the lake, locked in the trunk of his own car."

Jimmy O'Neil then outlined the testimony that would be given by Alma Jessup, the live-in maid. And finally he said that at the trial itself, he would put Lucca back on the stand.

"The sergeant will give testimony," he said, "about his interrogation of the defendant. And we will run a video of part of that interrogation—the part in which the defendant uses these words in reference to Slade: 'I would kill him.'"

Even in the carpeted hush of the courtroom this caused a

considerable stir, and Baird's heart sank. Judge Swanson gaveled
for quiet. The prosecutor meanwhile had closed his notebook
and sat down.

"That's the gist of our case, Your Honor," he said.

The judge looked dolefully up at the wall clock. "There's
still an hour before lunch break," she observed, looking at
Steiner. "Would you like to start now, Counselor, or wait till
after the break?"

Steiner was up on the balls of his feet, rocking precariously.
"No need to wait, Your Honor. Considering the state's case—or
lack of a case, I should say—I can start and finish well before the
break."

"Then we shall be grateful," the judge said, gesturing for the
little lawyer to proceed.

Small though he was, Steiner had a voice that needed no am-
plification in the sound-deadening room. Right off, he conceded
most of the prosecution's case, admitting that Baird had a motive
for killing Slade—"as did every other decent Northwest man
with a daughter," he added. And he admitted that Baird had ini-
tiated contact with Slade and had been out drinking with him on
three separate occasions.

"And the prosecution wonders why!" he thundered. "*Actually wonders why!* Even he admits you couldn't find two less likely
drinking buddies if you scoured the earth for them. Mister Clean
and this ex-con, this drug-dealing rapist, this bisexual whore to
the gay community."

Steiner turned and looked at Baird, threw out his hand as if
he were an emcee introducing a Hollywood star. "And yet, this
man—this one-time teacher and now successful businessman,
with scores of friends who will testify that he's the absolute tops,
the tower of Pisa, the flat-out best there is—this family man
with a lovely wife and two beautiful kids who love him dearly—
this man goes out bar-crawling with . . ." Up on his toes again,
Steiner looked to the ceiling for inspiration. ". . . with this sewer
creature! With this bottom feeder!"

Judge Swanson leaned toward her mike. "Again, Counselor,
I remind you that this is only the preliminary hearing. There is
no jury present."

"I apologize, Your Honor," Steiner said. "It's just that this case, it really gets to me. That a man such as this could be tried for murder on so little evidence. It's not easy to be calm."

"Try," the judge advised.

"I certainly will." Steiner bent to his papers, shuffling them to no apparent purpose. Then he returned his attention to the bench. "So my client goes bar-hopping with this . . . this Jimbo Slade. Why? Why on earth would he do such a thing? After all, Slade was stalking his daughter. Slade had burglarized his house. Slade had a long history as a sexual predator and was even the chief suspect in the brutal rape of another local woman whom he had stalked in much the same way as he had Mister Baird's daughter. Also, he was a viable suspect in another recent rape in our city, as well as two unsolved murders! Yes, that's right— *murders!* So why on earth would this man—Jack Baird—have anything to do with such a character?"

Pausing to straighten the hairs across his pate, Steiner looked from the prosecutor's table to the bench, as if he expected a response.

"Why else," he shouted suddenly, *"except to befriend the man?* To get to know Slade! To let Slade get to know him! All in the hope that this monster might stop thinking of him and his daughter as mere objects in his life—*things* actually, mere things that he could step on or not step on, depending on his whim of the moment. So, in a word, Jack Baird tried to co-opt the man. He tried to neutralize him with friendship. If in time old Jimbo—as Slade called himself—if old Jimbo just had to go out and find himself some beautiful young woman to rape and kill, just maybe he would overlook his new friend's daughter. Like the Angel of Death himself, just maybe Jimbo Slade would pass over Jack Baird's door."

Though the judge looked as if she were about to drop off, the crowd was quiet and attentive. And Steiner obviously was confident that he had them, the way he began to strut out in front of the tables now.

"Let us stick to the facts," he said, beginning to count on his fingers. "One, we concede that Jack Baird did go out drinking with James Slade on three separate occasions, the last one being the alleged night of the murder. So the state can forget about its witnesses in that regard—the dancer and bouncer who claim to have seen my client leave the strip joint with Slade around eleven on the night of August twenty-four. We concede that. And two: as for the other witness—the stripper, Satin—the first time she viewed the defendant in a lineup, she could *not* identify him. *Absolutely did not know him from Adam.* The arresting officer, Sergeant Lucca, will testify to that—as a hostile witness, I presume. So which Satin are we to believe? The one who never saw my client before, or the one who is apparently going to come into this courtroom and testify—for the moment anyway—that she did see him after all? I know which one I'd believe—*neither!*"

Steiner paused there to take a drink of water and rearrange his hair. Then he proceeded again, moving on to his third finger.

"And three, let us keep in mind that this youthful stripper—Satin or Terri Dean or whatever else she calls herself—even she does not claim to have seen the murder victim after-hours outside her apartment house, as one of the two men alleged to have assaulted her on the night of August twenty-four. Whoever he was, this assailant, she admits she never laid eyes on. He seized her from behind, she says, and punched her into unconsciousness. So even if she erroneously identifies my client as having been on the scene that night—as the assailant who saved her life, I believe that's how she puts it—that still doesn't put my client and the victim together in Bothell early Tuesday morning, just a few minutes before the killing is alleged to have taken place! Remember that!" The little lawyer turned from the crowd at that point and faced the bench again, moving on to his pinkie finger.

"And four, Your Honor, we will hear from my client's wife, who will testify that her husband came home between eleven and eleven-thirty that night and was safely in bed beside her when the victim—the rapist-murderer Jimbo Slade—met his maker a good ten miles away, on the other side of Lake Washington!"

The little lawyer was again rocking on the balls of his feet, weighing his next words, when another voice, clear and strong, was heard.

"I beg your pardon, Your Honor, but that is not quite true."

Lights flashed, cameras whirred, and a wave of sound—spectators whispering to each other—swept through the courtroom. Judge Swanson banged her gavel, and Baird turned to look, though he already knew that it was Ellen who had spoken.

She was on her feet now, resting her hands on the partition that separated the spectators from the participants. Her short hair was neatly coiffed and she was wearing one of her handsome tweed suits. She looked as calm as ice, unlike Kathy and Kevin, who were sitting next to her. In their shock and surprise, they looked to their father for an answer, but all he could do was shrug, signaling that he didn't know what was going on either—though he was afraid he did. It was payback time, he imagined. A sweet few minutes of revenge, and in public, for all the world to see. He thought of that overworked line about revenge being a dish best served cold.

Steiner by now had regained his voice. "Hey, what is this?" he bawled. "This is my witness, Your Honor! And what she told me earlier—what she swore to—that's the only testimony this court should hear!"

The judge's eyebrows arched higher. "Even if it's not true?" she said, looking past Steiner now, at Ellen. "You're the defendant's wife?"

"Yes, I am."

"And the testimony the defense counsel expected you to give at the trial—you wish to amend it?"

"Yes."

Steiner looked as if he were about to have a stroke. He banged his fist on the table, then advanced on the bench, his hands lifted, imploring.

"Your Honor, this woman can't testify here now! As you yourself have pointed out, this is not a trial! The only proper way to handle this matter is to call a recess so I can confer with the witness again and clear up this matter. I've had no indication of any contrary testimony."

"But we have that indication now," the judge said. "And since it appears that this witness has already lied once—to you— I see no reason not to put her under oath and get to the bottom of the matter. If you don't like her testimony, maybe the prosecution will. And that's what we're here for—to learn what each side has." She looked again at Ellen. "Will you come forward, Mrs. Baird, and testify under oath?"

"Yes, of course."

"I take exception!" Steiner bellowed.

The judge nodded. "So noted."

Baird watched Ellen as she sidled past Kevin and came through the gate, heading for the stand. He didn't hate her for what she was doing, but it surprised him that she hated him enough to do it. After taking the oath, she sat down in the witness chair.

Judge Swanson leaned toward her. "All right now, Mrs. Baird. The defense counsel stated that in the coming trial you will testify that your husband came home between eleven and eleven-thirty on the night of August twenty-four—the night the prosecution claims that James Slade was murdered. Will that be your testimony?"

"No, it won't be."

"When did your husband come home?"

As hushed as the courtroom now was, Ellen was able to speak at her normal level, almost conversational.

"For a number of weeks he had been keeping late hours, usually coming home long after midnight. On the night in question—which happens to be my parents' wedding anniversary—I was unhappy and suspicious, and I couldn't sleep. So I got in my car and drove around. I went past my husband's favorite bar, but I didn't see his car outside. And then I tried to think, wondering if he was actually seeing another woman, just who that woman might be. And the only one who came to mind was someone whose address I already knew—I'd looked it up before and had driven past her house one other night when my husband was out late. So I knew where it was. Anyway, I drove past the house again—oh, it must have been about eleven-forty-five—and this time I did see him. He evidently had just arrived. He was up on the porch, knocking on the door. Then the door opened and I saw the woman inside. My husband entered the house, and the door closed."

Judge Swanson squirmed. "I realize we're getting into a rather delicate area here," she said. "But then, this *is* a murder case. Mrs. Baird, can you identify the woman your husband was with that night?"

Ellen raised her hand and pointed directly beyond the prosecutor's table. "Yes," she said. "It was that woman, Your Honor. It was Detective Lee Jeffers."

NINETEEN

There was a brief tumult in the courtroom after Ellen named Lee Jeffers as the woman Baird had been with at the time of the killing. While the judge gaveled for silence, Baird glanced back across the aisle and saw Lucca staring at his partner as if she had turned into a pillar of dung. And the sergeant's mood did not improve at all when Lee, replacing Ellen on the stand, testified that she had thought Baird's first visit to her home had occurred on the night of the twenty-fifth, not the twenty-fourth.

"Which is why I never mentioned it," she went on. "I didn't feel it was relevant."

"And is that your testimony here?" the judge asked. "That the defendant visited you on the twenty-fifth, not the twenty-fourth?"

Lee paused for a moment, looking straight at Baird. Then she shook her head. "No, I can't swear to it. I'm not that positive."

After dismissing her, Judge Swanson leaned close to her microphone and announced acidly that since the police working on the case were now the defendant's alibi, and since there was no other solid evidence against him, she was dismissing the murder charge.

"As for the assault charge," she went on, addressing the prosecutor, "your witness waffles on the I.D. a bit too much to suit me. So I'm dismissing that count too." Still not smiling, the lady then looked at Baird and told him he was free to go.

Ten minutes later, under the massive portico of the courthouse, there was no judge to quell the tumult. Kevin had run on ahead to get the car, so Baird and Ellen and Kathy, along with Steiner, had to stand and wait, much to the joy of the media. The reporters and cameramen were in a mild frenzy, surging back to the portico after having chased Satin and her co-workers halfway down the street. Their hunger seemed at least partially to mitigate Steiner's obvious disappointment at the sudden turn of events. Baird wasn't sure what the little lawyer mourned most: losing the income from an extended trial or losing the starring role he would have played in the trial.

As exhausted as he was, Baird gave the media all the platitudes they wanted. Yes, he was immensely relieved at the outcome of the case. And yes, he was very proud of his wife, that she had come forward and "saved his bacon," especially in such difficult circumstances. Would there be a reconciliation between the two of them now? No comment, Baird said. As did Ellen. As for Kathy, the reporters wanted to know how she felt about her father. Had she always thought him innocent?

"Of course," she said, holding onto Baird's arm, smiling shyly. "How could he be anything else?"

Though Steiner was left without much to talk about, he did not let that discourage him. The reporters and cameramen who happened his way probably got more words and footage than they wanted. And they promptly abandoned him when they saw Lucca and Lee coming out of the building, moving past the huge Doric columns and heading for the street. Like driven sheep, the media poured across the broad stone stairs, trying to intercept the detectives, but failing with Lucca, who shoved his way forward and practically ran toward the police station, in the next block. Lee kept moving too, though without hurrying, smiling coldly as she made her way down the steps, through the reporters and photographers. They kept asking questions and sticking microphones in her face, but she continued to ignore them. In her dress, a blue polka-dot silk, she looked elegant and beautiful.

As Baird watched her, she glanced his way just once, and at that distance he could not read her expression. He wanted to run after her and explain that he had never meant to put her in such a predicament, making her choose between him and her career, between her lover or committing perjury. As she walked on, he wondered if she would ever forgive him, ever again let him be the lover he still wanted to be.

It was a beautiful day, bright and crisp, with the noontime sun pouring into the canyon between the courthouse and the building across the street. The sidewalks were filled with people on their lunch break, stylish women and well-dressed men as well as hookers and felons and bums. And Baird was beginning to wonder what had happened to his feelings of pessimism and despair. For the moment anyway, they seemed to have lost their grip on him.

In the courtroom, when Ellen took the stand and gave her surprising testimony, he had been thoroughly confused at first, wondering where the dagger was hidden in her words. He could not figure out what devious form her revenge was taking. Then it began to dawn on him that she was not trying to hurt him at all but to save him, and he felt stupid and ashamed. For a time he was not sure whether she had made an honest mistake, confusing the two nights—the twenty-fourth and the twenty-fifth—or whether she had deliberately lied in order to give him a better alibi than the one he had concocted on his own.

But when Lee took the stand and claimed she was unable to swear which night Baird had been with her, then he began to understand. It occurred to him that both women—and for that matter, the judge too, given the swiftness of her rulings—might have joined in a kind of visceral, unconscious conspiracy not so much to save him as to ratify what he had done, each woman affirming in her own way that the time had come to do battle against their common enemy: all the twisted, violent men, all the butchers and rapists and killers.

True or not, Baird found it a pleasant thought. He loved women. His sudden gift of freedom would not have seemed half so precious had he not been able to contemplate spending most of it in the company of women. Yet, at the moment, the women in his life seemed to be walking out of it. Lee was already gone, already across James Street and heading for the police station and whatever career he had left her. And Ellen would not look at him. She smiled at the reporters but continued to say nothing, just stood there watching the street, waiting for Kevin and the car.

For that matter, even Kathy seemed uneasy at his side, probably only because of the crowd still pressing in around them. But Baird recognized that she could have been feeling the first stirrings of revulsion toward him as someone who possibly had taken a life. Yet even in that case, he knew he would not feel remorse or regret, for he finally had come to the point where he understood—where he truly believed—that he had done only what he had to do, no more and no less. He had protected his child. It was as simple as that.

Still holding onto his arm, Kathy looked up at him and smiled. He kissed her on the forehead and hugged her close, reflecting that he could always do that at least.

"Are you okay, Daddy?" she asked.

"I'm fine," he said.